CASTAWAY COVE

Also by JoAnn Ross

Shelter Bay Novels
Sea Glass Winter
Moonshell Beach
On Lavender Lane
One Summer
The Homecoming

High Risk Novels
Freefall
Crossfire
Shattered
Breakpoint

CASTAWAY COVE

A SHELTER BAY NOVEL

JoAnn Ross

A SIGNET BOOK

SIGNET
Published by the Penguin Group
Penguin Group (USA) Inc., 375 Hudson Street,
New York, New York 10014, USA

USA | Canada | UK | Ireland | Australia | New Zealand | India | South Africa | China

Penguin Books Ltd., Registered Offices: 80 Strand, London WC2R 0RL, England

First published by Signet, an imprint of New American Library,
a division of Penguin Group (USA) Inc.

 REGISTERED TRADEMARK—MARCA REGISTRADA

ISBN 978-1-62490-695-4

Printed in the United States of America

To Maureen Hallett. (This time I got it right!)

Once again, to all our military men and women and their families for their service and sacrifice.

Also, with admiration and great affection to Operation Write Home, Cards for Soldiers, and Cards for Hospitalized Kids, who deliver so much handmade love with every card.

And, as always, to Jay, who reminds me every day why I write romance.

ACKNOWLEDGMENTS

Once again, I want to give thanks and a huge shout-out to the best publishing team in the business:

At NAL: publisher Kara Welsh, for her unwavering support over so many years; editor extraordinaire Kerry Donovan, who's not only too sweet and supportive for words, but hands down the most brilliant brainstorming editor ever; Jesse Feldman, who's always been there to take care of details and does the best tweets; editorial director Claire Zion, who rescued my manuscript from her slush pile one memorable fall day in 1982 and literally changed my life; Mimi Bark, who, with watercolor illustrator Paul Janovsky, has wrapped my Shelter Bay stories in such beautiful covers; Erin Galloway, who takes care of publicity with such aplomb; and all the other super people in production, sales, and marketing who actually get my books onto shelves.

And last, but certainly not least, publishing matchmaker, lunch maven, stellar agent, and friend Robin Rue, and superwoman Beth Miller, who's always kept everything running so smoothly!

I truly heart you all and I hope you've had as much fun working together these past years as I have!

CASTAWAY
COVE

1

Afghanistan

Disney Drive, the main drag of Bagram Airfield, was about as far from the Magic Kingdom as a person could get.

A river of bumper-to-bumper vehicles was headed out of the base, packed together like salmon swimming upstream.

"I swear it'd be easier to just get out and walk," Staff Sergeant Mac Culhane remarked to the cameraman and the female Airman correspondent from the American Forces Network who were traveling with him.

"Is it always this crowded?" asked the journalist from the *Seattle Examiner*, who'd been waiting for Mac when he arrived at the radio station that morning.

Apparently someone above Mac's pay grade had decided that some positive, warm-and-fuzzy Stateside press was in order, which was why they were traveling to the village for a meet, greet, and schmooze photo op with the locals.

"Actually, you're seeing it on a good day," Mac said.

"At least we're moving." Though at nothing near the posted twenty-five-miles-per-hour speed limit.

"So, is there a story behind why this street's named after Walt Disney?"

Jeez. You'd think the guy would've at least done some homework on the flight from the States.

"It's not. It's named for an Army specialist who died here when some heavy equipment fell on him," the AFN reporter said. Although her voice remained neutrally polite, Mac could tell from the very faint edge to her tone that she was as irked by the guy's question as he was.

"You definitely don't want anything on this base named for you," Mac said. "Because that means that you're dead." Another example being the Pat Tillman Memorial USO.

Mac might be a deejay, assigned to play songs and impart news and information, but like all the others he worked with, he took the AFN motto—Serving those who serve—seriously. Whenever he could, he'd go outside the wire and travel to some of the world's most dangerous war zones to entertain the troops and to film footage that was not only shown on AFN television but also sent home to family and loved ones.

He was now on his second tour in Afghanistan, where along with entertaining with music and banter, he also delivered the news of troop deaths. More during the surge, but lately the bad guys had stepped up their game.

"Damned if you didn't jinx us by saying we were moving," the cameraman complained as the river of vehicles on the lane leading out of the base came to an abrupt halt.

In less than a minute, the driver of one of the white pickups that civilian contractors tended to drive leaned on his horn.

Yeah. Like that was going to help.

Not wanting to be left out of the fun, a utility four-wheeler, looking like a combat golf cart behind Mac's MRAP (Mine Resistant Ambush Protected vehicle) got into the act, adding his horn to the cacophony, which wasn't helped by the roar of jets streaking overhead.

Meanwhile, pedestrians were packed as tightly together as the vehicles. Military personnel jockeyed for some semblance of personal space with civilian contractors and Afghans. Some, trying to speed up the process, had taken to walking or jogging in the street.

Finally, they got beyond the gate and headed out into the countryside, where the roads were even more of a joke. Bagram was definitely not a country club base—rocket attacks came so often that diving into bunkers became routine, not to mention the constant threat of insurgent attacks, and more recently "green on blue" violence from Afghan forces—and Mac often thought that you really took your life in your hands by traveling on any of the narrow, winding roads.

The base was in a valley surrounded by the Hindu Kush, where sunshine had the snow on the mountains gleaming like diamonds. There'd been a time, a thousand years ago, when Bagram was a wealthy, bustling city on the silk route. These days it was a village dependent on farming, base employment, and fighting.

Still, the drive past the fields with the mountains in the distance could have been pleasant were it not for the metal signs warning of land mines leftover from Soviet occupation hanging on wires along the road, and the constantly blowing sand that had the consistency of talcum power. Even when you couldn't see it, you could feel it in your eyes, nose, and throat whenever you went outside.

The market was bustling. Children, some of the boys wearing blue Cub Scout uniforms supplied by one of the officers at the base, who'd set up a scouting program for the local population, dodged the traffic as they ran through the streets. Giggling, remarkably carefree girls jumped rope and played hopscotch with stones on courts drawn in the dirt.

Women in dark burkas were focused on their shopping, while local police, trained by allied forces, patrolled past the food stands. As the translator gave the reporter the tour, Mac chatted in his less than fluent Dari with the shopkeepers and his fans, who, every time he came to town, treated him like a celebrity. At first he'd been surprised by that; then he came to realize that while Freedom Radio might consider the troops its target audience, a good portion of the civilians listened as well. And even if they couldn't understand all the banter, music proved universal.

As he bought some goat meat and yogurt from an elderly man whose eyes were nearly black in his dark, sun-weathered face, a brightly colored vehicle, locally referred to as a "jingle truck" because of the bells drivers put on the top of their cabs, pulled up to deliver a load of *kaddo bourani*, Afghan pumpkins.

Which led to Mac telling the Seattle reporter how he and his crew were going to set up a catapult for Freedom Radio's Thanksgiving pumpkin-hurling competition. He was just thinking how much he freaking loved his job when the world exploded in a fireball that sent him flying through the air.

Mac didn't know how long he'd been unconscious. But when he heard the Airman calling his name over the ringing in his ears, he managed with difficulty to open his eyes, which were even grittier with sand than usual. He hoped that explained the fact that trying to focus on anything was like looking through fractured glass.

"I'm okay," he called out.

If you didn't count the crushing headache, the nausea, the blood he could feel pouring down his face, and the fact that he felt as if his body had been peppered with fiery birdshot.

He wasn't sure whether he'd managed to get the words out of his mouth or had just thought them. And although he could sort of hear the Airman shouting, either she'd begun speaking in a foreign language or his brain wasn't decoding what she was trying to ask him.

As disoriented as he was, one searing thought flashed through Mac's mind. *Please, God, let my brain not be permanently scrambled.*

"Okay," he repeated, flinching as he turned his head to try to look around.

His left eye seemed to have been flash-blinded, while the vision in his right was hazy, but that didn't keep him from seeing that the explosion had ripped through the heart of the market, clearing a wide swath. At the periphery, burned and bloody bodies were piled up like so much cordwood.

He heard the cries and moans, but was grateful that along with the obnoxious ringing in his ears, whatever had happened to his hearing made the voices sound distant, like when his grandfather had taught him to listen to the sound of the sea inside a conch shell.

A mob of distraught people was rushing toward the scene, trying to dislodge the bodies, desperately searching for the living.

The Airman and her cameraman lifted him up and ran toward the MRAP vehicle.

He had wanted to assure them that he was fine, that they should leave him and go help the civilian women and children, when his right eye caught sight of what appeared to be a small arm wearing Cub Scout blue stretching out from beneath a jumble of human pickup sticks.

As he felt himself being carefully placed into the vehicle, a burning pain began washing over him in hot waves. Even as he fought against it, as the MRAP roared away, horn blaring loudly enough that even he could hear it, Mac surrendered to the darkness.

After having shrapnel painstakingly picked out of his arms and legs, and being treated for second-degree burns by the medical crew, he was airlifted from Bagram to Landstuhl Regional Medical Center in Germany.

"So, here's the deal," the doctor, a captain from next-door Ramstein Air Base, told him. "You were lucky."

The weird thing was that although every part of him hurt like one of the lower circles of hell, even through the IV drugs they were pumping into him, Mac knew she was right.

At least he was alive, unlike the Afghan translator he'd worked with for the past eight months, or the newspaper reporter, who'd had the bad luck of joining the growing ranks of journalists killed while covering the war.

"You've got lacerations on your chest and arms, and shrapnel in your thighs, legs, and shoulders, but fortunately your helmet, armor, and fire-retardant uniform prevented serious injury to your body."

"What about my eyes?" Which were currently wrapped in sterile gauze.

"It's too early to tell." Mac listened for optimism in the female doctor's tone, but heard only exhaustion. "But they're intact. Which is really amazing, given how close you were to the blast, even with your ballistic goggles, which I heard were toast."

"I should've seen it coming," he muttered.

"Yeah, with your X-ray eyes and superhero powers," she said dryly. "I know it's difficult for you warriors to get it through your heads, but you are, when it comes right down to it, human beings. Like the rest of us."

"I'm not a warrior. I'm just the guy on the radio."

He'd always been aware that his job was a walk in the park compared to those of so many others he'd served with. The troops worked damn hard, some risking their lives every minute of every day. His job, as he viewed it, was to always be there for them. To provide a little bit of home and bring some semblance of normal to a life that was anything but.

"Yet you were blown up, which I doubt would've happened if you'd chosen to remain a civilian deejay working in Albuquerque or Topeka."

Despite the pain, Mac smiled at that. "And how boring would that be?"

"Just what I need. Another adrenaline junkie." She sighed as she pulled back the sheet and began examining his wounds.

"Explosions can work in inexplicable ways," she said. "We never know what we're going to be looking at when we get the call for incoming.

"At the instant of detonation, shrapnel and heat rush out at supersonic speeds. They should have been picking pieces of you out of the dirt into the next century. But there's no order to explosions. Some areas are thick with shrapnel. You could have just as easily been cut in half by a door or the hood of the truck that suicide bomber set off. But you happened to be standing in a partial seam that was empty of any lethal debris."

Unlike his translator and the reporter. Mac knew that if he lived to a hundred, he'd never be able to unsee the images of the bombing's aftermath.

"The surgery released the swelling in your brain," she continued. "We'll keep an eye on you for a couple more days, to make sure you're out of the woods, then

ship you back to CONUS for continued treatment."
CONUS being military-speak for Continental United
States. "Your liaison will be visiting as soon as I leave,
but wanted you to know that your father called. My
suggestion, not that you asked, is unless you feel you
need immediate family support, it makes more sense
for him to meet up with you at Travis, where you're
ultimately headed."

"I'm fine," Mac lied, as he had been doing since he'd
found himself lying on the ground surrounded by
chaos. "If I'm only staying a couple days, there's no
point in having him fly all the way here, only to turn
right around and fly back again."

"That was my thinking."

Mac debated asking if his wife had called. But he
figured the doctor would have mentioned it if Kayla
had felt moved to contact the hospital.

Maybe his father filling her in was enough. Perhaps
she was still speaking to her father-in-law, even though
she hadn't e-mailed or Skyped Mac for three months.

Two days later, he left Germany, spending a one-
night layover at Andrews Air Force Base in Maryland
before continuing on to David Grant USAF Medical
Center at Travis Air Force Base in California.

His father was waiting there for him.

His wife was not.

Three weeks after his arrival at Travis, two weeks
after he'd begun climbing the walls, he was transferred
to outpatient status.

Although the bandages had been removed, his vision was still blurry. The retina tear on his left eye had
been repaired and the doctors assured him that with a
cornea transplant, his right eye should be as good as
new.

His father had wanted to accompany Mac to Colorado Springs, where Kayla, having landed a part-time

job as a Saturday news anchor, had moved with their daughter, Emma.

Not knowing what type of reception he'd receive, and needing to concentrate on repairing his wounded marriage, Mac insisted on going alone.

His wife had a right to be pissed, since after promising her that he would come home he'd reenlisted yet again. Mac realized that he was going to have to pull off some serious groveling to repair his fractured marriage.

2

From the stilted phone conversations they'd shared while he'd been at Travis, he wasn't surprised when Kayla didn't show up to greet him at the airport. He gave the cabdriver the address of the house he'd never seen, then sat in the backseat, practicing what he was going to say that might make things right again.

The neighborhood was typical of American suburbs, with neatly trimmed front lawns and tidy houses on either side of a street lined with trees that blazed with fall color. Even through his still-blurred vision, the high blue Colorado sky and red, yellow, and bronze leaves on the trees seemed blindingly bright after Afghanistan's unrelenting brown.

Most of the houses were flying the American flag, which was to be expected in a city that was home to the Air Force Academy. Mac couldn't help noticing that the flag flying from the front porch of the white rambler the cabdriver had pulled up in front of was not the Stars and Stripes, but a banner that boasted three fall-themed pumpkins.

He rang the bell, then waited for what seemed an eternity.

"Hi." His wife's tone, when she did finally open the door, wasn't angry, as it had been the last time they'd spoken in person. Nor was it the least bit welcoming. What it was, he decided, was disinterested.

"Hi," he said back, standing there, holding his duffel bag while she subjected him to a slow examination.

"You look good," she said. Since his mirror revealed that he was gaunt and gray, and sported a bald spot where they'd shaved his head for surgery, Mac translated that to mean that he didn't look nearly as bad as she'd expected.

"So do you."

It was the truth. She looked much the same. But different. Her long, straight slide of chestnut hair had been cropped to chin length, now a blazing mahogany that echoed the leaves of the tree on the small front lawn, and the snug purple sweater and skinny jeans revealed that although she'd always claimed to hate exercise, she'd been working out. A lot.

Silence settled over them as they stood there, she inside the ranch-style house, he on the narrow front porch. The only sound came from the blower the elderly man across the street was using to attack a mountain of leaves.

He glanced past her. "Where's Emma?"

"At a neighbor's." The unfamiliar glossy bright hair swung as she tilted her head toward the house next door. "You can make up for all the parenting time you've lost later. Right now, I thought it would be better if she wasn't here for this long-overdue conversation."

Mac's internal siren, which had failed to go off when the suicide bomber had driven his jingle truck into the marketplace, began to sound. But feeling the leaf guy's eyes on them, he wasn't going to stand out here in public and point out that the child Kayla was referring to was *his* child, too. Ever since waking up to find himself in the Bagram ER, he'd gotten through the pain, stress, and guilt by staying focused on getting back home and holding his daughter in his arms.

Although patience had admittedly never been his strong suit, Mac held his tongue and refrained from starting yet another argument as he walked into the small foyer.

Where the flowered suitcase sitting by the front door suggested that whatever conversation he and his wife were about to have was probably not going to go his way.

3

"So," Mac asked, with a casualness he hoped would conceal the IEDs going off inside him, "are you taking a trip?"

Her eyes had gone from disinterested to sad. But he recognized the glint of determination in them as well. "I'm leaving."

"Can we talk about it?"

His shrapnel-riddled leg was aching, but since she hadn't invited him to sit down after leading him into the living room, he remained standing. It didn't escape his notice that the living room of the rented house didn't have a single personal item in it.

She shrugged. "What's to talk about? We've been over this again and again, Mackenzie. Ever since you decided to go off to play war."

The scorn in her tone hit a hot button, but rather than get into an argument about the fact that no one in a war zone was *playing* at their job, he didn't jump at the bait he suspected she'd thrown out there just to get a rise out of him.

"You broke your word to me. Yet again." She folded her arms beneath her breasts, which, perhaps because she was so toned, seemed larger than they'd been. Or maybe, along with changing her hair, she'd gotten implants.

Not a good sign.

"I'm not going to argue that." Since it was true. "Does the fact that I honestly intended to leave the Air Force count for anything?"

"Only if you *had* left. Which you didn't."

Frustration rushing through him despite his exhaustion, he raked a hand through his hair, flinching as it hit on the stitches that had him looking like Frankenstein's monster. They'd been due to come out today, but since she hadn't shown up in California and he didn't want to let things go further downhill, he'd come to Colorado Springs, hoping to make things right.

"I'm sorry. You're right. I broke a promise."

He paused, waiting for her to accept his apology. When the silence yawned between them, a deep and foreboding chasm, he forged on.

"But it's a moot point, since my military career is pretty much washed up."

It needn't be that way. He had done stories on soldiers who'd returned downrange after being wounded. A Marine sniper who'd lost an eye had sworn he could aim better with one. Others had lost legs, including an Army helicopter pilot who returned with ones he claimed were better and stronger. Like a real-life Six Million Dollar Man.

But while lying in that bed in Germany, Mac had realized how close he'd come to dying. Which probably wouldn't have been any big deal for him, because he'd be dead and wouldn't be around to throw himself a pity party.

But the unappealing fact that had come crashing down on him was that many of the accusations Kayla had thrown at him like Molotov cocktails over the years were true. He'd been driven by ambition and selfishness as much as by patriotism or duty. And by enjoying being at the top of his game, the guy with a worldwide audience, he'd nearly left his daughter without a father.

"So you only came here because you've nowhere else to go?" she countered.

"No. I came here because I want us to be a family. Which we haven't been for a long time."

"And whose fault is that?"

"Totally mine." Not that she'd been a saint. But even though he might be clueless when it came to reading women's minds, Mac knew this was no time to start comparing personal faults. Especially since he couldn't deny leaving her alone for so much of their marriage. "That's why I'm willing to do whatever heavy lifting it takes to make things work."

"Heavy lifting," she murmured, suggesting that she wasn't exactly enamored of the term he'd chosen. Her gaze drifted out the window. She dragged a hand through her hair. For a brief, suspended moment, Mac thought he felt an encouraging bit of indecision.

"You look like shit," she said finally, turning back to him. "Sit down before you fall down. I need to make a call."

With that she left the room.

Since he felt about as bad as he probably looked, Mac lowered himself into a flowered wing chair and stretched his stiff, aching leg out in front of him. And waited.

Early on in his radio life, he'd developed an internal clock that kept him from accidentally ending up with one of the things every deejay dreaded . . . dead air. Which was why he knew she was back in just under five minutes.

"I'm honestly sorry, Mac." She'd dropped the

"Mackenzie," which she only used when she was pissed. Her tone, lower and less acidic, sounded as if she was speaking the truth. But her expression suggested that anything he might be about to say was too little, too late. "About what happened to you. And what happened to us." Her fingers slid through that unfamiliar glossy red hair again. "But I'm done."

He didn't need to be able to read his wife's mind to know she was telling the truth. At least what she thought was the truth. He could win her back.

Somehow.

"Where are you going?"

She paused. Just long enough to have him thinking that she'd prefer him not to know.

Then she shrugged. "You know I've wanted out of entertainment news, but I kept finding myself typecast in California. Ironically, you being in the Air Force helped me land this job, which was a good way to break in. Meanwhile, I've been sending out tapes and was offered a morning news anchor spot in Phoenix."

Even as he considered that Kayla was proving every bit as ambitious as he'd been, Mac felt a sense of relief. It could work. Phoenix was a big city with a bunch of radio stations. One of them was bound to hire him, especially since there were two air bases outside town that would provide a built-in loyal audience.

"I've always liked the desert," he said. Which had once been true. Before all that time in Iraq and Afghanistan.

"Maybe I haven't made myself perfectly clear. I'm going to Arizona. You're going . . ."

She paused, as if realizing that by moving here, she'd essentially left him without a place to live. "Wherever you want."

"Even if you don't want to be married anymore, I want to be where Emma is." Maybe he wouldn't stay

Kayla's husband, but he'd be damned if he'd give up his parental rights.

"Well, then, you have nothing to worry about. Because I'm leaving her with you."

"What?" The bombshell hit with much the same force as the explosion in that marketplace. If he hadn't been sitting down, Mac figured it would've staggered him.

"I've spent five years being responsible for her twenty-four/seven while you've gallivanted around the world playing music on the radio," she said. "It's your turn to pick up the slack."

Mac's first thought, and it wasn't a good one, was how she'd so cavalierly referred to their only child as *slack*.

The second was that just as he wouldn't have wanted Emma to grow up without a father, surely a daughter needed a mother as much, if not more.

His third thought, and the most unpalatable one, was to wonder what kind of woman could so blithely abandon her own flesh and blood. Maybe she'd changed during their years apart. Or maybe he hadn't ever really known her.

Maybe he didn't want to try to fix things after all.

But neither did he want Emma to become collateral damage in the war that her parents' marriage had become.

"Okay, I get that you're pissed at me," he said, trying a new tack.

"Make that fed up," she countered.

"Roger that." He got the message loud and clear. "I also understand that it couldn't have been easy handling everything on your own. But how the hell can you just walk away from our daughter?"

"It's not as if Emma's going to end up in some Dickensian orphanage. She has you. I'm not abandoning her, Mackenzie. Obviously she'll visit me in Arizona. And while our divorce lawyers will have to work out the details, she'll undoubtedly end up spending much more time with me than she ever has with her own father."

That accusation was tinged with enough acid to peel paint off the walls. "Bull's-eye," he said.

She glanced out the window again. As a car rolled up to the curb, she picked up her bag. "As I said, she's next door. The house with the rocker and mums on the porch. The neighbor's name is Jami Young. She's expecting you. I also boxed up your things when I left our California apartment. They're in the garage."

With that she left the room. And the house.

Pushing himself to his feet, Mac followed, standing in the doorway, watching as the driver climbed out of the car, took the bag from her, and put it in the trunk.

Once, after he'd joined the Air Force, because she'd kept pouring wine during an hours-long argument, Kayla had taken a cab to a local hotel, where she'd spent the night cooling down.

But the black BMW parked in front of the house was no yellow cab.

And the guy wearing the gray sweater, black slacks, and what were probably Italian tasseled loafers sure as hell didn't look like any taxi driver Mac had ever seen.

She climbed into the passenger seat without looking back.

Mac watched the car until it turned the corner and disappeared from sight.

Leaving him all alone. And wondering what the hell he was supposed to do next.

4

It wasn't supposed to turn out this way.

Radio had always been one of the few things he and Kayla had in common. She had, as she'd told him many times, fallen in love with the guy on the radio. The guy he'd wanted to be, ever since his days as a kid growing up in Portland, Oregon, when he would lie in bed in the dark, listening through the static and fades of all those far-flung radio stations riding the nighttime airways.

It didn't matter whether the station was rock, country, disco, or R&B. Even, on occasion, pop, which he'd mostly thought of as "girlie music." It was the personalities of the guys spinning the records that fascinated him. They were as much a part of the show as the music they played, and they seemed to be having fun. What was most amazing was that they all seemed to be talking directly to him as if they knew him personally.

All of the men Mac knew as a child had real grown-up jobs. His father had been a fighter pilot. His adoptive father, Boyd Buchanan (whose own father had been a fisherman), was a doctor. The guy across the street went to work every day in a fire-engine-red pickup to build houses, one next-door neighbor sold insurance, and the guy who lived on the other side, the father of Mac's best friend, taught history at the University of Portland.

All of them were so damn serious about their work. Which was a huge contrast to the excitement he heard from the radio guys. Whether they were talking about the record they'd just played, reading a commercial touting a local bank or car dealership, or just talking about cars, or sports, or what they'd done that weekend, you could tell they were having a high old time.

By the time he was fourteen, the hook had been set. Mac had decided that he wanted to be one of those guys on the radio, to reach thousands of listeners who would hang on his every word, who'd laugh at his jokes, all while probably being paid, like, a million dollars a year.

And they weren't just on the air. They made personal appearances, too, where they were treated like rock stars. Whenever he showed up at these occasions, it did not escape Mac's notice that deejays were really, really popular with girls.

When he was fifteen, he built a ham radio and spent hours listening to all the conversations between people in distant places. Growing even more convinced that radio could form bonds between people only cemented his determination to have a career on the air.

After two years at Oregon State University's KBVR station, impatient to get started with his life, he dropped out of college and landed his first professional job, at a country station in Alturas, a town with a population of less than three thousand near the California-Oregon border. He didn't make enough to live on, but it didn't take him long to figure out how to game the system.

When the volunteer firefighters wanted him to mention their Friday fish fry fund-raiser on the air, he suggested they bring some by the station, so he could tell everyone in broadcast range how hot-damn delicious the fish was. And sure enough, the firemen showed up with a platter of beer-batter-dipped fillets, which were as good as advertised.

After glowing mentions for three days, people arrived in droves at the firehouse. Not only was it a good deal for him, since he didn't have to buy dinner; it was beneficial to the community and only drew in more listeners.

Which made advertisers happy.

Which, in turn, made management happy.

And got him a raise.

Not a huge one. But, hey, every bit helped.

Having a pancake breakfast to raise money for new bleachers for the school's gym? Bring some pancakes and fried eggs by and he'd fill that gym with pancake-buying fans.

Win/win.

Unlike most deejays, Mac was never fired from a job, but he did swiftly jump from station to station in bigger and bigger markets, until that memorable day while he was in Fresno, when the clouds parted, angels sang hosannas, and damned if he wasn't offered a gig that landed him in sun-drenched, California-beach-bunny clover at San Diego's KSUN.

He'd achieved a career beyond his wildest boyhood dreams, and been given more freedom than he probably should've been allowed—playing music, making jokes, staging stupid contests, talking about pretty much whatever he wanted to. The days of begging for food on the air were in his rearview mirror.

Like the billboard with his grinning face on it towering over the freeway near Balboa Park, Mac was living larger than large: bantering with listeners on the radio

during morning commutes, making public appearances in the afternoon, partying at beach bars late into
the night, living on too little sleep and too many of the
Advils he ate like jelly beans for the inevitable morning-
after hangovers.

Fortunately, once that red control light went on and
he was on the air, despite the pounding head and roil-
ing stomach that were the result of living too large,
Mac easily slid into his Radio Guy persona, and there
was never a hint of complaint from the management
guys.

By the time Kayla had arrived on the scene, he was
growing tired of burning the candle at both ends. A
former Miss San Diego whose title had won her a job
as entertainment reporter for *San Diego News in the
Morning*, she'd appeared at a fund-raising gig he was
doing for Wounded Warriors at the Naval Medical
Center.

She'd let him know from the moment they were introduced that she was attracted. Which wasn't that unusual. In his early days on the radio, he'd viewed his
groupie fans as a perk of the job. Like a tasty buffet—
and he'd certainly sampled his share of delights.

It had never made sense to get into a relationship
when he knew he'd be moving on to the next station.
The next town.

But in San Diego his career was finally exactly where
he wanted it to be. So when the stunning beauty queen,
who'd warned him up front that she wasn't into one-
night stands, invited him back to her apartment at the
end of the fund-raiser, Mac couldn't think of a single
reason why he shouldn't move on to the next stage of
his life.

And now, it seemed, he was moving on again.

He also realized that he was clueless about how to
be a single father to a five-year-old girl.

Who was waiting next door for him.

Reminding himself that having survived a suicide bombing, he could certainly handle this situation, Mac took a deep breath, left the house, and walked across the front lawn to retrieve his daughter.

5

Jami Young was a pretty woman in her late twenties with brunette hair pulled into a side ponytail. She was wearing jeans and a University of Colorado sweatshirt, and holding a toddler on one hip. Both her smile and her eyes, as she invited him into the house, held hints of the sadness and pity she felt toward him, which did nothing to boost Mac's mood.

"I'm sorry," she said. "About what happened to you. And . . ."

She shook her head. "Well, you know."

"I think that's going to take some time to sink in," he admitted. "But right now, I'm here for Emma."

"Of course. She's in the backyard playing with Riley. He's our beagle. She loves dogs, by the way."

"Thanks. That's good to know."

She paused, as if trying to decide how much of what Kayla had shared to tell him. When she put a hand on his arm, Mac braced for yet more bad news.

"She doesn't know her mother's leaving."

"What?"

The woman sighed, and shifted the now wiggling toddler to her other hip. "Kayla said she wanted to avoid the drama of a good-bye. But she plans to call Emma from the road to tell her good night."

"That's big of her." An icy anger flowed over the initial flare of heat.

His daughter was standing with her back to him, throwing a blue ball to the brown and white beagle, who would race to it, baying with joy, then return to drop it at her pink-sneaker-clad feet.

"Good boy, Riley!"

As she picked up the ball and was about to throw it again, Mac said, "You've got a great arm! Are you, by any chance, a famous baseball player?"

She spun around, dropping the ball. "Daddy!" Lights on her shoes flashed as she raced toward him across the leaf-scattered lawn, propelling herself through the air and into his outstretched arms.

She flung her arms around his neck, her legs around his waist, and held on tight. "You're home!"

"I'm home," he said, not wanting to get into the fact that he had no idea where *home* might turn out to be. He smoothed his hand down her flyaway blond hair. "For good."

"Really?" She leaned her head back to look up into his face. Her blue eyes, as bright as sunlight on an alpine lake, searched his face. "Truly?"

"Really, truly."

"Cross your heart and hope to die?"

"Cross my heart." Holding her with one arm, he managed to make a cross on his chest between them with the other.

"Yay!" She wiggled free and began running toward the house. "Let's go tell Mommy!"

"Good luck," Jami said as the toddler, who she'd put down on the grass, headed toward the beagle, who was ripping the ball apart with enthusiasm. "If you need backup, or anything, just give me a call."

She pulled a sticky note with her phone number on it out of her jeans pocket.

"Thanks. We'll be fine."

Mac hoped. But he took the paper anyway, because if there was one thing years in war zones had taught him, it was that it was always good to have backup.

He caught up with Emma just as she reached the front porch. "There's something I need to tell you," he said, scooping her off her feet again. "About Mommy . . . She just had to go away. On a trip."

"But she didn't tell me." Tears welled up in those lake blue eyes and her rosebud lips began to tremble.

Terrific.

"She needed to leave right away, but she figured it would be okay, because then we'd have time to ourselves after me being away for so long."

"It was a *long* time," she agreed as he carried her into the house. "What happened to your head?"

"I got dinged up a bit."

"When you got blowed up?"

Although he'd received a handmade get-well card from Emma, Mac realized he had no idea what Kayla had told her about the attack. Which made this conversational minefield even more dangerous.

"It wasn't that bad. And I'm fine now."

"I heard Mommy telling Mrs. Young that you could've died."

"Nah," he lied. "That wasn't going to happen. Because I had you to come home to. And your special card made me get better a lot faster."

"I'm glad. . . . When is Mommy coming back?"

"I don't exactly know."

It wasn't the whole truth, nothing but the truth, but given their past, there was an outside chance that Kayla might change her mind. Maybe not for him, but for their daughter. Surely he could hope for at least that much from her?

"Meanwhile, what would you say about the two of us going out for dinner?"

Mac had no idea what Kayla had left in the refrigerator and pantry, and since if it wasn't an MRE, bacon, burgers, or hot dogs, he was pretty much clueless, going out seemed like the answer to his most immediate problem: feeding his daughter. "Anywhere you want."

Her mood turned on a dime.

"Yay! I want pizza!"

Thirty minutes later, surrounded by ringing, flashing arcade games, animatronic singing figures led by a guitar-playing mouse, amusement rides, climbing equipment, tubes and slides, and hordes of kids who appeared to have morphed into perpetual-motion machines with high-pitched voices that the military would probably love to be able to duplicate in order to puncture enemies' eardrums, Mac realized that this parenting gig could make his tour in Afghanistan seem like a cakewalk.

But he couldn't deny, as he wiped a bit of tomato sauce off his daughter's face, that her dazzling smile was worth it. He also suspected that the frantic activity helped keep her mind off her mother's "trip."

He'd worried about more questions about Kayla's departure, but fortunately Emma was wiped out by the time they returned home with the booty he'd helped her win from the arcade games. Whatever other lack of maternal behavior he might be putting on his wife, he couldn't deny that their daughter was well behaved.

She didn't argue about going to bed in a pink room that looked as if a bottle of Pepto-Bismol had exploded all over the walls, other than letting him know that "Mommy and I always read a story together."

After dutifully brushing her teeth with a Disney Cinderella toothbrush, she changed into a nightgown featuring a red-haired archer who was, Emma informed him, Scottish, and the "bravest princess of all!"

Apparently Jami Young hadn't been kidding when she'd told him that his daughter loved dogs. Emma's white spindle bed was covered with plush toy dogs of every size and color.

After making space, he lay down beside her and listened as she read aloud the story of Ferdinand, a fierce-looking but gentle bull that would rather just sit in the meadow and smell the flowers than fight. Which had Mac wondering what would happen if some government declared a war and no one showed up.

"And he is very happy," Emma recited the last line. Having proven a failure in the bull ring, Ferdinand had been sent back to sit beneath his cork tree and smell his flowers.

"So is Daddy." Mac dropped a kiss on her head.

"Me, too." She sighed, then wiggled beneath the Disney Princess coverlet, settling into a comfortable position as he put the book back on the shelf. "I'm *sooo* happy you're home. Will you be here when I wake up in the morning?"

"Absolutely."

"Good." Her eyes were already at half-mast. She was asleep before he'd turned off the light.

6

Two hours later, having given up on the idea of his wife calling, as she'd assured her neighbor she would, Mac was sitting in the dark with the radio tuned to a country station, working his way through a pricey bottle of single malt Scotch he'd found in a cupboard. Since Kayla had never liked the taste of hard liquor, he had to deduce the bottle belonged to BMW guy.

As Dustin Lynch sang plaintively about cowboys and angels, Mac wished he still smoked, as he had when he'd first started in the business, partly because all the other deejays did, so it seemed cool. If there was ever a night for whisky and cigarettes, this was it.

"And wouldn't that be a friggin' lame cliché," he muttered. He took another hit of the Scotch, enjoying the burn of it sliding down his throat like a velvet flame, and thinking back to that seemingly perfect first morning together.

Over a fluffy asparagus omelet, he and Kayla had shared family stories. He told her about his birth father, an Air Force pilot whose fighter jet had crashed into the Arizona desert when Mac was eleven. And how the doctor who'd later married his mother and adopted him had encouraged him to keep his hero father's name.

Her father was career Navy, which meant she'd lived a gypsy existence growing up. Despite living in a city where you couldn't throw a stick on the beach without hitting a sailor, she was firm about the fact that she would never, *ever* marry a military man.

Mac assured her he had no plans to run off to sea.

Having been an only child who'd always wished for a brother or sister, Mac wanted two kids. Maybe three.

An only child herself, Kayla had cheerfully agreed that three was a perfect number. Later, he would realize that she'd never disagreed with a single thing he'd ever said. At least before the marriage.

Their brief courtship led smoothly to the altar, and since they were both young and enjoying life, Mac had gone along with Kayla's desire to spend a few years just playing before they got down to the serious business of parenting.

Then, two days before their second anniversary, he'd been working a remote radio gig at the San Diego County Fair when an Air Force recruiter had dropped by his broadcast booth, professed to be a fan, and invited him out for a beer after the show. Two beers later, persuaded by the argument that he'd be serving his country by bringing a sense of home to lonely troops stationed overseas, Mac had decided to join the flyboys.

When he'd gone home and announced his decision to Kayla, she'd hit the roof.

"I grew up in the damn Navy," she'd shouted at him. "You knew I didn't want to be a military wife!"

More furious than he'd ever seen her, she had picked up a Waterford vase that had been a wedding present. "I married the hot guy on the radio! Not the man terrorists are going to try to kill!"

He had ducked as the vase went flying by his head and shattered against a wall.

They fought for hours, long into the night, until finally, after they'd both run out of words, as the stuttering pink and white light of dawn began to slip into the room, they had sex. Not makeup sex, because nothing had been resolved. Nor did the furious coupling that moved from the couch to the floor in any way resemble love.

She told him, as they were standing side by side in the bathroom, getting ready to go to work, that she'd leave if he went ahead with his plans.

"You've got to understand where I'm coming from." He had tried to explain his decision as he cut a swath down the foam on his face with his razor. "I've always had things easy, sliding through life, living in the moment. And sure, I've done promos for the military, and gigs like that Wounded Warrior event where we met, but it never really sank in that there are people out in the real world actually putting their lives on the line so I can play songs on the radio and you can dish entertainment gossip on morning TV."

"We both do our share of charity work." She'd frowned and begun to attack the circles beneath her eyes with concealer. "Like you said, much of it for the military. Surely that should count for something."

"Maybe it should. Hell, sure it does. And I can understand why you'd be worried, but it's not as if I'm going to be out there patrolling dangerous streets or flying helicopters. I'm going to be doing the same thing I'm doing here. In a nice, safe, well-protected studio on a military base surrounded by armed guards."

"I work on a morning news show," she had pointed out. "Just because I'm an entertainment reporter doesn't mean I don't listen to what's reported during the hard news segment. Troops *do* die on military bases."

"I won't get killed."

"I'm sure that's what your birth father said when he climbed into that cockpit before his plane crashed."

"I guess you had to have been there when I was talk-ing with the guy."

After shouting at him that she didn't have to have been there to understand, she had thrown down her foundation brush.

"I'm not kidding, Mackenzie. You wouldn't be the first person to fall for a slick recruiting spiel. And you damn well won't be the last. But if you go through with this, I'm out of here."

She stormed out of the bathroom. While he was in the shower, he heard the front door slam.

And by the time he returned home from the recruit-er's office, where he'd gone after his morning shift, his wife was gone. Two days later, having cooled down, she was back.

Mac quickly came to realize that military life, espe-cially with all the multiple deployments during two wars, was not conducive to marriage. In fact, whenever a call came in asking for a breakup song, he found him-self waiting for his own "Dear Mac" letter.

The first time he informed her, over a crackling phone line from Iraq, that he'd decided to reenlist, she'd threatened divorce. Certain that his marriage was finally over, Mac had been surprised that, even as he hated the idea of failing, he was mostly okay with that.

Until, two months after he'd returned from a two-week leave, she e-mailed him with the news that she was pregnant.

Prepared for a battle to convince her to keep their child, he had been both surprised and relieved when she'd told him that abortion wasn't a personal option. Since her unwillingness to be a single mother appar-ently proved even stronger than her dislike of being a military wife, their rocky, roller-coaster marriage stumbled jerkily along.

There'd been times over the years when Mac had thought the only reason they'd managed to stay together was because he spent so much time deployed. It was when they were together that old wounds reopened, allowing long-seething anger to explode.

Apparently, he thought, as he lifted the bottle to measure the amount of Scotch left, this time the wound had been fatal. As he refilled the glass, Toby Keith was proclaiming to be not as good as he once was.

And couldn't Mac identify with that?

His cell phone rang. Digging into the pocket of his jeans, he pulled it out and struggled to focus on the illuminated caller ID.

"Hey, Dad." Although his father couldn't see him, he sat up straighter and set the glass down on the side table. "What's up?"

"Kayla called me earlier."

"My wife?"

"That would be her. Unless you've gotten another one you failed to mention," Dr. Boyd Buchanan said dryly. "She suggested I call you." He paused, as if to allow Mac the chance to fill him in on what had happened.

"She left."

"Ah." The man who'd become even closer to him than his own birth father, whom he could barely remember, the man he'd called *Dad* since his teens, didn't seem all that surprised. "Well, that was certainly a possibility, wasn't it?" They'd discussed the situation while Mac had been a patient at Travis.

"True." Mac raked his fingers through his surgically butchered hair, then said, "She left Emma behind."

Silence. The only sound was the *tick tick tick* of the wall clock coming from the kitchen.

Then, finally, "With you?"

There was some hesitation in his dad's voice. As if he didn't think Mac could take care of his own daughter?

"Yeah. So, the good news is that although she said her lawyer will be contacting me about visitation rights, it appears she's giving me custody."

The breakup of his marriage, which Mac took responsibility for, was proof that he hadn't been the best husband. And, although it hurt like hell to admit it, he hadn't been a good father, either.

Nothing like his dad, who'd somehow managed to juggle a high-pressure career with marriage and fatherhood. He'd always found time to check homework, ask about Mac's day, and sneak in some fishing on weekends.

"The bad news is that I've no freaking idea what to do next," Mac admitted.

Showing the rapid, confident decision-making skills that had always served him extraordinarily well in the operating room, his father didn't hesitate. "Why don't you come to Oregon?"

Mac's mother had died suddenly two years earlier. Her warm and generous heart had simply stopped one day while she was out weeding her beloved garden, and nothing his famed physician father, the paramedics, or the doctors in the emergency room could do had been able to get it going again.

Professing that he needed a change to shake him out of his widowed depression and apathy, Dr. Buchanan had resigned his medical practice and teaching position and moved back home to the small coastal town where he'd grown up, to live with *his* father.

"Actually, that doesn't sound like such a bad idea," Mac admitted.

He might be a grown man, far different from the

self-centered college dropout who'd left Oregon to seek fame and fortune, but right now, the child he hadn't even realized was still lurking inside him wanted his dad to make things better.

"But what about Pops? Are you sure he'll be okay with a five-year-old girl living in the house with him?"

This time the pause was long enough that Mac wondered if his cell had dropped the call.

"Dad? Are you still there?"

"Yes." His father sighed. "Actually, there's something I've been meaning to tell you. About your grandfather."

"Okay." Mac didn't like the sound of that.

"I had to move him to a memory care facility."

"What?" Could this frigging day get any worse? "Are you talking about a nursing home?"

"It's a residence facility. But it's not like it sounds."

"Shit." Mac reached for the glass again and tossed back the rest of the Scotch. After his mother had married Boyd Buchanan, Mac had begun spending several weeks each summer in Shelter Bay and his grandfather Maguire had always been the toughest guy he'd ever known. And one of the wisest.

One memorable year, over Thanksgiving dinner, while riding high on the heady self-importance of being an OSU freshman, Mac had asked the older man, a fourth-generation Oregon fisherman, if he regretted not having been able to attend college, which would have allowed him to do something other than fishing.

"Why would I want to give up fishing?" Charlie Maguire had asked. "If you love what you're doing, boy, you'll never work a damn day in your life."

And hadn't Mac thought the same thing about his own work?

"What the hell happened? Last time we talked you told me that he was doing fine." His grandfather had been diagnosed with Alzheimer's disease two years earlier, but whenever Mac had spoken with his father he'd never picked up on a problem.

"I said his condition was being managed," his father said, correcting him. "As well as could be expected. If you remember, I told you when he was first diagnosed that it's not like even five years ago, when Alzheimer's was a sure death sentence. With all the new advances being made, it's quite likely that your grandfather will eventually die *with* Alzheimer's, not *because* of it."

Mac didn't even want to think about his grandfather, who'd been the solid, unmoving rock of their family, dying. "Then with all that positivity, why the hell is he in a nursing home?"

"Memory care residence," his father qualified. "There's a huge difference. And he's there because he kept wandering off. With the house located right across the street from the harbor, that put him at even more of a risk. He also left a gas burner on. Twice. Once in the middle of the night."

Okay. Those were definitely dangerous behaviors.

"Plus, although he's still engaged and can still carry on a conversation, he's easily confused. There are times he thinks I'm his doctor."

"Not surprising. Since you *are* a doctor."

"True. But *his* is thirty years younger."

"You've always looked young for your age," Mac said, still trying to wrap his mind around the idea of his grandfather losing his mind.

"Dr. Parrish is also a woman."

Damn. Another sign that the older man's symptoms had gotten worse. "Why the hell didn't you tell me?"

"I was going to tell you," his father continued. "But then you had the bad luck to get blown up and I figured you were dealing with enough without having to worry about your grandfather. Who is, I assure you, being very well taken care of. . . ."

Mac heard another long sigh and realized that this wasn't the least bit easy for his father. Putting himself in his dad's place, Mac knew the situation would be tearing him apart.

"He's happy there, Mac. He's in a bright and cheery home staffed with dedicated professionals who practice a gentle care philosophy dealing with varying stages of dementia. It's nothing like warehousing, locking people up to stay lost in their thoughts. Everyone has taken time to get to know him, his life experiences, even his sleeping routine, to work out a schedule of activities that are keeping him active but still allow enough rest for him to recharge.

"When he was still living in the house, I put one of those tracking bracelets on him, which he said made him feel as if he were under house arrest. All the daily, minute-by-minute decisions that were confusing him and making him anxious are now being taken care of at Still Waters, which relieves a lot of stress. Not just on me, but on him, too.

"And most of the time, when I visit, he sees me as his son. Not as the mean doctor who was always telling him what to do. Or as his jailer who was trying to keep him locked up. Which was only so he couldn't drown himself or get run over walking down the middle of Harborview in the middle of the night."

"Hell, I had no idea it had gotten so bad."

"That was the point. I didn't want to throw more problems on your plate."

Mac's father was a kind and generous man of sterling character. Despite his successes in so many areas, he'd always considered family the most important thing in his life. If Dr. Boyd Buchanan believed this was the best thing for *his* father, Mac wasn't about to second-guess him.

"I'd like to be able to be with him," Mac said. "Have Emma meet him." *Before it's too late.* He didn't say the words aloud, but knew his father heard them.

"That pretty little girl would bring a smile to his face and sunshine into his heart," Boyd agreed. "And there's nothing I'd love more than spending time with my incredible granddaughter. Especially with the holidays coming up."

It wasn't as if Mac had anywhere else to go. And his father, who knew a lot more about parenting than Mac did, could help during this rocky transition.

"I'll book the flights in the morning," he said. "And, Dad—thanks."

"I'm the one who should thank *you*. Your grandfather built this house with his own hands when he and your grandmother got engaged, then added on to it as each of his four kids were born. With my brothers busy with their own families around the country, I'm left here rattling around all alone in all these empty rooms. I'd be grateful for the company."

With at least one thing in his life settled, Mac said good night, turned off the radio, and went upstairs to the bedroom, stopping to check in on his daughter.

Emma was lying on her side, clutching a spotted Dalmatian toy. Since it had been dark when he'd put her to bed, he'd forgotten to close the curtains. In the silvery moonlight streaming through the window, she looked so small. So innocent. So vulnerable.

Which had Mac feeling as helpless as he'd felt when that truck bomb had sent him flying through the air.

She'd kicked off her covers. When he bent to pull the Barbie-pink blanket up, he brushed a kiss on her cheek. She murmured something in her sleep, then rolled over onto her back, taking the stuffed animal with her. But she didn't wake up.

Not wanting to smell his wife on the sheets of the bed in the master bedroom, Mac found a small guest room across the hall. After kicking off his boots, he fell facedown onto the too-soft bed.

His last thought, before he crashed into sleep, was that at least things had to go uphill from here. Because they damn well couldn't get any worse.

7

Shelter Bay, Oregon
Eight months later

Located on one of the hills overlooking Shelter Bay, Still Waters didn't look like your typical nursing home. Because, Annie Shepherd thought as she walked toward the building brightened by hand-painted murals of the Oregon coastal town, it wasn't. Instead, it was a thoughtfully designed residential home created especially to keep diminishing minds active, while at the same time quieting them. Thus the name.

When Sedona Sullivan, who led the monthly cookie-decorating group at Still Waters, had first suggested she volunteer here, Annie had been hesitant. What did she know about Alzheimer's? Other than that it was a horrible disease.

But then when she'd brought Sedona's suggestion up at Adèle Douchett's knitting circle, the elderly woman, who'd suffered her own form of dementia after a head injury, had been encouraging.

"Don't think of them as Alzheimer's patients, dear," she'd said as her needles rapidly click-clacked away, creating yet another blanket for Project Linus, a children's charity the knitting circle contributed to. "Think of them as individuals with years of life experience to share."

As Adèle herself continued to do. While the older woman's memory might not be as sharp as it once was, she remained a powerful force. "I started a knitting group at Still Waters while having cognitive therapy there, and I know you'll fit right in," she assured Annie. "And, as it happens, a widower I became friends with during my group therapy sessions moved in last fall. I'm sure you'd find his stories entertaining, and that you'll brighten his day like a ray of sunshine."

While Annie wasn't sure about the sunshine part, though she did her best to remain unrelentingly upbeat—even on the days when she secretly wanted to weep—Adèle had been right about the elderly residents having so much to share. Perhaps because she'd grown up without any family of her own, Annie had, over the past months, begun to think of many of them as the grandparents and great-grandparents she'd never had.

After being buzzed in by the doorman—the building was kept locked to prevent residents from wandering away, which was one of the reasons people came to live here—she paused to pet the huge cat lying in a sunbeam atop the reception desk.

Still Waters embraced the growing belief among caregivers that people were less depressed and lonely if they lived with animal companions. Which especially made sense when you considered how many residents had been forced to leave their own pets behind.

Since Turtle, named for his tortoiseshell markings, had arrived, two other cats and a golden retriever (appropriately named Goldie), all rescues from Dr. Charity

Tiernan's shelter, had joined the residents of the memory care home.

Annie paused to chat with two women who were sitting in the brightly lit library and enjoying the view of the colorful garden out the tall windows, then skirted around Goldie to walk down a cheerfully painted hallway, stopping outside the room of a resident she'd become especially close to. The widower friend of Adèle's.

After retrieving family photos from his son, together she and Charlie Buchanan had created the burlap-covered bulletin board posted in the hallway next to his door. At the top were his name and date of birth. Below that was a sepia photo of an outrageously handsome young man wearing the classic sailor uniform of white shirt, bell-bottom trousers, and "Dixie cup" hat. Tacked in one corner was a black-and-white snapshot taken aboard a ship. This time he was wearing a blue chambray work shirt and denim pants.

Below those was a wedding photo. The bride was dressed in a lovely white gown, while the groom looked proud, though a bit dazed, in that same Navy uniform.

"Good afternoon, Charlie." She greeted him with a smile as she entered the room brightened by crayoned drawings she knew had been done by his great-granddaughter. They were taped to the buttery yellow walls. He was sitting in a chair by the window, looking out at the courtyard garden, where a profusion of red, yellow, and white tulips brightened the misty Oregon day. He was wearing a cardigan sweater that matched his faded blue eyes over a gray T-shirt, a pair of khakis, and sneakers. "How are you?"

Having apparently been taught by his mother to always stand up when a woman entered the room, Charlie managed to push himself to his feet as he always did, using a combination of arm pressure and momentum, even though she'd insisted it wasn't necessary.

His brow furrowed for a moment as he tried to place her. While Charlie's long-term memory was as sharp as a tack, his short-term memory was decidedly less so. Which was one of the things she'd been working on with him.

"I'm Annie," she said gently. "Annie Shepherd."

His expression cleared, just a bit. "Of course you are. You're the nurse who has the same name as my wife." His tone didn't carry quite as much conviction as his words, as he lowered himself back into the chair, but not wanting to cause him any stress, Annie decided to focus on today's plan rather than get bogged down in names and the fact that she was actually a volunteer, not a nurse.

"I thought we'd work on your scrapbook today," she said, going over to the dresser where it lay open to a page showing a reprint of the wedding photo that was on the hallway burlap board. "Your wife was very beautiful," she said.

"Annie was the prettiest girl in Shelter Bay." He puffed out his chest with husbandly pride. "Let me tell you, she sure turned heads when she walked down the street. . . . Her parents didn't want her to marry me, you know."

"No, I didn't realize that."

He gave her a long look. "You must not be from here, then," he said finally. "Because everyone in town knew her parents wanted her to marry Walter Mannington. His family milled nearly all the timber in three counties, which made them about the richest folks on the coast. While I was just a fisherman with a boat owned mostly by the bank."

Annie pulled up a chair and sat in front of him. "But she chose you."

"She did." He chuckled, more to himself than to her. "Mannington was too stuffy. She liked to have a good time. Same as me. Good-Time Charlie, folks used to call me."

"You're still a charmer." She smiled back at him. "A bit like Rhett Butler. But without the mustache."

"Funny." The laughter left his eyes as they became slightly unfocused. And shiny. "Annie used to say that. Since she had a thing for Gable in those days, I wasn't about to point out that I was better-looking." A deep, rich laugh rumbled up from his chest.

Enjoying the discussion, Annie laughed with him. Of all the residents she worked with, Charlie Buchanan was, hands down, her favorite.

"She made that wedding dress herself," he said. "Out of a Japanese parachute I sent back home."

"That's a parachute?" Unable to stitch a straight line, Annie was more than a little impressed.

"Yup. I found it on one of the islands in the Pacific during the war. I sent it home to her, and since silk was rationed, she used it to make the dress. The veil was mosquito netting."

"That's ingenious."

"She was a clever girl. She worked as a dressmaker for a lot of rich women in town. Including Mrs. Mannington. Walter's mother. Which is how they met. He lived in a big house, and his boat was a rich guy's Chris-Craft mahogany runabout that sure as hell didn't smell of fish, like mine did. And he had himself a red Cadillac convertible, which I never figured made much sense with all the rain we get here. But the girls sure seemed to go for it." Deep lines furrowed his brow. "Dang guy was used to getting everything he wanted without having to work for it."

"But he didn't get the most important thing," Annie

pointed out as she heard the edge of old grievances creep into his tone.

"True enough." He narrowed his gaze and studied her. "What did you say your name was?"

"Annie. Annie Shepherd. I run Memories on Main. It's a scrapbook and paper-crafting shop. We made this book together," she reminded him. As she did every week. "And I brought some more photos of your trip to the Newport aquarium."

"Why in the blue blazes would I want to go to an aquarium?" he asked. "I spent my life with fish. Don't need to see any of 'em locked up in fancy glassed-in boxes."

The trip had been two days ago. Regretting that she hadn't switched her schedule around to come yesterday, when the outing may have been fresher in his mind, Annie forged ahead.

She ran tape over the back of the photos, inviting him to paste them onto a new page she'd prepared ahead of time, all the while keeping up a nonstop commentary about what she'd been told the group had done when they'd been at the aquarium.

"See," she said, pointing at the photo of him standing next to a giant Pacific octopus exhibit. "There you are."

"Seem to be." He scratched his head. Then frowned. "This dang Alzheimer's."

"It's difficult." She placed a hand on his arm. "But a visit to the aquarium isn't all that important in the great scheme of things."

"Do you know the definition of Scottish Alzheimer's?" he asked, not for the first time.

"No. What *is* the definition of Scottish Alzheimer's?" She'd found that if she repeated words back, people were more likely to remember them.

"You forget everything but your grudges."

She laughed, as he'd meant her to. "Well, you're better off than that. You have lovely memories of your Annie."

"Is she coming today?"

"She passed on," she reminded him, as she did at least twice every week. "Ten years ago."

"Oh. Yeah." He said the correct words, but she could see a lingering doubt in his eyes. "You look a lot like her," he said.

"I'll take that as a compliment." She wasn't nearly as dramatically beautiful as Annie Buchanan had been, but she wasn't about to argue.

"It's in your eyes," he said. "They're that same color. I always told her they remind me of the sun shining through the rain. . . . I should introduce you to my grandson. He's a doctor."

The stress caused by his struggle to remember the field trip, and the unwelcome memory of his wife's death, seemed to drift off his handsome face, weathered by years of being outdoors on the sea. His eyes, clouded by the disease, brightened. "You could do a lot worse."

Annie knew that his son was the doctor, while his grandson was actually deployed in the Air Force, but rather than correcting him, she merely smiled and patted his arm. "If he's even half the man you are, Charlie, I'd definitely have to agree."

They worked for a few more minutes. Annie felt a burst of optimism when, with a bit of coaxing, he was able to remember eating the ice cream in the photo taken of him at the seawall in town on the way back from the aquarium. She always sent an update to his son, Dr. Boyd Buchanan, after each of their sessions, and it was nice to be able to report positive news.

She was on her way out of the building when she

dodged a scooter—whose rider had swerved to avoid hitting Daisy, a calico who'd jumped down from a chair—and plowed into a man who'd been entering the building. Distracted by a display on his phone, he hadn't seen her coming.

"I'm sorry," she said as she was brought to a sudden stop by the rock-hard wall of his chest. The wheeled bag carrying her craft supplies tipped over onto the floor.

"It was my fault." Sounding anything but apologetic, he shoved the phone into the pocket of his jeans. "I wasn't watching where I was going."

Although she couldn't see his eyes because of the wraparound Ray-Bans, she could feel the laser glare he aimed at the cat. Who was calmly licking her paw, either unaware or uncaring of the potential disasters she'd caused. "Especially in this place with all the animals underfoot."

His sexily beard-stubbled jaw was firm, his chin ruggedly square and marked with a deep, delicious cleft.

Although the local joke went that Oregonians rusted instead of tanned, his tan suggested he spent a lot of time outdoors. Maybe he was a fisherman, like so many men in town? Or in construction? After a real estate dip due to the recession, in the past few months you couldn't go anywhere in town without seeing signs of a construction boom, mainly beach houses and condos for wealthy weekenders

He was tall, lean, and hard enough that she'd felt as if she'd run into a wall of unyielding steel when her chest slammed into his.

Annie took a step back and lifted her purse strap, which had slid down her arm, more securely onto her shoulder. "I take it you don't like cats?"

"I don't exactly dislike them." He shrugged shoulders clad in a black T-shirt that showed off that muscled male body in a way that supported the idea that he did some sort of physical work.

And heaven help her, when he combed his fingers through his shaggy, sun-streaked chestnut hair, she had a moment of what the nuns who'd taught in her high school would've referred to as an "impure thought." A picture of his broad, dark, workingman's hands on her body flashed wickedly through Annie's mind.

"I just don't *get* them." His baritone voice roughened with exasperation. "They're not like dogs, who let you know exactly what they're thinking."

Damn. He might be testosterone on a stick, but with that disparaging comment, his sex appeal plummeted several degrees. Not only did Annie love cats, but she was currently owned by a twenty-pounder she'd adopted at Charity Tiernan's Christmas pet fair.

"That's part of their appeal. They're mysterious." She started to bend down to pick up her bag, but he was faster. "They prefer keeping their thoughts to themselves."

Wasn't she the same way? Life in the revolving door of the foster care system and then her failed marriage had definitely taught Annie to keep what she might be thinking to herself.

"More likely people just mistake stupidity for inscrutability."

"I suppose that's one way of looking at it."

Well, wasn't he just Mr. Sunshine?

Deciding that the hottie in Ray-Bans was the male version of beauty going only skin deep, Annie felt sorry for whomever the man was here to visit. Feeling that she'd wasted enough time, she grabbed hold of her rolling craft bag, and after a momentary tug-of-war, he released it.

"Well, again, I'm sorry to have run into you." Since she was all too aware of the fact that they'd suddenly begun to provide entertainment for a group of residents sitting at a table putting a jigsaw puzzle together, she managed, just barely, to keep the annoyance she was feeling out of her voice. "Have a nice evening."

With that, Annie squared her shoulders and walked past him, toward the door. For some inexplicable reason she was tempted to look back to see if he was watching her, but she resisted the impulse.

8

Mac watched the woman hold up her pass card to the electronic eye that opened the glass doors. She was tall and slim, but what curves she had were definitely in all the right places. Her hips swayed enticingly in a simply cut sleeveless dress covered with a splash of flowers that reminded him of the garden his mother had so lovingly tended. They also had him thinking of starlight and tangled sheets.

Even as he tried to shake off that distracting thought, he watched her pull the flowered bag down the sidewalk to the parking lot. With a new job, a grandfather sinking deeper into dementia every day, and a daughter who, once she'd realized he really wasn't going to leave her again, was proving to have a very strong mind of her own, he had no business even thinking about tangling sheets with a woman. Which hadn't happened in so long, sometimes days would go by before he'd even miss it.

When her pert breasts had pressed against his chest like a wake-up call to his too-long-celibate body, every thought in his head had immediately gone south. He presumed that was why, instead of some clever, casual pickup line, his sex-battered brain had come up with cat insults. More proof that he'd definitely lost his touch. Even some alien landing from Mars would undoubtedly know that most females actually liked cats.

"You could've at least gotten her name," he muttered to himself as he used his coded key to enter the first-level memory care wing, where his grandfather's room was located. "Asked her out for a drink. Maybe even dinner."

Or to his bed.

"Don't go there." Besides, the invisible wall that had shot up between them after he'd insulted the cat wasn't all that encouraging. Although he did feel like he owed the cat a thank-you for causing the close encounter with the sexy stranger.

Assuring himself that the sudden jolt of lust was proof that all his guy parts were still in working order, despite the suffocating sense of survivor guilt that had been hanging over his head these past months since the explosion, Mac plastered a smile he was a long way from feeling on his face as he paused at the desk.

"Hey, look at you," he greeted Analise Peterson, the floor nurse. She was wearing her signature brightly patterned scrubs, which she'd once told him helped keep residents engaged by initiating conversation. Today's green shirt and pants were printed with— wouldn't you just know it?—kittens. "You're tan."

"Kelli Douchett was right about Hawaii being the best place ever for a honeymoon." She dimpled prettily. "The beaches were amazing. Including one we stumbled across on Molokai that looked like something out of a movie. It had this one gorgeous stretch with white sand that looked like spun sugar, and amazingly, there was no one there! We could've been the only two people on the planet. . . ."

When the new bride's voice drifted off and her

cheeks flushed bright pink, Mac had a very good idea of how they'd spent that stolen private time.

"Well, it's good to have you back," he said. "You were missed. . . . So, how's he doing today?"

"Pretty well," Analise said, morphing from blushing newlywed to the efficient, caring RN who kept the wing running so smoothly. "The other day's outing must have energized him. He's been quite chatty."

"That's definitely good news." One thing Mac had learned about Alzheimer's was that what might have once been small, mundane things were events to be celebrated.

He reminded himself of that as he walked down the hallway, past the doors with the bulletin boards covered with bright-colored burlap and photos of the residents' lives in happier, more optimistic times. The boards had begun appearing a few weeks ago and although he understood that it helped staff and visitors personalize the patients, there were times when he found himself wondering if the subjects of all those photographs would have been smiling as brightly if they'd known what was lurking in the hidden shadows of their futures.

Shaking off that depressing thought, he knocked on the door to his grandfather's room, then walked in.

"Hey, Pops."

He'd been coming to visit every day since he'd arrived in Shelter Bay eight months ago, and although at first he'd been relieved that his grandfather wasn't in as rough shape as he'd feared when his father had told him about the illness, there was no way to ignore the fact that there seemed to be less of him than when Mac and Emma had first visited. Despite the good days, the disease was relentless as it slowly stole its victims away. The phrase *the long good-bye* was heartbreakingly accurate.

On the plus side, Mac was learning the power of memories. How stories of the past made people who and what they are. His grandfather was, more and more, living in the moment. Which Mac, wishing he could forget a lot of his own past, had decided did have its pluses.

He'd begun hugging Emma a little tighter when he kissed her good night. Held her hand a little longer before she raced into her kindergarten class. And more and more often he found himself pausing to drink in the amazing, fiery beauty of the sun setting over the ocean, or the shimmering arc of a rainbow after a spring rain.

Or the seductive sway of feminine hips in a flowered dress.

"So." He turned a straight-backed chair around, sat down, and put his arms on the back rail. "How're things?"

"Same as they were yesterday," Charlie grumbled. "And the day before. And the day before that. This place reminds me of the Navy. Everything is scheduled the same. Over and over."

"Like *Groundhog Day*."

When his grandfather's expression revealed not a hint of understanding, although Mac knew he'd seen the movie, he merely shrugged. "It's a movie where time gets stuck and the same day keeps repeating."

"Yep. Sounds a lot like here," Charlie said.

"You went to the aquarium day before yesterday," Mac reminded him. "And got ice cream."

Puzzlement drifted across Charlie's eyes. Eyes that had once sparkled like sunlight on blue water, but were now more tinged with shadows. He tugged on the sleeve of the cardigan he was wearing despite the warmth of the room. At one time he would've filled out the shoulders of the blue sweater, but no more. It now swamped him—yet another change. The broad-shouldered, barrel-chested man who'd spent his life hauling in traps and fishing lines was being whittled away.

Mac noticed the scrapbook on the table beside the chair. There were new photos that hadn't been in it when he'd visited last evening.

"See," he said, pointing one out. "Here's you eating ice cream at the seawall."

The confusion dissipated, like morning fog over the harbor burned away by a summer sun. "Rocky Road." Charlie nodded with satisfaction, certain of this fact. "It's always been my favorite."

"I know." The disease might be robbing his grandfather of many things, but not of his love of ice cream.

"Annie liked strawberry." His smile was reminiscent. Wistful. "I always said it was because it was the sweetest. Just like her." He tilted his head, thinking. "We didn't have as many flavors in those days. Nothing like now. It's near impossible to decide what to choose when you just want a damn cone."

"You're not alone there, Pops."

"Annie liked strawberry," he said again, as if for the first time. He picked up the book and turned the page until he'd come to a photo of Mac's grandmother, posed on a driftwood log like a 1940s cover model, smiling into the camera. "I always said it was because it was the sweetest. Just like her."

"That's a good memory."

"Yeah. It is." He paused again, whether lost in that memory, or just lost in the labyrinth of his mind, Mac wasn't certain. "Your Emma likes strawberry best, too."

Mac had found it puzzling that the one thing his grandfather was never confused about was Emma. He always talked about her, always remembered what she'd told him, even recalled the names of her friends that she'd chatter about during their visits.

"She does," Mac agreed. "But I think it's because it's pink as much as for the flavor."

"Probably so. The girl does have a fondness for pink. Annie used to like it, too. Did I ever tell you about the time she surprised me by painting our bedroom?"

"I don't think so." He had, several times. But knowing it was one of his grandfather's favorite memories, Mac didn't mind hearing it again.

"She painted it bubblegum pink because she thought it'd be more romantic than the beige I'd painted it when I built the addition. Well, when I came home from crab fishing up in Alaska and walked into that room, the first thing that hit my mind was that the guys would never stop ragging me if they knew I had a foo-foo girlie-pink bedroom. But she was so happy about her surprise, I decided that I liked it, too. And it wasn't as if any of the guys on the boat were ever going to see our bedroom. Plus, she turned out to be right. We did have some fine romantic times in that pink room. . . .

"Mac, you need a wife."

The change in topic was abrupt and unexpected. Like so many of his conversations with his grandfather these days. Aware that there would come a time when the older man would disappear completely behind the veiled curtain that would cut him off from his friends and family, Mac was grateful whenever Charlie initiated conversation. As Analise had said, this was definitely a chatty day.

"I *had* a wife," Mac reminded him.

"You did?" Narrowed eyes sharpened as the past tense seemed to sink in. "What happened to her?"

Although they'd been through this numerous times before, Mac settled on the short answer. "She left me. Eight months ago."

And except for three phone calls to their daughter— one the day after she'd left Colorado Springs, the second on Christmas Day, and the third on Emma's recent sixth birthday—Mac hadn't heard a word from her. He had, however, received the divorce papers from her attorney, then the official notice that the State of Arizona had declared their marriage ended.

"Humph. Sounds like she wasn't the forever-after one . . . your soul mate, like Annie was mine. So maybe you need a new wife."

"I'm doing okay."

"So you say. But I'll bet my great-granddaughter could use a mother. Now, I'm not saying that you and your father aren't good caretakers," he said, sounding a great deal like the decisive, outspoken man he'd once been. "But little girls need a woman in their lives. And this is your lucky day, boy, because I've got just the woman for you."

"You do, huh?"

"I do." His grandfather folded his arms across his chest and nodded. "My nurse."

Unfortunately, his nurse was Analise, who'd just returned from her honeymoon. Damn. For a while there, they were on a reality roll. One step forward, two back.

"I'll take that under advisement." There was no point in reminding his grandfather that his nurse was newly married, since he would undoubtedly forget this conversation by the time Mac reached his truck in the parking lot.

"You do that. Annie—that'd be the nurse—is pretty, smart as a whip, and sweet. She'd make a perfect mother for little Emma. And you could do a helluva lot worse."

Now he was confusing Analise's name with that of his late wife.

"Like I said, I'll keep it in mind," Mac said, fighting back a long, deep sigh. Then, needing to change the subject, which was getting increasingly depressing, he asked, "Want to watch *Western Angler*? I brought along a DVD."

Although Mac had never understood the appeal of watching other people fish, apparently a lot of folks, like his grandfather, did. How else to explain a mind-blowing number of more than nine hundred fishing shows available on TV?

"Always up for fishing."

About five minutes into the show, which was all about fishing on the Clackamas River, his grandfather said, "She's waiting for me."

"Grandma?"

"Who else would I be talking about? Of course your grandmother . . . I keep telling her I want to be together again. But she keeps insisting it's not my time." He folded his arms and glared at the TV. "She made me wait six damn months after I proposed before she'd marry me so she could plan herself a wedding."

"Women like weddings." Kayla had certainly planned one with an attention to detail that had reminded him of the Joint Chiefs orchestrating an invasion.

"Yeah. I figured that out for myself when she had me choosing between chocolate and vanilla wedding cakes."

"Which did you go with?"

"We split the difference and went with marble. Woman never was on time a day in her life, so I spent a lot of time waiting. Which I never minded, because she was worth it. But dammit, here I am now, stuck in this place, waiting for her again."

As a fisherman hauled in a fifteen-pound steelhead that had put up one helluva fight, Mac's grandfather's words caused a stir of concern. "You're not thinking about speeding up that timeline, are you?"

The rise in military suicides had made Mac extra vigilant during his days on AFN whenever men and women would call in to his program with personal problems. Now he was attuned to every nuance.

"Of course not," Charlie huffed, sounding offended that Mac had even asked. "I was just making conversation."

"Okay. But you'd let someone know if . . . "

"I *said* I was just making conversation. So can you just shut your piehole and let me watch my damn program?"

"Sure." There was no point in arguing. But Mac did make a note to call his grandfather's doctor as soon as he left. And to stop again at the desk on the way out and ask Analise Peterson to request that the staff keep an eye out for any signs of depression.

They watched the rest of the thirty-minute program, which proved about twenty minutes longer than his grandfather's attention span.

After promising to be back tomorrow evening, he was leaving the room when Charlie tried one more time. "You think about my nurse. Not right for a man to be alone. And Annie would be just the right little gal for you."

"Yes, Pops," Mac said obediently, even as his mind drifted back to that woman he'd literally bumped into earlier.

She hadn't been wearing a wedding ring, and yes, he'd noticed, but that didn't mean that she wasn't attached.

He didn't even know her name. Didn't know a thing about her except for the fact that she liked cats. And didn't like men who didn't like cats.

Well, he did know that her eyes, behind a way hot pair of sexy black-framed librarian glasses, were an intriguing swirl of silver and pewter, that her nose tipped up a bit at the end, and that her kiss-me-big-boy mouth had had him on the verge of doing exactly that.

He also knew that during that fleeting moment of impact she'd awakened vital parts of himself that he'd begun to fear had gone dormant.

9

"I'm so glad we could get together," Annie said to Sedona Sullivan as they worked their way through an appetizer plate of popcorn shrimp and clam strips at Sax Douchett's Bon Temps Cajun restaurant.

"Me, too." Sedona took a sip of her wine. "Sometimes it seems as if we're the only two single women left under the age of fifty in Shelter Bay."

"At least in our circle of friends," Annie said as she dipped a piece of popcorn shrimp into the restaurant's signature Come-Back sauce. "I'm honestly glad everyone's happy. Especially Kara and Phoebe with their babies. But although I really am over my divorce, I'm happy with my life and have no inclination to jump back into the dating pool again anytime soon."

She'd managed to move beyond the divorce, and the pain of failure had eased. But she'd spent the past two years rebuilding her life, establishing her business and becoming part of the community, which didn't leave her with the time or energy for a relationship. There was also the fact that these days men, or at least the ones in Shelter Bay, actually seemed interested in creating families. Something that was a non-starter for her.

For a fleeting moment earlier, at Still Waters, when she'd felt that jolt like heat lightning, she'd been tempted. But then the guy who'd caused that red alert to all her feminine parts had opened his mouth and proven himself to be just another jerk. Which she so didn't need in her life. She'd been there, done that, and hadn't even gotten a T-shirt out of the deal.

"Smart woman," Sedona said. "It's also what I've been telling my parents. Until I caved in for one of their fix-ups last night."

"Your *parents* fixed you up? Aren't they some sort of hippies?"

"They are that. For some weird reason, they're starting to work into seemingly every conversation the complaint that I'm never going to make them grandparents. It's a little spooky how two former flower children, who still live in a commune, would start acting so abnormal."

"I'm not sure, but I think it's normal for most people, once their kids grow up, to start looking forward to becoming grandparents," Annie said mildly.

"Maybe. But my parents are definitely not *most people*. It almost makes me want to fly down to Arizona and check out what's gotten into their well water."

Personally, Annie had always found it unusual that after such an unstructured childhood, Sedona had grown up to become an accountant. But, of course, hadn't she walked away from the six-figure income and big-city high-rise corner office to bake cupcakes in Shelter Bay? Much the same way Annie had walked away from wealth and privilege and what was actually a stiflingly boring country club existence to move across the country and open a scrapbook store.

"People always have the wrong conceptions of commune living," Sedona complained as she snagged a shrimp from the pile on the plate and dipped it into the Come-Back sauce. "Contrary to conventional wisdom, most communes aren't refuges for aging flower children, but well-ordered, financially solvent, non-hierarchical, socially and ecologically involved communities. When I went to college, guys all figured that I grew up surrounded by free love, so naturally, I'd be easy."

"But you didn't." Annie had secretly wondered, but had never wanted to delve into such a private topic. Especially since, having grown up as a foster kid, she had no idea what constituted a "normal" family. "Grow up surrounded by free love?"

Although she'd never admit it, there were times when she thought that if people's lives had sound tracks, Sedona Sullivan's would be a medley of "Aquarius/Let the Sunshine In" from the musical *Hair*.

"No. I dislike conflict and drama, so I pretty much stayed on the boring straight and narrow. And my parents, while not the Cleavers, were, as far as I know, absolutely monogamous. They're very different people, actually. My mother, who taught me to bake, is mellow and calm and goes with the flow, while my artist dad's pretty intense.

"But as I got older and started thinking about boys and men and relationships, I realized that each of their individual parts fit together perfectly to make a much stronger united entity. I'm certainly not holding my breath, since I enjoy my life exactly as it is. But if I ever met a guy I meshed with as well as my parents do, I'd latch on to him in a heartbeat."

"I take it the guy last Saturday wasn't Mr. Right?" Annie often thought that it would be next to impossible for any man to live up to the required qualities Sedona had plugged into her unbelievably detailed Excel "dateable male" spreadsheet. The first time Kara Douchett had told her about the spreadsheet, Annie had been sure she must be kidding. But then she'd actually seen it for herself.

Sedona might have grown up in a commune, but apparently, despite her change in careers, there was a CPA still lurking somewhere inside her.

"Hardly. For any woman. Unless she was into vampires."

"You're kidding, right?"

"I wish I were." Sedona sighed and leaned forward, about to share the story, when their server arrived at the table to take their dinner orders. Crab jambalaya for Annie, shrimp étouffée for Sedona.

"He seemed normal enough when he kept coming in to buy a cupcake," she said. "Granted, I don't get many customers who come in *every day*, but I was admittedly flattered when even after I turned him down twice, he didn't stop."

"Some might consider that close to stalking," Annie suggested.

"True, it's a thin line. But I didn't get any weird vibes from him. He dressed like a normal guy, no black cape or upside-down cross necklace, he didn't have oversized incisors or ask for blood-flavored cupcakes. He was also walking around in the middle of the day, and from what I could tell didn't sparkle."

"So when and how did you discover his vampire tendencies?"

"After I finally caved in and agreed to lunch at the Sea Mist. When we first walked in and the hostess led us to a table by the windows overlooking the harbor, he said it was too bright."

"Which is unusual for here, but maybe his eyes are sensitive."

"Exactly what I thought."

"So, after we were seated, before we even got our menus, he informed me he was taking a trip to Tran-

sylvania. Since it's not one of your usual tourist desti-
nations, I asked him if he had family there, and he
said, 'Not exactly.'"

"That's odd."

"Agreed. But then he told me that he got into
fifteenth-century history after reading Bram Stoker's
Dracula."

"Aha! A clue. But not an indictment."

"Again, we're in full agreement." Sedona shrugged
and took another sip of wine. "I mean, it's not as if all
those millions of people who read vampire stories or
visit Forks up in Washington because of *Twilight* believe they're actually vampires."

"Lucky for the rest of us or we'd be overrun with
people wanting to suck our blood."

"Extremely lucky. When the waitress came to take
our drink orders, since I had to go back and make a
bunch of pies, I stuck to tea. He ordered white wine."

"Nothing unusual there. Given that the Sea Mist is a
seafood restaurant, I've ordered white wine a lot with
my meals there."

"Ah. But I didn't tell you his reason."

"Which would be?"

"White wine 'dilutes the bloodlust.'"

Annie paused in lifting her wineglass to her lips,
held it out, and studied the straw gold Chardonnay. "It
does?"

"Of course not. Because vampires, excuse me, don't
exist. He also told me that he only ate red meat."

"Which makes the Sea Mist an odd choice."

"Not if you order the burger off the children's
menu . . . So, while we were waiting for his rare ham-
burger and my seafood salad, he decided he could trust
me with his secret."

"I'm afraid to ask."

"Wise. Because it just so happens that he's a direct

descendant of old Vlad the Impaler. And it gets better. He's the first person in his American family to make the pilgrimage back to their homeland."

Annie nearly choked on her wine. "He comes from an entire family of vampires? Who live here in Shelter Bay?"

"No. We can rest easy. Apparently he's the only one for generations who inherited the count's powers. In fact, despite his showing supposedly irrefutable evidence from three different genealogists to his relatives, they all deny their heritage."

"Whew! I feel much relieved." Annie waved her hand. "So, continue on."

"Well, as I said, he seemed normal enough whenever he came into the shop, so for a few minutes I thought I might be getting punked. I couldn't imagine who'd go to the trouble to set up such a practical joke, but I decided to play along and see how far he'd go with the story. So I asked him if he had super vampire powers."

"And?"

"Supposedly he does, but he only uses them in times of great need. He can hover."

"Cool."

"And allegedly slow time down."

"Okay, that one might be worth having lunch with a vampire if he could pull it off for me for even a day," Annie decided.

What with her business, and her volunteering at Still Waters, the evening classes she taught at Memories on Main, the card group she led, which made blank-inside greeting cards for troops to send back home to friends and loved ones through Operation Write Home, as well as for the Cards for Hospitalized Kids charity, she could definitely use at least another two hours in her day.

"Unfortunately the blood power's been diluted through the centuries. Which is why he's going back to his so-called homeland. Because once he's in his ancestor's castle, he'll have Vlad's strength."

"Gotta love his optimism. Even if it might involve him looking forward to impaling tens of thousands of innocent people. So, is this where you got up and left the restaurant?"

"I hadn't had my salad yet. Which I'd been looking forward to all morning. As I said, he wasn't outwardly creepy. And, in a way, in the beginning, he was entertaining."

"But that changed?"

"Absolutely."

"If he'd leaped over the table and sunk retractable fangs into your neck, I would've heard about it," Annie decided. "Because someone would've called the sheriff, and Kara would've arrested him."

"No, it was just that being a vampire was all he wanted to talk about. I asked him what sports he liked, and he said that he couldn't do sports because even though his strength might not be up to his ancestor's, it was more powerful than humans', so it wouldn't be fair to compete. He is actually pretty buff."

"Probably from sweating blood in the gym."

Sedona laughed at that. "Trying to change the subject, I mentioned being homeschooled in the commune, which usually sparks some conversation, but it was as if he didn't have any real interest in me, because his response was that he'd always been smarter than anyone else in school due to his hyper-speed brain power, which had made him an outcast growing up."

"Not that telling everyone he was a vampire would've had anything to do with that. Especially once his classmates all started wearing garlic necklaces," Annie said dryly.

They laughed, then changed topics to the residents of Still Waters, and the upcoming sand castle and kite festivals on the beach as the weather warmed up.

Although Annie enjoyed the dinner, by the time she got home to her dark house on Castaway Cove, which she'd painted a cheerful sunshine yellow the first month she'd moved in, a tinge of the all-too-familiar blues had settled over her shoulders.

She'd been telling the truth when she said she wasn't ready to jump back into the dating pool. Partly because she couldn't see how she could fit in the time for a relationship between all of her professional and volunteer commitments. And partly because one of the problems with small towns was that the pool of single, available men was limited. Sedona might have gone out with the only vampire in Shelter Bay, but none of the men who'd hit on Annie since her arrival had her wanting to let them into her life.

Nor, she'd discovered, was she the kind of woman to settle for booty calls or friends with benefits.

After being abandoned shortly after birth in an anonymous drive-by dumping at a Eugene hospital, she'd spent the first eighteen years of her life in transient family relationships, and although she knew that many would think her hopelessly old-fashioned, what she wanted was the kind of happily-ever-after marriage that Charlie had shared with his beloved Annie. That Sofia De Luca, another friend of Adèle's, who ran Lavender Hill Farm, had reportedly shared with her husband. And that Adèle herself and her husband, Bernard, continued to share.

"Dream on," she murmured, as she scooped up the cat who'd jumped off the couch, not so much to greet her as to allow itself to be petted.

Pirate, named for his black eye patch and the fact that he'd supposedly been found feral on this very cove where Annie's house was located, where seamen from ships reportedly taken by Sir Francis Drake had waded ashore, personified feline independence. Which was one of the things she loved about him.

Dogs admittedly had their appeal, including unqualified love for their owners, but with some cats, like Pirate, you had to work to gain their respect. And affection.

She had a good life. Correction: a *great* life. Friends, a business she loved, volunteer work that made her feel as if she was contributing to her adopted town, and an oversized cat who occasionally would even deign to purr his approval.

But that didn't mean that sometimes she wasn't lonely. And more often, with so many of her friends settling down, more than a little wistful that she might never achieve the family she'd spent her entire childhood and teenage years dreaming of.

Although she'd fallen in love with the Victorian four-bedroom, two-bath cottage the moment she'd seen it, it was admittedly more space than one person—and one cranky cat—needed.

She'd turned one of the extra bedrooms into a craft room, but when she'd first seen the dream nursery Kara and Sax Douchett had created for their newborn, she couldn't deny having felt a momentary, unwanted twinge of envy. As honestly happy as she was for her friend, that didn't stop Annie from occasionally imagining those empty rooms filled with her own children. Playing, laughing, loving.

Bygones.

As much as she enjoyed her independence and the life she'd created for herself here in Shelter Bay, as she poured a glass of wine, lit a fire, and settled down to try to find something on her DVR, it crossed Annie's mind that sometimes Saturday nights really sucked.

10

Mac flat-out hated Saturday nights. The only two things worse, he decided, as he pulled into the KBAY radio station parking lot, were Valentine's Day and New Year's Eve, when the bar to have the best time ever was raised so high, you'd need a pole to vault over it.

Apparently his was a minority opinion, because everyone at Bon Temps, where he'd stopped in for a late supper after putting Emma to bed, had seemed to be having themselves a high old time. Sax Douchett had brought in an Alabama cover band from Corvallis for Country Night at the restaurant and the small dance floor had been crowded. One guy and his date had stood in the center, ignoring all the couples doing the boot-scootin' boogie around them as they'd slowly swayed, lost in their own lovey-dovey world.

And although he would fling himself off the Shelter Bay bridge before admitting it, the sight of the guy's hands on the woman's jeans-clad butt had sent a sharp, hot spike of lust through him, not unlike what he'd felt when he'd run into that woman at Still Waters earlier.

When he'd muttered to Sax that they ought to get a room, the former SEAL had laughed, put a bowl of fiery hot nuts on the bar in front of him and suggested that he just needed to get laid

Easier said than done. But he wasn't interested in going back to one-night hookups, especially now that he was a single father. The last thing Emma needed was for a parade of strange women to traipse through his life.

Besides, if he was to have sex, it'd have to be nooners, because his nights were no longer free. Although he'd originally taken the night gig, leaving Emma with his father, so he could be home during the day with her, Mac had discovered that whenever he was alone in the dark, his ghosts visited, dragging with them a litany of negative choices, failed promises, and *what-ifs*.

At least when he was on the air, he was connecting with other people—night-shift workers, long-haul truckers, and lonely people who, like him, were struggling to avoid that dark ride on the night train of regrets.

"Next up is Wade Bowen's 'Saturday Night,' a definite tears-in-your-beer song. And I'm asking the same thing Wade is: Why is everybody so in love with Saturday night?

"If you're not doing anything wild and fun—and hey, if you are, you're probably not sitting around listening to me spin tunes—why don't you pick up the phone, dial 555-9806, and let me know how you feel. And FYI, I don't exactly have the biggest staff in the world, so we're recording conversations for playback after the songs."

At the larger stations where Mac had worked, he'd have a producer fielding the calls. The best ones had an internal red-alert warning system that filtered out long-winded callers, foul-mouthed ones, and BS artists, like the guy who'd called last week to say he had photographic proof that Bigfoot was living up at Rainbow Lake outside of town. But KBAY was a small FM start-up station that just broadcast up the coast, which cut down on advertising revenue, which also cut down on staffing.

During the day, when the ad sales staff of two were working, and secretaries were getting coffee for the people the day producers would round up for interviews, and those producers were handling the extra calls that would come in during what was laughingly referred to as "Drive Time," the station almost seemed to be bustling.

But from midnight to four a.m., there was just Mac, his microphone, and his small but loyal night owl audience, which wasn't large enough to allow for the cost of a producer.

In some ways, working at KBAY was like his first job in Alturas. He'd worked the board himself back then, and although computers had changed a bit over the years, this wasn't that different. Besides, it kept him from having to spend the shift interacting with anyone. Since he'd gotten out of the hospital, he'd kept pretty much to himself, with the exception of Emma, his father, and his grandfather. Having already done the fame thing, and realizing what it had cost him, he avoided personal appearances. Nor did he allow the station to put up posters for his show, which, he realized, made him a bit of a mystery man in a town where everyone seemed to know everything about everyone else's lives.

He did eat frequently at Bon Temps, and so he occasionally made small talk with Sax, but when it came to his time in Afghanistan, Sax didn't ask and Mac didn't tell.

Besides, the former SEAL was so besotted with his baby daughter, always showing off the newest photos on his phone screen and going on and on about whatever new milestone she'd soared over that day, Mac wasn't really required to say more than "Wow," or

"That's cool." Or "Yeah, she is beautiful and yep, she does look exactly like her mother." All of which were true.

The song went three minutes and twenty-nine seconds. Add in another thirty seconds for a commercial for the Crab Shack, and Mac had about four minutes to record a call he could play after going back on the air.

The light on his console lit up before Bowen's song got to the bridge.

"So, who've we got?" Mac asked, picking up. "And hey, turn off your radio, okay? Because you won't be able to hear because of the feedback . . . Great."

"I'm Travis, from Depoe Bay, and I'm KBAY," the voice said, stating the tagline that the station owner had wanted to make sure all the deejays got people to say.

"Hey, Travis. So, how do you feel about Saturday nights?"

"They suck."

Well, that was succinct. As the dreaded dead air dropped like a rock, Mac tried to lure the guy into expanding on the story.

"Want to tell us why?"

"Yeah. I was cutting timber up Astoria way when the sawmill decided they'd had enough for the day and ours was the last truckload. Which meant I got to go home about two hours earlier than I'd told my wife."

Mac figured he could see this one coming, but since they weren't live, he decided to go with it a little bit longer. "I guess you went straight home?"

"Yeah. She'd been ragging on me for not spending enough time with her, but, hey, when you've got a contract to cut timber, it's not like you can blow the job off just to be home in time for dinner with the old lady every damn night."

Mac might not have been the best husband on the

planet, but even he knew that referring to your wife as "the old lady" wouldn't exactly win points.

"She'd been making more and more noise about wondering if she wanted to stay married, so I decided maybe an opportunity had dropped in my lap. I stopped by Fred Meyer and picked up some flowers, a box of wine, and those Belgian chocolates they sell there. My wife really liked the coffee ones."

"Can't imagine any woman not being happy to receive all that."

"Yeah. That's what I thought. Then, okay, I figured I'd get lucky and get some makeup sex, because she'd been really hot under the collar when I left the house."

There were getting into dangerous FCC territory, but Mac decided that the guy hadn't gone too far. Yet.

"Wanna guess what happened?" Travis from Depoe Bay asked.

"She was out with some girlfriends when you got home?" Mac hoped that was the answer.

"Oh, she was home, all right. But not with a girlfriend. I caught her in bed with a guy I'd known since high school. A guy who was supposed to be my effing best friend."

As Travis launched into a tirade that might've actually made a sailor blush, Mac hung up.

Then said, "Oops. Seems we lost the connection with Travis. But I think we can all understand why he might not be a fan of Saturday night."

There were another two minutes. Rather than risk the guy calling in again to get back on the air, Mac picked up on the call that had been on hold.

"Hey. Who are you and where are you calling from?"

There was a slight hesitation. Mac was about to risk Travis being back on line three, when a female voice said, "I'm, uh, Sandy. And I'm from Shelter Bay. Oh, and I'm KBAY."

She sounded nervous. Which wasn't that surprising. She wouldn't be the first person to sound flustered calling in to a radio program.

"Hey, Sandy. So, what do you do in Shelter Bay?"

"A little of this. A little of that."

"Ah. A lady with secrets."

"Not exactly secrets . . . I had dinner with a friend at Bon Temps earlier."

"Hey, me, too. What did you have?"

"Crab jambalaya."

"I had the gumbo and sweet potato fries. Then you came home and turned on the radio?"

Either she'd been out with a girlfriend or some guy had struck out. He also wondered if she'd been eating while he'd been in the restaurant. Because her voice sounded vaguely familiar. Maybe she'd been sitting at a nearby table and he'd caught a drift of her conversation?

There was a slight pause, which the clock in his head told Mac lasted three seconds. Another one and he would've jumped in to fill the gap.

"I sat alone in the dark for a while, thinking about mistakes," she said quietly. "Then I turned on the radio."

Part of Mac liked knowing that he was doing his job so well that someone had found his show to be a balm to what sounded like loneliness. And couldn't he identify with the regret he heard in her voice?

Hell, maybe that's what had his numbers soaring. Maybe he wasn't the only one who sat alone in the dark thinking of all the *what-ifs* strewn alongside the wrong roads he'd taken.

The clocks were ticking down. The one on the production board, the one on the wall, along with the one in his head.

"We've got to go to the network for a news segment," he said. "Would you mind staying on the line, Sandy? Then you can give your view on Saturday night."

Another hesitation. He could practically feel her arguing with herself over the phone line. Which perversely made him want to talk to her even more.

"All right," she said finally. Her laugh was soft and more than a little sad. "It's not as if I've got anywhere all that exciting to go."

"And here I thought I was Mr. Excitement," he said, sliding back into Radio Guy mode.

He made the connection with the network feed, and then, as a story about the war in Afghanistan, which he could do without hearing, came on, Mac returned to Sandy.

"And, just so you'll know, I'm not recording this part of our conversation for the air," he said.

"Why?"

She didn't sound thrilled by the personal attention.

"I don't know." That was the truth. The only time he ever talked to callers off the air was when they sounded as if they might prove to be a threat to themselves or others and he was trying to talk them off some ledge. "Maybe because we have something in common."

"Oh?"

Damn. Her voice was definitely familiar. That single syllable had sent a bell ringing, but it was deep enough in his mind he couldn't place it.

"The reason I asked the question in the first place is that I was thinking the same thing tonight," he said. "About my own past screwups."

"What kind of screwups?" She drew a quick breath. "I'm sorry. I shouldn't have asked that. It's personal. And none of my business."

"It's not that unusual a story." Unfortunately. "I was a lousy husband."

"I'm sorry." He'd gotten good at judging people by their voices, and hers was sincere. "From your use of the past tense, I guess you're divorced, too?"

Ah. A clue. So, the lady with the dulcet tones wasn't married. Though if she was sitting in the dark, dwelling on regrets, she probably wasn't any more ready for a relationship than he was.

"Yeah."

"I'm sorry."

"I was, too." He paused and although there was no reason to expound on that answer, he decided to go all in. "But if I hadn't been putting myself first for a long time, she probably wouldn't have left me."

The red light on his board had begun to flash. "Damn. We're about to come off the national news in twenty seconds. Would you mind hanging on a little more?"

She paused again. He wondered if her thoughts were as evident on her face as they were over the phone. He also guessed that since he'd been in Shelter Bay eight months and this was the first time they'd talked, she wasn't one of those people who normally called up radio stations.

"I think I'd better get to sleep," she said. "I have a busy day tomorrow."

"At your business."

"Yes."

"Which would be?"

"I'd rather not say."

"That bad?" She had a sexy voice. Low and lush and husky. Sort of like Lauren Bacall in all those old black-and-white movies. He wondered if maybe she ran a phone sex business out of her house. Then decided she didn't sound comfortable enough on the phone for that.

"No. It's just that . . . well, I don't know, but I think I'm more comfortable with us just talking like this."

Mac kicked himself for opening up enough to admit

he'd been a lousy husband. Which had probably cost him any chances with Sandy whatever her last name was.

"A mystery woman . . . I can handle that." For now. "As long as you promise to call in again."

Silence.

Then, "I just may do that."

"I'll be looking forward to it. Oh, and what do you think?"

"About what?"

"Saturday nights," he reminded her.

"Oh. When I first called I was going to say I wasn't a fan. But I guess there's something to be said for them, after all."

"Great. So if you can hang on just a another minute longer to share that opinion in tonight's poll, we're going back on the air in five . . . four . . . three . . . two . . . one second.

"We've got Sandy, from right here in Shelter Bay. So, Sandy, how do you vote?"

"Some Saturday nights make up for the others," she said, making him wonder if she was talking about their off-the-air conversation.

"So that's a yes vote?"

Another pause. "I guess it is." She sounded surprised.

Mac watched the green light disappear off the board, only to immediately be replaced with a blinking red one as she—damn it—hung up.

"So far we've got one thumbs-down from Travis and an affirmative from Sandy. After Jake Owen's "The One That Got Away," we'll see if we've got any tiebreakers out there. . . .

"This is KBAY, FM ninety-eight-point-six. And never forget, cowboys and cowgirls, friends don't let friends listen to pop."

While the next caller told him what was essentially a country song about his wife leaving him on a Saturday night, driving away in his truck with his chocolate Lab in the backseat, Mac registered that as a no vote and wondered if, wherever she was, Sandy was thinking about him. The same way he was thinking about her.

11

"Oh, my God!"

As soon as Annie hung up the phone, she buried her face in her hands. What on earth had gotten into her? She had never, ever in her *entire* life called in to a radio station.

But after being unable to find anything on TV or her DVR that she wanted to watch, she'd taken her glass of wine upstairs to bed, where she'd turned on the radio and listened to *Mac at Midnight* on KBAY as the moon rose over the ocean, casting the shipwreck outside her window, just beyond Castaway Cove, in a silvery mist that made it look a little like Sir Francis Drake's pirate ship.

And speaking of pirates . . . Granted, she had no idea what Mac Culhane looked like, but if that deep voice was any indication, Captain Jack Sparrow had nothing on him.

And why oh why had she told him about her failed marriage? Not only did she not call in to radio shows, she *never* talked about those days. Well, except a bit with Sedona, who for some reason seemed to encourage personal conversations from her. Perhaps it was because Sedona, having grown up in that commune, wasn't the least bit judgmental.

In the beginning, the CPA-turned-baker was mostly a friendly acquaintance in town who'd been recommended to help her set up a business plan for Memories on Main. But in the past year, they'd grown closer, so much so that Annie often felt Sedona was the nearest thing to the sister she'd always dreamed of.

In fact, they were so close, she was tempted to call Sedona right now. But then, realizing that it was nearly two in the morning, she nixed that idea.

"Which means you have no one to tell," she said out loud.

Tell what? Even as she said the words into the darkness, Annie had no idea what there *was* to tell. She'd called up a radio deejay. No big deal. Lots of people did that every day. Or every night, in his case. She heard his regular callers to his show all the time when she listened to the station.

But she'd also mentioned her failed marriage. Though with fifty percent of marriages ending in divorce, a lot of his calls revolved around that topic. The logger who disliked Saturday nights had certainly used his breakup as a reason.

So why did *their* conversation seem like a very big deal?

Because keeping it off the air, as he'd done, made it more personal?

So why did you lie about your name? And not tell him the name of the store? an argumentative voice in the back of her mind piped up.

Why, indeed?

She was, after all, proud of the way she'd reclaimed the abandoned retail space that had been stripped down to the bare walls by previous tenants. She had turned it into a cozy shop with a classroom where customers could also try out different paper-crafting machines before buying.

The only answer she could come up with was that she'd sensed some sort of emotional connection with Mac Culhane that had made her uneasy. Although it didn't make an ounce of sense, he always managed to make it sound as if he was talking to each individual listener while on the air; once they'd gone to just the phone, the connection had deepened.

She'd felt her face flush when he'd called her a mystery woman. And had the song he'd played after she hung up—"The One That Got Away"—been chosen for her? Or had it already been on his playlist and was only a coincidence?

Whichever, it had left her feeling edgy, which was more unsettling, since talking with Charlie about marriage and families had already jumbled her feelings.

Deciding that the conversation must have opened old wounds she'd thought were healed—it was the only explanation she could come up with for behaving so uncharacteristically—she reached over, turned out the light, and, exhausted from her roller-coaster day, fell like a stone into a deep, dreamless sleep.

Until sometime just before dawn, when a pirate came to her in the dark. As if possessing the power to read her mind, his midnight voice crooned the exact words she'd so longed for her former husband to say, and his wickedly clever pirate hands touched her in all the places she'd ached to be touched.

Unfortunately, when the sun filtered through the slats of the white wooden blinds of her bedroom window, her dream pirate was gone and except for the feline Pirate, who was sprawled heavily across her legs, Annie was, as she had been even during all the days and nights of her marriage, alone.

12

Although statistics he'd read kept saying that there were more and more stay-at-home dads, Mac had yet to meet another one in Shelter Bay. He always seemed to end up being the only father at the park in the mornings. At first all the mothers had looked at him with suspicion, but after a time, though he still might not have been totally accepted, at least they no longer seemed to be keeping a closer eye on their children whenever he and Emma showed up.

A few single moms had even invited him to dinner, making it clear that they were offering more than pot roast or fried chicken. Although so far he thought he'd been pretty adept at dodging the offers, Barnie Nagle, who ran Barnie's Barbershop, located at the end of Whale Watch Drive, had said that *his* wife had told him that there was starting to be some speculation that the bomb blast had damaged more than just his eyes.

Although Mac's ego had wanted to set the record straight right on the spot, another, more pragmatic part of him had decided that if it kept those playground moms at bay, he could live with the rumors circulating about possible injuries to his junk.

"Isn't it a lovely day?" asked one woman as she sat down beside him on the blue bench. Connie Fletcher, a newly divorced single mom who'd moved into the summer home she and her former husband—an estate lawyer in Eugene—had bought three years earlier, either hadn't gotten the memo about his rumored sexual handicap or was perhaps one of those people who had to check things out for herself. Of course, it could be that maybe she was just lonely. Like so many other people, including, he admitted on the days when he let himself get down in the dumps, himself.

"It's a great day," he agreed with enthusiasm. "And the weather's supposed to hold through the holiday." From all the announcements he'd been given to read on the air, Shelter Bay definitely believed in going all out for holidays. Including the upcoming Fourth of July.

"I know. That's so sweet of you to promote our women's group picnic basket raffle." Her Southern drawl, unusual for this part of the country, brought to mind wide white porches and mint juleps. "I'm on the committee and we've been selling more tickets this year than ever. Which I'm sure has something to do with all the promotion you've been giving us."

"Always happy to help a good cause."

Although he knew that to many people in the cities the idea of people creating picnic lunches to be raffled off to raise money for the school's arts, creative writing, and music programs might seem like a flashback to the nineteenth century, it was turning out to be one of the most popular of the holiday activities when people called in to say what they were looking forward to.

"I'm making Southern fried chicken, macaroni salad, and since where I grew up you can't have a picnic without deviled eggs, I'm making my mama's recipe, but I've added a twist with a topping of fresh crab."

"Sounds like a winner."

Which was definitely true.

Emma, who'd just raced over from the swings, had now begun scampering up the brightly colored monkey bars.

"And the pièce de résistance is my red velvet cake, which is even better than Sedona Sullivan's recipe. Not that I'm one to toot my own horn, but it makes sense, since she grew up in Arizona. In that commune."

The derision in her voice suggested the blond baker could well be Shelter Bay's sole communist.

"And, of course, there has to be sweet tea. I always make enough for a crowd," she said significantly as her gaze drifted across the rose garden, past the statue of the woman waiting for her husband to return from sea, to her son, who was currently sitting atop the colorful jungle gym, talking to Emma. Who, Mac noticed, was no longer smiling as she'd been only moments earlier.

"That's a good idea. Since a lot of people are probably bidding for their family supper," he said distractedly as his daughter tossed her sunshine-blond head in a gesture he'd come to recognize as a warning of impending temper.

"I was thinking that perhaps you and I, and Kenny and your darling little girl, might like to share it together before the fireworks."

Before he could respond to that suggestion, his daughter, clad in pink jeans, a pink T-shirt studded with rhinestones that spelled out DADDY'S GIRL, and a new pair of pink sandals, suddenly drew her thin arm back and hit Kenny smack on the nose with a left hook that while totally socially unacceptable, was pretty damn effective. Especially for a six-year-old girl.

Mac's father had always taught him that you never, ever hit a girl. Although seemingly provoked, Kenny apparently had never had that little life-lesson talk with his lawyer father, since he hauled off and hit her back. Mac cringed as the small male fist connected with Emma's right eye.

"Emma!"

"Kenny!"

Both parents shouted at once and took off running as the two combatants tumbled to the cork pad beneath the jungle gym and began rolling over the newly cut green grass.

Mac got there first, grabbed his daughter up, and held her tight against his hip even as she squirmed to get away and her fists continued to flail.

Kenny's mother went the cajoling route, which didn't seem to be working, since the boy leaped to his feet and charged at Emma.

"That's enough," Mac said, even as he lifted Emma higher. He'd pulled out his military voice, which apparently still possessed some authority—Kenny stopped in his tracks and Emma quit swinging. "Stop. Now."

"She started it," the boy insisted, shoving his hands into the pockets of his jeans. "By hitting me first."

"Because he said bad things about me and Poppy," Emma countered. "He said that no one should be allowed to play with me because I could give them the Alzheimer's. Like chicken pox. I told him Alzheimer's was not catching but he kept saying that Poppy was dangerous and it was a good thing he was locked away in that home."

Mac felt his own temper rising and resolutely tamped it down. Kids, he remembered from his own school days, could be unbearably, often casually, cruel. And many, as it seemed Kenny did, knew just what buttons to push to get a response.

"Kenneth Fletcher," his mother said, her moonlight-and-magnolia-sugar tone sharpening, "that's a very cruel thing to say. And absolutely not true. What happened to Emma's great-granddaddy is very sad and you owe her an apology, young man."

"She hit me first," he repeated sulkily, wiping his bleeding nose with the back of his hand. "And Peter Potter said that *his* grandfather has the Alzheimer's and had to be locked away because he kept getting mad and getting in fistfights with strangers and that he even hit a man in the checkout line at the grocery store. So *he* was dangerous."

"Poppy wouldn't hurt a fly," Emma insisted. "Just because Peter's grandfather got in fights with people doesn't mean my poppy would. He just has a sick head. But his doctor is giving him medicine for it. Right, Daddy?"

"That's right. Alzheimer's affects everyone differently and your poppy might get a little grumpy from time to time, but he's never hit anyone." Deciding that the combatants seemed to have reached some sort of detente, he put Emma back on the ground.

"See." Unwilling to totally surrender, she jutted her chin out and stuck both small but surprisingly dangerous fists on her hips. "I told you so."

"But you still owe Kenneth an apology for hitting him," Mac said.

Emma stuck out her bottom lip in a pout that he was getting used to seeing. No longer was she the totally acquiescent little girl who'd greeted him with such joy when he'd returned from war. Mac's father told him that was a good thing, that it meant she was trusting that he wouldn't leave her again, so she no longer felt as if she needed to be on her best behavior. But there were times, like now, when he wished she didn't possess such a strong streak of both her parents' stubbornness.

Not quite ready to wave the white flag of surrender yet, she folded her arms across the front of the grass-stained T-shirt. One elbow, he noticed, was skinned, probably from falling onto the cork below the jungle gym.

"First he has to take back what he said about Poppy."

"Emma." Mac had learned that his military tone could roll right off his daughter's back. "Hitting people is never the way to solve a problem."

"Sometimes it is," he heard her mutter beneath her breath.

"What was that?" he asked, giving her a second chance.

Truthfully, he didn't blame her. If he'd been six years old, and someone had said anything against either of his parents or his grandfather, he'd probably still be rolling on the ground, fists flying.

Her long, exhaled breath ruffled her corn-silk bangs. "I'm sorry I hit you." Her tone held all the sincerity of a politician trolling for campaign dollars. "But Poppy's *not* contagious. He just forgets things sometimes, right, Daddy?"

"That's right." Mac decided to try to turn this event into what Dillon Slater, a former EOD-guy-turned-physics-teacher-and-basketball-coach, would have referred to as a *teachable moment*.

He turned to Kenny, whose nose was still bleeding. The boy's cheeks were flushed with anger and probably embarrassment at being punched by a girl.

"Not many people know much about Alzheimer's, so it's understandable that your friend Peter is confused, but just because Emma's great-grandfather has it doesn't mean that she's going to get it. Or that it's catching. Because it's definitely not like chicken pox or the flu."

"See?" Connie Fletcher's voice regained its chirp. "You need to let Peter know, so he won't go on spreading such falsehoods. While I'll have a little chat with

Mrs. Potter and make sure she talks with him. And you must never, ever hit a girl again."

"Even if she hits me first?" Since his nose was still bleeding—though fortunately it didn't look broken—Mac could understand the kid's incredulousness.

"Even then," Connie said, with a flash of steel magnolia. She turned toward Mac. "I'm truly sorry. My son's been having a few issues since the divorce."

"I understand."

Emma didn't talk about her mother much, but he often wondered if she missed Kayla more than she let on.

As much as he loved the man who'd adopted him when he'd married Mac's mother, he'd never forgotten that day the two men in dress uniforms had arrived at the door to tell them that his dad's plane had gone down. There were still times, years later, when although he'd never seen the crash, he would dream about it.

"Well, I'm glad we got that all settled," Connie said. She placed a soft, manicured hand on his arm. "My basket's the white wicker one," she said. "I distressed it myself and made the big red, white, and blue sequined bow. . . . In case you'd feel inclined to bid on it."

"It sounds great," Mac hedged. "And since I think we've reached detente, it's time for Emma and me to go visit her great-grandfather at Still Waters."

"Of course." She leaned down and patted Emma's cheek. "Poor little thing. Having your mama leave you and your daddy, then your dear poppy losing his mind all in the same year. Maybe someday you and I could have a spa day together to take your mind off your troubles."

His daughter's shoulders stiffened at that obviously less-than-appealing invitation, which Mac, grandson of a fisherman, knew was a shiny lure to pull *him* in. But his daughter saved the day by flashing a bright, totally fake smile, and saying, "Thank you, ma'am. Maybe someday."

As embarrassed as he'd been by the public fight that had drawn the attention of every other mother at the park—within hours they would be spreading the word about what a wild daughter the clueless single father was raising—Mac couldn't help smiling when he heard his own words, which he'd admittedly been using to put off getting Emma a pet, now being pulled out to avoid hanging out with the mother of the obnoxious, though understandably troubled, Kenny.

"It's a date," Connie Fletcher said, her own Miss Cotton Queen smile returning Emma's feigned one. "I'll give your daddy a call one of these days soon and we can set things up."

"You're not going to go out with Mrs. Fletcher, are you, Daddy?" Emma asked as they drove to Still Waters.

"I hadn't planned to," Mac responded mildly.

"Good. Because the only reason she was being nice to me is that she wants you to marry her."

"I think we were just talking about a picnic basket." When did she get so damn perceptive? Not only was she no longer unrelentingly cheerful, but somehow, before his very eyes, she'd become six going on thirty.

"That's just what she says. When I was over playing Barbies, I heard Peggy's mom tell Mrs. Tyler that every single woman in town wants to marry you."

"I'm sure that was an exaggeration."

"Kenny's mom sure was after you. She was looking to trap you the same way people do those crabs they pull up off the dock. You need to watch out," she warned. "Because having a bad mom would be a lot worse than not having my mom live with us."

"Is that hard on you?" he asked with a casualness he was a very long way from feeling.

"I miss Mommy sometimes." Her voice was small and sad, which reminded him of himself so many years ago.

Their situations weren't exactly the same, but he sure hadn't talked to any grown-ups about losing his dad. And although his mother hadn't dated all that much, he remembered resenting any man who'd come to the house. Until Dr. Boyd Buchanan, who had not only possessed the patience to ignore Mac's less-than-compliant behavior, but had proven to be the real deal.

He might not have been a fighter pilot with a cool uniform and helmet, but he had taught Mac how to build a radio, and encouraged him to follow his own dream instead of going to medical school, like Mac sometimes suspected his mother would've preferred.

"I love your grandpa Buchanan a whole lot," he said. "But that doesn't mean I've forgotten my first dad. And sometimes I wish he could see what a wonderful granddaughter he has."

"Poppy says people who die go to heaven and can see everything. So Grandpa Culhane probably knows all about me." Her small forehead furrowed as she considered that for a minute. "I hope he isn't disappointed that I hit Kenny."

"He'd understand. I would've done the same thing," Mac admitted. He wasn't certain that was the right lesson to teach his daughter, but he'd promised both her and himself that he would never lie to her.

"Poppy always says family's the most important thing," Emma said. "And it was wrong what Kenny said."

"True. But you have to promise me, no more hitting."

She sighed again in a way that had him wondering

if all little girls could be so expressive, or if, just perhaps, he had a budding actress on his hands. More to
worry about, as visions of his innocent daughter moving to Hollywood and running into guys like he'd once
been flashed through Mac's mind.

13

Emma loved visiting her daddy's grandfather. Unlike her daddy and granddaddy, who she knew sometimes got busy and weren't paying her their total attention, Poppy always leaned forward in his chair, his eyes right on hers whenever she'd tell him things. Sometimes his lips even moved right along with her, as if he knew just what she was going to say before the words came out of her mouth.

"What the blue blazes happened to you, girl?" he'd asked as soon as she walked into his room at Still Waters, where he lived with a lot of other grandmas and grandpas who'd gotten the Alzheimer's. There were also cats and dogs living there, which sometimes was her favorite part of her visits.

Although her daddy had made her go home and change out of her dirtied clothes and put a Disney Princess Band-Aid on her elbow after he'd washed it and put cream on it, her poppy's eyes had gone straight to her *eye*. Her grandpa, who was a doctor, had put frozen peas on it, but she could still feel it swelling up.

"I hit a mean boy. Then he hit me back."

"Did he deserve it?"

"He said a bad thing about your Alzheimer's. That it was like chicken pox and people could catch it. So I gave him a bloody nose." She may have had to apologize, but the memory of that moment still made her smile.

"Good for you," he said.

"Pops," her daddy said in that quiet, warning way of his.

"Girl was sticking up for family," her poppy said. "Which was exactly what she should do."

Emma beamed as she reached into her book bag and took out the picture she'd drawn for him. "It's the Fourth of July fireworks," she said. "I'm sorry you won't be able to come see them with us. But maybe you can see them from the window."

"Don't worry about me. I've never liked fireworks since I was in the war."

"Really?"

They were one of Emma's favorite things, right after cats and dogs and Christmas. She loved the music and the way they lit up the sky, and this year was going to be the best of all because her friend Angel had told her that Shelter Bay always ended the fireworks display by shooting off a cannon.

"Why not?"

"Because they remind me of when I was on those ships in the South Pacific during the war and the damn Japs kept trying to sink us," he said.

"Pops," Mac repeated quietly.

"*Japanese.*" Poppy corrected grumpily. "Like you never called that bastard who blew you up names?"

"Not in front of my daughter."

"Humph."

"I have a friend who's Japanese," Emma volunteered. "Her parents have a tulip farm and grow the prettiest flowers. Her name is Mai, and she's really nice. You'd like her."

"If she's a friend of yours, I know I would. And I've bought some tulips at their farm. So your daddy's right. I shouldn't have used that bad name.

"But it's a beautiful picture. Maybe your best yet. So from now on, when I think about fireworks, I'll think about you," her poppy said. "Which will probably make me like them now."

"I'm glad." Emma grinned and threw her arms around his neck and gave him a big hug. The way he always told her that each picture was her best yet was another reason she loved her poppy.

She could also tell him secrets, and she believed him when he told her that he'd never, ever tell anyone a single thing she told him. Which was good, because she'd had the most exciting idea that she couldn't wait to share with him. But she couldn't do that with her daddy in the room with them.

"Daddy," she said, "I have a something important I need to talk with Poppy about."

"Okay," he said.

She liked the way her daddy's eyes crinkled up when he smiled. Peggy Murray, one of her new best friends, had a big crush on him. Emma still wasn't sure how she felt about that. Sometimes she was proud to have the most handsome dad of any kid in kindergarten. But other times, when Peggy came over to her house with Angel Tiernan-St. James, her other BFF, and would keep trying to get his attention, Emma would get jealous.

Which was why Angel was her number one BFF, because Angel was going to marry Trey Douchett, so she didn't make those stupid cow eyes at Emma's dad.

Sometimes they'd even rehearse how Angel's wedding would be, with Angel playing the bride, Emma playing the groom, and Peggy being the priest. Once, during a sleepover at Peggy's, Peggy had insisted that the groom had to kiss the bride. So Emma and Angel had tried to kiss, but had ended up giggling so hard that Emma had almost wet her pink Powerpuff Girls underpants. Peggy got mad, said they were both so stupid neither one of them would probably ever get married, and went to the other side of the room and began playing with her Bratz dolls.

"It's really, really important," she stressed now to her father. "And private."

She could tell her dad wasn't real happy about that idea, but she'd also figured out that if she used the special coaxing voice Peggy had taught her, she could usually get him to go along with whatever she wanted.

Sometimes her grandpa said that her daddy was spoiling her. Emma didn't understand what the problem was with that.

She *liked* being spoiled.

"Let the girl have a little privacy," her poppy said. "I'll be here to watch out for her."

Her daddy's brow furrowed like it sometimes did when he was trying to decide something. "You promise not to leave this room?" he asked.

"Cross my heart and hope to die." She crossed her sparkly fingertips on the front of her new glittery pink and purple Princess Merida T-shirt that she'd been going to save to wear to her first day of first grade, but when she'd been changing clothes after the playground fight, she'd decided it would cheer her poppy up.

"Okay. I'll go get some coffee and be back in ten minutes."

"We'll be here," her poppy said. "It's not like we have a lot of places to go."

Once the door closed behind her daddy, Emma asked, "Do you like living at Still Waters, Poppy?"

"It's okay."

"My friend Peggy said her grandpa is in a home and he says it's like a jail."

"It's not that bad." He picked up a scrapbook and held it out toward her. "I went to the aquarium and out for ice cream. See."

"Oh. That's nice. I saw that octopus when Daddy took me. It's really big."

"It is that."

"Do you think you could have caught it on your boat?"

"Wouldn't have wanted to," he said. "But, yeah, I could catch about anything, back in my time. Well, except a whale, maybe."

"I like whales. They sing. . . . Not like people, with words, but it's still pretty. Daddy bought me a CD of them when we went to the aquarium. So you don't want to run away?"

"Guess I won't today."

"Okay." She blew out a breath. "But if you ever want to, I have the bestest place for you to hide out."

"Where would that be?"

"My friend Angel showed me this cave down on the beach when I went there one day with her family. It's got diamonds in the walls and when she was a foster kid, she was going to run away and live there with her big brother, but then they got adopted so they didn't have to.

"So I was thinking, that if you ever wanted to run away from here, you could go there and I could visit every day and bring you food and stuff."

"That's an idea," he said, rubbing his chin, which scratched a bit when he kissed her cheek, but Emma didn't care. "But you have to promise me never to go down to the beach by yourself. Or even with your friend. Because the sea can be dangerous for little girls, and you never know when a sneaker wave is going to wash up."

"Okay." Happy that her poppy wasn't unhappy and didn't want to run away, she perked up, reached into her Barbie backpack, and pulled out the paper and crayons she was never without. "Want to color?"

14

"I did something really, really stupid," Annie confessed to Sedona.

She was planning a card-making party for a book club group to be held at the store, and Take the Cake's cupcakes always made any occasion more festive. Since they were all alone in the bakery, except for the workers in the kitchen, she felt free to share what she'd nearly called her friend about last night.

"You couldn't be stupid if you tried," Sedona said as she put the dozen assorted prettily frosted cakes into a pink box.

"That's what you think. I called in to KBAY last night and talked with Midnight Mac."

"You were *Sandy*, who voted yes for Saturday nights?"

"You heard me?"

"Well, I didn't realize it was you, since for some reason you're going to have to explain, you were using a fake name, but, yeah, I was listening and for a second I thought it sounded a little like you."

The idea that people who knew her might be listening to *Mac at Midnight* was something Annie hadn't even considered when she'd impulsively picked up the phone and punched the station's call-in number.

"I don't know why I used a fake name, either," Annie admitted. "When he asked, it just popped out of my mouth." She didn't, couldn't, even with such a close friend, share where that particular name had come from.

"It gets worse. You didn't hear our entire conversation, because he kept me off the air when it got a little personal."

"Seriously?" Sedona put down the scissors she'd been about to use to cut a piece of white ribbon. "You talked about personal stuff with Midnight Mac? When it's like pulling teeth to get you to tell your friends anything about your life before you landed here in Shelter Bay?"

"I tell you stuff."

Although she'd moved beyond her foster-child days, the previously necessary and now ingrained habit of keeping secrets remained strong. She'd only skimmed the surface of those years last summer, when she'd joined other women in volunteering at the annual camp for separated foster siblings at Rainbow Lake.

And while Sedona, Chef Maddy Chaffee, and Kara Douchett all knew her husband had left her for another woman, Annie admittedly hadn't exactly gotten into her part in the downfall of her marriage.

"Like how personal?" Sedona asked. "Did he flirt with you? Or, wow, don't tell me he was risking FCC violations by fooling around with phone sex?"

"Of course not!"

Color flooded into Annie's face at that idea. Partly because she'd never, ever had phone sex in her life. Nor could she imagine being so emotionally open with anyone. One thing she and her husband had had in common was that neither one of them said anything during sex.

"We were just talking about regrets. And both having been married."

"Ah. I guess he told you he's divorced. "

"Yes."

Although Sedona was nearly as close as a sister, Annie decided against telling her that Mac Culhane felt responsible for the breakup of his marriage. That was so personal, she suspected it wasn't a story he told everyone. Which had her wondering why he'd shared it with her.

"His little girl is just precious," Sedona said. "If I wanted kids, she's exactly the type of daughter I'd want."

It was Annie's turn to be surprised. "You don't want children?"

"It *is* allowed, you know," Sedona said mildly as she picked up the scissors again and snipped the ribbon. "Not everyone has to buy in to motherhood."

"Well, of course it's allowed." Another thing Annie had failed to share was her own dismal experience with pregnancy. "It's just that I've watched you with Kara's and Phoebe's babies. And from how patient you are when it's taking kids ages to select a cupcake flavor, I never would've guessed you didn't like children."

"But I *do* like children. A lot. Just other people's." She tied the ribbon in a bow as perfectly as she seemed to do everything else.

Annie had often thought that even her friend's cupcakes looked as if they belonged in a museum display. Like the Limoges painted porcelain boxes Annie's husband had always bought her as gifts. At first she'd loved them. Once she found out it was his assistant who'd simply called the Park Avenue store and had them delivered, they'd lost their appeal.

"If I wasn't an only child, I'd probably be that favorite aunt who'd swoop in with lots of presents, spoil the kids rotten for a few hours or, at most, a couple days, then leave while still adored."

Sedona sighed, giving Annie the impression that she'd had this conversation too many times over the years. "It's just that growing up as the eldest girl in that commune left me being a part-time surrogate mom to a bunch of younger kids. Although I haven't entirely closed my mind to the idea of motherhood, I'm pretty sure I burned out on the idea of having any children of my own."

"That makes sense."

Especially since Annie had often played the same role for younger foster children in some of her placements. Though *she'd* loved playing the role and had always dreamed of having children of her own.

Different strokes.

"What does he look like?" she asked, bringing the conversation back to its original track. Unlike some of the other station deejays, Mac never seemed to do personal appearances, and there were no posters advertising *Mac at Midnight* in any store windows.

"Who?" Sedona asked with feigned innocence.

"Mac Culhane."

"Ah." An exquisitely shaped blond brow lifted. "You're interested."

"It's just easier to talk with someone when you know what they look like," Annie hedged.

"He's tall, about six-two, I'd guess, and lean, but not skinny in any way. I've never seen him without a shirt, but some mornings we're both running on the beach at the same time and I can see he's really ripped beneath his T-shirt."

When that comment sent Annie's unruly mind swirling up a picture of the man she'd run into at Still

Waters, she shook off the mental image. *He'd* been the complete opposite of the warm and caring deejay. "What else?"

"Let's see, when he runs, his gait is a little off, as if he might have an injured leg. Not enough to be all that noticeable if you're not looking carefully, but it caught my eye one day when he was running a few yards ahead of me. Well, to be perfectly honest, it was *after* I noticed his very fine butt."

Annie told herself that she was *not* going to think about Midnight Mac's butt.

Major fail.

"He's got thick, wavy black hair, blue eyes, and some scars beneath his eyes that for some reason, maybe because we were running on your beach in front of that shipwreck, had me thinking of pirates."

Just the mention of pirates, which brought back her erotic dream, sent a hot flash blazing through Annie from the roots of her hair down to her toes. Was it possible to go into menopause at thirty-three?

"So he's as sexy as he sounds on the radio?"

"Even sexier. If you're into wounded, gruff warrior types, which I'm so not. I'm always surprised when I hear him talking so easily on the radio, because he's never said more than a half dozen words at a time to me."

Annie's foolish fantasy about possibly someday meeting Mac Culhane in person died an instant death. Sedona might be one of the smartest people in town, but that didn't stop her from also being one of the nicest and looking like, as Annie had heard her described, Malibu Barbie. If the middle-of-the-night radio deejay hadn't displayed a bit of interest in the sexiest woman in town, Annie wouldn't stand a chance.

It was just as well. She'd learned the hard way that reality never lived up to the fantasy. And, she reminded herself, she wasn't in the market for a relationship.

"He does adore his daughter, though," Sedona allowed as she rang up the sale. "It's more than apparent that she's the most important thing in his life. Just as it's obvious that she thinks he hung the moon, so he can't be as surly at home as he comes off." She shrugged, then put a tropical piña colada cupcake topped with coconut in an individual box. "For you," she said. "To savor while you're lying in bed, listening to your fantasy man tonight."

Annie accepted the box, knowing from experience that when Sedona Sullivan decided to give you one of her world's best cupcakes, she would refuse to take payment for it.

"He's *not* my fantasy man."

"Really?" That blond brow arched again. "If that's true, you're probably the only woman in Shelter Bay who hasn't fantasized about the guy."

"I thought you said he wasn't your type."

"For a relationship," Sedona clarified. "There's enough heat simmering below the cool, aloof surface that if he'd even noticed I was alive, which he hasn't seemed to so far, I wouldn't mind indulging in a brief, hot fling. I don't really like a lot of conversation during sex and he would definitely be an improvement over Dracula."

They shared a laugh over the baker's most recent date fail. Then Annie picked up both of the cupcake boxes and went on her way.

As she pulled out of her parking space in front of the bakery, preoccupied with planning what supplies she was going to set out for the book club members, she failed to see the black pickup, driven by a dark-haired man with a little girl sitting on a booster seat in the back, pull into the space she'd just vacated.

15

Mac had been on edge all day, waiting for tonight's show. So much so that he'd snapped at Emma while she'd been dithering for what seemed like an eternity in picking out a cupcake at Take the Cake. Fortunately, as his daughter's blue eyes had begun to fill, Sedona Sullivan, who looked like she belonged surfing on a California beach instead of serving up cupcakes, came to his rescue with a trio of miniature cakes that solved the chocolate/strawberry/banana dilemma.

Knowing when she had him at a disadvantage, Emma had no problem talking him into stopping at the Crab Shack for the panko fried prawns she'd come to love. After getting a family meal order to go, he'd dished up supper, washed her hair in the tub, tucked her into bed, and briefly told his father about his visit to his grandfather, all the time feeling as if the hands on the kitchen clock had come to a stop.

By the time he went on the air, he felt as if he'd drunk eight triple espressos.

"So, gang," he started out, "the burning question for tonight is a scary one for a lot of people. . . ."

He played the opening clip from *Jaws* to underline his point.

"We're going to talk about love. Is unconditional love a thing of the past? Did it ever exist or is it one of those made-up Hollywood 1950s impossible ideals of couples like Bogie and Bacall, Rock Hudson and Doris Day, or Katharine Hepburn and Spencer Tracy? These days, when divorce seems to be like a flu virus that can hit everyone, even those who think they're inoculated, does it keep you from getting involved again?

"Pick up the phone and give me a call while we listen to Dierks Bentley's 'Thinking of You.' "

Mac wondered if Sandy was listening. Wondered if she would get his message that he'd spent the entire day thinking of her. Something about her had gotten under his skin and into his mind.

He could've just googled her by her phone number, which had shown up on the caller ID, or checked to see if her name was listed on the local Chamber of Commerce Web site. Then he would know what business she ran and he could have casually dropped in and checked her out.

But that would be too easy. And, as he knew too well, reality often didn't live up to the fantasy. Which was why he'd chosen this topic for tonight. He knew that he was using work, his grandfather, and Emma as excuses not to even put himself in a position to get involved with anyone. But he'd spent much of the day wondering if, deep down, he was afraid.

Afraid that if he did meet her and felt even half as strongly about her in person, she might shoot him down. What if he discovered that he'd imagined the connection between them? Or maybe it had been real, but she'd just been using him as a fantasy man. A disembodied male voice coming out of her radio that she could mold into some ideal of masculine perfection.

Which he was anything but.

The light flashed on. Mac tensed, then blew out a breath when he saw the caller was a regular.

"Hey, Cowboy. So, what about it? Do you believe in love?"

"I believe love can be great," the caller, a bull rider who was stuck home in Shelter Bay this summer with a shattered shoulder and broken leg keeping him off the rodeo circuit, responded. "One weekend at a time."

"A girl in every rodeo town?" Mac guessed. Since rodeo cowboys had to pay their own expenses on the circuit, being able to sleep at a girlfriend's house saved on motel bucks.

"It's the easiest way. Everyone has fun, no one gets hurt or angry."

The other two lines immediately lit up.

"You ever think of trying for a bit more commitment?" Mac asked. "Like maybe a week or two?"

"Nah. Why would I want to do that? With gals it's all about looks. Same as with us guys. So, if you click, you get together, have some fun, then move on before things get too intense. No harm, no foul."

Mac remembered a time when he'd behaved much the same way as he'd moved from town to town. "I wonder if the women think the same way?"

"Who knows what the hell women think?" Cowboy said. "Here's the way I look at it. They go for the bad-boy types because they're looking for the wrong guy."

"Not Mr. Right?"

"What would be the point in that? Gals date guys they want to change into a good person. It's like Beauty and the Beast or all those other fairy tales they grow up reading. If you're the kind of guy who goes out of his way to treat a woman right, with flowers, candy, and overpriced dinners at the Sea Mist, they think you're a wuss and won't look at you twice.

"But forget to call, or ask them out at the last minute, or show up at their door at midnight for a booty call, and hey, man, they're all over that."

Nothing like starting the night off with a bang. Normally Mac liked it when a caller threw out a grenade like Cowboy was doing. But if the phone rang as much as he suspected it would, he probably wouldn't get any decent Sandy time.

"Well, now, pardner, that's a real interesting take on it," he said. "Thanks for starting things off with a bang. And our next caller is . . ."

He hung up the first line, which immediately lit up again, and picked up the third, leaving the second hanging for a time, since the caller ID showed it to be another guy and he wanted to hear a woman's response to Cowboy's take on romance.

"Hey, Sophie. Thanks for calling in. Where are you calling from?"

"Depoe Bay and that Cowboy's a douche."

"Why don't you tell us what you really think?"

"Women aren't stupid. We can tell real life from fairy tales. And let me tell you, I can't imagine a woman spending five minutes with such a brain-dead misogynist."

"So, are you in a relationship?"

"Not at the moment. Because I made the mistake of marrying Cowboy's evil twin. I was young and stupid and, and yeah, maybe I thought he'd change."

"Making Cowboy's point," Mac felt obliged to note.

"No. I figured that once he was married, he'd feel the same way I did. That 'until death do you part' also included monogamy."

Mac was guilty of many marriage sins. Fortunately not that one. "That's tough."

"It was at the time," she admitted. "But, hey, his loss, right? And I ought to be thankful because I'm now working on self-love."

"That sounds like you're in a good place."

"It is. But it's more like a journey of self-discovery, and I'm enjoying every step of the way."

"Good for you. Good luck with that, and thanks for calling in, Sophie."

As soon as he answered line three, two lit up again. Yep. It was going to be a busy night for a Sunday, which was usually slow.

"We've got Dale on the line. So, Dale, do you agree with Cowboy? Or Sophie?"

"I think it's all about timing," the caller said. "If you're out there scamming on women for the short term, yeah, you hit on enough of them and you'll get lucky. But eventually random sex with women whose names you can't even remember in the morning gets old, you know?

"Like going out drinking tequila shots with your buddies every night. Now that I'm in my thirties, I'm ready to settle down, but I figure if I just be who I am, and not try to be what I think women want, and generate positive energy, eventually love will find me."

"And you'll settle down and have two-point-five kids?"

"Something wrong with that?"

"No. It's still probably the ideal. At least for a lot of people." It had been for him. Until his marriage had died. Which, he acknowledged, was more his fault than Kayla's.

"So, thanks for calling and, hey, if you meet that perfect woman for you, be sure to call back and let us know, okay?"

"Sure."

Another woman was on line two.

"Can you give Dale my phone number? Because people are drawn to positive energy and I just know I'm the perfect woman for him."

"Sorry, I'm not into the matchmaking business, but—"

"That's okay," she broke in. "Dale, I'll be at the Stewed Clam tomorrow night at eight. If you want a woman who appreciates a man who's into commitment, come on by."

She hung up before Mac could decide whether to cut her off. Since she was recorded, he could leave out that last part, the way he'd kept his conversation with Sandy private. Then again, he thought with a shrug, unless Dale turned out to be a serial killer, what could it hurt?

"Just a reminder that we're not the *Love Connection* here," he said. "After a word from Tony Genarro from Genarro's funeral home, who, around here is referred to as 'the guy with the plot, the guy with the plan,' we'll be hearing Brad Paisley's 'Waitin' on a Woman.' Meanwhile, you all keep those calls coming in."

The commercial took thirty seconds. Mac decided he'd run three minutes of calls. Then Paisley's song went four minutes and forty-five seconds. Which gave Sandy eight minutes and fifteen seconds to call in.

As Genarro rattled off a list of reasons for pre-planning funerals, Mac sat back in his chair and, just like Paisley in the song, found himself waitin' on a woman.

16

Annie jumped when the phone rang. She'd realized after she'd first called the station that Mac would have her caller ID and could either call her or, if he went to a bit of trouble, in this day and age with everything on the Internet, even track her down.

But, no, it wasn't him.

"So, why haven't you called him?" Sedona asked when Annie pressed *Talk.*

"Who?"

"Oh, don't give me that innocent act. Midnight Mac."

"What makes you think I haven't? I told you, he records the conversations off the air while the music is on, then plays them after the song's over."

"If you had called him, why would he be sending you those messages? He opened up with 'Thinking of You.' Then now he's playing 'Waiting on a Woman.' Who else could that be?"

"You never know. He probably has a lot of women calling him all the time." Women far more interesting than her. Hot, sexy women like Sedona.

"Right after you hung up last night, he played 'The One That Got Away.' It's *you*, Annie."

"Maybe."

A secret part of Annie, the part whose fingers had been itching to pick up the phone, hoped Sedona was right. But why did he have to choose that topic, of all things? Couldn't he have talked about sports? Or the best country video ever? Or the weather, which had been unseasonably balmy for an Oregon June?

He'd been right on the money when he'd said love was scary. Scary to talk about, even scarier to fall into. And too painful when it ended.

"Call him." Sedona pressed her case. "It's obvious he's made time just for you. Put your big-girl panties on and call the guy. You know you want to."

With that she hung up, leaving Annie listening to dead air.

Annie waited another few seconds. Then, unable to resist the phone's siren call, she punched in the number she'd already memorized.

"It's about time," the roughened voice said after the first ring. "Do you know how crazy I've been going waiting for you to call?"

"*This* is crazy," she said. "You don't even know me."

"I told you. We can remedy that. I've got tomorrow night off. Let's spend it together."

All night? "You have a daughter."

"I also have a live-in babysitter. Who's my dad. And, just to make sure we're on the same page, I'm not talking about spending the entire night together. Just dinner. Maybe a twilight walk on the beach. We'll talk, trade life stories. See if this connection between us, whatever it is, exists in real life."

"I don't know. . . ."

"You know how we were talking about regrets? Of things we wish we hadn't done?"

"Of course I do. It was only last night." And this relationship, whatever it was, was happening way too fast for Annie's comfort level.

"Well, do you really want to go through life regretting what we didn't do?"

"I'm not sure I want to go through life with a man who'd stoop to such a cliché to get me to go out with him."

"Touché. I'm not asking for a lifetime. Or even more than one dinner. Just a couple of hours uninterrupted by commercials, callers, and music . . .

"How about this? . . . If I promise not to propose, will you have dinner at the Sea Mist with me?"

Yes.

No.

Yes.

No.

The warring responses bounced back and forth in Annie's head.

"We're running out of time," he said.

"I'm sorry. But no."

Then, before she could change her mind and give in to temptation, Annie quickly hung up.

Then called Sedona, who she knew would be waiting.

"Okay. I called him."

"And?"

"He asked me out to dinner. At the Sea Mist."

"So he's willing to spring for the big-ticket meal," Sedona said. "Well done, you."

"I turned him down."

"Why would you do that?"

"Because there's no point."

"It's just dinner," Sedona said, with an uncharacteristic huff of exasperation. Maybe they didn't have a lot of free love in that commune where she'd grown up, but Sedona Sullivan was normally the most easygoing person Annie had ever met. "Not a damn marriage proposal."

"Funny, he said the same thing. But I'm not interested in just hooking up with some stranger. And it can't go anywhere further than that, so what's the point?"

"Why can't it go anywhere?"

"It just can't."

Annie might not have a crystal ball, but she could see the future. A future where Mac Culhane would start thinking about giving Emma a little sister or brother. Better to guard all their hearts, she assured herself.

"You're not still legally married, are you?"

"Of course not." She might not have been totally forthcoming about the breakup of her marriage, but she hadn't lied.

"Then what's wrong with sharing some intelligent, interesting conversation over a great meal?"

"I already have that with you. And Maddy, and Kara, and the others."

There was a long silence as Sedona thought that over. "Damn. This conversation is making me wonder if just maybe my mother was partly right."

"About what?"

"That if I'm not careful, I'm going to end up eighty years old, living all alone with a houseful of cats. What she had no way of knowing when she warned me about that was the equally depressing fact that if *you* keep refusing to date, we could end up as old lady roommates with doilies all over our furniture and fur balls everywhere."

"That *is* depressing." And it hit home for her even more than it might usually have, considering her recent conversation with Charlie, which admittedly had her thinking more and more of marriage and soul mates. "Especially since we both already have cats."

"Ah, but only one each. At the moment. Which means we're not in danger of becoming cat ladies. But over time, if we're not careful, that could change with the way Charity is always pushing those homeless animals on everyone in town. . . .

"Maybe it's time to get proactive. Instead of waiting for Mr. Right to show up on his prancing white steed, maybe we should just make the first move. Women *are* allowed to ask men out these days."

"You may have a point."

Having discovered the pleasures of independence, Annie had no intention of ever getting married again, but after all the work she'd done to overcome the debacle of her marriage, didn't she deserve some fun?

But not with a man who had a child. Because no way was she going to allow herself to fall in love with a little girl, or worse yet, allow a little girl to fall in love with her, when there wasn't any path to a happy ending.

"You also happen to have a dating-expectations spreadsheet that no mortal man could ever live up to," Annie said.

"Well, there is that." Sedona sighed. "Thus is the curse of a perfectionist. But maybe it's time to do a bit of editing on it."

"That would be my advice. As for me, it's already late and I have to change the shop window display to a Fourth of July theme, so as for what to do about my romantic life, or more specifically, lack of it, I'll guess I'll just sleep on the idea."

"Alone."

"Unless George Clooney suddenly shows up at my door, I'm afraid so."

"We should be so lucky," Sedona said with a laugh as she hung up.

The clock radio sat on the bedside table, within reach. All she'd have to do was reach out, hit the button that was already set to KBAY, and she wouldn't be exactly alone.

"You're close to needing an obsession intervention."

Resisting the almost overwhelming urge, she turned off the light, rolled over on her stomach, and covered her head with her pillow, as if to shut out the deep baritone voice she didn't need the radio turned on to hear.

17

Emma loved watching her daddy shave. She loved the way he swirled the wooden-handled brush on the soap, which turned into frothy bubbles on his face. But today, sitting on the edge of the bathtub, she was wishing that he would just hurry up.

"Daddy, we're going to be late," she complained.

"The party's not for another three hours." The razor cut through the white foam, leaving a trace of skin she knew would be soft and smell like soap. Not like her poppy, whose chin was scratchy. But she never minded because her grandpa had explained that was how old men were.

"I know when it is. Grandpa taught me to tell time," she reminded him.

Peggy was having her sixth birthday party at the store called Memories on Main. They would all be making cards to hand out to soldiers who were marching in the Fourth of July parade. Emma felt as if she had ants marching under her skin as her daddy seemed to be moving as slow as the tortoise that was her kindergarten class pet.

"But we still have to have breakfast and visit Poppy

and I'll just die if I'm the only girl who's late and misses something fun."

"You won't be late. I promise."

He hadn't broken a promise to her since he'd come back from the war. But Emma still worried. Her mother used to accuse her of being a fretter. Once she'd asked her teacher what the word meant and was told it meant someone who fussed a lot about unimportant things.

But Emma didn't think she fussed. At least not nearly as much as Peggy. And the first party she was invited to since she and her daddy moved to Shelter Bay was *not* an unimportant thing.

"Why don't you go get Peggy's present while I get dressed? I'll be down in five minutes."

Recognizing the tone as the no-arguing one he sometimes used, Emma huffed a big sigh and went to get the Race Car Barbie Peggy had been talking about forever. Before they went to the store, her daddy had called Peggy's mother to make sure her parents weren't getting her one. Even though Emma thought that having two race cars would be better because then they could actually race each other.

While they were at the store, she'd pointed out the Pet Vet Barbie she wanted. After she'd had a playdate at Angel's house and met her mom, who took care of sick animals, Emma had decided that she wanted to be a vet, too. Especially since Angel's brother, Johnny, was going to be a veterinarian. Maybe they could get married and open an animal hospital together.

She'd begun playing vet with her stuffed animals and even, just last week, she'd cut open her Saint Bernard and sewn him back up again. Unfortunately, the only thread she'd been able to find in the house was red, but her grandpa was a doctor and sometimes cut up real people to save their lives and he had told her that her stitches were real straight for a first-time surgery.

Maybe if she took her daddy to the store again and told him how much she really, really wanted the Barbie who came with her own animal hospital supplies, he'd listen when she explained how much they needed a dog. Or even a cat.

Instead of always saying "One of these days." Which seemed to mean "No." Because they'd been living here in Shelter Bay since right before last Thanksgiving and the only real-life animals she had were two goldfish—who mostly just swam around in circles in their bowl with the fake plastic palm tree, which got boring after a while.

She was sitting on the bottom step when he came downstairs. "Ready to go?" he asked.

"I've been ready for *hours*."

"Well, then, let's get going. And I have a surprise for you."

"We're going to Dr. Tiernan's shelter to pick out a dog?"

"One of these days," he said.

"When?"

"Soon. Don't you want to know what the surprise is?"

"Okay."

He reached down and ruffled her hair. "I called ahead to the Grateful Bread and had a RESERVED sign put on the bus. Just for us."

Emma loved the booth that was made out of the front of a real van painted all over with flowers and other fancy designs, some of which her daddy told her were peace signs, meaning that the world should stop having wars. But as much as she liked eating in the bus, she decided that she deserved a pout since he was probably going to make her wait forever for a dog. Maybe even until she was in third grade.

"Okay."

He rolled his eyes up toward the ceiling, where a

spot still needed to be painted over from when she overflowed a bubble bath last week.

Then, since he could never stay frustrated with her for long, he laughed, picked her up, flung her over his shoulder, and carried her out to his pickup.

The same way he could never stay annoyed at her, Emma couldn't stay mad at her daddy. By the time they reached the restaurant, she was looking forward to the strawberry waffles and telling her poppy all about Peggy's party.

Maybe she'd even be able to make him a Fourth of July card. Her daddy said he'd helped save the world from bad guys when he was a sailor. A really, really long time ago. In the olden days before computers or even TVs.

In the scrapbook her poppy had been making with the lady who ran the store where Peggy's party was going to be there was a picture of him when he'd been a little boy, not much older than her, sitting on the grass beneath a tree, his arm around a white dog with a big black spot around its eye. If she could get Poppy talking about *that* dog, maybe her daddy would decide that *one of these days* could be now.

18

After insisting that she was in a hurry to leave the house, Emma had taken ages to make up her mind between her usual strawbetty waffles and the marionberry-stuffed French toast. Finally, after some assurances from the owner of the restaurant that she would love the toast, she'd ordered it. And she did love it. But although the delay had them running late, Mac wasn't about to skip the visit to Still Waters.

There were more and more days when he wondered if his grandfather had even remembered he was coming, but having belatedly realized the power and importance of family, Mac wasn't going to risk failing Charlie the way he had his wife and daughter.

After yesterday's night off, Mac's mind was on tonight's show when he entered his grandfather's room and found her there. The woman he'd run into last week. Today's sundress was white silk, with a full skirt bordered in tulips like the ones blooming in the gardens outside the window. And while he remembered reading somewhere that tulips were unique in the flower world for not having a fragrance, underlying the scents of institutional disinfectant she smelled like a summer garden.

Since her back was to him as she filed away her scrapbook-making materials in her wheeled bag, Mac spotted her before she did him. When she turned around, instead of looking annoyed as she had the last time he'd seen her, her gray eyes widened and she looked strangely stunned.

Her gaze went immediately to his eyes, which, thanks to some optic surgery and a corneal implant, were nearly as good as new. While he would never be recruited to be a Marine sniper, his vision was nearly as strong as it had always been. He did still have a tracing of scars beneath his eyes, where the goggles he'd been wearing hadn't completely protected his face from burns, but the plastic surgeon had done a good enough job that people didn't look shocked at his appearance.

But she did.

Okay, maybe not shocked as if she'd just seen a zombie or a vampire.

But definitely surprised.

"'Bout time you showed up," Charlie greeted him. "I was afraid you'd miss meeting Annie. This is the nurse I told you about," he said slyly, proving that some things *did* stick in his mind. "The one you should ask out."

While his memory might be hitting on all cylinders today, Charlie's filters were down, allowing him to speak his mind, whatever he might be thinking. Mac watched the soft color, the same hue as the pink tulips on her skirt, bloom in her cheeks.

"Hi." Seeming to recover, she managed a forced but polite smile. "I'm Annie Shepherd. I've been working with your grandfather on his scrapbooks."

"You've been doing a great job." It was the truth. He'd sensed an improvement in his grandfather since the scrapbook project had begun. While Emma's poppy might still live mostly in the moment, the photos seemed to be helping him hang on to the old memories and family ties. "I'm Mac Culhane."

"*You're* Midnight Mac?"

"You listen to the show?" He couldn't imagine a woman who looked this good and smelled so luscious having any reason to be alone at midnight.

"From time to time," she said casually, knocking his rising ego down a peg. Apparently not finding him all that much more appealing than the first time they'd met, she bestowed a genuine, sunshine-bright smile on Emma.

"You must be Emma, the artist your great-grand-father keeps telling me about," she said. "The one who drew all these beautiful pictures." She waved a grace-ful hand at the walls that were becoming more and more covered with Mac's daughter's drawings.

When Mac imagined that hand, which wasn't wear-ing an engagement or wedding ring, creating a happy trail down his bare chest, then beyond, he felt as stunned as she'd looked when she'd turned and first seen him standing in the doorway. Her voice sounded vaguely familiar, which he wrote off to that conversa-tion they'd had when he'd dissed cats.

"I *was* going to be an artist," Emma said, her little face beaming as if someone had turned on a lightbulb inside her. "But now I decided to be a vet. Like Dr. Tiernan."

"That's a very good goal. I adopted my cat from her shelter."

"You have a cat?"

Mac nearly groaned at the excitement in his daugh-ter's voice. Wouldn't it just figure that this woman had a cat? No wonder she'd put the Arctic chill on him the last time they'd met.

"I do," the woman said. "His name is Pirate because he was found in the cove where pirates used to hang out."

"Real pirates?"

"So the story goes. I run a shop called Memories on Main," she told Emma, who looked enthralled. "And even if you've decided against being an artist, have you ever thought about making cards?"

Emma's sky blue eyes widened. "I'm going to a card-making party there today!"

"Peggy Murray's party?"

"That's it!" While Emma had been excited about the party all week, she was suddenly behaving as if she'd just won a golden ticket to Willy Wonka's chocolate factory. Or a trip to Disneyland. "We're going to make cards for soldiers in the parade!"

"I know."

Well, of course she did, since she ran the store and was putting on the party, but Mac liked the way she validated Emma's enthusiasm with an equal pleasure of her own.

"We usually send our soldier cards overseas through Operation Write Home and Cards for Soldiers, but I thought this would be a nice personal touch to thank our local military men and women."

"Poppy was in the Navy," Emma said. "And Grandpa was a doctor in Vietnam. That was a war."

"I've heard of it."

"Then Daddy got blown up in Afghanistan. That's another country that's far, far away, which was why he was gone a long time. But he's all okay now." She reached out and tightly clutched his hand. "And he's going to stay home with me forever."

"How lucky for both of you." She lifted her gaze from Emma back to Mac. Although she was still smiling, he recognized that invisible wall going up again. "I realize it's come to sound like a cliché, but thank you for your service, Mr. Culhane."

Although the Purple Heart he'd received was nothing like the Navy Cross Sax Douchett had been awarded, since coming back Stateside, Mac had begun to understand why his friend was always visibly embarrassed when people brought up his hero status.

"Hey," he said with a shrug, "I was just the guy on American Forces radio who found myself in the wrong place at the wrong time."

"That may be, but I suspect the troops who tuned into your program appreciated you being there for them." Her gaze swept over his face again, lingering for a moment on the scars. He waited for the pity and was relieved not to see it. Then again, her expression had gone oddly unreadable, making it impossible to sense her thoughts.

Mac studied her in return, from the top of her dark head down to her feet, clad in pink flats with bows on the toes. When his gaze got up to her breasts, he remembered all too well how they'd felt against his chest. Which, in turn, had him feeling like a sex-crazed, hormone-driven sixteen-year-old now. Not that he'd actually experienced sex when he'd been sixteen, but he'd sure as hell thought about it a lot. The same way he was thinking about dragging her outside in the summer rain that had begun to fall so he could see what she'd look like wet, with that flowered dress clinging to her body.

Would the silk turn transparent? A question that got him thinking about what kind of underwear she had on beneath it. A woman who looked that hot wouldn't be wearing practical cotton. It'd be lacy, and maybe her bra would be one of those half-cup things that revealed just an intriguing hint of dusky nipple, and . . .

Hell.

His fevered mind stopped just as his lips were about to taste heaven when he realized that all three people in the room were looking at him and decided that either he must have been staring too long or they were waiting for a response to some question. Hopefully none of them had noticed his totally inappropriate hard-on.

"I'm sorry," he said. "My mind wandered off for a second. . . . To a work problem . . . down at the station."

"Well," she said briskly after a short pause, "I'd better get over to the shop to set up all the supplies and card-making kits for the party. We're also having punch and cupcakes," she revealed.

Emma clapped even as Mac figured that after that breakfast and the party, his daughter would be bouncing off the walls all night long from the impending sugar high. "From Take the Cake?" she asked.

"Where else?" The genuine smile was back, suggesting it was only him she had a problem with, since she was also friendly with his grandfather. Surely she wasn't still pissed about the damn cat remark?

She bent down and brushed a kiss against Charlie's cheek. "See you soon, handsome."

Her tone was jesting, but it still had an effect on Charlie, because beneath the red-and-white-striped flannel bathrobe he was wearing over a bright green, blue, and yellow Hawaiian shirt covered with palm trees, his shoulders squared and he sat up straighter, looking much more like the proud young man in that photo of him on the bulletin board outside his door.

"And I'll see you soon," Annie told Emma as she ran a finger down the slope of his daughter's nose. Then paused. "Perhaps you might want to have your daddy stop by the drugstore and pick up some concealer to help cover up that eye."

Emma's shiner was definitely getting more vivid by the moment. Worrying that it might cause the other girls to tease her, Mac was thinking he ought to have gotten something to try to cover it up when Emma surprised him yet again.

"Thank you," she said politely. "But I like it because it shows everyone that I was sticking up for family." She went over and put her arms around her great-grandfather. "Poppy says that family is the most important thing there is."

It could have just been a trick of the light, but Mac thought that the woman's eyes, which reminded him of the sun shining through rain, misted up a bit.

"Your poppy's a smart man," she said. "You should listen to him."

Then pulling her roller bag behind her, she walked out of the room. Leaving behind the scent of flowers and Mac wondering, yet again, what she was wearing beneath that summery sundress.

19

"You're never going to believe what happened this morning," Annie told Sedona as she picked up the order of cupcakes for little Peggy's birthday party.

"Unlike my mother, who's claimed, with some validity, to be psychic, I'm not," Sedona, who was wearing an apron with three cupcakes printed across the front, said as she retrieved the pink box she'd had waiting beneath the counter. "So, why don't you just save me having to play twenty questions and tell me?"

Fortunately, the front of the store was empty, providing privacy for this all-too-personal conversation. Except . . .

"Denise is in the kitchen," Sedona said in answer to Annie's unspoken question. "And she's got the radio on, which will keep her from hearing anything you say. So spill the beans."

Denise Rogers had recently graduated from the culinary school Chef Maddy had set up at Lavender Hill Farm. The former resident of Haven House, a home for victims of domestic violence, had demonstrated a talent for making light-as-a-feather pastry crust. Since Sedona had added pies to her menu, she'd hired Denise right after graduation. Then, using her former CPA skills, she had helped her new pastry chef plan a budget that allowed her to rent an apartment within walking distance of the bakery.

"I just met Mac Culhane. At Still Waters."

"Really?" Sedona ran Annie's credit card. "That's right. Although he hasn't shown up at the cookie-decorating group I run there, I remember Emma mentioning her great-grandfather was a resident."

"I've been working with Charlie since you and Adèle talked me into volunteering, and get this—he's been trying to set me up with his grandson."

"Didn't he say who his grandson was?"

"No. He tends to get confused from time to time. . . . Well, a lot, really. And he kept saying his grandson was a doctor. So, of course, I figured he was talking about his son, Dr. Buchanan."

"Dr. Boyd Buchanan is Mac Culhane's father? I wonder why they have different last names."

"I wasn't about to ask. But don't deejays often use professional names?"

"I think they might," Sedona agreed. "Perhaps because they tend to jump around from station to station and town to town so often. Which makes it even funnier that *you* decided to use an alias, too."

"I told you, it just slipped out."

"But it is something you both have in common." She tapped a short, buffed fingernail against her lips. "Well, this is certainly interesting."

"That's one word for it. It gets worse. He's coming to the store today."

"Why?" Annie watched as comprehension dawned in Sedona's eyes. "Ah. He's bringing Emma to Peggy's party."

"Exactly. So, what do you think I should do?"

"What do you want to do?"

"Nothing. I definitely don't want him to figure out that I'm Sandy from Shelter Bay." She dragged a hand through her hair. "I think, from the way he looked at me so intently for a minute, he may have recognized my voice."

"He probably looked at you like that because he's a male and you're a gorgeous woman."

"Please."

Although Annie knew she was attractive enough, she certainly wasn't the kind of woman who turned heads or had men walking into walls, as she'd seen happen with Sedona. "Besides, it wasn't *that* kind of look."

"Boy, your ex must've done a number on you—I'd kill for those exotic black curls and the fact that you seem to be able to eat whatever you want without having to run miles every morning to work the calories off."

Annie didn't want to talk about her marriage. But the comment, Sedona actually comparing her own amazing looks to Annie's, momentarily stunned her into silence. If there was one woman on the planet she would never have suspected of possessing body-image problems, it was Sedona Sullivan.

"But he didn't say anything about suspecting who you were?"

"Not a word. But that may have been because his grandfather and daughter were in the room. She has the beginning of a really bad black eye from some boy hitting her."

"I hope she hit him back."

"Apparently she hit him first. For saying mean things about her great-grandfather."

Sedona nodded with satisfaction. "Good for her."

"I thought you were firmly anti-violence."

"I am. On principle. But one thing I learned during

my admittedly unorthodox upbringing was that family should always stick up for family."

"That's what Charlie Buchanan told Emma."

"Sounds like the old guy's still got some of his mental faculties. Along with a romantic streak that's really sweet. Now that you know who he's talking about, are you going to take him up on his fix-up plan?"

"Of course not."

"Why not? What could it hurt?"

"The first time I met Charlie's grandson at Still Waters, we definitely didn't click."

"The first time?" Sedona folded her arms. "I thought you didn't know who he was."

"I didn't. At least not then. He wasn't exactly wearing a stick-on badge saying, 'Hi. I'm Midnight Mac.' The truth is that although he's admittedly probably the hottest single guy in town, I found him totally unlikable and if he'd asked me to go out right then, I would've said no. I'm pretty sure he feels the same way about me."

The moment he'd introduced himself, Annie had felt shaken by the idea that the warm and empathetic man she'd come to feel an emotional nighttime bond with was also the same rude, cat-hating individual who'd caused an instantaneous, and definitely unbidden, spike in her pulse. It was as if while her heart might be falling for Dr. Jekyll, her rebellious body was hot for Mr. Hyde.

"Could you tell if he knew who you are?"

Before Annie could respond, the glass door opened and a sixtysomething woman entered. "Good morning, Ms. Sacchetti," Sedona greeted her after shooting Annie a sharp *We'll talk about this later* look. "Don't you look dashing."

The woman patted her Lucille Ball fluorescent-hued hair. "Thank you! I did it myself from a box. It only took twenty minutes, and just like magic, I was a new woman."

"Well, it's certainly a new look. And quite appealing with your coloring. So, are you having your regular today?"

"No. I decided to think outside the box and go with the marionberry cheesecake."

"That *is* a change from your usual vanilla with buttercream frosting." Sedona took a cheesecake cupcake topped with bright berries from the glass-fronted display counter.

"I was listening to Midnight Mac talk about taking risks and falling in love," the woman said. "When I woke up, I realized I'd gotten into a rut, and decided to make some changes.

"So I drove over to the market as soon as it opened, bought the hair color and went home and, although it recommended a twenty-four-hour test, I just mixed it up, applied it, and voilà! I was a redhead.

"After I leave here, I'm going to walk down the street to Passages travel agency and book one of those seniors' Alaskan cruises and have myself a shipboard romance. Just like Deborah Kerr and Cary Grant in *An Affair to Remember*. But without the part about getting run over at the Empire State Building. Because that scene always makes me cry like a baby."

"Wow!" Annie entered the conversation. Maureen Sacchetti was also one of *her* customers. The elderly woman always reordered her favorite supplies, and had never indicated any desire to attend a class or try some new technique or paper-crafting tool. "When you decide to shake up your life, you don't fool around."

"I'm sixty-eight years old, dear," the older woman said. "And I come from sturdy peasant stock, which means that I've still got a lot of years of living to do. No way do I want to end up being one of those boring, dried-up centenarians content to be rocking on my front porch when the mailman shows up with a birthday card from the White House. And as nice as it would be to have the president wish me a happy birthday, by then all the glaciers might be gone.

"And with women outnumbering men, at my age there aren't nearly enough of them to go around, either. Which is why I'm also stopping by the Dancing Deer Two and having the twins set me up with cruise outfits that'll knock some hot geezer's socks off."

"I think that's a grand idea," Sedona said.

"So do I. You know what they say about regretting the things you don't do more than the things you do," Ms. Sacchetti said.

"Funny," Annie murmured, "someone said the same thing to me just the other night."

"Well, whoever it was, you ought to listen," Maureen stated firmly. "Or you'll end up like me, living in your dead mother's house, surrounded by all her antiques, spending your free time knitting and making sympathy cards for all the widows and widowers of your friends who are passing away left and right."

And wasn't that a pleasant thought?

After Mrs. Sacchetti had left with her adventurous cupcake, which Sedona had insisted was on the house because a change-your-life day deserved a celebratory cupcake, Annie remembered their conversation about the two of them ending up being elderly cat lady roommates.

"You know," Sedona said, "although she might be going overboard just a bit, she really does have a point. So, what are you going to do about Mac Culhane?"

"Nothing. I'm also going to stop calling the show."

"Why? Was it because of what I said about him not seeming all that friendly?"

"No. Although my first impression was admittedly

negative, you were right about him being very sweet with his daughter. He was also very patient and loving with his grandfather."

Which gave him major points in Annie's book. Which was part of the problem. He was exactly the type of man she could fall in love with.

"But it can't go anywhere."

"For heaven's sake, would you stop staying that?" Sedona, who was usually the epitome of calm, blew out a breath. "If you only date men you think you'll end up marrying, you're going to lead a very lonely life. Do you really want to wait until you're nearly seventy, like Maureen Sacchetti, to have yourself a fling? Or to get married again?"

"Hello, Pot. This is the Kettle, pointing out that you're getting a bit rusty yourself. Besides, getting married again is definitely not on my agenda."

"Ever?"

"No." Of that Annie was very sure.

Sedona tilted her head, narrowed her eyes, and subjected her friend to a long, judicial look. "Do you have any idea," she said, "how frustrating you can be at times?"

"Me?"

"Yes, you." The blond Barbie ponytail bobbed as Sedona nodded decisively. "We're supposed to be friends."

"We are."

"So you say. And it's not that I don't really like you, but sometimes it drives me crazy that you never share anything about yourself with me."

"That's not true." Not exactly.

"Of course it is. You know all about me. Including the fact that one of the reasons I quit my job in Portland was that the guy I worked for expected to be a boss with benefits."

"You could've gotten another job at any other firm in Portland. Or Seattle. Or even San Francisco."

"True." Along with her beauty queen looks, Sedona had a mind like a steel trap and an innate confidence that she wore like a second skin. "But I really hated working in the city, and I prefer working with cake batter to working with numbers all day.

"But my point is, I told you all about it. Including why I decided not to file a sexual harassment suit. But all I know about you is that you were abandoned as an infant, went to college, headed off to D.C., where you married your rich lobbyist boss, and when it didn't work out, you moved back home to Oregon. Hell, I don't even know why you opened Memories on Main. Instead of a flower shop."

"Maybe because I have a black thumb."

"That's not what I meant and you know it. Shelter Bay isn't exactly a town you stumble across. It's literally on the edge of the continent and you have to make the decision to go out of your way to move here. Plus, people don't go to all the trouble and expense of opening a business if that business doesn't mean something important to them."

"I'm not sure that's always the case," Annie argued. "It could have been purely an economic decision. All you have to do is go into any big-box craft store to see that paper-crafting items are taking up more and more room."

"I haven't noticed, since I'm always there for baking supplies. But I've seen you in action. You're every bit as dedicated to making scrapbooks as I am to making the world happy one cupcake at a time."

"I like making scrapbooks." Annie didn't share how, for many years, one particular scrapbook had been her anchor in the storm-tossed sea that was her life.

"So do a lot of people. But they don't spent all their

divorce settlement money and go into debt in order to sell pretty paper and rubber stamps."

"I went into debt to fix up the house." As Sedona well knew, since she was the one who'd helped Annie achieve the funding for the lovely but decidedly run-down Victorian on Castaway Cove that Annie had spent the past eighteen months refurbishing.

Before Sedona could respond to that, the door opened again and a rush of German-speaking tourists flooded into the shop.

"Later," Sedona said, handing her the pink box of cupcakes. "And hey, have a great party."

"Thanks."

Sedona's tone had been conciliatory. But as she left the store, Annie realized that while her friend looked as sweet as one of her own cupcakes, Sedona possessed a will of pure forged steel, and now that the subject had been broached, she wasn't going to be able to keep her personal secrets to herself for much longer.

20

"Does Poppy's head hurt?" Emma asked as they drove down Harborview from Still Waters. Unlike winter, when Shelter Bay could look like a ghost town, at this time of year the sidewalks were crowded with tourists. Even more than usual since the upcoming Fourth of July festival had grown into such a popular event.

"No, you don't have to worry about that. Because it doesn't."

"But you said it's sick."

"Not the kind of sick like when you fall down and skin your arm," he said.

"Or get a black eye." She reached into her pink purse, took out the Barbie compact, and studied the purplish-blue skin surrounding her eye with a feminine satisfaction that suddenly, God help him, gave Mac a fleeting glimpse of what she would look like as a teenager.

"Which isn't going to happen again," he felt obliged to warn, putting aside the idea of checking out the availability of chastity belts once she hit puberty.

He didn't admit that he had certainly earned his own share of black eyes growing up. Although he'd never considered himself a nerd just because he liked working on radios, a small group of school bullies had. And they, like Kenny, had learned the lesson that neither Culhanes nor Buchanans backed down from a righteous fight. Apparently his daughter took after him in that regard.

"When I pushed Poppy's wheelchair down to the ice cream machine, some old lady wagged her finger right in his face and told him he should never wear a striped bathrobe with a Hawaiian shirt."

No way was Mac going to admit that he'd thought the same thing when he'd first entered the room. His grandfather's choices of clothing had definitely become more eclectic lately. There were days, even as the weather warmed, when Mac would find him wearing three sweaters over an ancient Oregon State sweatshirt.

"Your poppy always liked going to Hawaii."

Charlie had been a young sailor stationed at Pearl Harbor during the attack. Mac felt long-buried emotions stir as he remembered visiting the memorial to the sunken *Arizona* with his grandfather. The thought of all those sailors buried beneath the sea had had Mac thinking about his own father's death on that Arizona desert.

Now, after losing his Air Force father, and seeing war up close and personal himself, Mac had an even better idea of what his grandfather had experienced. He wondered if Charlie was ever visited by ghosts other than that of his beloved Annie.

Like so many veterans, he seldom talked about his war experience.

Maybe, Mac thought, he could ask Annie Shepherd if there were any more photos of Charlie's Navy days that might spark some memories of stories about to be lost to the mists of time. His grandfather had been a member of the Greatest Generation; decades from now

Emma, and her children, along with future descen-
dants, should be able to read those stories and learn not
just about Charlie Buchanan but about the times that
had formed him.

"We'll have to go to Hawaii someday," he said.

"That would be lots of fun," Emma agreed. "Maybe
I could get a grass skirt, like Peggy did when her parents took her to Hawaii. We hadn't moved here yet,
but she wore it to the kindergarten Halloween party
and everyone says it was the best costume ever. And
we could get you a shirt with palm trees, just like Poppy's."

Although Emma had proven to have a mind of her
own, it hadn't escaped Mac's notice that she seemed
happy to do anything that involved being with him,
even if it was just hanging out together. Which triggered more guilt about the years he'd spent away from
home.

"I told that lady who said bad things about Poppy's
outfit that I like to wear stripes and flowers together all
the time. Because I'm a creative artist," Emma said,
drawing his mind back to their conversation. "So it just
means that Poppy's creative, too."

"Good for you." His grandfather was right about
family standing up for family. "I hope you were polite."

"She was very annoying. But I didn't yell. Or hit her."

"Well, there's a positive," Mac said, stifling his
laugh.

"Are you going to get married?"

"What?" Her question had him slamming on the
brakes too fast and too hard as a young couple, obviously in love, jaywalked over to the seawall after buying a bag of saltwater taffy.

"Mrs. Fletcher told Peggy's mother that she thought
it was a shame I was growing up in a house with two

men. That girls needed mothers, so you should get married again."

Mac wasn't surprised that his single-father status was garnering conversation. Gossip was part of life in Shelter Bay.

"Are you unhappy living with your grandfather and me?"

"No. Though I miss Mommy, even if she did wish she'd never had me."

"That's not true." Some lies were justified.

"Sometimes, when I'd make her mad, she'd tell me she wished that. She said if she just left for good, the Air Force would have to make you come home and take care of me."

Her matter-of-fact tone hurt more than the idea that Kayla had shared her unhappiness with their innocent daughter. "She also told Mrs. Young, the lady who lived next door in Colorado, the same thing right before she went away on that trip the day you came home from war. . . .

"And then she did it. Left for good."

Her voice trembled, revealing that she was close to tears. Mac put a hand on his chest, surprised, not for the first time since his life had literally blown up, that a heart could actually ache from emotional overload.

Maybe Sax and his brothers, J.T. and Cole, were right. All three were war vets and they had advised him to get professional help instead of trying to gut out his survivor guilt himself. But isn't that what his grandfather and father must have done? And they seemed okay. Well, except for Charlie losing his mind to Alzheimer's.

Of course, none of the Douchetts talked that much about what *they* did while in Iraq and Afghanistan, either. Mac figured each generation of warriors probably had that in common.

"Your mother loves you."

He was also beginning to realize that little girls, at least his Emma, were far more aware of what was going on around them than he ever would have expected. Apparently eavesdropping on adults was something she did often. And well.

"I know," Emma said. "That's why she sent me presents for Christmas and my birthday. And mommies always love their children. Like Bambi and his mommy. But sometimes, when I acted up, or when she couldn't afford a babysitter, I just made life hard on her. . . ."

"Poppy says that she probably wants to give you and me time together to make up for when you were gone at war."

"Now there's a thought."

"And that she's probably having to work all the time because of her new job in the big city."

"It's always hard changing jobs. If you want, we can call her tonight."

"No." She exhaled a soft little sigh. "That's okay. I don't want to make life hard on her. And besides, I have you and Poppy and Grandpa."

As grateful as he was that Emma had Charlie to talk to about her feelings, when you factored in dementia, delusions, and just general confusion, his grandfather wasn't exactly the most credible adviser these days.

Plus, dammit, that was Mac's job. He was her father. And it hurt like hell that his own daughter didn't feel free to share her innermost thoughts and feelings with him.

Could she be worried that he would leave if she wasn't always perfect?

And wasn't that a freaking shitty thought?

That provoked him to decide that he would ask his father for a referral to a child psychologist.

Passing the taffy couple, who had crossed the street and were now sitting on the seawall sharing their treat and a kiss, he continued beyond the colorful buildings flying their bright wind socks to Annie Shepherd's scrapbook store. Which he must have passed several times before and never noticed.

"Maybe you could marry Sedona Sullivan," Emma suggested helpfully, returning to the topic he'd hoped she'd forgotten. "Then we could have cupcakes every night for dessert."

"They might not be such a treat if we had them every day." He liked the cupcake baker, and couldn't deny she made the best cakes and pies he'd ever tasted, but as gorgeous as she was, he had never felt even the smallest spark whenever Emma would drag him into Take the Cake.

Not like the spark he'd felt with Annie Shepherd earlier.

"Poppy's nurse, Analise Peterson, at Still Waters, is really pretty. But she just got married." Emma continued mulling the problem of his single state as he pulled into a parking space in front of the cheery white store with its yellow-and-white-striped awning and window filled with red, white, and blue patriotic displays. Which reminded him that he *had* noticed the store before, a few months ago when it had been decorated with yellow chicks, brightly painted eggs, and bunnies, all created from various colored papers.

He'd thought at the time that he should bring Emma here for drawing supplies, since she was obviously so into art, but then he'd gotten wrapped up in his new gig at KBAY and it had slipped his mind.

Old habits, it seemed, died hard.

"She went to Hawaii on her honeymoon. But I don't know if she got a grass skirt while she was there, because she always wears her nurse's outfits at Still Waters. . . .

"Ms. Shepherd's pretty," Emma pointed out as she

climbed down onto the sidewalk from her backseat booster seat. "She smells like flowers and Poppy likes her a lot. Maybe you could ask her out on a date. Somewhere nice. Like the Sea Mist, where we celebrated Father's Day with Poppy and Grandpa."

"There's a thought," Mac said.

Unfortunately, it was one that was way too appealing, since in contrast to the strong emotional connection he felt toward Sandy from Shelter Bay, which had him inviting *her* to dinner at the Sea Mist, he'd felt the same sort of deep, almost painful physical pull around Annie Shepherd.

Although he might not have been a warrior, he'd had to go through basic training with the rest of his recruiting class and had spent a lot of time drilling. Mac hoped to never have to shoot a weapon in battle, but the one thing the military had driven home was that with enough repetition, muscle memory would always kick in. The electrical charge he'd been hit with when Annie had turned around today could've won him a Boy Scout tent-building badge for the boner it had sparked beneath the fly of his jeans.

As he parked in front of the store, a white crossover pulled up behind him and two little girls piled out. Assuring Mac that now that she was a big girl of six years old, she didn't need him to go inside with her, Emma was out of the truck like a shot, running toward the pair dressed in frilly dresses.

They were chattering away like magpies as they literally skipped on shiny patent leather party shoes into the store. Mac decided the fact that she didn't stop to wave good-bye was a good thing, showing that she'd gotten over her earlier sadness.

He also decided, as just the memory of his two meetings with Annie Shepherd had him adjusting his jeans, that it was just as well Emma hadn't wanted him to come into the store, because one thing he didn't need was having his body respond like that of a hormone-driven teenager in front of a bunch of little girls.

Driving over to Bon Temps for a game of pool with Sax to kill time before he returned to pick Emma up, he wondered what kind of man could be so attracted to two women at the same time?

A normal one, he reassured himself.

As he turned onto Harborview, Mac felt, for the first time in a very long while, as if, just maybe, his life, which had literally been blown out from under him, was getting back on track.

21

The crafting room at Memories on Main looked as if a typhoon had hit it. The glass-topped tables were covered with sheets of designer paper, embellishments, ribbons, various punches, inks, stamps, and pens. Papercrafting was often a messy prospect, but fifteen little girls had brought an entirely new chaos to creation.

Still, the love they were putting into their cards was so obvious that Annie knew the recipients would be able to feel it. Which was all that was important.

There was a slight problem when Emma Culhane had plucked a marker from the box and begun signing *Love, your friend, Emma* in Day-Glo pink.

"You can't use a girlie color like pink for a soldier," declared Peggy Murray, the birthday girl, who'd already proven to be more than a little bossy.

"Can, too," Emma said, putting that card away and reaching for another she'd made, this one with a smiling dog sticker on the polka-dot-covered front. "I always sign the pictures I draw for my poppy in pink and he loves them." She tossed her blond head. "And he was a sailor in a big, big war, so he should know a lot more than *you* do about what soldiers like."

She looked up at Annie. "Isn't that right, Ms. Shepherd?"

"Your poppy does love those pictures," Annie agreed. For a moment she'd considered suggesting that Emma, who obviously loved color, use a red pen for her careful childish printing, but then she decided she wasn't about to stifle the young artist's creativity. "I'm sure all you girls' cards will make our soldiers happy."

And who wouldn't smile when they saw that blindingly bright pink ink and think of the little girl who'd made the card for them?

"See?" Emma told Peggy, whose scowl suggested that wasn't the answer she'd wanted to hear.

"As soon as all the cards are signed, we can move on to the cupcake-and-ice-cream part of the fun," Annie said.

Her attempt to smooth the troubled waters paid off when there was a loud cheer and everyone started calling out their favorite Take the Cake flavors.

Except for that brief little ripple between Emma and Peggy, the party had gone well. *Better than well,* Annie thought as she cleaned up the paper scraps, scrubbed the glue off the glass-topped tables, and tucked the cards the girls had made into the box where she'd been storing the cards for the schoolchildren to hand out to troops during the Fourth of July parade. Although Shelter Bay didn't have enough veterans for every child to be able to hand out a card, before the school year had ended a couple weeks ago, two names had been drawn from each class, and—wouldn't you know it—Emma Culhane had won one of the tickets for her kindergarten class.

Because Emma had rushed out of the store as soon as she'd seen her daddy's truck pull up in front, Annie had avoided running into Mac Culhane again today.

But, since Emma had won that ticket, like it or not, Annie would be forced to come in contact with the man again. Which was why she'd sworn not to listen to his program.

After ten minutes of NPR talk, and another ten of a jazz station from Newport, she'd given up and tuned in to KBAY, where he was talking about the challenges of being a single dad trying to comprehend a daughter's mind.

"You have to understand, this is a girl who could be the poster girl for pink. Not the singer but the color. Her bedroom looks as if a bottle of Pepto-Bismol exploded all over the walls, and even the red, white, and blue cards she made at a party today at Memories on Main to give away to soldiers during the parade this week were signed in pink ink."

Annie smiled at the memory

"So, you can imagine the reaction when we returned home to a letter informing her that her new grade school has a uniform code," Mac was saying. "White blouses and plaid skirts, and no, like I tried to explain to her, neither can be pink."

The sigh floated over the airways like an arrow straight into Annie's heart.

The child was not only darling; she was an original.

Just like her father.

Yet another reason Annie was *not* going to call.

"So, a day that began with French toast topped with whipped cream in the Grateful Bread's bus and was highlighted with a little girl's card-making birthday party, complete with cupcakes, ended in tears."

Another long male sigh.

"And speaking of tears, here's 'Someone Else's Star,' a tearjerker by Bryan White about a guy who's been spending too many nights alone, wishing for a love of his own, when he finally comes to the conclusion that he must be wishing on someone else's star because it seems like everyone around him is in love with everyone else. But unlucky him."

Less than twenty seconds into the perfectly described tearjerker country song, Annie's phone rang.

Expecting Sedona, she snatched it up.

"I'm not calling him," she insisted yet again.

"Yeah, I got the idea when you gave me that chilly reception at Still Waters," the all-too-familiar voice said.

Oh, God. Why hadn't she taken that one extra second to check the caller ID?

"I was *not* chilly toward you."

Okay, so maybe she wasn't exactly enthusiastic, but she'd certainly been polite to deter Charlie or Emma from picking up on the fact that he was the last man on the planet she wanted to run into.

"Sweetheart, the second you figured out I was the guy Charlie's been trying to hook you up with, there was enough ice surrounding you to freeze the bay."

"That's an exaggeration. And I'm *not* your sweetheart."

"Point taken. That was admittedly chauvinistic. What can I say? Men are pigs."

"How did you figure out who I was?"

"Your voice sounded familiar the first time you called. Then I had the same feeling today at Still Waters, though it took a while to sink in that you and Sandy were the same person. . . .

"But here's the thing. We have less than three minutes and eighteen seconds before I have to pay the bills with a promo spot for Bennington Ford. So I have one question."

"What?"

"Are you making a basket for the Fourth of July picnic charity deal?"

"Yes. Why?"

"What does it look like?"

"It looks like a basket. The old-fashioned wicker kind." Perhaps she had embellished it a bit with some stamped flag images, but he didn't need to know that.

"Is your name on it?"

"No, because it's supposed to be a blind drawing. And that's technically three questions and why are you asking?"

"Because I intend to bid on it."

"Why?"

"Because I figure it's the only way I'm ever going to get you to go out to eat with me."

"Even if you did win my basket, the rules clearly state that the maker isn't required to eat with the winner. The auction isn't a date fix-up. The idea is to raise money for school arts, creative writing classes, and music education. And given that your daughter is so artistic, you should be all for that."

"I am. But are you telling me that if I win your basket, you're going to refuse to eat with my daughter, who couldn't stop talking about how much fun she had at your store today?"

"That's playing dirty. And you've gone way over your question limit. Plus you're running out of time."

"So give me a hint. Not only do I still want to spend time with you, even though you did, for some reason we'll talk about later, lie about your name, but you've got to protect me from Connie Fletcher."

"Ah." Annie laughed at that. Connie's intense quest to snag husband number four was providing a great deal of grist for Shelter Bay's gossip mill. It only stood to reason that she'd have zeroed in on the way hot midnight deejay as her next target.

"Don't tell me that after having served multiple tours in war zones, you're afraid of a mere female."

"Hey, I've seen females capable of wielding automatic weapons better than a lot of guys, so I know exactly how dangerous you people can be. But this particular female's a barracuda. And I wasn't fighting while I was deployed. I was just the— "

"Guy on the radio. I know. And I also don't believe it. Sedona told me that Kara told her that Sax told her that you used to go outside the wire all the time to report on troops stuck out in forward operating bases."

"The troops didn't get a lot of visitors out there in no-man's-land. Those guys were working their tails off, so those of us who'd landed easy duty just wanted to show them we appreciated it.

"But you're right, the clock's ticking. So yes or no, and I'm giving you fair warning, if we're still on the air when this song is over, I'm risking having the entire late-night audience of Shelter Bay hear my manhood crumble when you turn me down on live radio."

"Somehow I suspect you'd survive." She also suspected he was unaccustomed to being turned down by a woman. Which made her wonder why his wife had left.

"And how did you figure out who I was?"

"It was partly your voice. And partly because, ever since leaving Still Waters, I've been trying to figure out how I could have such a strong response to two different women. "

"You wouldn't be the first man to have feelings for more than one woman at a time."

"That's not me. Not anymore, anyway. Then, driving to the studio tonight, it finally dawned on me that both women were you. . . .

"Say yes, Annie." His voice deepened seductively.

"What could it hurt? We'll be in a public park with not only most of the town around us, but my daughter, too. I realize you don't want to spend any time with me because of how we first met, but surely you're not going to take the fact that I dissed cats out on a six-year-old motherless little girl?"

It was Annie's turn to sigh. "You really don't fight fair."

"Believe me, Annie Shepherd, fighting is the last thing I want to do with you." Images of tangled sheets and hot female flesh flashed through Mac's mind. The woman was flat-out driving him insane. "Say yes."

Mac could feel her debating with herself. Every nerve ending in his body was tingling like they used to whenever he'd leave the supposed safety of an Afghan base.

"All right." She finally caved. Then she described her basket with its flags.

"Sounds appropriately patriotic."

"But less than original. Everyone else will probably put flags and a red, white, and blue ribbon on their basket. I'll go with yellow. For the troops all coming back home again."

"See? Something we can agree on. Don't look now, but we're on a roll."

She made a sound that could've been a snort. Or, better yet, a muffled laugh.

"But just in case someone else gets the same idea, why don't you put your initials on the bottom?"

"That would be cheating."

"Twenty seconds, Annie. Please make my daughter the happiest girl in town. Not that she's the only reason you sharing your basket with me would make my day."

Mac wasn't used to begging any woman. But for some weird reason, he was willing to beg this one.

She expelled a short, quick breath. "Okay. For

Emma. Because she's a doll and I know how it is to grow up without a mother."

He wondered if she realized that she'd just given him a clue to the enigma that was Annie Shepherd, aka Sandy from Shelter Bay. But, damn, now that he was down to less than fifteen seconds, Mac had no time to delve into it. He'd have to come up with a plan to have a more intimate conversation before the Fourth.

"Terrific." He looked up at the digital countdown clock. "I'll call you tomorrow. We can work out the details."

Before she could object or he could say good-bye, the light flashed and he was back on the air, pushing the great deals to be had at Bennington Ford's Fourth of July Sellathon.

22

Fortunately, the next morning was busy, which kept Annie from dwelling too much on having agreed to spend the upcoming Fourth of July celebration with Mac Culhane. Although she knew all the people would be coming downtown for the holiday's events, after having spent years in D.C. where it seemed the lobbyist lifestyle went on twenty-four/seven, she'd come to realize that there was a great deal more to life than work. Which was why, unlike Sedona, who was staying open and would be baking cupcakes like crazy, Annie had decided that Memories on Main would be closed for the holiday.

"Can you believe this?" Kim Nance, a divorced single mom who worked part-time for Annie while attending Coastal Community College, asked as a busload of senior citizens on their way to the Chinook Winds Casino Resort in Lincoln City swarmed into the store. "It's like the invasion of the AARP."

"Don't knock them," Annie said as she watched a group of women oohing and aahing over a display rack of sea-themed paper and accompanying embellishments, including, for Shelter Bay, the obligatory whales.

"They probably all have grandchildren whose photos need scrapping. By the time they get back on that bus, they'll have paid our rent for this month."

"It's not that I'm ungrateful," Kim said. "It's always good to be busy. Though I sure can't understand why anyone would want to spend a gorgeous summer day inside a casino, pulling a lever on a slot machine."

"Different strokes," Annie said. Which was why she also always kept casino-themed kits in stock.

"OMG. Be still, my heart," Kim said as the bell on the front door jingled and Mac Culhane sauntered in.

Kim wasn't the only one who'd noticed. One by one, the women all stopped chattering and digging through the sale baskets to stare at the sole male in the shop, who looked every bit as hot as the other times Annie had seen him.

Rather than his usual black T-shirt, he was wearing a blue button-down oxford-cloth shirt a few shades lighter than his eyes, and although he was still in jeans, the crease was sharp enough to cut through the sheets of designer paper covered with seashells that Annie had been in the process of bagging.

Every female eye in the store followed as he walked toward the counter. It was only because Sedona had mentioned it, and Annie was watching him so carefully, that she detected a slight limp.

"Is he not the most gorgeous male animal you've ever seen in your life?" Kim said under her breath.

"I could just eat him up with a spoon," the customer, whose hair was dyed a shade remarkably similar to the fluorescent red that Maureen had shown up with the other day, said. "My late husband had a rock-hard body like that once upon a time. Everyone in Salem thought I was marrying him because he was running for the state senate and I wanted to be a politician's wife."

"But they were wrong," Kim guessed as Annie watched Mac pause to treat a trio of women with varying shades of snowy hair to a dazzling smile that had them giggling like schoolgirls.

"You bet they were. I married my Arnold for the sex." She sighed again, causing Annie to wonder if she was remembering that sex with her late husband, or imagining indulging in it with the midnight deejay.

Which, as a tsunami of impure thoughts swept over her, Annie found herself imagining as well.

"He's good-looking," Annie said, managing to keep her tone cool and composed even as her body flared hot and bothered. She wouldn't even need the spoon. She had a sudden urge to lick Midnight Mac. All over. "If that's your type."

Another woman had just come up to the counter carrying a basket filled with glue runners, a box of metal whale brads, and a wooden-handled rubber stamp of a whimsical flower-spotted whale.

"Since when is tall, dark, and sexy as sin not every woman's type?" the customer asked. "If I was twenty years younger, I'd be tempted to jump him right here."

"Make that thirty years," the first woman said. "Not only do I know exactly when you were born, since I'm your younger sister, but you'll always be older than me."

"Like two years makes that much difference at our age."

"If *I* weren't wearing this ring"—Kim waggled her left hand to show off the diamond she'd received from her fireman fiancè for Valentine's Day—"I'd do him in a heartbeat. . . . Which is why we're all going to have to live vicariously through you," she said to Annie.

"Me?"

"Well, none of us have called the show under a fake name," Kim said.

"I don't know what you're talking about." Annie

had always been a lousy liar. If she'd been testifying under oath in a trial for her life, the blatant lack of truthfulness in her voice would've had a jury sending her to the Big House.

"Don't try to deny it," Kim said. "It's all over town. They're even taking bets at the market on when you're going to show up together in person."

"Looks like now," the late senator's wife said.

"It's not 'showing up together' to have a customer come into the store," Annie muttered. "And people call radio stations all the time."

"I wonder what he's doing here. He doesn't look like a scrapper or a cardmaker to me," the redhead said.

"Nor to me," her lavender-haired sister agreed.

"Which means," Kim said, "the hottie deejay is here to see you."

Which appeared to be the case when he stopped in front of the counter.

"Hi." How could that one word, consisting of merely a single syllable, have the air between them crackling like heat lightning before a squall?

"Well, hello." They were now the center of attention. Given the conversation that this encounter would generate once everyone got back on that blue and white bus, Annie felt as if she should be charging admission to the show. "This is a surprise."

"Emma came home from yesterday's card-making party with a wish list," he said in a voice every bit as dark and rich as the chocolate fudge sold along with the saltwater taffy at the candy shop next door.

Every gaze in the place followed his hand as he pulled the notepaper from the front pocket of those jeans, which, though knife-creased, were still worn thin in some very eye-catching places.

"Great marketing ploy." His grin, which caused the thin white scars beneath his eyes to crinkle, was unreasonably cocky. Even as she warned herself of its dangers, Annie felt her knees weakening. "Holding parties to get people hooked on more supplies."

Reining in her thoughts, which had wandered into hot and treacherous territory, Annie lifted a sharp gaze to meet his laughing one. "It's not a ploy. Your daughter's a very talented artist. If you'd been aware enough to want to help her develop that talent, you would have bought her some decent drawing pens or pencils before she had to make you that list."

The minute she heard the words escape her lips, Annie wanted to pull them back. Knowing from last night's show how overwhelmed he seemed to be, suddenly a single father of a six-year-old girl, she shouldn't have been so uncharacteristically snarky to the guy, who really seemed to be trying.

"I'm sorry," she said as she led him to the back of the store where the pencils, pens, and inks were displayed. Fortunately it was at the far side of the wooden shelves, out of sight of the counter, where everyone seemed to have gathered to chatter about the invasion of testosterone into the cozy store. "That was uncalled for."

"But true," he said. "I have to admit that I'm pretty much on the low end of the single-parent learning curve."

"You appear to be doing well enough. Emma seems very well adjusted." Annie believed in giving credit where credit was due. She also suspected that it was natural for a little girl to want a mother. She certainly had. And, if she were to be perfectly honest, there were times she still felt that lifelong loss.

"This is quite a list," she said, looking at the items printed in pink on the piece of paper. "And these alcohol pens are wonderful. But perhaps pricey for this stage in her coloring. Though putting these on her list suggests she wants to try blending, which would probably be too advanced for most people her age. But from the drawings on Charlie's wall, I think you ought to just let her go for it."

"We," he corrected. At her puzzled look, he clarified. "After yesterday I got the feeling that she views you as a mentor as well as a potential mom candidate."

"She did suggest I should marry you," Annie admitted. She hadn't been going to bring it up because she had no idea what his daughter had been discussing with him.

"That's another list, and while you were definitely in the mix after your meeting at Gramps's room, after the party I think you've now claimed the top slot."

That idea, just as it had when Emma had brought it up yesterday, triggered memories and dreams she'd been trying, without success, to forget.

"I'm sorry if she was overly persistent about wanting a new mother," he said. "I'm discovering a stubborn streak beneath all that girlie pink."

"Gee, I wonder where she got that from?" Annie asked.

"Unfortunately, from both of her parents, so I suspect the teen years will be interesting. And I didn't mean to make you unhappy."

"You didn't."

"So you say." He reached out and rubbed at the lines she hadn't realized were creasing her forehead. "But your face is telling me something different."

"I'm just getting a headache." She brushed away his touch, which was leaving sparks on her skin, and got back to business.

"So . . . what I'd suggest is this basic set of less-expensive watercolor pencils. Along with these colored ones."

"They both look pretty much the same to me," he said. "What's the difference?"

"The colored ones are more waxy and glide more smoothly across the paper." She handed him one. "Try it on this sketch pad." She kept the pad hanging on the display so people could try before buying.

He took the red pencil she handed him and drew a stick figure holding out a flower. *Talk about smooth,* she thought as he tore the paper off and handed it to her.

"Apparently while your daughter may have gotten her parents' stubbornness, she doesn't seem to have inherited her artistic talent from you."

The little cloud of depression lifted as she looked down at what, if she'd been Emma's age and received from a boy, she would have considered a love note.

"True. The drawing sucks. But it's the thought that counts, right?"

"So they say." Deciding that she didn't want to share even a few of the thoughts she'd been having about him, she took one of the watercolor pencils from the bin. "As you can see, this is a harder pencil."

This time he drew a rectangle with a square on top, then added arms and legs and a smiling face. Then drew a heart in the center of the rectangle and filled it in with a red watercolor. Next he drew a second robot, adding loopy lines that she took to be long curls and lips to its face. Reaching into the bin, he selected a pink pencil, which he used to shade in the ultra-feminine mouth.

Beneath the robots he wrote, in a broad, scrawling script, *Robot Love.*

"Very cute." Which, dammit, was true. It also helped her connect the fun Midnight Mac on the radio with the dangerously dark exterior of the man she'd met at Still Waters. Layers. The man definitely had them.

"Now, you could've dipped the tip in water and done the same thing, or brushed it with water, but when I used to keep a spray bottle here, I found that sometimes the kids used it for water fights. So here's another way to show you the difference."

She took a blending pen and moved it across the heart of the female robot, which gave a softened water-color effect.

"Cool," he said. Taking the pen, he did the same on the lips. "They're the same color as yours," he said, pointing out what she'd already noticed. "And here's where I tell you that they've been almost all I've been thinking about since yesterday. And wondering if they taste as good as they look."

Growing up as a nomad, Annie had always tried her best to be the "good girl." The kid that her foster parents might want to adopt for their very own. Or at least keep for more than a few weeks or months.

She'd stuck with that behavior through college, then into her marriage, being cheerful and acquiescent so as to never make waves.

But as those dark blue eyes settled on her lips, which had suddenly gone desert dry, Annie decided that perhaps there was something to be said for wave making. As Sedona had pointed out, she'd moved to the very edge of the continent.

So why not carry living on the edge just one step further?

After all, lips that firm and chiseled were designed to tempt even the most levelheaded woman. Dragging her gaze from his mouth, she saw a storm brewing in his eyes, his irises darkening until they were nearly as black as his pupils.

A bad girl she hadn't even known was lurking inside her smiled at him. A slow, you-know-you-want-me smile that was as much dare as temptation.

"Well," she said, in a husky voice that wasn't as

moonlight-and-magnolias-drenched as the one Connie Fletcher always pulled out when she was flirting with men (which was nearly always, from what Annie had been able to tell) but was a very long way from her usual calm and almost logical tone, "I suppose there's only one way to find out."

23

Reminding himself that this wasn't why he'd come here to Memories on Main today, as well as taking the extra precaution of putting both hands on the shelves on either side of her, to keep them from getting into trouble, Mac leaned forward, lowering his head.

The sky outside had been a brilliant coastal-summer blue, without the sign of a cloud, when he'd entered the store. So why was he suddenly hearing the rumble of thunder?

He was a breath away. A slight shifting of their heads and their lips would meet. Even as he was telling himself that this could end up being a major mistake, she licked those glossy pink lips with the tip of her tongue, and, slam bam, he was toast.

She tasted like cherries and temptation, and sex on a summer's night, bringing up mental images of the two of them on a blanket on the beach while the waves rolled onto the sand, and the stars whirled overhead, and she moved beneath him, mouth to mouth, hot flesh to hot flesh, long legs wrapped around his back, telling him *yes*, and *yes*, and *oh, yes*.

She'd shout his name even as she begged for more.

He'd expected to feel sparks. But what he hadn't planned for was an early explosion of Fourth of July fireworks.

He might claim to be just the guy on the radio, but Mac was no stranger to risk. Nor danger. If he were to be perfectly honest, he'd even have to admit that part of the reason he went outside the wire more than most AFN deejays was that he enjoyed it.

But he'd always recognized his own strengths. Along with his own weaknesses. And the emotions that Sandy from Shelter Bay, or Annie Shepherd, or whatever the hell she wanted to be called, stirred in him represented more risk than a horde of Taliban or a dozen terrorists with armed jingle trucks.

As the sweetest lips he'd ever tasted parted beneath his, even as a low moan flowed from them straight into his mouth, he forced himself to pull away.

"Wow." Her cheeks were flushed, her lips swollen, her eyes dark and clouded with a tempting blend of confusion and unfulfilled need. "If Connie Fletcher knew you could kiss like that, you'd never be safe."

"Connie Fletcher doesn't have anything on you." He knew the flirtatious redhead couldn't, on her best day, knock his socks off the way this woman had with one mere, too short kiss.

He lowered his hands, which were practically itching with the need to touch her. All over. "That really wasn't what I came here for."

"Okay." She glanced down at the pencils she'd been holding that had fallen to the floor between them. "And, for the record, I don't usually kiss customers behind the display shelves."

"Usually?" Mac lifted a brow, feeling foolishly like laughing. Not at her. But at their situation and because suddenly he was feeling so damn good.

She drew in a deep breath that did interesting things

to the front of today's sundress, a cheery yellow-and-white-checked number with delicate little hearts for buttons. As he imagined unfastening each of those little white hearts, Mac found himself slipping closer to the edge of that dangerous cliff again.

"Actually, I've *never* kissed a customer."

"Which makes me your first." He grinned. "I like that idea."

"You're impossible."

"Actually, I'm hungry. Which is why I dropped in, to see if you wanted to go to lunch."

"With you?"

"Well, we could go separately. But that doesn't seem like a real good way to get to know each other."

"And that's important why?"

"Because we're going to be spending the Fourth together. And although I'm pretty sure you're not a serial killer or anything like that, I guess I'm sort of an overly protective father and I'd like to know a little about the woman that my daughter is pushing me to marry."

"I told you, marriage is off the table. And it's lovely to know that you don't suspect me of being some sort of murderer, but I'm not buying your story."

"That bad, huh?"

"Let's just say you're not going to be winning any Nobel Prizes for literature anytime soon."

"Okay." He took a deep breath. Blew it out again as he wondered why the hell he was feeling like the high school nerd asking the head cheerleader to the prom. "Here's the deal. I like you. My daughter likes you. And although you might keep trying to make me think otherwise, that kiss just revealed that you're interested, too."

She folded her arms across the front of the yellow gingham. "And your point is?"

Mac was encouraged that she hadn't tried to lie about the connection between them.

"But you don't want to be interested," he guessed.

"No. I don't. It's nothing personal, and I've honestly no idea why I just acted that way, but the thing is . . . I've pretty much given up men."

"Is that like giving up chocolate for Lent?"

"No. Merely a lifestyle choice."

"Does that mean that anyone with a Y chromosome is now out of the running?"

"No." Black curls bounced as she shook her head. "I didn't mean that at all. It's just that, well, relationships tend to complicate things too much."

Damn. Something about him was making her skittish, so the first thing he had to do was get her to relax around him. To trust him. To prove to her that he wasn't anything like her ex must've been.

"I'm just talking about lunch. You have to eat."

"In case you didn't notice, the store's packed. I have to work."

"Well, we're in luck. Because that bus is getting ready to take off," he said.

She glanced out the window, watching as several seniors who'd been visiting other Main Street shops dutifully climbed back on the blue and white tour bus.

"If you're worried about that poll they've got going at the market and Barnie's—"

"They're betting at the barbershop, too?"

"According to my dad. And Van, down at the Grateful Bread, says we're suddenly topic number one at Cut Loose."

"Which means, since it's the only salon in town, I'm never going to be able to get my hair cut again," she muttered.

"There'll be another story for everyone to fixate on in a day or so. Meanwhile, if you want to try to avoid any gossip—"

"Which is impossible in this town."

The upside of living in the small coastal town was that everyone cared about everyone else. The downside, he'd discovered, was that they also cared about everyone else's business.

"I can pick up some takeout at the Crab Shack and we can eat on the beach." He continued on his mission to get her alone. "I know this place where Sax and his brothers used to hang out growing up, it's totally private, and—"

"I don't think that's such a good idea. But you're not going to let up, are you?"

"No, I'm not. As you've already pointed out, tenacity runs deep in the Culhane genes. You've already nixed the Sea Mist. How about Lavender Hill Farm's restaurant? I heard they've got an organic grass-fed American Kobe burger that's the best thing walking around on four hooves. "

"That's a bit rare for my taste."

"Ha-ha." He liked that she actually made a joke instead of glaring at him. He was beginning to win her over. "It's not actually walking around. Anymore. But Ethan Concannon is friends with the rancher, who's down in the southern part of the state, and while some of us guys were shooting hoops over at Sax's house the other day, he told us it's unbelievable."

"It may be. But I'm more into salads."

"Lavender Hill has the best salads in town." At least that's what the commercials he'd been running for the combination herb farm, restaurant, and cooking school said.

She glanced down at her watch. "Thirty minutes," she said. "That's it."

Damn. Since his dad had taken Emma out fishing with Cole and Bernard Douchett, Mac's afternoon was his own. He wanted more. But having made inroads, he was willing to take whatever he could get.

"Thirty minutes from when we sit down." While it probably took all of eight minutes to get to the farm from here, he wanted as much time as he could get.

"I just realized something," she said.

"What?"

"Nearly every one of our conversations comes with a time clock."

Which had been one of his major frustrations whenever she'd called the station. Of course he hadn't realized it was her. But that didn't alter their situation.

"We can change that today," he suggested.

"Thirty minutes," she repeated firmly.

"You've been working too hard." Annie's assistant, who apparently had been lurking close enough to hear their conversation, appeared from the other side of the shelves. "Take an hour. Relax and enjoy the day."

"Don't you have anything better to do than eavesdrop?" Annie asked the young woman, who didn't appear at all apologetic.

"Not at the moment."

"What about that order of paper that came in this morning?"

"What we didn't sell is already shelved. Since there was more red, white, and blue paper in there, I added it to the window display."

"There was also a box of stamps and adhesive."

"Logged into inventory and shelved. And it's too late in the day for any buses to stop in town, unless they're here for a whale-watching tour, in which case everyone's going to be dashing in line to get the best seats." The clerk grinned. "So I'd say we're pretty much in the lull of the day. I figure I can handle things. For an hour. Or more."

If it hadn't been for that small, sparkly diamond on the fourth finger of her hand, or that Annie, who was obviously vacillating, would've gotten the totally wrong idea, Mac would have kissed the young woman on the spot.

"Why don't we split the difference?" he suggested as he watched Annie gathering her resolve again. "Forty-five minutes would be a good compromise. And allow time for dessert."

"Let the man take you out and feed you," said the redheaded senior, who apparently had decided to buck the driver's instructions to immediately board the bus.

"Don't be such a stick-in-the-mud," the woman's lavender-haired sister said. "And having eaten there, I can highly recommend the Dungeness crab on field greens, with grapefruit and avocado salad." She made a shooing motion with a hand that was laden with some serious jewelry. "Just go."

Which started the rest of the women in still the store shouting, "Go to lunch! Go to lunch! Go to lunch!!"

At which point Annie closed her eyes and appeared to be counting to ten.

When she opened them again, she did not exactly look like a woman thrilled to be going out to what Frommer's had described as a restaurant that epitomized the best of Oregon Coast cuisine, one of those gems that travelers dream of discovering. The reviewer had even gone so far as to call it "a foodie's paradise."

"It seems to be unanimous," Mac said.

"Does anyone ever say *no* to you?" Annie countered with a huff of frustration.

Then she sighed, apparently remembering the personal story he'd shared during the first of their late-night conversations.

"I'm sorry," she said again. "This seems to be my day for putting my foot in my mouth."

He glanced down at the foot in question. Today's sandals had some sort of cork wedge heel and were covered in flowered fabric. Her toes had been painted the same glossy pink hue as her mouth, and although he'd never had a foot fetish, he suddenly wanted to suck them, one by one.

"Don't worry about it," he said. "I'm not the first guy whose wife left him. And unfortunately, I won't be the last. . . . So, how about it?"

"I'm minoring in retail business for when I run my art gallery," the young woman reminded Annie. "I can certainly handle this place alone."

"I know you can."

You could've heard one of those little metal things from a nearby bin drop as everyone in the place, including him, waited for Annie Shepherd's answer.

"Forty-five minutes. But I'm counting the time we spend waiting for a table. Since the restaurant doesn't have any lull this time of year."

"No problem. I already have a table booked by the windows. With a view of the gardens and ocean."

"Oh, that's so romantic," one of the women said.

"That's one word for it." Those frown lines furrowed her brow between her remarkable pewter eyes again. "No one could ever accuse you of a lack of self-confidence, Mr. Culhane."

"It's Mac," he reminded her. "And it wasn't over-confidence. I was merely hopeful. And Maddy assured me that if you didn't agree, she'd have no trouble giving our table to someone else."

"You know Maddy Chaffee?"

"Sure. Not only is this a small town, but my family would come here from Portland to visit Charlie during Christmas and summer vacations when I was a kid. I was even around when Lucas pulled that lame-brained stunt that broke the two of them up for so many years.

"So," he said, wanting to get on with the fun part of the afternoon, "why don't you just have your assistant—" He paused, realizing he didn't know her name.

"Kim," she said helpfully with a sexy smile that suggested while she might be engaged, she wasn't beyond a light flirtation.

"Hi," he said. "I'm Mac Culhane."

"Everyone knows that," she said. "I'm a big fan."

"Thanks. You'll have to call in some night."

She dimpled prettily. "I might just do that."

"Anyway," Mac said, continuing his original thought, "if you could take care of gathering up the rest of the things on this list, and any other stuff you think a six-year-old with artistic talent might like, I'll pick them up when I bring your boss back from lunch."

"Sweet," Kim said. "Do you want to become a member?"

"Member?"

"We put you on an e-mail list," Annie explained, "and then let you know of new products, sales, special customer coupons and discounts."

"Sounds great." Not only would Emma love shopping here, but it would give him an excuse to come see Annie. He gave her his most encouraging smile. "Ready to go?"

"Do I have any choice?"

"You two have fun now," one of the nearby older women called out, waggling her fingers as she and her sister finally left the store.

"And don't worry about hurrying back," Kim said. "Everything's totally under control."

"You do realize that you're impossible," Annie said as they walked up the hill to where he'd left his truck, in front of Tidal Waves Books, where a fat yellow cat dozed in the window. The last time Mac had brought Emma to the bookstore, she'd badgered him for a week about why they needed a cat.

"You're not the first person to suggest that," he said as he opened the door of the truck for her, enjoying the flash of smooth thigh as she climbed into the high passenger seat.

"And I doubt I'll be the last," she said when he joined her in the pickup.

Having gotten what he'd gone to Memories on Main for, Mac wasn't about to argue. Especially when it was true.

"Probably not," he agreed as he started back down the hill toward Harborview, heading out to Lavender Hill Farm.

24

Maddy Chaffee came out of her kitchen to greet Annie and Mac after they'd been seated at a prime table by the tall windows and served drinks and a basket of warm, fragrant herb bread. Coincidentally, Annie saw Sedona at the far side of the room with a man she didn't recognize. He wasn't nearly as sexy and handsome as Mac, but he was good-looking in a buttoned-up kind of way.

She caught her friend's eye and waggled her fingers; Sedona did the same; then, although maybe it was a trick of the sunlight glinting off the tumbling water of the stacked stone fountain, she thought perhaps Sedona rolled her eyes.

The gardens were in full bloom and beyond the yard there was a view of sailboats skimming across sun-brightened water that almost had Annie wishing she knew how to sail. Maybe she could take lessons someday.

The house she'd bought had come with a dock at the edge of the cove. It was rickety and would probably need either repairing or replacing, but Maddy's contractor husband, Lucas, who'd done the major work in restoring the pretty yellow Victorian to its earlier beauty, could probably take care of that.

"It's so good to see you both," Maddy said. "I have to admit, I'm honored that my restaurant is where the two of you decided to show up. I couldn't *buy* advertising like this."

"Is the fact that I called in to the radio all over town?" Annie asked.

"You know we pride ourselves in keeping up with the news here," Maddy said mildly. "There may be some who aren't talking about it. But they're probably buried in Sea View cemetery.

"There hasn't been much to get people excited since Phoebe and Kara had their babies during last winter's ice storm. A new romance always adds spice." She folded her arms over her black chef's jacket and said, "And believe me, I know my spices."

And her scandals, Annie thought. After all, a couple years back Maddy had been living the high life in New York City, when her celebrity chef husband's sex video went viral. At least Annie's own divorce had been fairly private, notable only among their own circle of friends.

No, not friends. Because in the high-powered world where Annie had been living, she hadn't had friends. Not close ones like Sedona. Or even Kara Douchett and Maddy, with whom she'd also become close through Sedona's friendship with them. Or Charity Tiernan, from whom she'd adopted Pirate.

The only people she and Owen had ever associated with were her husband's business contacts, clients, or legislators whose votes were important to his clients. And thus to his success.

Shaking off the pall of those days that she'd left behind, Annie surrendered and laughed along with Maddy and Mac about gossip being part and parcel of the town.

Wasn't this what she was looking for when she'd moved to Shelter Bay? This sense of community? So how could she complain about people being interested in her life?

"Speaking of spices," Maddy said, "I just put a tequila lime marinated prawn salad on the menu today. People are saying it's like the best of a margarita on a plate."

"I'd been planning to go with the crab salad," Annie said.

"Another good choice. In fact, that's what Sedona ordered. The crab's just off the boat this morning."

"But you got me with the margarita comparison," Annie decided.

"Excellent." Maddy smiled and instead of calling over a server, took the order herself. Then she turned to Mac. "Why do I suspect you're not here for the salad?"

"Called it. I'm one of those Neanderthal basic meat-and-potato guys, which is probably a bit of a heresy here in seafood land. I've been hearing great things about your Kobe beef."

"In the interest of full disclosure, it's not legitimate Kobe," Maddy said. "There's a lot of mislabeling out there, so I insist on being specific in my own place. In order to be designated true Kobe, it would have to originate from Wagyu stock and be slaughtered in the Kobe region of Japan. Which may be too much pre-lunch information for anyone but a foodie," she admitted.

"I lived on a farm," Annie said. "I know where my food comes from."

"Well, the Bar M, in the southern part of the state, crossbred their already fabulous Angus with a herd of Japanese Wagyu, which is why it's called *American* Kobe. It's beautifully marbled and so tender you can cut it with a butter knife." She grinned. "End of lecture."

"You almost had me opting for a steak with that butter knife line," Mac said. "But I think I'll go with the burger for lunch." He smiled at Annie over the top of the menu. "Then next time we come here, you can have the crab salad, and I'll have the steak."

"I don't believe I've agreed to a next time," Annie pointed out.

"Yet," he countered with a sexy-as-hell wink as he handed Maddy Chaffee his menu.

"So," he said, taking a drink from a frosted mug of beer after Maddy returned to the kitchen with their order, "you grew up on a farm?"

"I *lived* on one. For a few months."

"Your family move around a lot?"

"No." Annie ran her fingernail around the rim of her glass of basil lemonade—she'd declined to order wine since she was going back to work. "I was left in a box at a hospital when I was a few weeks old, which landed me in the state foster care system, which had me moving around a lot."

Including the farm she'd mentioned, where she'd discovered the first day that she and the other three foster kids living there had been taken in to work as unpaid hired hands.

"That sucks."

"Not always." She thought about the scrapbook habit that had provided comfort for so many years, eventually changing her life. "How about you? I know your father's a doctor and your grandfather was a fisherman. What about your mother?"

He gave her a look that let her know that he knew she was changing the subject, but wasn't going to call her on it. "She was a university librarian. Dad's her second husband."

"Oh, that explains the difference in last names. I thought perhaps you took Culhane as a professional name."

"Culhane's my birth dad's name. He was an Air Force pilot who died in a training flight outside Tucson when I was a kid. When my mom married the guy who became my dad, he gave me the choice of taking his name or staying with my dad's, which he thought would be a way to help me remember my roots and honor a hero."

"That's an incredibly generous gesture."

"Dad's an incredibly generous man."

"So I've noticed. According to the rumor mill, he's a very popular doctor as well."

Mac laughed. "That's true, though a lot of physicians would consider changing from being a world-famous pediatric cardiac surgeon to treating chicken pox and giving booster shots a demotion, he seems to be really enjoying his part-time work as a family physician. And I've got to say, we've probably got enough cakes, cookies, and casseroles in our freezer as gifts from women suffering an epidemic of mysterious symptoms to last until the end of the world. Or an earthquake or tsunami, whichever comes first."

"It's always handy to be prepared." Although she wasn't about to admit it, the blue and white tsunami evacuation road signs still made her a bit nervous. Especially since she lived right on the water, and not up on a cliff like Sax and Kara Douchett. "As for the women, they're probably lonely, so I guess you can't blame them for trying. "

From the way the women of Still Waters flirted with the handsome, sixtysomething silver-haired Boyd Buchanan when he came to visit his father, Annie suspected he could be one of the more eligible bachelors in town.

"It's always worth a shot. And who knows?" Mac shrugged as he tore two pieces of bread off the loaf and handed her one. "But my money's on him being a one-woman guy. He always said Mom was his soul mate."

"That's sweet." She dipped the bread into the flavored olive oil pooled on a white rectangular plate.

"Yeah. Maybe he picked the idea up from Charlie. Or maybe it's genetic.

"So," he said, returning the focus of the conversation to her, which she'd hoped to avoid, "have you always lived in Oregon? And why did you move to Shelter Bay?"

"I grew up in Oregon." Those days were not her favorite subject. Annie took a sip of lemonade. "After graduating from the University of Portland, I moved to D.C." She smiled a bit at the naiveté of that young girl she'd once been. "I actually thought I was going to be the new Woodward. Or Bernstein."

"I imagine that's probably the goal of most journalism majors," Mac said. "And you should do that more often."

"Do what?"

"Smile." His eyes slid down to her lips, which she hadn't even realized had curved, and then back up to her eyes. "It's pretty damn amazing."

"It's just a smile."

"Yeah. That's what da Vinci's model probably said when he was painting the *Mona Lisa*."

"Are all you radio guys born to be such smooth talkers?" she countered. "Or is it something you learn in deejay school?"

"Although it wasn't a line and I meant what I said, as for the radio business, you can have all the training in the world, but mostly you learn stuff by doing. Which is probably pretty much the same as journalism. Or," he said as he saw a server headed their way with lunch, "cooking."

The conversation broke off for a moment as plates

were delivered. Annie thought her salad of brilliantly colored field greens dressed with a tequila lime vinaigrette could have appeared on the cover of a cookbook. Or framed on the wall in some chichi art gallery or museum.

And Mac's burger, which included caramelized onions and blue cheese from a nearby farm, served on a toasted roll topped with black and white sesame seeds, was definitely manly food. As were the fries and what had been described on the menu as a house-made dill pickle.

"Did you?" he asked after he'd taken a bite of the burger and declared that it lived up to its billing.

"Did I what?" The tequila-grilled prawns were heaven, the greens from Lavender Hill Farm gardens as fresh and crisp as they looked.

"Did you take Capitol Hill by storm and uncover political scandals? You've got to remember, I was out of the country for much of the past decade, so I could've missed something."

"No." She put down her fork and took a longer sip of lemonade, wishing it were something stronger. She kept hoping to put her past behind her. "Breaking into the political beat right out of school isn't that easy. I'd interned at the *Post* the summer of my junior year, but so do a lot of other, way more connected students. And I didn't want to try to break out as a blogger."

"So?" He crunched one of the fries that had come with the burger. "What did you do?"

"I went to work on K Street for a lobbyist who represented educational interests."

"A noble pursuit."

"At times." She'd learned, her first weeks on the job, that watching government in action really lived up to that old adage comparing it to sausage making. Sometimes it was better not to know what went into the final product. "Then the short story is that I married the boss. Divorced the boss. And moved back west."

"Why didn't the marriage work out?"

"I didn't realize I was having lunch with Dr. Phil."

"We've already shared more than most people do before a first date." He reminded her of those late-night conversations. "We both admitted to regrets. I'll be the first to admit that I was a lousy husband. I was running around the world, all wrapped up in my own self-importance—"

"I imagine what you were doing for the troops was a far more important thing than writing lobbyist press releases," Annie said.

"Nothing wrong with press releases," he replied. "And yeah, I like to think I made a difference. But somewhere along the way, it went from being about the troops to being about me. As Kayla told me more than once."

"Kayla being your ex-wife."

"That would be her. We'd been the golden couple. She was a former Miss San Diego who used her title to get a gig doing entertainment news on a local station. I was the morning drive-time guy on the top-ranked station in San Diego. We were living the American dream, and everything should have been perfect, but then I started thinking that there had to be more to life than making money and having fun."

So Sedona either hadn't known, or had neglected to mention, that he'd been married to a beauty queen. If Annie was so determined not to get involved, why did that little news flash bother her? "Which is when you joined the military?"

"Yeah. I went out for a beer with a recruiter after a gig for Wounded Warriors. He could probably make your Washington lobbyists look like amateurs. He was good at his job."

"And you were good at yours."

"And you know this how?"

"Because you're good now. You connect with your callers in some personal way." Hadn't he gotten her to call in? "It's as if you're all alone, just one on one. That's an admirable talent."

"Thanks. Kayla was less impressed. Then again, she was the one left back home trying to keep it all together."

"I've always heard that the most difficult job in the military is being a military spouse."

"That's probably true. It didn't help that she'd grown up a Navy brat and had always sworn not to marry a military man."

"So, essentially, you altered the contract."

"Pretty much blew it up."

As he polished off the beer, Annie's heart went out to him, as it had that night when he'd told her, when they'd been talking alone in the dark, about regrets.

"When my marriage broke up, I blamed myself." It was the first time she'd said those words out loud to anyone. It worried her that the person she'd chosen to tell was the one person she'd vowed not to get involved with.

But maybe that was better? Couldn't it make him more impersonal if she could think of him more along the lines of a fellow survivor than a potential lover?

"I honestly can't imagine anything you could do that would give a man any excuse to leave."

"No one's perfect. We all have flaws."

Had it been her unrelenting hunger to have a child at all costs that had driven her husband into the arms and bed of another woman? Or would he have left anyway? She had, after all, been his third wife.

Something she hadn't known when she'd married him, since he'd neglected to mention wife number one, whom he'd married right out of college and who'd been there with him in those early days when he first started setting up his business. She'd even, Annie had found out during the divorce proceedings, been the first person to hold the job Annie had taken over, writing the press releases and working on crafting legislative bills.

"But I've come to realize that life's often messy," Annie said. "And random."

"If that's true, why did you blame yourself?"

"I wanted children. My husband had already raised a family with his previous wife. He had children older than I was when we married. If I hadn't been secretly afraid that he would say he didn't want another family, I would have, should have, brought it up before we got married. By the time I finally realized his mind was made up, he'd already found someone else."

"His loss," Mac said.

Damn. She was talking too much. Stalling for time, Annie took a bite of shrimp. "I've no idea why I'm telling you all this."

"It's called sharing. It's what friends do."

"Is that what we are? Friends?"

"I'm not saying I wouldn't like to be more," he said.

"Friends with benefits?" Didn't it just figure?

"No, friends with chemistry, because although you're unwilling to admit it for some reason, we seem to have a chemistry that rivals a supernova. Which is a really big responsibility."

Being the terrible liar that she was, which had been one more reason she'd failed as a lobbyist's wife, Annie wasn't going to try to deny the chemistry. Even that first meeting at Still Waters, when she'd decided to dislike him, there'd been something. . . .

"Because of Emma," she guessed.

Sedona had filled her in on what she knew about Mac Culhane, and apparently he hadn't gone out with anyone since arriving in town. Annie suspected that was because he didn't want his daughter to get emotionally involved with a woman only to have *her* disappear from their lives as well.

"No. Well, sure, Emma, too. But you can't overlook that there could be repercussions for the entire world."

She put down her fork and looked at him across the wooden tabletop. "The world?"

He had a way of turning even the most serious conversation to a lighter topic. Another thing that worked so well on the radio. And encouraged people to call in.

"Yeah. Didn't you feel it? During that kiss? The ground rumbling beneath our feet?"

"No."

He pointed his fork at her. "Liar," he said without heat. "And my point is that if we can make the earth move, if I ever do get you naked and horizontal, we could risk blowing up the planet."

"Does that line work for you very often?"

"I wouldn't know. I've never tried it before, because I've never felt it before. And *that*," he said, "isn't radio guy hyperbole but the absolute truth. But if you want to keep things light, it's your call."

"Thank you."

"You're very welcome. Besides, you'll be saving me money on power bills with all the cold showers I'll be taking."

The fact that he'd brought up the kiss had her sharing something she'd been thinking about ever since it had happened.

"Speaking as a friend, I have to admit I'm worried about spending the Fourth of July together."

He put down the burger he'd been about to take another bite of. "You're backing down?"

"Emma is obviously looking for another mother. I

don't want to get her hopes up, only to have them dashed."

"We'll be careful," he promised. "Keep things casual around her. There'll be no tonsil tangling in public with my daughter present. And my dad'll be with us, so it'll be more like a family outing than a date."

"But we're not a family."

"Correction. A friendly gathering."

"I suppose that sounds safe enough," she replied.

"Emma's my entire life right now," he said, turning serious again. "I'll admit to having some survivor guilt from Afghanistan. Nothing that serious, just your run-of-the-mill nightmares and stuff I've put in a box in my mind that I mostly keep locked."

"That makes sense." Especially since he'd admitted blaming himself.

There was a long moment of silence as he fiddled with his cutlery, as if trying to decide how much he was willing to share with her.

Then he said, "Oh, hell with it . . . What if all the women in town who are talking about us are right? What if we're somehow letting Emma down, having her growing up just with two men in the house? What if little girls really do need a mom?"

"If that's not a rhetorical question, you're asking the wrong person," Annie pointed out. "Because I wouldn't know. Never having known my own mother. But I did have a handful of foster parents who were better than others, and I learned there are lots of ways women can influence a child's life without being her parent. I think that saying about it taking a village is true. And you've certainly brought her to the right place."

"Yeah." His smile wasn't as sexy as it had been. More reflective and a little sad, she thought. "This town is pretty much Mayberry on the bay. Which is why when Dad first suggested my bringing Emma back here to live, I jumped at the chance."

He dragged a hand down his face.

"Hell, I'm sorry. And there I go again, slipping into a damn it's-all-about-me mode. You're right. You didn't grow up with a mother *or* father, and look how great you turned out."

He blew out a breath. "So next time I fall into old selfish habits, you have permission to just smack me."

Despite the seriousness of the topic, Annie found herself laughing at that idea. "I've never hit anyone in my life; there's not much likelihood of that happening. Besides," she admitted, "given the choice, I'd much rather kiss you."

25

Sedona had been thinking more and more about her spreadsheet of qualifications that any future husband would have to possess. Perhaps Annie had a point. Perhaps it was a bit too stringent.

After all, who'd have thought Shelter Bay's sheriff would now be living in matrimonial bliss with the town's former bad boy? Or that J. T. Douchett, the college history teacher son of a fisherman, would marry an Irish movie star and screenwriter? And those were just two of the couples who'd become her close friends that she wouldn't have thought stood a chance in the beginning.

Which was why, when a customer, who'd moved to Shelter Bay to work on a new start-up tech company asked her out to lunch at Lavender Hill Farm's restaurant, she impulsively accepted.

Minutes into the lunch, Sedona was beginning to miss Dracula. At least that date, while admittedly weird and a bit creepy, had been unique.

She felt certain that her entrée was wonderful and delicious. Maddy Chaffee was incapable of preparing anything less than superb, which is why Sedona—

who'd always preferred the precision of baking, where exact measurements not only mattered but were vital to success—had taken a few classes and was now actually, if she did say so herself, a fairly good home cook.

But it seemed that every time she was about to take a bite, the man across the table, who'd seemed so friendly, though a bit earnest, when he'd come into the bakery for his daily cupcake, would ask her yet another question.

"What's your favorite movie?" he was asking now.

"Easy. *Truly, Madly, Deeply*. The way Alan Rickman comes back from the dead to help ease the pain of his grieving widow is probably the most romantic thing ever written. Which is why I always cry when she finally has to send him and the other ghosts away."

"So, you'd consider yourself a romantic."

There he went, typing away into that damn BlackBerry he'd put on the table as soon as they'd arrived.

"Not really. I'd consider myself a logical, rational woman who can also appreciate a hot guy, great acting, and a well-written romantic plot."

More thumb tapping.

"What's *your* favorite movie?" she asked, deciding to turn the tables on what had begun to feel more like an interrogation than a getting-to-know-you lunch.

"*The Goonies*," he said without looking up from his typing.

"Isn't that the one that was filmed up in Astoria?"

"Yeah. At least some of it was. A lot of the exterior scenes were shot down here and in Cannon Beach, but a bunch of us still get together in Astoria every year as a tribute."

"Well. That's a nice tradition." If a bunch of crows were called a murder, and whales traveled in pods, she idly wondered what a gathering of nerds was called.

"It's even better than *Revenge of the Nerds*," he said,

unknowingly validating her thought. "It's based on an archetypal adventure like you find in all the video games today. There's a map and keys to unlock the location of the treasure. It's got pirates and the Goonies are on this quest to save their Goon Docks neighborhood from being turned into a golf course by the evil villains, which has them constantly having to invent cool stuff. . . .

" 'Hey, I've got a great idea, you guys!' " he said, raising his voice loud enough to have heads at nearby tables turning toward them. " 'Slick shoes!' "

When she looked at him uncomprehendingly, he explained, "It's a line from the movie. The invention Data uses to shoot oil out of his shoes so they can escape the evil Fratellis. Though actually, the substance special effects created was made of glycerin, water, and food coloring. Isn't that interesting?"

"Very." Not.

"Yeah. Since Data didn't have Q to supply him with fancy spy stuff like James Bond does, he was forced to invent his own gadgets, like slick shoes and Pinchers of Peril. Which may seem kind of silly, but hey, they end up saving lives when the Goonies go into the caves in search of One-Eyed Willie's treasure, which ends up saving everyone's homes." He smiled for the first time since they'd sat down. "That movie changed my life."

"That's quite an impact for a single movie to make."

"It's true," he said earnestly.

At least now he seemed engaged. Unfortunately, his enthusiasm wasn't directed toward her.

"After watching it, I began taking stuff apart. It drove my mother crazy when I dismantled the toaster, the microwave, and the video recorder, but it's how I learned how things work, which eventually is how I was able to invent a computer program that made me a multimillionaire before I was twenty."

"And now you're working on a new project."

"Yeah. Some guys would probably just sit back and enjoy the bucks with yachts and private jets and all the women that are attracted to rich guys."

"But not you."

"I'm like a killer shark," he confirmed. "I have to keep moving or I die."

The way she was about to die of boredom.

"That's all very fascinating," she said. "I'll have to try to catch it sometime."

"I've got the expanded Blu-ray 25th Anniversary Edition," he volunteered. "Maybe you can come over and we'll watch it together. It's got some awesome extras with *all seven* Goonies showing up to talk about the film."

He frowned. "Though Sean Astin just walked out in the middle. Which was kind of weird. But maybe it was meant to be a secret to get people talking and wondering about. Like the giant killer octopus scene being deleted from the DVD."

"I'm sort of in my busy season right now," she hedged, having not a single clue what he was talking about. "What with all the tourists in town."

"Maybe after they all leave. I probably watch it at least once a month anyway."

As he went on asking more questions, methodically recording her responses, Sedona's mind wandered and her gaze drifted back over to the table where Mac and Annie appeared to be having a fairly serious conversation. When it seemed to ease up, she caught Annie's eye and pointed toward the restroom.

She might not own a pair of "slick shoes." But it was definitely time to escape this seemingly endless lunch.

26

Sedona had no sooner followed Annie into the rest-room than Maddy joined them. "I guess someone forgot to notify me that we were having a meeting?"

"I just had to get away," Sedona said. "Before I screamed and everyone would probably think there was a mouse in the restaurant, or a fire, or something, and I'd have caused a stampede of lunch customers."

"All leaving without paying their checks," Maddy said. "Which would not have made me all that happy." She locked the door, leaned against it, and folded her arms. "So, what's going on? You"—she pointed at Annie—"looked about as serious as you have since I've known you.

"While you," she said, turning toward Sedona, "appeared to be undergoing a tax audit."

"Worse," Sedona said. "I was being interviewed for this business the guy's setting up."

"So it wasn't really a date? He's not into you or your cupcakes?"

"No. Apparently all my customers who were betting on when he was going to ask me out had the wrong idea. He was merely trying to get up the nerve to ask me to lunch. The guy might be rich enough to buy the entire town, but believe me, communicating with the opposite sex isn't high in his skill set."

"He looks familiar," Annie mused. "He's not bad-looking. Sort of like Clark Kent before he changes into Superman."

"Yep, he is good-looking. In a nerdish sort of way. Maybe you saw him on the cover of *Fortune* magazine a few months ago. He's a member of that illustrious one percent of the wealthiest people in the country, having made gazillions in the tech business. He's working on a new start-up. Which is the only reason he wanted me to have lunch with him."

"He wanted financial advice?"

"Hardly. No, he's doing this personality interview thing, then plugging all my answers into some computer program he's developed that, according to him, will set people up with compatible partners. With, he assured me, ninety-nine-point-six percent accuracy."

"Are you talking an online dating service?" Maddy asked.

"Exactly. He's calling it 'My Matrix Match.' Apparently, although he's been collecting e-mail interviews from subjects for the past year, I'm the first daughter of former flower children he's run across."

"Not surprising, in his line of work," Maddy said.

"True. Plus, the fact that I made such a major change in occupations apparently adds a variable element outside the mean, to fit into his mathematical model."

"Wow, and doesn't that sound like a fascinating lunch conversation for a lovely summer day?" Maddy said.

"It seems that you being a CPA-turned-baker would make you more difficult to plug into any niche," Annie mused.

"Possibly. But I really don't care whether he can fit

me into his metric niche. I just want to get out of here."
She looked pleadingly at Maddy. "Couldn't you set off
a fire alarm or something?"

"It can't be that bad."

"Believe me, it is." Sedona sighed, reached into her
purse, took out a zippered mesh bag, and repaired her
lipstick. "As much as I was really hoping for some of
that seasonal marionberry ice cream you've got on the
menu, I'm just going to go back to the table and tell him
there was some sort of emergency at the bakery. If I
have to spend another minute with Goonie Guy, I'll go
stark raving mad."

"He likes *The Goonies*?" Annie asked.

"Apparently the movie changed his life. Why?" Her
gaze sharpened. "Oh, don't tell me—"

"I thought it was fun," Annie said. "Except for the
giant octopus at the end. Which made no sense to the
story line."

"That's *exactly* what he said. Maybe we ought to
switch lunch dates."

"As much as I value our friendship, and you know I
think of you as the sister I never had, I'll pass on that."

"I would too, in her place," Maddy said. "After all,
every woman in town has been throwing herself at Mac
Culhane. And here our own Annie has him hooked."

"It's just lunch," Annie insisted.

"You've always been the worst liar," Sedona said.
"I've no idea how you survived foster care. From the
little you've said, life there sounds like the pilot for a
Survival of the Fittest show on the Nature Channel. You
two have a *lot* more than lunch going on."

"She's right," Maddy agreed. "If the chemistry between the two of you had gotten any hotter, you
would've set off the sprinkler system."

Fortunately, Annie was saved from answering when
the doorknob jiggled.

"I've got to get back to the kitchen," Maddy said.

"I need to escape." Sedona said. "Like yesterday."

"And I'm going to go back and try to remember all the reasons I'm not going to have a hot, sexual fling with Midnight Mac," Annie said.

"Good luck with that," both women said in unison as Maddy unlocked the door and they all walked out past the waiting woman, who said, "Thank you," to Annie.

"You're welcome. For what?"

"They set up a pool down at Bennington Ford, where I work in customer relations, about when you two would first get together in public. I guessed here, for lunch. Today. Which means I win. So not only did you and hottie Midnight Mac pay for my lunch, I'm going to be able to buy that Coach bag I've been coveting at the outlet mall in Lincoln City."

Apparently Mac hadn't been exaggerating when he'd told her they were the topic du jour everywhere in town. She'd realized, early on, that everyone in Shelter Bay lived in each other's pockets, which was mostly a good thing, since the flip side was that everyone cared about everyone else.

Until she'd made that late-night phone call to Midnight Mac, she'd managed to fly comfortably under the radar.

As she walked back to the table, suddenly aware that nearly every eye in the place was on her, Annie tried to wrap her mind around the idea that people were actually betting on her and Mac's relationship.

Not that they actually had a relationship.

Damn.

As he looked up at her and smiled, Annie knew that Sedona was right. She *was* a lousy liar. Especially when she tried to lie to herself.

27

What the hell are they doing in there? Women, Mac thought, as he tapped his fingers on the table, were dangerous enough by themselves. When they got together, well, it was time for a guy to be scared, because they were definitely plotting something.

He would have been scared. Hell, maybe he should've been. But the fact was, he was too freaking turned on by what she'd just said, right before Sedona had the bad timing to call her into the ladies' restroom for some kind of girl confab.

The guy the cupcake baker had been having lunch with didn't even appear to be missing her. Instead, he was busily drinking his fizzy water and typing away on a BlackBerry as if he was in some sort of bubble. Like the Cone of Silence in *Get Smart*.

When Maddy had headed for the ladies' room as well, Mac decided he might be in for a long wait. He glanced down at his watch, making note of the time, because although patience had never been his long suit, he was willing to wait as long as it took for Annie to return. But he damn well was going to deduct the time she spent in there with the other two women from the agreed-upon length of their lunch date.

Finally, Maddy emerged and headed back to her kitchen, while Sedona returned to her table, where BlackBerry guy didn't even bother to look up. Which was proof that he was either blind or some sort of robot.

Since their table was the farthest from the small alcove leading to the restrooms, Annie had the longest distance to walk. Which allowed him to drink in the sight of her, the sway of that yellow gingham skirt, the crest of her breasts swelling above the dress's neckline, those thin little straps that he'd discovered, while following her to the shelves in her shop, crossed on her smooth bare back.

Today's cat-eye glasses reminded him of the ones Marilyn Monroe had worn in *How to Marry a Millionaire*, which he'd caught late one night on TV when his ghosts had kept him from sleeping. Although Annie might not have Monroe's voluptuous curves, that didn't stop her from being every bit as sexy.

"I'm sorry," she said, as she sat back down across from him.

"No problem." His only problem was that from the way his guy parts had gone on red alert, he wasn't sure he was going to be able to walk out of this restaurant without giving the town a new scandal to talk about. "Is everything all right?"

She slid a glance over at Sedona, who was signing a credit card receipt. "It is now."

"She deserves better," Mac said.

"You'll get no disagreement with me there." She picked up the handwritten menu, which changed daily. "The raspberry crème brûlée certainly looks good."

"Yeah. It does."

"Though maybe the blackberries with the crème fraiche," she mused. "Did you know that if you mix heavy cream with buttermilk and let it rest for twelve hours in the refrigerator, you get crème fraiche?"

"No. That's not something they taught us in the Air Force."

"I learned it in one of Maddy's classes. We made a three-course French dinner."

"Sounds great." Telling himself that this lunch was all about getting to know each other, he stomped down the fantasy of ripping that dress off, spreading crème fraiche all over her body, then licking it off. "Did you mean it?"

"About the cream and buttermilk?"

"No. About what you said, just before you went off to the women's summit. About wanting to kiss me."

"I shouldn't." She was pretending a deeper interest in the menu.

"That wasn't the question."

"Yes." She sighed heavily, then looked up at him. How had he never realized he had a thing for women in glasses? "I shouldn't," she repeated.

"Why not?"

"Because I was serious about not wanting to get into a relationship."

"I think it's a bit early to worry about that." Though he was beginning to. Mac hadn't decided how he felt about this complication. "And believe it or not, I'm no longer the party animal deejays are made out to be, so I don't tend to sleep with women on the first date. But if you want to just use me for sex, hey, I'm okay with that, too."

She didn't immediately answer as those faint lines appeared between her brows again. "I'm trying to decide if you're serious or not."

"That makes two of us." Then her big gray eyes

dropped to his mouth, as if remembering that kiss she'd said she wanted, and all his good intentions to take things slow went south. Straight from his brain to below his belt.

"So," he managed. "Which sounds good? The blackberries or the crème brûlée?"

He nearly groaned when she licked those lips he was dying to taste again with the tip of her tongue.

"I'm not really in the mood for dessert," she said.

"How about a drive out to the beach?"

"To that place you told me about earlier?"

"Yeah. Or we could go to your place."

"No." Her response came quickly, giving him the impression that while she might be up for another kiss, or hopefully more, she wasn't ready to jump into bed. Which was probably the wise, sensible decision.

Unfortunately, he wasn't feeling either wise or sensible at the moment.

"The beach," she decided. "But I really do need to get back to the store soon."

"Deal." He waved the server over for the check, and to save time, rather than waiting to go through the credit-card-charging routine, he tossed some bills into the lavender folder.

Playing the gentleman, he pulled her chair out for her. Then, with his hand on her smooth, bare back, they walked out of the restaurant together.

28

"You realize we've probably just landed ourselves on the front page of the *Shelter Bay Sentinel*," Annie said as they drove away from the restaurant and back toward town.

"You're overestimating our importance," he said. "We'll probably land somewhere between the notice of the Taste of Shelter Bay festival and the police report."

"Which last week consisted of a call about a suspicious car stopping at mailboxes, which turned out to be the mail carrier," she said. "Another mailbox was vandalized when someone painted a yellow smiley face on it and a domestic disturbance reported by a neighbor next door to a home where the couple who lived there turned out to be engaging in 'vigorous sexual role-play.'"

"Don't forget the pool of blood on the pier," he said.

"Which turned out to be spilled Pinot Noir." She'd laughed when she'd read that one. "So, the top crime on the Shelter Bay police report hit parade was two cars stopping on a Forest Service road outside of town, some teenage boys getting out, having a fistfight, then getting back into their cars and driving away."

"The first rule of Fight Club is never talk about Fight Club." Mac glanced over at her. "And you don't sound all that upset."

Annie shrugged. "It was a little unsettling, since I'm not used to being in the spotlight. But everyone was already speculating about us. At least we've livened things up until the next excitement."

"Someone's bound to get drunk on the Fourth and do something stupid," Mac said encouragingly. "That should take the heat off us."

"I'm not sure. Especially since the mayor made that proclamation declaring Shelter Bay the 'Romance Capital of the Oregon Coast' and decided to add a matchmaking fair as part of the Fourth of July weekend festival."

"That's a plus. There'll be lots of other couples to focus on, so we won't be stuck in the bull's-eye."

Annie wished they'd be so lucky, but she doubted they would, especially once they showed up with Emma and Mac's father. Wouldn't that get speculative tongues wagging? She suspected Dottie and Doris, the elderly owners of the Dancing Deer Two boutique, would immediately start looking through wedding dress catalogs. With so many people getting married lately, their stock would have to be depleted.

"Though Sedona and her date didn't exactly look as if they're going to be part of those festivities," he said as he turned onto Harborview, which ran along the bay. Most of the commercial boats were out to sea, though more sailboats were skimming across the water, sails raised to catch the wind.

"He's some rich tech guy who was interviewing her for a start-up he's doing," she explained. "A matrix match-up service that supposedly fixes you up with your perfect partner. Like that's going to work."

"You never know." He opened the sunroof, then

rolled down both front windows enough to let the fresh air in. "Look at us."

"We didn't meet online."

"No. But the situation was much the same. We probably talked more honestly because we *didn't* know each other than if we had, at least that first night you called in."

And wasn't that what she'd been thinking herself?

"We did skip past all that early getting-to-know-you stuff," she said. "Like favorite foods, music, top three fave movies—"

"That's an easy one. *The Godfather. Platoon.* And *Die Hard.* Oh, and I'm adding a fourth. *Butch Cassidy and the Sundance Kid.*"

"Ah, the usual guns, guts, and glory." She wasn't the least bit surprised.

"I *am* a guy. We like that stuff." The hot-guy look he shot her spurred a bone-melting desire that had her re-thinking her moratorium on men. "Your turn."

"It's hard to pick just three. Or even four. But I tend to lean more toward the classics. *Breakfast at Tiffany's. When Harry Met Sally. Dirty Dancing.*"

"'Nobody puts Baby in a corner,'" he said, quoting the famous line from her third choice.

"You've seen it?" Unlike his choices, that one didn't have a single weapon in it.

"Since women usually end up choosing the video for movie nights, once you reach a certain age, odds are you've seen that one." He made the right turn toward the iron drawbridge leading out of town. "Swayze was always pretty much a guy's guy, even when he was dancing, which made watching it not that much of a sacrifice."

Annie was thinking that she wouldn't mind if Midnight Mac put *her* in a corner. Up against the wall, with her skirt hitched up, and her legs wrapped around his waist . . .

And she was totally losing her mind.

"Favorite ice cream," she said, desperate to change topics.

"Vanilla."

Which came as a surprise, since there was nothing vanilla about him. Then he flashed her a wicked grin. "With chocolate sauce and whipped cream on top."

The way he was looking at her, as if she were a hot fudge sundae that he'd like to eat up, made her feel as if she were coming down with the flu. How else to explain her swimming head and the swarm of butterflies flapping their wings in her stomach?

Not to mention that tingling under her skin when he put a tanned hand on her thigh as if it had every right to be there.

"We're just talking about a kiss," she insisted. "Nothing more."

"Agreed."

"That first one was pretty good," she admitted. Which was a major understatement, but it was important to keep this relationship, whatever it was, on somewhat equal ground. "But it could've been a fluke."

"What happened wasn't any fluke." The loud blast of a warning horn shattered the air; a gate went down in front of the truck, and a moment later the bridge began going up to allow a ship to pass through. "Which I'll prove to you soon enough."

Those wickedly clever fingers slipped beneath the hem of her dress, continuing upward, making little circles that were leaving sparks on her skin.

"We're going to be stuck here for a while," he said as a gleaming white yacht headed toward the bridge. "Let me give you a sample. To help you make up your mind."

He unfastened his seat belt.

"Driving without a seat belt is illegal," she felt obliged to point out.

"I'm not driving."

To accentuate his point, he twisted the key, turning off the engine. Then leaned toward her, and with unnerving sensual intent, took off her Marilyn Monroe glasses and put them carefully on the black leather dashboard.

With that out of the way, and radiating testosterone, pheromones, and a dangerous male vibe that, instead of making Annie want to run, had her holding her breath, he inched closer to her.

He cupped his warm hand at the back of her neck, then closed the gap between them.

This wasn't their first kiss. She should have known what to expect. She'd *told* herself that she could handle Mac Culhane. After all, as the song lyrics from *Casablanca*—another movie she would've added if she'd cheated like he had and gone for four instead of three—went, "a kiss is just a kiss." Right?

Wrong.

The instant his mouth claimed hers, hot, hard, demanding, she realized she'd miscalculated. And even as she told herself this was crazy, that she barely knew him, she lost her ability to think and was clinging to him as if he were a lifeline in a storm-tossed sea, which it felt like as their tongues tangled and her heart started beating so hard and fast she wouldn't have been surprised if it had burst out of her chest.

She had *so* miscalculated. *This* kiss was not just a kiss. And the rough male groan that rumbled from his chest as his open mouth moved down her throat was definitely not just a sigh.

Oh, wow! The man could kiss.

Really, really kiss.

A blaring sound reverberated through the roaring in her ears.

"Damn," he muttered against her mouth, "the bridge is going back down."

Now *that* was a sigh as he pulled away, refastened his seat belt, and started the engine. A deep, ragged sigh that, as she shoved her glasses back onto her face (which didn't do a whole lot of good because her vision seemed to still be blurred from rampant lust), assured her she was not the only one who'd felt on the verge of drowning.

"Okay," she said after they'd crossed over to the other side, when her head had stopped spinning and she was pretty sure she could speak again without sounding like Minnie Mouse. "You win. That kiss in the store? It wasn't a fluke."

"I'm taking that as a compliment," he said. "But it takes two. And, sweetheart, you are one hot babe."

She knew women who would have taken offense. There'd even been a time, when she was struggling to become a proper Washington Junior League matron, that she would have at least attempted to pretend annoyance.

But not today. Because today, for the first time in her life, she actually *felt* like a hot babe.

"We're still not having sex," she felt obliged to warn him.

"That's your call. But may I ask a question?"

She didn't entirely trust him. Oh, she knew she was in no physical danger, but she'd already heard the way he had of getting people to say things they'd never told anyone else. Hadn't she done exactly that herself when she admitted to at least partially blaming herself for the breakup of her marriage?

"All right."

"Are you talking about a sex moratorium for this afternoon? Or no sex ever?"

"Ever. I told you, I'm not into the idea of a friends-with-benefits relationship." At his arched, disbelieving brow, she said, "All right. You're right."

"Did I say anything?"

"No. But you were thinking that if we keep this up, we're going to eventually end up in bed."

Or on a floor, or up against the wall, like in that flash of a fantasy, or on the beach, beneath a sky of whirling stars . . .

"I sure as hell wouldn't object if you take me up on that offer to use my body for sex."

"I've given up men." She wasn't sure which of them she was trying to convince. Him or herself.

"Not that I want to get into an argument on such a nice day, but I don't think you're doing real well with that game plan," he said easily.

"It's you," she muttered. "You mess with my mind." Not to mention her body.

"Join the club. And, just in case it's slipped your mind, *you* called *me*. I was just sitting there in the dark, in a shitty mood, trying to do my job on the radio, when Sandy from Shelter Bay gave me a reason not to hate that Saturday night."

In the hormonal fog that had clouded her mind, Annie had forgotten that he'd sounded depressed and all alone that night when he'd asked the question. The same way she'd been feeling when she'd picked up her phone and made the call.

"It's complicated."

"Someone once told me life's messy. And often random. Which, by the way, I'd pretty much figured out for myself. Before you had me feeling like a sixteen-year-old with a perpetual boner."

"I didn't like you at first," she said, still struggling for a lifeline to avoid getting in over her head. "I don't mean when I called in. I meant when I ran into you at Still Waters."

"You didn't *want* to like me," he corrected as he turned onto a narrow, sandy road. "But, like we've both already discovered, you don't always get what you want."

And wasn't that the truth?

But today, for just this stolen moment in time, Annie wanted Mac.

And for now, she decided, as this time *she* was the one who reached across the console and put her hand on his jeans-clad thigh, it would be enough.

29

"Oh, it's lovely," Annie said after Mac stopped the truck at the edge of a beach she hadn't even known existed. Stretching out in both directions, the sun-gilded ribbon of golden sand was completely deserted. "You hung out here with Sax and his brothers?"

"Yeah. His grandfather built that picnic table," he said, pointing toward the grayed wooden table and benches. "Although the weather's done a number on it over the years, you can still see where he and Cole and J.T. carved their initials in it."

He didn't mention that his were there, too. Along with Jared, Kara Douchett's first husband's, who'd been Cole's best friend in high school and had gotten himself killed on a domestic call as a cop after returning safely home from Iraq. Proving that life wasn't always fair and often sucked.

One memorable night, before Cole and Jared had graduated from high school, they'd snagged some beer from Bon Temps, which the Douchetts had owned at the time, gotten drunk, and sworn to be best buddies for life. Whatever might happen, wherever they'd end up, they'd always be there for each other.

And there were other nights. . . .

"What's funny?" she asked, making him aware that he was smiling at the memory of the night he and Sax had double-dated and, after a movie he couldn't remember, had driven out here for a make-out session. That was the night, in the backseat of Sax's Camaro, when Mac had rounded second and nearly gotten to third base with Debbie Henley. He might've made it, too, if Kara's father, who'd been sheriff at the time, hadn't pulled up behind them and flashed his red and blue cruiser lights.

"Just remembering old times," he said.

"I suspect I'm not the first girl you've brought here."

"Hey, I was in high school."

"Which answers the question." Instead of appearing offended, she gave him a knowing smile. "I always used to envy people like you," she admitted.

"You didn't know me."

"You all seemed the same, as I was looking from the outside in. Confident, having a good time, going steady, breaking up, living like you were all part of the cast of *Happy Days*."

"Appearances can be deceiving."

Mac thought back to Kara getting pregnant her senior year of high school, and Lucas and Maddy breaking up. And, how, if they'd actually been living a *Happy Days* life, Sax would've been the Fonz. On steroids.

"I suppose so. But there's such a sense of continuity about you all. Of connection." She sighed. "This probably is a terrible mistake."

"I've made mistakes a helluva lot worse," he said. "It's just a kiss."

"We've already kissed twice. In the store and on the bridge."

"They don't count." He brushed a thumb against her lips, which parted slightly at his touch. "The first was public, so I couldn't really do my best. And the second was just a test. Let's see what happens when we both really put our minds to it."

"If my mind was even halfway working, I wouldn't have come out here," she complained.

She dragged her hand through those thick curls and looked out over the water. Fishing boats were chugging along the horizon, while another trio of boats, with tourists standing on the decks, had gathered around what he guessed was the pod of Shelter Bay whales. The familiar scents of seaweed and salt rode on the air.

Being the father of a six-year-old had taught Mac patience. So, although it wasn't easy, he waited, as seagulls whirled noisily over the boats and pelicans flew by the windshield.

After what seemed like forever, apparently having made a decision, she unfastened her seat belt, then leaned toward him, touching her fingertips to his cheek.

Her eyes were as fathomless as the sea. A stormy sea as turbulent emotions swirled in those gray depths. Feeling himself drowning as she moved closer to him, Mac cupped her chin in his fingers. Then tangled his hands in her hair and tilted her head, covering her lips with his, kissing her lightly at first, nipping, teasing, tasting.

A low moan of arousal trembled against his mouth as she parted her lips, offering more.

Being male and human, Mac needed no further invitation. His mouth conquered hers as he hauled her onto his lap, held her tight against him, and deepened the kiss.

He'd known there would be pleasure. But never before had a kiss brought him pain. For the first time in his life, every atom in his body ached. His blood heated, pounding in his head. Boiling in his veins.

The passion that had been simmering since that first kiss in her pretty little store surged through him. As she responded, hands grasping the front of his shirt while her avid mouth drove him to the brink of sanity, Mac was struck with an almost overwhelming urge to touch her. Everywhere.

But the one thing he'd learned since returning from Afghanistan was that sometimes a guy just needed to be a grown-up. Which was why, instead of ripping her yellow and white dress apart, sending those little heart-shaped buttons flying all over the cab of his truck, with hands that were not as steady as he would have liked, he cupped her bare shoulders and set her a little bit away, breaking the heated contact.

"The deal was a kiss," he said, as her unfocused eyes stared into his.

"That wasn't just a kiss." She glanced down at her hands, which were still clutching his shirt, and slowly loosened her fingers. "That was foreplay."

"Sweetheart, if you think that's foreplay, your ex wasn't doing it right. That was like a warm-up to the preview of foreplay."

"Has anyone ever told you that you can be more than a little arrogant?"

"Sure. I took it as a compliment."

"You would."

"I may be arrogant, but you're lethal."

He could tell that surprised her. "I am not." She shook her head. "Damn. I knew this was a mistake. It can't go anywhere."

"Here's a surprise for you. . . . You're not going to get any argument about that. You deserve a guy who can put you at the center of his life."

He'd already suspected it from their phone conversations. But what she'd said over lunch had pretty much nailed his belief that he really should stay away from this particular siren call. Which didn't explain what he was doing here with a woman who represented trouble.

"To treat you the way you deserve to be treated," he continued. "Right now, Annie, I'm not that guy."

She lifted her chin, surprising him by seeming annoyed at that. "Did I say anything about wanting to be at the center of anyone's life?"

"No. But face it—you're not the kind of woman who'll settle for a hot one-night stand or booty calls. You're a settle-down-in-a-nice-little-house-with-a-picket-fence type of woman."

"As it happens, I already have a very nice house," she said. "Which also has a picket fence. So, if you think I need you to provide one—"

"No, that's not what I was trying to say. And I know I'm going to regret turning down anything you might be inclined to offer, but you've got a point about chemistry not being enough. Not for you. And right now, that's all I can offer."

"And to think that I actually liked chemistry in school," she muttered.

His body was aching and his mind was engaged in a full-scale war between what he wanted to do and what he *should* do. Because he was tempted, too tempted, he merely said, "We'd better get you back to work."

"I suppose so." Her annoyance faded, like morning fog lifting, as she scooted over and fastened her seat belt. "What are we going to do about the Fourth?"

"What about it?"

"I don't want to bail on spending the day with Emma."

"We're grown-ups." He was reminding himself as

much as her. "It isn't like we'll be having any hot make-out session on the lawn in front of everyone. There's no reason we can't still be friends."

"As long as we stick to being together in public," she amended, revealing that she was every bit as tempted as he was.

"Deal."

As they drove back to town in silence, Mac decided that the Fourth of July was looking to be a very long day.

As Mac and Annie were leaving the beach, they passed a white Subaru that was just arriving.

"Is that who I think it is?" Aimee Pierson asked.

"Looks like Midnight Mac and Ms. Shepherd, from the scrapbook store," sixteen-year-old Matt Templeton said.

"I've been hearing they're an item." Aimee glanced back over her shoulder at the black pickup truck. "What do you think they're doing all the way out here?"

Matt grinned. "Probably the same thing we're doing."

"That'd be cool." When she smiled back, Matt decided he had to be the luckiest guy on the planet. "Annie Shepherd's really nice. She deserves to be happy." She reached across the space between the bucket seats and took hold of his right hand, which had been resting on the knob of the gearshift. "Like us."

He'd nearly lost this girl due to his own stupidity, but fortunately, after he'd done some major apologizing, she'd taken him back, and now that he had his driver's license, he no longer had to depend on her driving him around in her mom's old Volvo.

When his mother had first dragged him from Beverly Hills to Shelter Bay last fall, he'd hated the small town with a passion as hot as a thousand suns. Now, as he brought the birthday car his mom and new dad had bought him to a halt at the sand's edge, Matt decided there was nowhere else on the planet he'd rather be.

30

Since he'd told his dad he'd be bringing dinner home, Mac stopped by Bon Temps after taking Annie back to Memories on Main. It was the slow time between the lunch and dinner crowds, so the restaurant was empty, with just Sax behind the bar, washing glasses.

"Hey, cher. I'm glad you stopped in," Sax said. "I was just about to call you."

Mac claimed a barstool. "What about?"

"The Fourth. Do you want a beer?"

Mac figured that after fighting back the urge to have crazy hot sex with Annie Shepherd, he could use something to cool him down. And he still had several hours before he had to go on the air.

"Sure. Make it Double Dead Guy Ale."

"That bad a day?" Sax reached into the cooler, pulled out a dark bottle, popped the top, and handed it over with a frosted glass.

"Actually sort of mixed. So, what about the Fourth?" he asked after taking a long drink of the ale straight from the bottle. Which cooled his throat, but did nothing for other vital parts of his body, which could heat up just at the thought of Annie.

"We lost Ollie Nelson last night," Sax said.

"Damn. That's a shame." The former vet was a favorite down at the VFW, being one of the few who would actually talk about his days in the war. And not just any war. The big one. WWII. "But he was, what, ninety?"

"Ninety-three."

"He looked okay when I saw him the other day."

"He died in his sleep." Sax pushed a bowl of what Mac knew to be red-hot beer nuts his way. "Seems his heart just quit beating."

"That's a bummer, but isn't it the way we'd all like to go?" Mac asked as visions of that arm with the blue Cub Scout uniform sticking out of the pile of bodies in the Afghan market flashed through his mind.

"I'd rather not go at all." Sax dipped another glass into the sink, swirling it around in the suds. "But it sure as hell beats a lot of stuff we've both seen." He rinsed the glass and dried it with a towel. "Ollie was going to ride on the parade float to represent his generation. He and your grandfather were the last Shelter Bay vets to have fought in that war."

"That's a sad milestone. To be down to one. I guess there's going to be a funeral?"

"A memorial service. Tomorrow. One in the afternoon at Genarro's, interment in the vets' section of the Sea View Cemetery, then a funeral lunch/supper thing back here."

"I guess I'd better tell Pops. Given that they were close friends."

"Yeah. You wouldn't want him hearing it from someone else. So how is Charlie these days?"

Mac shrugged as he snagged some nuts and felt the roof of his mouth burst into flame. Knowing that Sax saved the really hot ones as a test, he refused to let on that he felt on the verge of spontaneous combustion.

"He has good days and bad." He took another, longer drink of the ale, ignoring Sax's cocky, satisfied look. "He seems better with Emma. I swear his short-term memory goes up on the scale when he's talking with her."

"Interesting. Then again, little girls have a way of making everything seem better. Speaking of which . . ."

Mac saw this coming as Sax put down the towel, reached into his pocket, and pulled out an iPhone.

"We had Grace's six-month photos taken last week. I still can't believe she's mine."

He turned the screen toward Mac, showing off the photo of the six-month-old baby, her head covered with a red fuzz a few shades lighter than Kara's strawberry blond. Her eyes were enormous, seeming to take up much of her small face, and, while they were blue, rather than Kara's green, he saw her mother's serious nature in them. In contrast, her toothless grin was as wide as a slice of summer moon.

"She's really beautiful, Sax," he said honestly. She looked like a baby angel in a dress he figured had been purchased for the milestone occasion. There were so many white ruffles, her round little head, dimpled arms, and chubby legs appeared to be emerging from a cloud.

"Just like her mother. She started sitting up on her own the day before the shoot," Sax said, sounding as proud as if he'd just eliminated the last of the Taliban, single-handedly with his Super SEAL powers

"That's impressive." Mac had no idea how old Emma had been when she'd first sat up. He wondered if he would spend the rest of his life trying to make up for those lost years, and decided he probably would.

"Yeah. That's what Kara and I thought. Here's another one of her with Mikey." Michael Sean Concannon had been born the same day, during a rare ice storm.

Mikey's father, Ethan, was an organic farmer and his mother, Phoebe, who'd escaped an abusive first husband, had worked as a sous chef at Lavender Hill Farm restaurant before becoming a mother. According to the Shelter Bay gossip line, she was planning to return to the restaurant part-time when the season began slowing down after Labor Day.

The baby boy was wearing a blue shirt with a bright red Elmo on the front, tiny blue jeans, and white high-tops. Instead of looking at the camera, he was staring at baby Grace, seated beside him, with a glazed-eye look of bemused wonderment.

"Poor kid's already a goner." Mac wondered if he looked at Annie that same way and figured he probably did.

Sax laughed. "Yeah. Although they won't admit it straight out, I suspect Kara and Phoebe are already planning their wedding."

He flipped to another photo, which showed Kara, looking soft and pretty in a flowered watercolor dress that was a distinct contrast to the starched khaki sheriff's uniform she wore to work every day. Yet another photo showed the family together: baby Grace and Kara, Sax, and Trey, Kara's son whom Sax had adopted. They could have appeared on a poster for the perfect family.

"You are one damn lucky son of a bitch," Mac said.

"I tell myself that every day," Sax agreed. "I wasn't as bad off as some guys when I got out of the military, but I had my share of ghosts."

"I think everyone does."

"Yeah, but mine talked and followed me around all the time. And razzed me, just like when they were alive and we were all part of the unit. It was weird, but also kind of cool in a way."

"Like they weren't really gone. "

"Exactly." Sax shoved the phone back into his pocket and returned to washing glasses. "But once Kara and I got together, really together, not just the sex part, but the connection I'd always felt for her, they took off. And now, when I dream, I dream of her. And Trey and Grace."

"Lucky." Although he would never deny Sax his happiness, Mac found himself envying the former SEAL.

"You bet your ass. . . . So," Sax said, "getting to why I was going to call you—somehow I managed to get myself put on the VFW's parade committee."

"Maybe because you're the only recipient of the Navy Cross in Shelter Bay?"

"You know how I feel about that," Sax muttered. "I've learned not to see that damn sign outside town, but there are days when I forget and look at it and find myself wishing a tsunami would just wash the sucker away.

"Anyway, the Korean War guys are going to be on a float, along with some disabled vets from more-recent wars. Ollie was going to be with them, but now he can't. So I was wondering if you think your grandfather would be up to representing the Greatest Generation."

"I don't know." Mac rubbed his chin as he gave it some thought. "Some days, absolutely. Others . . ." He shrugged. "Hell, like I said, I don't know."

"Why don't you ask him?" Sax suggested. "And we'll leave it up in the air. If he's feeling good on the Fourth and you think he could handle it—the benches will all have seat belts, or we could work out a deal with a wheelchair—"

"Pops wouldn't use the chair. It's hard enough to get him into it when he's at Still Waters. His pride wouldn't let him use it in public."

"Okay. But there will definitely be seat belts. And we could put arms on either side of where he's sitting. Just for extra stability."

"Sounds good. Emma would be over the moon to have him take part. I'll drop by Still Waters in the morning and see what he has to say about it."

Something belatedly occurred to Mac. "The parade's early in the day, right?"

"At eleven. Before the noon basket raffle," Sax confirmed.

"Good. Because he can't handle fireworks."

Sax shrugged. "Been there. There are times they still get to me. But you don't have to worry. I'll have Kara and the mayor put a joint notice in the *Sentinel* that for respect of our vets, no one should set off even small firecrackers during the parade." Privately shot-off firecrackers were illegal in Oregon, but it wasn't always possible to keep them out of people's hands on holidays.

"Sounds good. I'll ask him." Mac polished off the beer. "I need some takeout."

"And here I thought you'd come to tell me all about your hot date with Sandy from Shelter Bay."

When Mac flipped him off, Sax just laughed and took his order.

31

"Sedona called," Kim told Annie as soon as she returned to the store. "She said to call her back when you got a chance."

"Okay. Thanks." She was grateful the other woman hadn't mentioned that she'd been gone an hour past that negotiated forty-five minutes.

Fortunately, business was brisk, which kept her from being able to think about Mac until closing. After saying good night to Kim and turning the OPEN sign to CLOSED, she picked up the phone.

"I know we both had a big lunch, but what would you say to stopping by the Sea Mist for a drink on the patio before going home?"

"You're on," Sedona said. "After my lunch, I'm in serious need of alcohol." She paused. "And you need to talk."

"I think I'm in trouble."

"I'll call Maddy and Charity," Sedona said. "Unfortunately, I don't know if Kara could get a sitter at the last minute."

Although Annie liked Kara Douchett, that was just as well. As confused as she was, she wasn't sure she could take looking at the baby photos the proud new mother would be bound to show off.

"It'd take time to fill her in," she said. "But since Maddy was there, too, it'd be good to get another opinion."

"She'll come," Sedona said without hesitation. "See you there in fifteen minutes."

And wasn't that the kind of friendship she'd moved to Shelter Bay for? Annie asked herself as she drove the two blocks down to the harborfront restaurant, where Sedona, organized as always, had already reserved them a table on the water.

Sedona arrived right on the dot, Maddy and Charity Tiernan two minutes later.

"I hope I didn't take you away from preparing for your dinner service," Annie said to Maddy.

"Not at all. Although Kyle isn't as good a sous chef as Phoebe, she'll keep things running smoothly while I'm gone. It's also a good test, because I don't want to be working all the time, which is partly why I decided to stay here in Shelter Bay after things fell apart in New York.

"I'm thinking of moving Phoebe into a general manager position once she's back full-time, which would allow Kyle to move into her slot."

Kyle was another successful graduate of Haven House, having landed in town from Massachusetts, the same way Phoebe had, through an underground railroad of women who, in many cases, were willing to risk breaking the law to save women from abuse.

Having lived in abusive situations herself as a child, Annie also volunteered at the shelter, helping its residents create scrapbooks depicting their progress from victims to self-sufficient, confident women. Those same women paid it forward by creating greeting cards for various volunteer organizations like Operation Write

Home, Cards for Soldiers, and Cards for Hospitalized Kids.

"If I had someone like your Lucas at home, I sure wouldn't want to be at work all the time," Annie said.

They chatted a bit about the upcoming Fourth of July festivities, including Charity's plan to bring some adoptable cats and dogs from her shelter to her festival booth, and then, once their glasses of wine and appetizer had been delivered, Maddy, the most outspoken of the three, said, "Well?"

"I kissed him."

"We already know about that," Sedona said, waving away the admission as she plucked a clam strip from the tower in the center of the table. "It's all over town that you were making out with him behind a paper display."

"It was a pen display. And we weren't making out. He merely kissed me. On a crazy dare."

"You dared him to kiss you?" Charity asked, looking pleased at that idea.

"What can I say? He makes me crazy," Annie muttered.

"Well, whatever. It's old news," Maddy said. "We're here for the juicy parts."

Annie leaned forward, lowering her voice in an attempt to keep any more of her personal life from becoming grist for the Shelter Bay gossip mill. "We went to the beach. To this private spot he knows."

The other women burst out laughing, drawing some attention from the surrounding tables.

"You've been there," Annie guessed.

"One of the advantages of being connected to the Douchetts," Maddy said. "The summer after I graduated from high school, Lucas and I went there a lot."

"And Gabe took me there for the Crab Shack's butter-roasted Dungeness crab picnic package," Charity said. "As good as it was, halfway through the meal, I just wanted to pour that melted butter all over him and lick it off."

"I know the feeling," Annie said. "But in my case, it was crème fraiche."

"That works, too," Maddy agreed. Her reminiscent smile was that of a cat who'd just finished a bowl of very rich cream.

"I don't miss the roller-coaster emotions that come with a relationship, but I do miss sex," Sedona said on a sigh.

"Me, too," Annie admitted. "I hadn't realized how much until Mac kissed me. I think if he'd decided to make a move, right then and there, I wouldn't have been able to think of a single reason why not."

"I *still* can't think of a reason," Sedona said.

"Maybe if it were just the two of us. But there's his daughter to think about," Annie said.

"Well, surely you're not going to be going at it like sex-crazed monkeys on the couch while she's watching *Dora the Explorer*," Maddy said.

"Of course not."

"It's not as easy having sex with kids around," Charity admitted. "But Gabe and I have three, and trust me, we certainly manage it."

"Which is obvious. After all this time together, you two still have that newlywed glow," Maddy said.

"So do you and Lucas," Charity said.

The chef dimpled at that. "Well, we had a lot of years of catching up to do."

"How's that going?" Sedona asked.

The smile widened. "We're still working on it."

"You two are just making this worse," Annie complained. "I'm trying to convince myself that sex is overrated."

"Good luck with that," Sedona said dryly as Annie

took a long gulp of the crisp, dry Chardonnay. "I thought we'd agreed that we were going to jump back into the dating pond."

"And how's that going for you?" Annie threw Sedona's own words back at her.

Sedona shrugged. "Not all that well, since instead of a prince, I definitely ended up with a frog today. But at least I hold out hope. If you decide you don't want Midnight Mac, I might give the guy a shot."

"That's the trouble." Annie sighed heavily and although she wasn't really hungry, she was in need of something fried, and began chewing on a breaded clam strip. "I do want him."

"Then go for it," Maddy advised. "You know what they say . . . you snooze, you lose."

"Ha." Annie took another clam strip from the stack and dipped it into the accompanying tartar sauce. "You're a fine one to be talking about making the moves. I've heard all about how Lucas got you to marry him. You weren't exactly the one pushing for the relationship."

"There's a good reason for that," Maddy argued. "Not only was I just coming off a public breakup, but Lucas and I had a history."

"And a really big misunderstanding that the guy had to explain," Charity said.

"Exactly." Maddy pointed a clam strip toward Annie. "While you and Mac are starting out with a clean slate. You can make your relationship whatever you want it to be."

"I don't want a relationship."

"Liar," the other three women said together, echoing that voice inside Annie's own head.

"What you want is not to want him," Maddy said knowingly. "Been there, done that." She waggled a gold-banded finger. "And look how that worked out."

"It's complicated," Annie insisted, still not convinced that she could have sex without risking her heart.

"Life's complicated," Sedona said.

"Especially when it comes to men," Maddy agreed. "Like Kara always says, if it's got tires or a penis, it's bound to cause you trouble."

Despite the fact that she was still horribly conflicted, Annie couldn't help laughing. "Amen to that."

32

"Well, you're here early," Analise Peterson said when Mac arrived at Still Waters the next morning. Today's navy blue scrubs were covered with sailboats.

"I've got some news I wanted to tell him before anyone else did." He didn't mention that after getting home from the station, frustrated from having waited in vain for Annie to call, he hadn't gotten any sleep. "How's he doing?"

"So far, so good. He opted for the early-bird breakfast, then went out into the garden."

So he wasn't watching the morning TV news. That was a good thing. "He didn't take the paper with him, did he?"

Charlie still liked reading the *Shelter Bay Beacon*, although Mac had been told that he frustrated some residents when he'd take part in the morning news group because he'd comment on a story, then three minutes later, comment on it again, and again, as if it were new. One newcomer to the group had finally yelled at him, but according to Analise, the others had stood up for his grandfather and later suggested the new guy was going to have to work on developing tolerance if he wanted to fit in.

"No. He's just sitting out there, looking through his scrapbook."

"Great." Mac wasn't looking forward to telling Charlie about Ollie, but better that than having him hit with the news without a careful buildup.

"Speaking of scrapbooking," the nurse said with a teasing smile, "I hear you've taken it up."

"Is nothing private?"

"Nope." She folded her arms. "I like Annie Shepherd. She helped me choose the perfect paper and embellishments for my honeymoon photo album. You could do a lot worse."

"We're just friends."

"Yeah." Analise laughed. "From what I heard you're really *friendly* friends. And personally, not that you asked, I think it's great."

"That's because now that you're married, you want everyone else to be married, too."

Although he would've thought it a mostly female thing, Mac had watched the same phenomenon with deployed guys. Once someone returned from leave with a wedding band on, he'd start preaching the marvels of marriage. Of course, usually those marvels revolved around daily sex and lots of it.

"Guilty," she agreed with a grin. The desk phone rang, allowing Mac to escape any inquisition.

He entered the garden, which was surrounded by walls covered with climbing vines to keep residents from wandering off. It was early enough that although the sun was rising in a clear blue sky, dew still sparkled on the dark green leaves. Mac knew his grandmother had loved gardening as much as his own mother, which, he suspected, was why Charlie, who'd never shown any interest at all in flowers, spent so much time out here.

He was, as Analise had said, looking through the scrapbook Annie Shepherd had helped him make. It was open to a photo of Charlie and his Annie, which Mac knew to have been taken on their honeymoon at Rainbow Lake.

She was seated on a log, with the waterfall behind her, wearing a pair of jeans and a red-and-white-checked blouse tied beneath her breasts. Her hair was blowing in the breeze, she was laughing at the camera, and even in the faded black-and-white photo, anyone could see the love shining in her eyes.

"Morning, Pops."

"Morning." Charlie didn't bother to glance up from the photo. "When I woke up this morning, Annie reminded me about when I rowed her across the lake from our rented cabin to the lodge on the other side," he said.

Mac knew Charlie was referring to *his* Annie. Not Mac's. Not that Annie Shepherd *was* actually his. As she'd made perfectly clear. And, he reluctantly kept telling himself, it was probably just as well.

"We were going to have breakfast," Charlie said. "It was early morning and the lake was smooth as glass. The fog was coming off the water, but we still couldn't see more than a few feet in front of the bow."

"Sounds tricky." Mac knew from experience that fallen trees lurked beneath that seemingly serene water, waiting to snag passing boats.

"What it was was nice." Charlie's eyes, which had brightened while talking about his deceased wife softened with the long-ago memory. "Being young, and having been away at sea for so long, we definitely set that boat to rocking."

Mac laughed. "Good for you."

"Being in a war taught me how short life can be. Which is why it's important to seize the carp."

Mac put aside the fact that he'd definitely failed on the carpe diem advice with Annie and instead decided, since his grandfather had brought up the subject of life and death, to tell him about Ollie.

He sat down on the bench beside Charlie and stretched out his legs. "I was talking with Sax Douchett yesterday," he said.

"Always liked that young fellow. I knew he wasn't near as bad as he liked people to think. He was just sowing his oats. Like a lot of us do while waiting for the right woman."

Which Kara definitely was for Sax.

Mac was beginning to feel a bit like that song he'd played the other night. About wishing on someone else's star because it sure as hell seemed like everyone else in town was all lovey-dovey, while he was just frustrated.

"He brought up the parade."

"Always liked the Fourth of July parade." Charlie frowned. "Guess this'll be the first year since 1945 I've missed being part of it."

"He was thinking you might like to take part again this time. On the float," he said quickly, in case his grandfather might get confused and think he'd be expected to walk.

"I sat on the bench with Ollie Nelson last year. We're the last two of our generation."

"That's another thing I need to tell you," Mac said gently. "Ollie passed on."

"He did? When?"

"Night before last."

"Oh." At first Mac was surprised when his grandfather seemed relieved. Then clarification came. "I was afraid he'd died some other time and I'd forgotten." He shook his head. "I might forget what I ate for breakfast, but if we'd lost Ollie and I'd forgotten, well, hell, that'd just be wrong."

Knowing the bond that war forges, Mac understood his pops' reasoning perfectly.

"Is he going to have a funeral?"

"Tomorrow."

"I need to go."

Mac wasn't about to ask if his grandfather felt up to it. Being battle buddies created an especially deep bond. "It's at one. I can pick you up at noon to give us plenty of time to get there and settle in."

"Make it eleven thirty," Charlie said with surprising clarity and decisiveness. "I'll need time to change into my uniform, which I'll need you to get from the house."

"Will do," Mac said.

Last year, in the parade when Sax rode in that convertible, looking as uncomfortable as hell in his spiffy Navy whites, Mac's grandfather had been proud to still fit into his uniform. He suspected that this year it would hang on him, but he also knew that Charlie would consider it a necessary sign of respect.

"You think any more about that nurse?" he asked. "Annie?"

"She's not a nurse, Pops. She's a volunteer."

"Makes no difference. She's pretty enough. And sweet as taffy. You could do a lot worse. You should ask her out to dinner. Wine and dine her. That always works."

Mac laughed, deciding there was no way he was going to share the fact that they'd already had lunch. No point in encouraging the old man about something that wasn't going to happen.

Though, he thought, as he waved good-bye to Analise, then drove away from Still Waters, it was strange how, along with always being able to remember his conversations with Emma, Charlie seemed locked onto the idea of fixing him up with Annie Shepherd.

Just proving that Alzheimer's might be a roller

coaster, but it wasn't one where all the cars were connected and everyone was on the same ride. Although
the end was certain, the one thing he'd learned over the
past eight months was that everyone's experience was
as unique as the people suffering from it.

As Mac passed the tidy shops with their colorful
wind socks blowing in the sea breeze, he saw Annie out
in front of Memories on Main, rolling down her yellow
and white awning.

He was tempted to stop, but the fact that she hadn't
called the show last night suggested that she really was
putting a stop to any relationship they might have going. Besides, since this was his father's day for working
at the clinic, Mac needed to get home, having promised
to take Emma to the park, then have a hot dog roast on
the beach.

So he merely slowed down, and honked once. She
turned around, saw his truck, and waved. Today's
dress was a stoplight red. When a sea breeze caught
and flared the flirty skirt high on her thighs, he was
tempted to pull over.

Although he hadn't been in Spec Ops, or anything
secretive like that, the military had taught Mac to keep
information close to his chest.

Working for AFN had also required that he keep his
emotions to himself, because when he was reporting
that day's casualties, or listening to some of the personal stuff people who called in to request songs would
tell him, he could've spent a lot of his deployments too
depressed to get up in the morning.

So, while he might seem all outgoing as Radio Guy,
concealing his feelings had become second nature. Until that first night with Sandy from Shelter Bay, and
again at lunch, when he'd found himself opening up in
a way he hadn't with anyone. Not even his father. Or

Sax, whom he'd always been closest with, back in the day.

She was probably right about not getting involved. But just watching her lips curve in that smile had him remembering her taste.

Despite the nightmares, and the ghosts, he'd told himself that compared to most guys, he was doing okay. He'd learned to deal with stuff, and things he didn't want to deal with got put in that lockbox in his mind.

Not much got to easy, breezy Midnight Mac.

But, as fucked up as this situation could turn out to be, Annie Shepherd had sure as hell gotten to him.

33

She wasn't going to call. Annie told herself that all day, trying to ignore the burst of pleasure she'd felt when he'd driven by. It had taken all her restraint not to give him an invitation to stop. But then what?

Fortunately the pods of whales, along with the local dolphins, had begun putting on quite a show, filling the whale-watching boats with tourists, who would rush into her store in search of paper, brads, and various other whale embellishments to create the memory pages they intended to make once they got back home.

During the off season, her sales tended to be local, along with an online base that was growing more every day. Enough so she was thinking she might have to hire someone part-time just to handle the mailing.

After closing the shop, she went home, took advantage of the low tide to walk a mile along the beach from her cove, then back home again. She fed Pirate, who was noisily demanding his dinner, nuked a frozen diet meal for herself, which tasted just barely better than the cardboard box it came in, and settled down with a romance novel that was just hot enough to keep reminding her of the kisses she'd shared with Mac Culhane.

So much for escapist fiction.

Giving up, she switched to a history of the cove where her house was located—it was a fascinating enough story, but had been written by a professor emeritus who'd retired to Newport, and seemed to have missed his calling. Because his technical, detail-heavy, dry prose style was definitely more suited to writing legal briefs, legislation, or computer manuals.

Finally giving up, and wondering how it was that a book that was so impossibly boring couldn't have at least made her sleepy, Annie poured a glass of wine and took it upstairs to bed, where she slipped between the sheets and turned on the radio.

"When I was growing up, spending my summers here in Shelter Bay," Mac was saying, "everyone knew the rules of dating. Among them bein' that it was always the guy's responsibility to make the first move at the end of a date.

"But with all the gains women have made in equality, is it still that way? Guys, do you still sometimes get conflicted about whether she wants you to kiss her at the end of a date? When you realize you're caught in a movie moment, but you're having a hard time decoding the scenario?

"And, hey, you women out there, are you still waiting on a guy to make the move? Or do you believe in taking the matter into your own hands. Or, in this case, lips?

"Give me a call at 555-9806 and let me know your thoughts. Meanwhile, we've got an ode to those guys who are responsible for making that move with Gloriana's "Good Night," or as most people call it, "Kissed You Good Night.""

Annie's phone immediately rang.

"He's doing it again," Sedona said. "Sending you a message. Talking about kissing you."

"Maybe," Annie allowed, even though she knew her friend was right. "Though it could be a coincidence. Most country songs are about kissing, drinking, falling in love, or breaking up."

"He wants you to call."

"I know."

Annie hitched up higher in the bed and took another, longer sip of wine. Pirate, sensing her anxiety and not happy that she shifted enough to slide him off her legs, shot her an annoyed glare and moved down to the bottom of the bed. In revenge, he began clawing the pretty woven wool throw she'd bought for a ridiculously low price at one of the artisan boutiques in the Cannery.

"Well?" Sedona said.

"I'm thinking about it."

"He's practically inviting you to make the next move," Sedona said, pressing her case. "He's already done *his* part. Now it's your turn."

"He drove by the store this morning. While I was out putting down the awning."

"And?"

"Didn't you hear me? He *drove by*. If he was all that interested, why didn't he stop?"

"Because you told him you didn't want him to? You're the one who said it wasn't going to work."

"And he agreed."

"That's what guys *always* say to protect their egos when they've been turned down. Would you have wanted him to get down on his knees, right there on Main Street, and beg?"

"Of course not."

Oh, God. Maybe she was one of those women who expected the man to make not just the *first* move, but *all* the moves. And how depressing, in this day and age, was that?

"It's complicated," she said yet again, reminding herself that she'd dared him to kiss her in Memories on Main, of all places.

"Life's complicated. Love even more so."

"Who's talking about love?" What she and Mac Culhane had was merely chemistry. Wasn't it?

"Don't get bogged down in details. Or ahead of yourself. He's putting himself out there, Annie. The question is, are you going to snatch him up? Or wait until someone else does?"

"I can't very well call the station if I'm on the phone with you," she said.

"Go for it," Sedona replied. Then cut the connection.

Wishing she'd brought the bottle upstairs, Annie polished off the rest of her wine, took a deep breath, and dialed.

34

The phone buttons had lit up. Mac figured Cowboy and the others could wait because there was one caller he was not going to risk keeping on hold.

"I was hoping you were listening," he said.

"I like country music," she said.

"See, we have something in common."

"Well, that and kissing," she admitted. He thought he heard a smile in her voice.

"That's a damn good start."

"I suppose so." She paused. Then said, "How long do we have?"

"The song runs four minutes, forty-seven seconds."

"That's a long one."

"Hey, I try."

"I'm glad you honked when you drove by today," she said.

"Can't not compliment a pretty woman in a red dress," he said.

"I thought maybe you'd stop." Another pause. Then a sigh. "And this is sounding so like high school."

He laughed because damned if he hadn't been thinking the same thing. "I wanted to. Especially when you flashed me."

"The wind caught my skirt," she countered, but he could practically see that cute color rising in her porcelain pale skin. "And it didn't go that high."

"High enough it had me wanting to bite your thigh."

"Don't." She almost moaned it.

Ha! He was getting to her.

"Just being honest. So, yeah, I wanted to stop, but I wasn't sure you wanted me to. I was also pretty sure you didn't want me kissing you on Main Street where everyone driving by could see."

"No. Of course I wouldn't." She didn't sound as if she entirely meant that. Which was a good thing. Wasn't it?

"I was coming back from seeing Pops," he said.

"So early in the morning?" She knew what time he got off work, which meant she also knew that he wouldn't have gotten much sleep. What she didn't need to know was that thanks to her bedeviling both his mind and his body, he hadn't gotten any. "Is something wrong?"

"No. Not with him, anyway. A close friend he was in the war with died. I wanted to break the news before he heard it from anyone else. He wants me to take him to the memorial service tomorrow, so I'm keeping my fingers crossed that he'll be having a good day when I show up in the morning."

"I'll keep mine crossed as well, for both of you," she said. "I assume you're talking about Ollie Nelson?"

Okay, that was a surprise. "How did you guess that?"

"Your grandfather talks about Ollie. A lot. Especially when we're working on his war scrapbook."

"What war scrapbook?"

"He hasn't shown it to you?" She sounded as surprised as he'd been to hear about it.

"No. I didn't even know it existed." How coincidental was it that he'd just been thinking he needed to get Pops' stories down? Apparently Charlie had already been working on that. With Annie Shepherd.

Which meant she knew really personal stuff about his grandfather that none of his family did. And how weird was that?

"The only ones I've ever seen are the family one and the new one you just started about his activities at Still Waters, like the aquarium field trip. Today, when I got there, he was sitting in the garden looking at the photo of my grandmother on their honeymoon."

"Ah, the one at Rainbow Lake. I love that one," Annie said. The smile in her voice had him picturing the one that would be shining in her eyes. "She reminds me of a 1940s cover girl. Like Rita Hayworth."

"Nailed it," Mac agreed as the damn clock he was beginning to hate ticked down. "I guess he told you about rowing across the lake."

"And stopping in the middle? Yes, he wasn't specific regarding the details, but I got the idea."

"We talked about you, too."

"Oh?"

"Yeah. He told me to seize the carp. Not that you're a carp, but—"

"I get the point. Especially since he told me the same thing. About you."

"So." He blew out a breath. "Here we are."

"It appears so."

"And, if that song is to be believed, it's up to me to make the next move."

"I called *you*," she reminded him. "Again."

"Good point. So, laying my ego out there on the line, here's where I tell you that you've gotten under my skin, Annie Shepherd. I think about you. A lot." Like most of the time. "Maybe too much."

"I think about you, too."

"But?"

"We agreed to be grown-ups."

"True. But I damn well don't remember agreeing to be a monk. And last time I heard, you hadn't joined a convent."

"No." Her soft laugh of approaching surrender hit him in the gut. And lower. Yes, he was definitely getting to her. The same way she'd already gotten to him.

"We already agreed to be friends," he reminded her. "So what's wrong with seeing each other socially?"

"Socially? Like a date?"

"I know you keep saying you've given up men," he said. "But you don't seem to be real invested in that plan. So maybe you're just out of practice."

There was another pause. Longer than the first. The clock was down to thirty seconds.

Just when Mac thought he was going to have to cut her off, and hey, wouldn't that win him a lot of points, she said, "After you take Charlie back to Still Waters tomorrow, give me a call. If you have time, I'll take the afternoon off and fix you a late lunch at my place."

Was she actually talking about a nooner?

Ten seconds.

Or, in this case, maybe a lunch was just a lunch.

Five seconds, and no time to investigate further.

"It's a deal," he said, just an instant before time ran out.

"You're tuned in to KBAY ninety-eight-point-six *Mac at Midnight* and we had ourselves some technical difficulties that screwed up the phone lines," he lied deftly as he went back on the air. "But I think we've got that situation fixed, so lines are now open.

"Question for the night being, Who's supposed to make the first move? The guy? Or the woman?

"While you're dialing, here's Sugarland, with "What I'd Give," a tune about a friend wanting to be more. Switch genders and it works just as well because I'll bet a lot of guys have found themselves in that situation, too. So let's throw that into the conversational mix."

Mac hit *Play*, rocked back in his chair, and as he watched the lines start to flash, he hoped Annie would get the message that while he was willing to settle for friendship, his ultimate plan was for a whole lot more.

35

The minute the hot, plaintive Sugarland song ended, the phone rang. Although Annie hadn't really expected Mac to call her with all the other people undoubtedly wanting to talk to him, she experienced a little stab of disappointment when she saw Sedona's name on the caller ID.

"So?" Sedona asked. "What did you guys talk about that had him move things to the next level?"

"We're negotiating levels," Annie insisted.

"You're not going to be able to hold things at the status quo," Sedona predicted. "Don't forget, I've seen you together. Even if Kim hadn't reported that kiss in the shop, the chemistry between you two had electricity sparking all over the restaurant. I was afraid you'd blow the circuit breakers."

"I invited him over to the house for a late lunch tomorrow."

"You do have condoms, right? Just in case he doesn't come prepared to dress for the occasion?"

"We're not having sex."

About this Annie was perfectly clear. Oh, she wasn't certain it wouldn't eventually happen. But tomorrow was about conversation. And, okay, even if she swore ahead of time it wasn't going to happen, there'd probably be more kisses.

But maybe once he heard what she had to say, he wouldn't want to kiss her again. "I'm having him over so I can explain why we can't ever have a long-term relationship."

"You're not the type of woman to just have a fling," Sedona said.

"Maybe I've been thinking about what you said about being proactive. As long as we keep things casual, it *could* work."

"Maybe." Sedona sounded skeptical. "I don't suppose you'd care to share with me why any deeper relationship is out of the question?"

Along with Mac Culhane taking up so much of her thoughts lately, Annie had been considering Sedona's accusation that she didn't share personal aspects of her life like true friends did. And, of all the women in Shelter Bay, Sedona was Annie's closest friend.

"Okay." She blew out a breath. It wasn't as if she'd been unfaithful or anything. "Let me run downstairs and get some wine."

"Are we going to need alcohol for this conversation?"

"Maybe you won't," Annie said. "But I've only recently admitted to myself the full picture of what happened to me. I'm not sure saying it out loud is going to be all that easy."

After retrieving the bottle she'd opened earlier, she crawled back beneath the sheets, dislodging a grumpy Pirate, who, as soon as she'd left the bedroom, had settled on her pillow.

She poured a glass and took a sip, hoping it would settle her nerves. It didn't. After all this time, it still hurt.

"You know I've always wanted children," she began.

"Of course."

"And that my husband was older."

"And that he was your boss who had children older than you," Sedona said. "What does that have to do with Midnight Mac? Or any other man you might be attracted to?"

"A lot of people thought that I married Owen because he was rich and powerful and I wanted to live that Washingtonian lifestyle."

"No one who truly knows you could ever think that."

"Thanks. Because that's true. I didn't want the wealth, or all the charity lunches and dinners with people I had nothing in common with. Or the Fairfax County stone mansion with the closet this bedroom could fit into. All filled with designer clothes and shoes."

"Okay. I have to admit I'm lusting after the shoes," Sedona said. "Not that there's anywhere to wear them in Shelter Bay, but still . . .

"So, you married for love."

"No," Annie admitted. "Oh, I thought I did. But I was twenty-two, barely out of college, and after a lifetime of moving from place to place, I've belatedly realized that Owen represented security."

"That makes perfect sense," Sedona agreed.

"I hated that house," Annie admitted. "It was so large we had a live-in housekeeper, along with a maid and a gardener, so I never felt as if we had any privacy. But it did have all those bedrooms—"

"Which you intended to fill with babies."

"Yes." Annie smiled softly at her youthful naiveté. "But when I hadn't gotten pregnant the first year, the doctor told me I needed to relax. And suggested I drink a glass of wine before sex."

"A male doctor, no doubt," Sedona said dryly. "A woman probably would've also looked for a physical cause."

"We tried for two years," she said. "Finally, although looking back on it, I can see that Owen was quite satisfied with how things were, he also wanted, in his way, to make me happy. So I went to a fertility specialist.

"And here's a little sidebar. When I was thirteen, I had these horrible pains in my lower side for days, which my foster mother at the time kept writing off as me merely whining about menstrual cramps."

"You're the least whiny person I know," Sedona said supportively.

"Well, she felt differently, so finally, after a week, my appendix ruptured."

"I hope the State took her license away. It'd be lovely if she was also sent to prison for child neglect, but that probably didn't happen."

"I don't even know if she lost her license," Annie admitted. "Because when I got out of the hospital a week later, I was moved to a different home. . . .

"Anyway, I had a diagnostic hysterosalpingogram, which showed that my fallopian tubes were too scarred from the surgery for my eggs to be able to make it through to meet Owen's little swimmers. Fortunately, since money was no problem, I talked Owen into IVF treatment."

"That's supposed to be tough to go through."

"It wasn't easy." Just the memory had Annie taking another drink. "After the first try didn't take, Owen told me that he hated the entire process. That it had made me seem more like some sort of wannabe incubator than a woman."

"Lovely guy, Owen. No wonder he's an ex."

"I didn't leave then," Annie said. "For the next couple years, even as his daughters both had children,

which, believe me, wasn't easy to watch, especially
since they didn't bother to hide how much they re-
sented me, I threw myself into becoming the perfect
D.C. society hostess."

Apparently Annie wasn't the only one drinking, because she heard a spewing noise on the other end of the
phone, and then Sedona began coughing.

"Sorry," she said. "I know it must have been a
wretched time for you, and I'm sure you must have
been a dynamite hostess, but I'm having a really difficult time envisioning you in that lifestyle. And I like to
think I have a pretty good imagination."

"That makes two of us. At least, unlike the political
parties, the charity work was for good causes, but it
still didn't fill that hole I had inside me."

"The one needing to be filled with kids," Sedona,
who'd professed not to even want children, said sym-
pathetically.

"That one," Annie agreed. "Knowing how many
children need homes, I was seriously considering
adoption, but every time I'd bring it up, Owen would
have a reason why it wasn't a good time."

"I'm disliking this guy more and more," Sedona
muttered.

"He's not as bad as I'm making him out to sound,"
Annie insisted. "Perhaps a bit passive-aggressive on
the issue."

"Jeez, you think?"

"Anyway, as I got near my thirtieth birthday, I decided to give myself a present that meant more than the
diamond necklace and matching earrings he had his
assistant buy, and I made an appointment for the two
of us with an adoption agency counselor.

"I wasn't certain he'd even show up for the meeting,
but he did, which was a positive sign. Until he finally
told me, flat out, in front of the counselor, that having

already raised one family, he had no desire to begin
again."

"And *that's* when you left."

"No." How foolish had that been? "I stayed for another year."

"Why?"

"You have to understand. Owen was the only real
family I'd ever known. Even if we didn't have my fantasy family, I was determined to make it work." She
sighed heavily and took another long sip of wine. "But
I could tell he'd already emotionally moved on. Then
one Sunday morning he surprised me with a date for
brunch at the Hay-Adams.

"At first I thought that maybe he'd decided to try to
bring a little romance back into our lives, but no sooner
than our mimosas were served, he told me that he'd
fallen in love with someone else."

"Damn. The bastard took you somewhere public he
knew you couldn't make a scene." Ironically, Sedona
sounded angrier than Annie herself had been at the
time.

"Which shows how little he knew me," she murmured. "Because I don't make scenes." She never had,
having watched what happened to foster kids who got
put on the "troublesome" list.

"I would've wanted to start throwing china. Which,"
the other woman admitted, "as much as it would've
killed me to play the lady, I probably wouldn't have."

"No. You wouldn't." Annie blew out a breath, relieved to finally get this story out. "I moved out of the
house, which I'd never liked, our long-overdue divorce
was as cold, dry, and unemotional as our marriage, and
less than two months after it was finalized, he and his
new trophy wife appeared in the Lifestyle section of the
Washington Post."

And in her former husband's circle, it was as if she'd

never existed. Something Annie was used to, having moved from home to home, family to family.

"Since I no longer had any connection to the capital, I decided to start over again as far away as I could. I'd grown up here in Oregon, so it made sense to begin with it as a destination point. And, as you pointed out, Shelter Bay is on the edge of the continent and as different from the inside-the-Beltway vibe as you can get. So I moved here, opened Memories on Main, and am happy with how things worked out."

"I'm truly sorry about the baby thing, but glad you managed to come out of all that happy. You still need to get laid, though," Sedona said.

Which made Annie laugh. Another reason they were friends.

"Same back at you," she countered. Then she thought about those kisses on the bridge and the beach. "And maybe I will. As soon as I can figure out how to look at sex as just another recreational activity and not a prelude to something deeper."

"I still don't see what the problem is," Sedona insisted. "I'm having an even more difficult time with it now that I know about your marriage breaking up over kids. You want a child. Mac Culhane *has* a child. That balances out nicely."

"Once a CPA, always a CPA," Annie said. "It's not all about checks and balances and bottom lines. There's a very good chance he'll want a brother or sister for Emma."

"And an equally good possibility that he won't. I'm an only child," she reminded Annie. "And look how good I turned out.

"Besides, even if he does want another child, you've already said you were considering adoption. Which, may I point out, has turned out wonderfully for Charity and Gabe. You'd never know that Johnny and Angel weren't their birth children. Having watched Mac with Emma, I'd bet he'd be totally open to adoption."

"This conversation is making my brain hurt." Unlike all her ones with Midnight Mac, which made all the other vital parts of her body ache.

"You just need to relax," Sedona said. "Nothing like some hot sex with a hard body to release endorphins. Try thinking of Midnight Mac as yet another important part of a healthy lifestyle."

With last bit of advice, she hung up.

Just the thought of getting naked with the man set off an all too familiar hot rush of desire.

Setting the empty wineglass on the table, she lay back on the pillow she'd reclaimed from Pirate, who immediately climbed on top of her legs, and closed her eyes, trying to practice the meditation techniques Sedona had taught them all late one night during a sixties-video-watching party at Kara's. At the time Maddy had been suffering from unfulfilled lust for Lucas, and like Elizabeth Taylor's Maggie the Cat, she'd spent a lot of time pacing the floor.

But even as Annie struggled to calm her body, her restless mind kept spinning. She'd never been good at living in the now, since the now had always been so unstable and fleeting. Having developed the habit of looking ahead, trying to garner control over an unknown future, maybe she *was* making too big a deal of this situation.

So what if whatever she had going with Mac didn't lead to a happily-ever-after ending?

That didn't mean she couldn't just do what probably any other woman in her circumstances would do: Go with the flow, enjoy the moment, and the very hot man.

And, as Sedona so succinctly put it, get herself laid.

36

Mac had never had sex with a friend before. It wasn't that he didn't have female friends. Despite radio being a male-dominated business, especially at the deejay level, which was essentially a boys' club, he'd become friends with women he worked with. But he'd always drawn a line in the sand. On one side were friends. On the other were lovers.

So now he was the one pushing to rub out that line with Annie. And, from the kisses they'd shared and the fact that she'd invited him over to her house, in the middle of the day, it suggested she was down with that.

He wasn't real sure it was the best idea he'd ever had. That line had always served him well. Kept his life from getting messy.

"Yeah, nothing messy about your life," he muttered as he whisked eggs in a bowl.

His dad, who usually made breakfast, had gotten a call from the trauma center at the Oregon Health and Science Univeristy, where he had practiced and taught for years, that they'd received three pediatric trauma cases, two with multiple internal injuries, from a tractor-trailer/minivan collision. If the legendary Dr.

Buchanan would only agree to scrub in, they'd send a helicopter to fly him to Portland.

Needless to say, he'd left like a shot, making Mac wonder if there were times his father missed the pace of life-and-death surgery, the same way Mac occasionally found himself missing the adrenaline rush of going outside the wire to play deejay for troops out there in no-man's-land at remote Forward Operating Bases.

Although he was glad that those children would have a better chance at life with his father wielding the trauma room scalpel, it did leave Mac with a dilemma about how to take his grandfather to the memorial service for Ollie, and have a late lunch, or hopefully more, with Annie, while taking care of Emma.

He was still pondering that problem, whisking Emma's scrambled eggs in the pan while the toast was browning, when a blood-chilling cry came from outside.

He raced out the front door, toward the sound, and saw Emma, still in her nightgown, at the bottom of the inclined driveway with a metallic pink bike lying on top of her. Although he was running as fast as he could, time took on a slow-motion aspect that had him feeling as if he was slogging through knee-deep quicksand while his heart was beating as fast as it had that time his Humvee had come under fire on the road to Kandahar.

"What the hell are you doing out here?"

Cool move, Culhane. The harsh tone, born from sheer fear at seeing her arm twisted in a way no one's arm should be bent, started the tears flowing. It also sent a vision of another blue-uniformed bent arm that he didn't want to think about flashing through his mind.

"I'm sorry, baby." He carefully lifted the bike off her, then crouched down beside her. "I didn't mean to yell. Don't worry. Daddy's here." Looking at her arm, he wished *his* dad was here, too. Of all the damn days for him to be away . . .

"I fell off my bike," she whimpered, the screams having stopped the minute he'd shot through the door like a rocket.

"I see that. But it's going to be okay."

"My arm hurts."

"We're going to get that fixed." Fortunately, from what he could see, there were no bones sticking through the skin. Which was a good sign. Right?

"Did you hit your head?"

She nodded. Then began crying. "It hurts. But not like Poppy's."

Christ. What was he going to do about Charlie?

First things first.

By now, Jackie Chamberlain, Mac's next-door neighbor, who'd been on her way to her law office, had come out, seen the situation, and crossed their adjoining lawns.

"Hey, sweetie," she said, lifting her pencil skirt to crouch down beside Mac. As she took a tissue out of her bag and wiped at his daughter's wet cheeks, a guy part of him, on some distant level, noticed her attractive legs. The dad part of him was too focused on Emma to feel anything but relief that a woman was on hand to help with the tears. "Looks like you took a tumble."

"I f-f-fell," Emma said.

"I can see that." She brushed Emma's blond bangs from her forehead. "I'm going to stay here with you while your daddy goes and gets a pillow for your head, and calls an ambulance," she said with a look toward Mac.

"Nine-one-one," he agreed as the fear fog cleared from his head. "I'll be right back, baby."

He grabbed the pillow from his bed even as he dialed.

"They're going to be here in a sec," he assured Emma as he slipped the pillow carefully beneath her head. He'd witnessed neck trauma before, and since she'd lifted her head when he'd come rushing out the door, he was pretty sure that part of her was okay.

"I'm going to get to ride in an ambulance?" she asked, her sobs decreasing to hitched breaths.

"Yeah. But it'll be okay," he assured her. "Even fun. And I'll be right there with you."

"Okay," she said, and promptly threw up on his cross-trainers.

Another advantage of living in a town the size of Shelter Bay was that the ambulance showed up in less than three minutes, lights flashing.

"That was fast," Jackie Chamberlain said.

"We ran the red light." The EMT jumped from the driver's seat and joined Mac and the lawyer next to Emma. "Isn't that the cutest nightgown?" she said. "My daughter Dani has the very same one. She loves that movie."

"M-M-Merida's the bravest princess of all," Emma said, still stuttering with a combination of what Mac figured was fear and pain as she wiped her runny nose with the sleeve of her good arm.

Damn. He should've thought to grab a handful of Kleenex. Or at least a roll of toilet paper. Yet more Dad fail.

"I know. And today, I think you're probably the bravest girl in all of Shelter Bay," the woman soothed as she ran her purple-gloved fingers over Emma's head, and down her neck, across her shoulders, frowning as she took in the awkward bend to the right arm. "Let's just put a splint on your arm, okay? Then we'll give you a ride to the hospital."

"O-k-kay."

Not wanting to get in the way, although it took every

bit of restraint he possessed, Mac stood back, letting the two EMTs lift his daughter onto the gurney and slide her into the ambulance.

He was about to climb in with her, when Emma lifted her head, and said, "I need you to take a picture."

"What?"

"Ms. Shepherd says that scrapbooks are a good way for being able to look back on your life. So I want this picture for the book I'm going to make."

He knew that telling her that it was more important to get the hell to the hospital would only waste more time, so he pulled out his iPhone and snapped the shot.

"Let me see," she insisted, sounding, he thought, a bit like the royal princess of Shelter Bay.

He showed her the photo.

"Okay. That's a good one." Despite the pain Emma had to be feeling, her lips curved upward in a smile. "Peggy is going to be *so* jealous."

37

Annie was getting ready to leave for Memories on Main when Mac called.

"I'm at the hospital and need some help," he said. "And you're the first person I thought to call, but if you can't do it, I'll understand, so don't feel obligated—"

His voice was stressed, ragged, and harried. Which meant he sounded nothing like himself.

"Just tell me," she said, her concern escalating to alarm. "Are you all right?"

"Other than about to go insane, I'm fine. Emma fell and maybe broke her arm. Or maybe just her wrist. Hell, I don't know." She could picture him thrusting his hand through his dark hair.

"Oh, no!" Which was bad, but not as bad as she'd first thought from his voice.

"And she might have a concussion."

"Poor little thing. What can I do?"

"Just like that? You're not going to ask what I'm going to ask?"

"Friends don't have to ask," she said. "What do you need? Do you want me to come to the hospital?"

"No. I need you to go over to the house. My dad's

house. Well, I guess it's mine and Emma's now, too, but it used to be Pops'—"

"Mac." He was coming as close to babbling as a guy with as much testosterone as he had could get. Which was, again, as far from the cool, easygoing Mac Culhane as she'd witnessed thus far. "I know the house. Is your father there?"

"No. That's the damn thing. He's off doing emergency surgery in Portland. So"—he took a deep, ragged breath—"I need you to go get Charlie's uniform, which is hanging on the closet door in my bedroom. I ironed it this morning. Then take it to Still Waters. I'll call Analise and let her know you're coming and she can help him get dressed."

"No problem. How will I get in?"

"I left my key under the mat."

"That's the first place thieves look," she said before thinking. Obviously burglary was not his main concern at the moment.

"If someone breaks in and empties the place out, I'll just have Kara arrest them and shoot them. And I hate to ask, but I need something else."

"Anything."

"I have to take Pops to Ollie's memorial service by one. Fortunately, it's looking like they're going to be done with X-ray pretty soon; then, because the doctor who'll put the cast on is a veteran, he's going to move her to the head of the line. I think if nothing else goes wrong, I can take Emma home, then make it to Still Waters in time to get him to Genarro's for the service, but—"

"I'll go back to the house and wait for you to get home with Emma," Annie offered without hesitation. "Then I'll stay with her while you take Charlie to Ollie's memorial."

"Thanks." The single word was said with a huge rush of relief. "I owe you. Big time."

"You don't owe me anything. As I said, that's what friends are for. Now, go be with your daughter."

As she drove over to the Buchanan house, Annie thought how, although she dreaded the idea of the little girl in pain, Mac's daughter's injury had just shifted her relationship with him yet again. It had also deepened it. Which could be a problem, but she decided to take Sedona's advice about living in the now and worry about that later.

She found both the key and the uniform, just where he'd told her they would be. The house, while tidy, showed none of the warmth of a woman's touch. As she walked to and from the bedroom, she mentally added some pillows on the oversized leather couch, hung some pictures on the bare walls, set a few decorative pieces on the fireplace mantel, and put a jar of wildflowers on the heavy wooden kitchen table that she could see from the family room.

After calling Kim to tell her that she was taking the entire day off, not just the afternoon, Annie drove to Still Waters and dropped off the uniform with the nurse, who assured her that Charlie would be ready when Mac arrived to pick him up.

Since Emma, whose X-rays showed a broken wrist and a wrenched, but not dislocated shoulder, still hadn't begun to get her cast made, Annie took a quick detour to the shop, where she picked up some stickers, an empty scrapbook, and papers for the little girl to record her misadventure.

Although she'd offered to give them a ride home from the hospital, Mac had told her that a nurse he was friends with had offered to drive them.

Tamping down an unexpected and decidedly unwanted twinge of jealousy at that news, and trying not to wonder exactly *how* friendly Mac and the nurse happened to be, Annie managed to get back to the house five minutes before they arrived in an SUV driven by a thirtysomething guy sporting a Marine haircut. Annie knew that many former medics were working as nurses these days, so when Mac's nurse friend turned out to be male, she felt a little foolish for having jumped to the wrong conclusion. It also brought home the point that she cared about this man more than she'd wanted to admit. Even to herself.

Emma, despite sporting a cast on her wrist, which was in a sling, and bandages on both knees and elbows, seemed to be taking the accident in stride.

"I was riding my bike with no hands, like Trey Douchett was doing the other day when he rode past the park, and I fell and broke my wrist," she said as Mac carried her into the house. Her voice was slurred, as if she'd been on a bender. "And it hurt a lot."

"I can imagine it does," Annie said, thinking that Trey, being all boy, had probably been showing off for the girls at the park.

Mac had decided that his daughter would stay in his room, because it had a flat-screen TV. Since he had his arms full, Annie pulled back the charcoal gray sheets.

"The doctor gave me a shot," Emma said. "So it wasn't too bad. And I was really brave, wasn't I, Daddy?" She looked up at him as he laid her on the bed, treating her as if she were a piece of delicate crystal that he was afraid of breaking.

His face was still an ashen shade of gray, revealing that although Emma seemed to be doing amazingly well, Mac obviously hadn't entirely recovered from the experience.

"You sure did, sweetie," he said. When his lips curved in what appeared to be more grimace than smile, Annie's heart turned as gooey as a chocolate-filled truffle. "You were like a super-heroine."

"Like Merida," Emma said. "She's a princess," she told Annie.

"I know. And, as it happens, I just happen to have a stamp and some Merida stickers I thought you might like on your cast. To let everyone know how brave you are."

"Really?" The resiliency of children was remarkable. "Can we decorate it now?"

"You need to rest," Mac said, shooting Annie a look of desperation.

"Your daddy's right." Annie leaned down and brushed the little girl's blond bangs back, revealing the Barbie Band-Aid adorning her forehead. "Why don't you take a little nap, and—"

"I'm not sleepy," she insisted, fighting it even as her eyelids were trying to drift shut. "It's not nighttime yet."

"I can read you a story," Annie suggested.

"Or I could watch *Brave*," she said.

Mac briefly closed *his* eyes. Annie had the feeling he was counting to ten.

"That's a good idea," he said when he opened them again. "There may still be a line in it you haven't memorized."

"Daddy was just joking," Emma informed Annie. "I know *all* the lines by heart."

"I'm not a bit surprised. But I haven't seen it, so this will be a treat for me."

Emma scooted over. "You can sit with me and we'll watch it together." She looked up at Mac, who still looked miserable. "Daddy, would you get Angus from my bed?" she asked. "That's Merida's faithful horse," she told Annie. "I think it would be fun to have a horse, but Grandpa said it would be impractical to keep one in the backyard."

"I think it would," Annie agreed as she sat on the edge of the bed. "Because horses need room to run."

"That's what Grandpa said. But I don't really want a horse. What I really, really want is a dog."

Her eyes, glazed from whatever medication they had given to her in the hospital, were limpid pools of blue as she looked up at her father. Then she whimpered, causing panic to flood into his dark eyes.

"As soon as you get your cast off, we'll go to Dr. Tiernan's shelter and you can have any dog you want," Mac said.

"Really?" The little girl's eyelids were getting heavier by the moment.

"Absolutely."

"Not just someday, like you always say?"

"As soon as you get your cast off," he repeated. "The doctor said, since it's just a crack, you should be able to get it off in three to four weeks. Then you'll be able to throw balls for a dog to fetch, and play tug-of-war."

"A dog." She sighed happily. "When I fell down I thought that this was going to be a terrible, horrible, no good, very bad day. But I got to ride in an ambulance and the nice lady even turned on the siren," she told Annie.

"Cool," Annie said.

"It was." Her eyes drifted all the way closed, but apparently her mouth hadn't yet gotten the message that her brain was turning off for a while. "And everyone at the hospital was so nice. I got a lollipop and the man who took my X-ray printed out a copy for me."

Her blue eyes popped open again and she looked up at Mac. "Where is it?" Her voice held the first hint of panic Annie had heard.

"I dropped the envelope on the couch on the way in," he said. "I'll go get it. "

"Okay."

"We can put it in the scrapbook I brought you," Annie said as Mac left the room, presumably to get the DVD and X-ray.

"You brought a scrapbook, too? With papers and stuff?"

"All kinds of papers and stuff." Although she knew she was just getting in deeper, Annie brushed a kiss onto Emma's satiny cheek. "We can look at it together later."

Emma wiggled into the sheets, as if barely able to keep from dancing. "This is my bestest day ever," she said on a happy sigh.

Then immediately fell asleep.

The phone rang as Annie heard Mac come back toward the stairs.

"What the hell?" His voice was loud enough to hear over Emma's soft breathing.

Moving as gingerly as she could, Annie climbed out of the bed and crept into the living room.

"I'll be right there," he said.

After hanging up without bothering to say good-bye, he scrubbed both hands down his already haggard face. "Fuck." His broad shoulders slumped, as if suddenly weary of carrying the weight of both his grandfather and his injured daughter.

"What's happened?"

"Pops just tried to beat up an orderly who was helping Analise get him into his uniform."

38

"I've got to get over there," he said. "From what Analise said, he got confused when he saw the uniform and thought they were trying to force him to go back to war. Which was when he began flailing away."

"So, it looks as if he'll miss Ollie's memorial service. And what the hell will we do if this gets him kicked out of Still Waters?"

"I don't think that happens unless fighting becomes habitual," Annie assured him. "Agitation is common with Alzheimer's patients, and outbursts of aggression aren't unknown as the disease progresses. Just last month I arrived there in time to see two elderly ladies rolling around on the floor wrestling over frosting tubes during Sedona's cookie-decorating class."

"And who knows if they're still living there?" he pointed out. "Would you mind staying until I get back?"

"I'd already agreed to sit with Emma while you and Charlie were at the memorial," she reminded him. "But I really think you ought to give me a shot at getting him calmed down."

"I'm his grandson."

"True. And family means a lot. But I still think I'm a better choice."

"What makes you think you'd be any better at settling him down than Analise, who's trained to handle dementia patients?" he asked as he headed toward the front door.

She didn't take offense at his less-than-encouraging tone. Although it wasn't yet noon, he'd already had what Emma had described as a terrible, horrible, no good, very bad day.

"I've been working on his war scrapbook with him for weeks. He's told me a lot of stories, especially about the day his carrier got hit by Japanese bombs and Ollie pulled him out of the ocean before it sank."

"Damn. How could I not know any of that? All he ever said was that he served in the Pacific with Ollie."

When he dragged his hand through his hair again, Annie caught it on the way down and held it for a moment in both of hers. "It's probably easier to speak with a stranger. Or," she said, "I'm certainly no expert, but I've come to realize that there's often no rhyme or reason when it comes to Alzheimer's.

"Maybe I just happened to be there the day his memories had spun him back in time and he felt like talking. Then, perhaps once he started, it became easier to keep going."

Something occurred to her. "Did they give him any drugs to calm him down?"

"No. They managed to get him into the sensory room without any. That's a good sign, right?"

The sensory room, designed for when residents became agitated or had difficulty sleeping, which was common with dementia patients, was a dimly lit room with a dark-painted ceiling lit with stars.

A machine provided soothing sounds: white noise,

rain, the surf, or a waterfall, which Annie knew Charlie liked best because it reminded him of the waterfall at Rainbow Lake where he and his Annie had honeymooned.

There was also a blanket—scented with lavender from Maddy's grandmother's Lavender Hill Farm—that could be warmed; a daybed, which the women tended to prefer; and a big vibrating recliner.

The room had been designed by experts in the psychology of dementia, and usually it took only eight to ten minutes to calm a resident.

"A very good sign," Annie confirmed. "And my point was that because I know all the history between Ollie and him, there's a chance that I can help him remember that it's in the past. Because if he later realizes that his actions caused him to miss the memorial, he could be really upset."

"He was afraid, when I told him about Ollie dying, that he might have forgotten it," Mac told her. "He said they'd been through so much it would've been wrong to forget. If you wouldn't mind—"

"Of course I wouldn't. I can't guarantee success, but I'll do my best."

She thought she saw him relax. Just a bit. "Thanks. I owe you."

She smiled at that. "Friends," she reminded him. Then went up on her toes and kissed his cheek.

Despite the seriousness of the situation, he hooked one arm around her waist, drew her up against him, and kissed her. Long and hard and so deep that, feeling as if she was drowning, she grabbed hold of his shoulders for a lifeline.

"This is insane," she said as she pulled away and retrieved her purse, which she'd tossed onto the entry table with the bag of scrapbook goodies when she'd arrived. "Crazy . . . I can't believe with all that's going on right now, as inappropriate as that kiss was at this time, dammit, I want more."

"Don't feel like the Lone Ranger." His voice was deep and bedroom-husky. Which had her mind following her rebellious body to places she had no business thinking about. Certainly not now. Maybe never.

As if to prove his point, he caught her arm and swung her around again for one more quick, hot kiss that sent her head spinning and made her knees weak and had her fluttering in parts of her body that Annie had forgotten even *could* flutter.

"I don't know what you had planned for lunch today," he said. "But I do know that we're not finished, Sandy from Shelter Bay. Not by a long shot."

"I've got to run."

And run she did, out to the car, then waited until she was out of sight around the corner before she pulled over to the curb. Needing a moment to regroup, she took a few of the long, deep yoga breaths Sedona had taught them all.

Although Charlie and Emma's accident had complicated their situation, Annie was really going to do it.

She was *so* going to do Midnight Mac.

"But first," she said to herself, pulling back onto the deserted residential street, "I have to bail Charlie out of Time Out."

39

Charlie was back in his room, clad in white boxer shorts, white socks, and a white T-shirt when Annie arrived. She was relieved that he was calm, but the fact that he wasn't dressed and was sitting in his recliner with his arms stubbornly folded over his chest wasn't a good sign.

"Hi," she said with a warm, but not overly cheerful smile. One thing she'd discovered was that when someone was depressed, having another person invade his or her personal space by being overly perky not only didn't help, but could actually make things worse.

He looked up at her.

"Who the hell are you?"

Annie pulled a chair up beside him and sat down so he wouldn't have to look up at her. "I'm a friend. Annie Shepherd. You and I make scrapbooks together sometimes."

"The hell I do. Scrapbooks are girlie things. My Annie makes scrapbooks." He gave her a long look. "You're pretty enough," he allowed. "But my Annie looks like a pinup girl."

"I know."

His brow furrowed. "You know my sweetheart?"

"Only by the pictures you've shared," she said, taking the family album from the side table and opening it to the wedding photo. "This is one of my favorites."

He stared at it for a long time. Annie realized that having been lost for a while in the confusing labyrinth of memories, he was having trouble figuring out what Annie was doing in her postwar wedding dress while they were trying to return him to war.

"She made that dress herself," Annie reminded him.

He nodded as a spark of comprehension dawned in his eyes. "From parachute silk."

"Silk you sent her home during the war," Annie said gently. "World War II."

"I know which damn war it is," he snapped. Then stopped. Looked down at the photo again. Then out toward the garden, where red, white, and blue petunias had been planted for the upcoming holiday.

"Which war it *was*?" he said tentatively. It broke her heart watching him struggle to pull himself back from those mists of time.

Annie had been working on living in the moment. She couldn't imagine the difficulty of trying to live in the moment when your mind had become like the shifting sands on the beach.

Another thing occurred to her as Charlie slowly turned the pages, taking in the photos she'd helped him put together. She'd only known Charlie Buchanan a few months. Mac had known him as being that strong, hardy, tale-telling grandfather for decades. How difficult must it be for him to watch the unraveling of a life? A life they'd made together after he'd already lost his father at too young an age? What helplessness and yes, at times, like today, what *hopelessness* he must be feeling.

When that idea proved too depressing, she turned her mind back to the project at hand.

"That veil is mosquito netting," she reminded him as he stared at a photo of the young and happy couple cutting a tiered white wedding cake. Charlie's now age-spotted hand was still young and strong atop his bride's on the knife.

"I brought that netting home for her," he said, more to himself than to Annie. "From the Pacific."

"It was very clever of you to think of it. And she looks beautiful in it."

"I wanted to get married as soon as my ship docked in San Francisco," he said. "But she made me wait because she said she'd already waited so long, a few more months wouldn't hurt to do it up right."

He ran an aged finger, bent and broken from various tangles with ropes and traps as a fisherman, over the faded black-and-white photo. "After all I'd put her through, worrying about me, especially after I nearly drowned at sea, there was no way I wasn't going to give her anything she wanted."

He lifted his eyes, which were wet with tears, up to Annie's.

"Ollie Nelson pulled me out of the water. Up onto the deck of the *Minneapolis*. Nearly fell into the drink himself doin' it. That's how we met."

"Yes," Annie said as her own eyes filled.

"He saved my life. And became my best friend." He looked down at another photo of the small wedding party consisting of bride, groom, and two attendants. "And my best man."

"He was a friend for many years," Annie agreed softly.

"Was." The word lingered between them as he processed that idea. "And now he's gone," he said finally. "And I'm the last one left."

She could only nod.

He sighed. A long sigh filled with reluctant acceptance and deep regret.

Then, with effort, Charlie pushed himself out of the recliner. "We'd best get going," he said. "I've got a memorial to go to."

40

Fortunately, although the largest room at Genarro's funeral home was filled to capacity with fellow veterans, the service didn't last long. Before driving Charlie by the house, so Mac could take over, Annie had called and given him a short version of how she'd gotten him back on track. Knowing how intransigent his grandfather could be, Mac suspected it couldn't have been easy, and now not only did he still want her, but he had even more reason to be grateful to her.

He had every intention of crossing that line between friends and lovers, but at this point Mac realized that what they'd begun to build between them was more than just friends with benefits.

Something deeper.

Something he was going to have to consider for both their sakes. Because while the chemistry between them was more powerful than he'd ever felt, he'd also learned the hard way that maintaining a relationship was difficult enough even before adding in the complexity of being a single father.

He no longer had just himself to think about. He'd

screwed up so much about parenting, he didn't want to mess up his daughter.

Although he'd realized that Annie had a point about wanting to be careful about not hurting Emma, having watched them together today, he realized that he was going to have to balance all the different relationships in his life carefully. Since he was used to being a just-go-for-it kind of guy, that wasn't exactly his long suit.

"You okay?" he asked Charlie as they left the service. Because of the way the day had started out, and because Mac was concerned about how his grandfather was doing, he was relieved when Charlie decided to skip the interment and the supper planned for afterward at Bon Temps.

"After getting through the war alive, I've always figured any day I'm aboveground is a good day."

"Got a point there," Mac agreed.

The older man didn't say anything on the drive back to the memory care residence. Which was just as well, since Mac didn't want him talking about anything that might cause battle flashbacks while he was in the truck.

It was only after Charlie was settled into his room that he said, "Did I ever tell you about how I met Ollie?"

"During the war," Mac replied, even though now, thanks to Annie, he knew more.

"I was on the *Lexington*. It was a carrier based out of Pearl. But we missed the attack because we'd been sent out on December fifth, two days earlier, to ferry some Marine dive-bombers out to reinforce Midway Island."

"Lucky," Mac said. Sensing a story coming, one he'd been hoping to hear, he pulled up a chair.

"Yeah. It all didn't seem real when we were called back to Pearl and saw the destruction. My first thought was relief we hadn't been there. Then I felt guilty for feeling that way. Finally, I just settled on being goddamn mad."

Which was smart, Mac thought. Since his pops still had a lot of war to get through and being dragged down with survivor guilt wouldn't have helped anyone.

"I had two friends on the *Arizona*," he said. "Jerry Long and Pete Novak. We'd met at the enlisted men's club and I've gotta admit I was real pissed when we got our orders to leave on the fifth, because there was going to be a big Battle of the Bands at the club on the next night.

"Jerry and Pete kept ragging me about all the pretty girls I wasn't going to get to dance with, not that I would've danced with any of them, because it would've seemed like cheating on Annie, but it would've been fun to have some beers and listen to the bands."

His gaze turned a little distant. "But I never saw either one of them again because they went down with their ship."

"You never mentioned that when you took me to the memorial on that trip to Hawaii."

Charlie shrugged. "Why talk about something you can't change?"

Or why talk about something that still hurt? Mac wondered if the increasing loss of time delineation between past and present might cause ancient survivor guilt to rise up again. Which could cause depression.

Another thing he was going to have to ask Analise to watch out for.

"Look in the bottom drawer of that dresser," Charlie instructed him. "The album's under some sweaters. It's the blue one."

Mac found it easily. It was, appropriately, navy blue, with *The United States Navy* in raised gold letters and the round Navy seal showing a bald eagle with spread wings perched on an anchor in the center.

Obviously more of Annie's work.

The first page showed the same photos that were on the board outside the door. Charlie in his recruitment photo, and another in his work dungarees on board.

Then the images changed as fast as life must have changed for Seaman First Class Charles Boyd Buchanan.

"This is the *Lexington*." He tapped a finger on a faded old newspaper photo of an aircraft carrier, its deck filled with planes. "My flattop . . . We sure saw our share of action over the next months." Although his tone was matter-of-fact enough, Mac figured his words were probably a major understatement.

Beneath the photo someone had listed the various battles the carrier had taken part in. "That Annie Shepherd looked those up online and wrote them all down," he said, confirming what Mac had guessed.

His pops turned the page. "And this is her during the Battle of the Coral Sea. May 'forty-two."

The carrier was engulfed in a cloud of billowing black smoke and she was listing dangerously. Although the paper had yellowed and cracked with age, Mac could see sailors diving off the deck.

"She'd been hit with some bombs, which caused a bunch of fires and explosions, but the crews were able to get all the fires out and we managed to keep refueling and sending planes up," he said.

"But finally there were just too many explosions, so the captain gave us the abandon-ship order. At that point, though I was always scared spitless of sharks, going in the water was preferable to staying on board.

"So, there we all were, two thousand plus, sliding down the monkey lines, but the problem was that when you got to the last twenty feet, there were no more knots on the rope, so you're trying like hell to hang on, but it's wet and you're sliding into the guy in front of you, and the guy above you is sliding into you and the rope eats up your hands something goddamn awful."

He held out his hands, palms up, revealing faint white scars that Mac had never before noticed, given how dinged up his grandfather's hands were from years of commercial fishing. It crossed his mind how they both carried physical reminders of their individual wars.

"Finally, I just said a real quick version of the Hail Mary and leaped into the water. The flattop was creating some heavy swells in an already rough sea while going down, which had me worried for a while she was going to tip over on me. But then I was pushed a long ways from the ship and from what I could see, I was all alone, which I'll have to admit didn't give me a whole lot of confidence about making it out of the water alive."

"I can imagine." Actually, Mac couldn't. At least *he'd* been mostly unconscious during his much shorter battle experience.

Charlie's eyes took on that soft, unfocused look that suggested he wasn't seeing the scrapbook, or the room, or the red, white, and blue garden outside the window, but miles of smoke-engulfed sea with oil and gasoline and God knows what else floating on it. Bodies? Likely, given what Charlie had said about the fires and explosions.

"It was strange," he said, sounding as far away as that day. "The swells rise up and carry you down, and keep you there until you're pretty sure you're never going to breathe again and you can't see another soul, or even the ship, until you manage to kick your way back up to the top."

"How long were you out there?"

"They said about two hours, but it seemed like forever. Finally, this whaleboat, which was a little wooden boat they used to ferry sailors on and off ships in those days, showed up alongside and they took me over to the *Minneapolis*, a heavy cruiser that was part of the fleet.

"There were all these guys, leaning over the railing, pulling us onboard. Ollie was the one who got me onto the deck, where my legs seemed to have gone out on me, I guess from all the treading water I'd done, so I lay there flopping around like a dead fish."

"No surprise there. And you became friends."

"And shipmates. The *Minneapolis* saw action in near every battle of the Pacific, winning seventeen battle stars."

"Impressive," Mac said, having no idea what that meant, but Charlie's pride was evident.

"Sure was. She also brought troops back to the West Coast at the end of the war.

"But I didn't know all that was going to happen that day. All I could do was watch with the others as the admiral sent the *Phelps* out to sink the *Lexington*. It took five torpedoes to finally send her down, which was a shame, because she'd performed valiantly, but giving her a decent burial was sure better than the way they sold the *Minneapolis* to some rich metal company for scrap."

The spark of anger, born from what must have been long-smoldering embers, seemed to bring Charlie the rest of the way back to the present. "Twenty-seven hundred and thirty-five men survived that day. Another two hundred and sixteen were killed.

"It's *them* I'm going to be in that parade for," he told Mac. "There's not that many of us old-timers left and the ones who weren't lucky enough to make it home need to be remembered. And if I get confused again, like I guess I did today for a spell, it's your job, as family, to straighten me out and make sure I get there to honor them. You and your Annie."

"She's not *my* Annie," Mac said.

"So you say." Charlie winked. "But I'm putting fifty clams on the line that says otherwise."

"You're not talking steamer clams."

His grandfather had always been a gambler. Fishing was, itself, a dicey occupation and he'd always enjoyed the poker games down at the VWF.

"You know better than that." He grinned like the Charlie who'd welcomed Mac into the family by tossing him into the bay. Mac had learned it was a Buchanan summer tradition. "I'm talking dollars, boy. And believe me, you're going down."

41

Mac returned to find Emma sitting up in bed, finishing off a bowl of tomato soup and crackers. The bed was covered with all sorts of stickers and papers and various other things.

"Annie brought me all this cool stuff," she said, crunching a cracker.

"That's way cool. But it's Ms. Shepherd."

"She said I could call her Annie. Because she's my newest best friend."

"'Ms. Shepherd' is so stuffy," the woman herself, who was anything but stuffy, commented.

"How are you feeling?" Mac asked his daughter.

"Okay. My wrist was beginning to hurt again, but Annie gave me some more medicine. She said that my bones will heal faster if my body isn't fighting pain."

"That's what the doctor at the hospital said," Mac agreed. "Why don't you let me take that tray into the kitchen and talk to Annie for just a minute?"

"Okay. Then you can come back and help me make my scrapbook from all the pictures you took for me at the hospital."

"Thanks," Mac said when he and Annie were out of hearing. "I really appreciate all you've done."

"I told you, it's no problem."

"Yeah. It is. I dumped a lot on you and for all I know you don't even like kids."

Annie wondered if he was serious. "If I didn't like children, I'd be in the wrong business," she said mildly. "Preserving childhood memories brings in nearly as much income as my vacation photo business. And kids are always coming by for stickers. I love them. And Emma's adorable, Mac. She's bright and funny, and talented. You should be really proud of her."

"I didn't have anything to do with that," he said.

"I think you had more to do with it than you're giving yourself credit for. Having her mother leave couldn't be at all easy for a little girl. Then with moving here and having to start a new school and make friends . . .

"Well, she seems amazingly well adjusted."

"Dad says kids her age handle divorce in chunks. I figure she must know Kayla's never coming back or she wouldn't be so set on finding a replacement mother."

Knowing that she currently topped that list had Annie struggling to think of something, anything, to say, but Emma rescued her.

"Daddy," a voice called from the bedroom, "are you coming? I want to get started on my scrapbook."

"In a minute, peanut," he called back. "How much do I owe you?"

"For what?"

"For all those things you brought."

"Don't be silly. You bought enough the other day to pay my electricity bill for a month. I just grabbed some theme papers and stickers for this occasion. They're a gift."

"Well, thanks. For them and for staying with her."

"That was a delight. And easy, since she slept most of the time you were gone."

Annie didn't add that Emma had insisted she lie down on the bed with her, and she knew that Mac's scent, from his pillow, was probably now permanently embedded in her mind.

"Are you going to be able to work tonight?"

"I don't go in to the station until after she goes to sleep. So, since Dad called to let me know he'll be back in the next hour or so, we should be fine."

"Good. Well, then, I'd best get going."

"I'm sorry we missed lunch. Or whatever."

"Another time," she suggested.

"Definitely," he agreed. "Wait just one minute." He held up a finger, then left the room and was back in seconds.

"She's asleep again," he said in a low voice.

"That's good. She needs her rest. Plus it gets you out of scrapbooking."

He leaned closer. His lips came so close to her ear she could feel his breath. "There is that."

Then he tangled a hand in her hair, sliding the other down her back, cupping her butt as his mouth covered hers and he kissed her deeply, thoroughly, letting loose the pent-up hunger as his tongue tangled with hers and he ground her against an impressive erection that couldn't entirely make up for the lost hot sex she'd so meticulously planned for at lunch.

The only problem was, as an echo of a whimper came from the bedroom, it would have to do for now.

Instead of immediately releasing her, he dragged his mouth along her jawline, down her throat, to where her pulse was beating like a jackhammer.

"I'm not done with you," he practically growled against her skin.

"I certainly hope not." When she was sure she could stand on her own, she lowered her hands, which had seemingly taken on a mind of their own and somehow become splayed across his bare back, beneath the shirt of the blue dress uniform he'd worn to Ollie's memorial service.

"Daddy," the voice plaintively called out again.

"I'd better go see what she needs."

"Absolutely."

He picked up the purse Annie had dropped on the floor during the heated kiss and handed it to her. Then they stood there for another long, aching moment, the air between them thick with passion and things not said.

Not wanting to keep him from his daughter any longer, she slipped the strap of her bag over her shoulder and said, "Have a good program," as she left the house.

"You going to call in?"

She shot him a flirty look over her shoulder. "Maybe."

"We can talk dirty during the commercials."

Okay, so maybe she wasn't as ready for all this as she'd begun to think, because she could feel the heat flooding into her face as she quickly glanced around, looking for any neighbors who might have overheard that, then escaped to her car.

A glance in the rearview mirror showed him still standing in the open doorway.

His words, specifically one significant word, came back to her as she drove to the shop.

Whatever.

She'd already set the scene for the *whatever*, having shaved her legs, slathered lotion on every part of her body, put on her hottest underwear, downloaded a must-have seduction playlist Kara had made up that both Maddy and Charity swore by, and with Maddy's help, planned a seduction lunch.

All three women had insisted she serve oysters as a first course, but not knowing whether Mac liked them raw and deciding there wasn't a man on the planet who wasn't a fan of bacon, she opted, at Maddy's suggestion, for smoked oysters wrapped in bacon. For the main course she'd intended to put together a pizza with the alder-smoked salmon, mushrooms, and thick white cheese sauce that Maddy had brought over. Dessert would be chocolate fondue with fruit.

As she'd planned the menu, Annie had realized once again how, although they'd shared so many things with each other, she didn't know the little everyday details that most dating couples learned early.

Which was something they were going to have to work on. Because it was crazy and just plain wrong that she knew more about Charlie Buchanan than she did about his grandson.

Unfortunately the lunch would have to wait. Along with the *whatever.*

"Best-laid plans," she murmured as she pulled into a parking space down the street from the store and tried to get her mind back into work mode.

42

Mac was going crazy thinking about that missed lunch. Not that he'd been all that hungry. Not for food, anyway. What he couldn't get out of his mind was the *whatever* part of the afternoon.

He'd been on the air for half an hour and Annie still hadn't called in. But he knew she was listening.

Time to make a move.

"You know that feeling, when you're climbing the walls, which isn't getting you anywhere but more and more frustrated?" he asked. "Well, Kenny Chesney sure as hell knows how it feels in this next one. For all the guys and gals out there lying all alone in a bed that's gettin' more and more cold, here's 'Come Over.'"

He didn't have to wait long.

"That's not fair," Annie complained when he picked up the line.

"Hey, climbing the walls sure as hell wasn't getting me anywhere. So, we've got four minutes and eight seconds. . . . What are you wearing?"

She laughed at that. "I am so not having phone sex with you."

"It was just a simple question to pass the time. Which is now down to less than four minutes," he reminded her. "Believe me, when we finally get together, sweetheart, I'm going to need a lot more than four minutes."

"When?" she asked. "What happened to *if*?"

"Is there any question?"

"No. There should be, but—"

"Annie." He loved saying her name. He'd also spent way too much time imagining her saying his while he drove her higher and higher.

No.

Make that *screaming* his.

"We've got complications," he allowed. "And messy personal histories. But like the song says, we don't have to fix each other."

He counted the time clicking away in his head as she considered that for a good ten seconds that seemed like a frigging hour.

"No," she decided. "We don't. As for what I'm wearing, since you left me feeling all turned on today, it just happens to be an itty-bitty babydoll nightgown." She paused to let him picture it. "I don't like to feel confined when I'm sleeping."

"What color?"

Five more seconds of torturous silence.

"Red," she said finally. "With black lace. And a red and black lace thong."

"Wouldn't want you to feel confined." Mac wondered if any deejay had ever been electrocuted by drooling into the microphone. "Too bad you're all alone," he said.

"I know." She sighed. "But the only man I want in my bed just happens to work nights."

"Maybe you need to find yourself a new guy."

"Or maybe he just needs to learn to multitask a little better," she suggested. "Not that he hasn't had extenuating circumstances, so I don't want to be too hard on him. . . .

"But like Kenny says in that song, it's hard to sleep in a cold, cold bed."

That did it. The thought of Annie Shepherd wearing something out of those Victoria's Secret catalogs, which were banned by some commands, but the guys would pass them around in Iraq and Afghanistan anyway, made Mac groan.

Two minutes.

"I'm sorry about screwing up lunch today," he said, wondering again how single fathers ever managed to juggle work, fatherhood, and a love life. And he even had his dad to help take care of Emma, which most guys—and women—didn't. With the divorce rate being what it was, and so many of those people having kids, it was a wonder people managed to carve out enough time to get horizontal together to keep the population growing.

"I'm sorry, too," she said. "But it isn't as if you blew me off."

"I really wish you hadn't used that particular word," he said.

She laughed. "Anticipation, they say, is a good thing."

"It's obvious you've never been stuck with a perpetual hard-on."

"Ah, there comes the dirty talk I'm risking having recorded for posterity," she said.

"The recorder's off."

"I certainly hope so. And, as it happens, it's your lucky night, because I'm handing out rain checks. For a limited, one-time offer."

"We both know one time isn't going to be nearly enough," he said.

She laughed at that. "You're running out of time. I'll see you on the Fourth."

Which was, damn, still two days away.

"And you have an injured daughter to be with and I have work to do during the day," she reminded him when he pointed that out.

Hell with that, Mac thought as he was left listening to dead air on the other end of the phone while Chesney finished up what had to be the ultimate booty call song.

As he queued up one of the Genarro's funeral home "man with the plot; man with the plan" commercials, Mac came up with a plan of his own.

A plan for Annie and him to get lucky together.

43

As long and occasionally unsettling as her day had been, Annie couldn't sleep. After Chesney's "Come Over" sexual invitation, Midnight Mac just kept playing more songs designed to leave his middle-of-the-night listeners hot and bothered. Or jumping each other.

She was seriously considering taking the edge off all by herself. But she resisted. Because although she had no idea when Mac was going to get a break from his responsibilities to Emma, especially now that the little girl had been hurt, and would obviously be more needy, Annie wanted to experience every bit of passion she knew he was going to bring to their lovemaking.

Sex, she thought, correcting herself. That was all this was about. But sometimes, she considered as the digital dial on her alarm clock clicked past two thirty in the morning, and Faith Hill and Tim McGraw were getting straight to the point, singing to each other about making love, sex was enough. Which had her wondering how the married couple ever actually managed to make love while living with three little girls on a bus.

At some point, during which Keith Urban had better

things to do on a rainy Sunday than making the bed, Annie finally dozed off, but was awakened soon after by her phone ringing. Groping for it in the dark, she came fully awake when she read the caller ID.

"I'm calling to give you fair warning that I'm tired of waiting," the all-too-familiar voice went an octave deeper than even his radio voice, melting every atom in her body.

"Okay." She hitched herself up in bed, already turned on and expecting more sexy phone talk. "So, what's your suggestion?"

"Open your front door."

"What?"

"I'm on your porch."

"You're kidding."

"I never, ever kid about sex. Look out your window."

She pushed back the bedding that she'd washed yesterday morning with this very man in mind and crossed the room to the window. He'd backed away from the door, out from beneath the roof so she could see from the dormer window. Just looking down at him, leaning against the railing in the spreading yellow glow of the porch light, caused her temperature to spike.

"Give me two minutes," she said.

"I'm really getting fed up with talking on a damn clock," he countered. "Make it one. Or I'm coming in."

Although she was certain he wouldn't actually break down her door if she didn't make it downstairs within his imposed time limit, and equally frustrated at not ever having enough time together, Annie grabbed a loudly protesting Pirate from the bed, tossed him into the guest room, shut the door, and hoped he wouldn't keep complaining but would settle down on the hand-made antique quilt that he seemed to enjoy ripping apart whenever she let him into that room.

Then she raced into the bathroom, brushed her teeth, ran a comb through the tangled curls that she'd barely managed to get to a mess slightly less wild than Medusa, raced down the stairs, twisted the lock, took a deep breath for calm, which didn't work, and opened the door.

"Hi," she said in a breathless, needy voice she didn't recognize.

"Hi yourself." With his eyes locked on hers, he pushed away from the railing and moved the few steps to close the gap between them. Again, it was only because she knew to look for it that she noticed the slight limp in his slow, determined, gunslinger's walk.

He'd gone into pure alpha male hunting mode and she was his prey. Thanks to the moves she'd learned in a self-defense class she'd taken when she first moved to D.C., Annie could've had any other man walking funny for a week.

But when her gaze drifted down to that bulge beneath the metal buttons of his jeans, an entirely different set of moves scorched through her mind and kept her standing exactly where she was.

Waiting.

Wanting.

He stopped, the tips of his black cross-trainers a whisper from her bare toes. His midnight-dark eyes made a long, slow perusal, from the top of her head to those toes, which Sally, who did nails down at Cut Loose, had painted a hot Charged-Up Cherry.

"I must look a mess," she said as his eyes returned to hers. She lifted a hand to her tangle of hair.

"I like it. You look soft. Warm. Approachable. And"—his gaze drifted down to her breasts—"definitely dangerous."

Oh, hell. Annie belatedly remembered the message written across the front of her cotton knit scrapbooker's nightshirt that she'd forgotten she was wearing: I RUN WITH SCISSORS. IT MAKES ME FEEL DANGEROUS.

"Okay." She folded her arms defensively across the nightshirt. "I lied. I wasn't really wearing a red baby-doll nightie and thong."

But the ridiculously expensive scraps of lace and silk that constituted the bra and matching panties she'd bought at Oh So Fancy to wear under the seduction lunch sundress had come close. Unfortunately, they were still in the top drawer of her lingerie chest.

"There goes the fantasy I've been having for the past four hours, imagining pulling that lacy thong off with my teeth. . . . You didn't lie about it being red, though."

"It's also not the least bit sexy," she said on a sigh, thinking of all the plans she'd made to turn this man inside out.

"Depends on the woman. Some don't need all the fancy trappings to be sexy as sin."

He didn't seem annoyed, or even disappointed that she wasn't dressed like a lingerie model. Instead, his lips quirked and laugh lines crinkled out from his eyes. "Don't worry." His hands settled at her waist. "It's not like you're going to be wearing it all that long."

That thought got an immediate response. As her nipples tightened beneath the silhouette of the running girl on her nightshirt, Mac's wickedly clever hands slid up her ribs, barely skimming the sides of her breasts.

"Are you cold?" As the fingers of his left hand brushed over her nipple, making it harder and even more sensitive, he smiled with blatant male satisfaction.

Part of her wanted to make him as crazy as he was making her. At the same time she had never felt as insecure in her life. Sex with Owen had been a paint-by-number exercise, and he'd never, ever ventured outside the lines.

As arousal stirred in her stomach, then lower, every

instinct Annie had told her that with Midnight Mac it would be anything but.

So, curious, excited, and yes, nervous about whether she'd be able to live up to his expectations, undoubtedly set by all the women he'd been with before her, Annie could only stand there.

Still waiting.

And, oh, God, still so wanting.

As if reading her mind, he smiled. It was slow and wicked, and it made her tremble with longing.

He cupped her breasts in his hands, his fingers rasping over them, until the soft, well-washed knit cotton between them suddenly seemed almost unbearably heavy. Annie wanted the nightshirt gone. She wanted to feel his touch, and his beautifully formed mouth, on her bare, hot skin.

She was shivering. Not from any night chill, but from need.

"You like that."

Until she'd met the man who had become her husband, Annie's sexual encounters had amounted to six weeks of being pressured into sex by the son of one of her foster parents when she'd been sixteen. Later, during her freshman year at the University of Portland, she'd foolishly tried to find self-esteem by having quick, totally unsatisfactory sex with guys too selfish to ever think about pleasing a partner. They'd taken what they wanted, what she'd eventually come to realize she was giving away too freely, only to leave her feeling worse about herself.

She'd accepted Owen's proposal partly because he didn't elicit any of those crazy sexual needs she'd suffered her first year out on her own.

But as she soon discovered, being stuffy in the bedroom didn't necessarily mean he was any more generous or less selfish than those callow college boys.

Owen had never talked while making love. He never complimented her, never asked what she did or didn't like. He did let her know by his actions and movements early in their relationship what he expected from her, and she, grateful to him for having married her, for giving her a chance to have an actual family of her own, honestly didn't believe that she deserved anything more, so she had willingly, *silently* obliged.

Those old lessons, she was discovering, died hard.

She swallowed. Then nodded.

"Tell me." He caught a nipple between his thumb and middle finger and tugged. "How about this?"

"Yes." The word escaped on a shuddering rush of breath.

"So far, so good."

His hands moved downward, down her ribs, continuing over her stomach, which she instinctively sucked in at his touch, then lower to cup her between her thighs, drawing a low, ragged moan.

Even as he explored her with his touch, he kept his eyes on hers. "I take it that's a yes."

Hanging on to her ebbing control, Annie nodded again. She was so turned on she didn't trust herself to speak.

His arched brow invited more. Oh, he was wicked. He knew what he was doing to her. But as much as her body was obviously his for the taking, he was insisting on hearing her say the words.

Annie drew in a breath. Then managed, through lips that had gone impossibly dry, to say, "You know it is."

"Good. Because after all this time thinking about all the things I want to do to you, I want to make sure I get it right."

"You know you are. But I'm not used to talking while doing . . . having . . . Well, you know. Sex."

"We'll deal with that later," he said. "Let's take it one step at a time. For now, what do you want?"

How was it that she could feel vulnerable, yet in control at the same time? Perhaps, she considered, because he didn't make any secret of the fact that he wanted her as much as she wanted him. That he found her as hot as she found him.

Which gave her the nerve to say what she'd been thinking for days.

"You. I want you."

"Far be it from me to deny you anything your sweet, sexy little heart desires." Before she could perceive his intention, he scooped her up, tossed her over his shoulder, and carried her into the house.

44

"I don't remember Rhett carrying Scarlett this way," she said from her upside-down position as he kicked the door shut, pausing only long enough to twist the lock.

"The guy didn't know what he was missing." Her nightshirt had slid down nearly to her waist, leaving her bottom bared to his touch. "I like this better."

Although it might not seem as romantic as Clark Gable carrying Vivien Leigh up that staircase, Annie, branded by his hand on her heated skin, decided she preferred this move, too.

"Where's the bedroom?"

"Upstairs. First door to the left."

He found it without any trouble, then set her back onto her feet beside the sleigh bed she'd found at Angie's Antiques and Collectibles. It had taken her weeks to sand the peeling white paint off it and to paint it a soft cream color as an accent to the sea blue walls. Although it was still more than an hour before dawn, she'd drifted off with the wooden blinds and window open, allowing light from the moon to stream in. The room seemed to grow smaller and smaller as he spent a long time looking down at her, as if seeking answers to some question he hadn't asked.

"Mac." She had never begged any man before. But at this moment, she would beg for him. "Please."

"Please what?" He bent his head and lowered his mouth to hers, nipping at her bottom lip. "Kiss you?"

"That's a start."

"Exactly. Just a start . . . Lift your arms."

His dark and dangerous tone possessed the power to fog her thoughts. When she did as he'd asked, he caught the hem of her very unsexy nightshirt and in one deft movement pulled it over her head and tossed it onto a nearby chair.

Leaving her standing completely naked, with the sea breeze from the open window whispering against her bare skin.

The night sky was atypically clear, free of clouds. Annie had never realized until now, when she felt as if she were standing in a spotlight, how very bright moonlight could be.

"The neighbors—"

"Live a very long way down your driveway and around the corner."

Which was true. One of the things she loved about her house was that except for the occasional sea kayaker paddling by, she had absolute privacy.

"I've been imagining you like this for days." The desire in his eyes echoed his words. "Since we first met at Still Waters."

"You certainly hid it well." Another first. She never pouted. But she did now.

He smiled, just a little, at her aggrieved tone. "I think I knew you were going to be dangerous."

"You were rude."

"Guilty. But maybe I can make that up to you." He

ran his hand from her shoulder to her thigh. "I'd never do anything to hurt you."

But he could, she realized suddenly. Her plan of living in the moment, of sex for sex's sake, of celebrating the now—or whatever trendy-modern-woman term she wanted to use for it—was backfiring.

She'd already begun to care. Too much. He could, without even meaning to, hurt her more than those thoughtless boys or Owen ever had.

His hands slid down her back, cupping her bare bottom, lifting her against him. He was hard and thick and the rough scrape of the denim against her bare skin had her wanting him inside her.

Now.

But before she could get the words out, he took her mouth in a kiss as hard as the body grinding against her. Her lips parted, inviting the thrusting invasion of his tongue, and as they pulled each other down onto the bed, she wanted to eat him up.

As he fed her slow, deep kisses, he touched her everywhere.

"Do you like it when I touch you here?" He cupped her breasts again, causing them to swell into his hands.

"Yes."

"And when I put my mouth on your beautiful breasts?"

He took first one, then the other, into his mouth, tugging, tasting, nipping at her nipples, causing a rushing pleasure just this side of pain.

"Oh, yes."

His hands and mouth continued their quest, taking the same path as earlier, but without the barrier of the cotton nightshirt. He licked the underside of her breasts, which she'd never realized could be such an erogenous zone, then down her stomach, causing her to arch her hips as his tongue dipped into her navel.

"You know what I was thinking about, all night at the station while playing those damn hot songs?" he asked, his words vibrating against her lower stomach like a tuning fork.

"What?" she managed, as she lifted her hips, wanting, needing, for him to touch her *there.*

"Touching you." His fingers skimmed lower, and yes, parted her *there.*

"Oh, God, yes." This time he didn't need to ask as pleasure and still more need tangled within her.

"And tasting you." With his hands spreading her thighs, he did exactly that, his tongue gliding over her center.

"Mac." Her hands felt inordinately heavy as they lifted from his back to tangle in his hair. She heard a ragged whimper, and belatedly realized it had broken free from her own parched lips. "Please. I need you." She was writhing beneath him. "Inside me."

"And you'll have me." She'd never known that any man could possess such patience. "But we're no longer on the clock, Annie my sweet." Oh, God, his teeth had replaced his tongue, having her on the verge of going off like a rocket. How did he know to do that? "And I'm not nearly done with you."

To prove his point, his mouth claimed her. *There.* Sucking, licking, nipping, devouring her, creating a pleasure so sharp, so acute, she could only plead, over and over, in a voice that sounded nothing like her own, for him to stop.

To never stop.

Until the pleasure grew too intense, and suddenly her entire world was spinning away, into that dark night sky, flinging her among the white-hot stars, where she scattered into a million little pieces of light.

Afterward, as she fell back to earth, Annie thought she might have gone blind. Perhaps she'd even fainted—because she couldn't understand how she'd ended up lying, chest to chest, against Mac as he held her close, his lips pressed against the top of her damp head.

"Okay." Her body was still suffering internal aftershocks. "If we didn't just have an earthquake, it's official."

"What?"

He smoothed the soaked strands of hair away from her face and touched his mouth to hers. In contrast to his earlier kisses, this one was as soft and gentle as dandelion fluff blowing on the wind.

"You're a sex god."

He laughed at that. A deep, rough sound she could feel rumbling up from his rock-hard chest.

"Hardly." His lips skimmed up her cheek as his hand moved down her back, his fingers tracing patterns that, amazingly, were getting her all hot and itchy again. "It's you."

She blinked to clear her vision and read the truth in his gaze. Truth and a very raw masculine hunger, which reminded her that while she'd been flying among the stars, she'd—damn—forgotten something elemental.

That it was only good sexual etiquette for the guy to get off, too.

"I think it's us." How else could she explain the chemistry that had sparked between them from the beginning? Or that he'd managed to do what no other man had ever done?

She slid her hands beneath his shirt. "But you're wearing way too many clothes."

45

Question, Mac thought, as he stood beside the bed, stripping off his clothes, risking endangering his junk with those damn metal buttons: *How many guys, in the history of mankind, ever got off talking about their relationship?*

He kicked off his shoes.

How about none?

Although his hormone-crazed body had tried to tune out his more rational mind, Mac knew, on some level, that Annie had a point about their situation being more complicated. Because any decision he made, for the next twelve years, would have to factor in his daughter.

Who obviously adored Annie Shepherd.

Which wasn't why he was here, in the woman's bedroom, stripped down to a pair of navy ribbed boxer briefs and on the verge of getting his brains screwed out.

He was here because whatever was happening to him—to his mind, his body, and yes, dammit, his heart, was beyond his power to stop.

While the topic definitely wasn't at the top of his hit parade of things to discuss, he and Annie were going to talk about where they were going. But right now, at this moment, looking down at her on those pretty flowered sheets, all naked and flushed and warm, all Mac could think about was how many times over the past days, and especially the nights, he had imagined her like this. Too many to count.

He wanted.

She wanted.

And as an early predawn light filtered into the bedroom, that was enough.

He'd never met a woman who managed to be both guarded and open at the same time. Although she was no virgin, there was something untouched about her, which was why, although he'd felt as if he was slowly killing himself, he'd forced himself to take his time, learning her secrets, teaching her the sensual pleasure of simply lying back and enjoying them.

Her body had been a banquet of sweet flesh, of hollows and curves, and he'd feasted, savoring every tasty inch.

But now it was her turn, and she proved to be a quick study as she moved over him, her breasts, then her lips carving a happy trail down his chest, then beyond, touching and tasting as he'd done to her.

She'd begun slowly, almost tentatively, learning his body as he'd learned hers, but as she picked up the pace, her hands and mouth streaking over him, Mac's mind fogged.

Needs battered away at him, and his hunger had claws.

Unable to hold back any longer, he reached out blindly and grabbed the condom he'd put on her bedside table. Although he hadn't fumbled with a condom since he'd had sex with Pam Wagner in the backseat the summer after his senior year of high school, not only had Annie managed to twist him inside out but she'd somehow turned all his fingers to thumbs as well, and finally, in desperation, he ripped the package open with his teeth.

"Oh, I like that," she said, saving him from complete humiliation by taking it from his hand. "Very caveman-like."

"I don't think cavemen had condoms," he managed as she took him in her hands.

"Probably not," she agreed as she rolled the latex down his length. "But without cable, I'll bet they spent a lot of time doing this."

With her hands on his chest and her eyes on his, she lowered herself onto him and began to move in a way that had him fearing he would blast off before they even got started.

"Give me a minute."

Her smile, in the pinkening light of dawn, was one of the sexiest things he'd ever seen. "I make you crazy."

"How about fucking insane?"

He cupped her hips, willing his body to slow down. To settle in. To make this last.

"We've already done sweet and slow," she said, leaning forward, brushing her breasts against his chest, her body tightening around him like a wet fist.

"What would you say to hard"—her hips began to rock—"and fast this time?"

That was all the invitation he needed. Holding her waist, he drove up into her. Hard and deep, so deep she gasped, but instead of pulling away, she met his pace, keeping up with him even as he rolled them over, arms and legs entwined.

Then, needing to regain some control, he caught her wrists, holding her arms above her head as he pistoned into her. Mindlessly. Recklessly.

"Look at me," he said on a deep, guttural growl. Yeah. Like a caveman.

She opened her eyes, which had fluttered shut, and met his gaze.

Then whimpered as he pulled halfway out, torturing them both.

"Now," he said.

"Oh, yes," she breathed. "Now."

He plunged into her, one long, strong stroke that had her weeping out his name even as what little was left of his mind exploded.

Empty, drained, and not sure he would ever be able to move again, Mac collapsed onto her, burying his lips against her throat.

"That was," he said—

"Wonderful," she said with a slow, satisfied sigh.

And, apparently as spent as he was, she immediately crashed into sleep.

Mac glanced at the clock's illuminated dial, calculating how much time he had before Emma woke up at home, needing her father.

Enough, he decided as he went into the adjoining bathroom and took care of the condom. Then he returned to bed, lying behind her, cuddled like spoons, and followed her, dropping like a stone into sleep.

He might not have been a warrior, but radio work had given Mac an internal clock in his head that told him when to wake up so as not to miss a shift. Even during those long-ago party days. His time on the FOBs had taught him to sleep quick.

Which he did, only to wake up to find Annie leaning on one elbow and looking down at him, a serious expression on her lovely face.

"How long have you been awake?"

"Only a few minutes." She smiled. "I was enjoying the view." He followed her gaze to his morning erection.

"It tends to do that," he said. "Even when I haven't been dreaming of the hot woman who managed to screw my brains out."

"I did, didn't I?" The smile reached those remarkable eyes, turning them to gleaming pewter. "It was mutual." She stretched lazily, like a cat, which had the rest of his body catching up to his penis. "Now, unfortunately, you have to get going."

He didn't need to glance at the clock to know that once again time was running out on them.

"Yeah. I'm sorry. I want to stay here, but—"

She touched a very un-Annie-like red fingertip to his lips. "I understand. I was just wondering if you had time for coffee." She skimmed a fingernail down the inside of his thigh, frowning a bit at the white scars left behind by shrapnel. "And maybe a shower." Her eyes drifted up to the part of his body he could've flown Old Glory from.

"It seems a shame to let that go to waste," she said, revealing the inner seductress that he'd suspected had been lurking inside her.

"Shelter Bay is nothing if not anti-waste," he agreed.

"And think of all the water we'll save."

"You've convinced me that it's our patriotic duty."

She was out of the bed, standing over him, all tousled and still glowing from multiple orgasms, looking like every guy's wet dream. "To save our country. And maybe even the planet."

Mac tried to remember the last time he'd felt this good. And decided he'd *never* felt this freaking good before.

"God bless America."

46

After a shower that was anything but quick, Mac was standing in Annie's tidy kitchen, drinking coffee before leaving. Which he didn't want to do. But he had no choice.

"Come to breakfast with me."

"You have to go home to your daughter. And I have to get to work. All the tourists will start arriving today for the Matchmaking Fair. If I'm taking the Fourth off, I need to be there to help Kim with sales."

"I get that. But we can eat at the house. With Dad and Emma. Then you can go to work and I can play Barbie, or tea party, or make a scrapbook or whatever little girls do when they know they've got their fathers wrapped around their little finger."

"Or their cracked wrist," Annie said with a smile. "And breakfast sounds wonderful. If you're sure your father won't mind."

"He'd love it."

"So would I." Even though she knew she was risking getting in over her head, Annie wanted to spend every minute she could with Mac. "Why don't you go ahead? I'll be over as soon as I feed my cat."

"See how much you've distracted me? I even forgot, when I came here last night, that you have a cat." He glanced around. "Where is it?"

"I put him in the guest bedroom when you first arrived because it takes him a while to warm up to people."

As if taking that comment as a test, he said, "I'd like to meet him."

"I'm not sure that's such a good idea."

"Annie." He leaned down and kissed her. He tasted of coffee and her minty, teeth-whitening, cavity-fighting toothpaste. "What I said about not liking cats? I didn't really mean it. I was just in a lousy mood."

"Okay. But don't say I didn't warn you." She went and fetched Pirate, carrying him downstairs.

The minute the cat spotted the interloper, he jumped out of her arms, hit the floor, and bristled his fur.

"Hey, Pirate." Mac bent down, his hand extended to pat the tiger cat.

"Oh, I wouldn't—"

Too late. Annie watched as Pirate moved first. Hissing, he took a swipe with his paw, his razor-sharp nails fully extended.

"Okay," Mac said, as they both watched the thin red line appear on the back of his hand.

"Oh, my God, I'm sorry." Annie grabbed a paper towel and began squirting antiseptic soap on it.

Meanwhile, the demon cat stared Mac down with yellow eyes, then, apparently satisfied that he'd made his point, claimed his turf, or whatever went through crazed feline minds, sauntered over to a sunbeam, plopped his big butt down, and began washing his huge, deadly paws.

"Don't worry about it," he said, as Annie dabbed madly at the wound. "He should probably get extra kibble, for watchcat duty."

"He's really quite docile," she said. "Well, maybe that's not the right word, exactly. He's admittedly territorial. I think because he was a stray for so long, he's decided that he's not going to risk anyone throwing him back out onto the street. But he does get used to people. In his way."

She hadn't gotten scratched in, what? A month? Six weeks?

"It's no big deal."

"He likes children," she said. "I've had card-making parties here at the house and he's always been a perfect gentleman."

Mac looked skeptical. Then he glanced over at Pirate, who hissed a warning, which didn't exactly help his cause.

"I'd better get going."

Oh, great. Her herculean grumpy cat was chasing off her boyfriend. And wasn't that just the perfect way to cap off a perfect night?

He kissed her again, quick this time, but it still made her toes curl.

"I'll tell Emma you're coming. You'll make her day."

This time it was Annie who stood in the doorway, watching as *he* drove away. Then she went back into the kitchen and glared at Pirate, who merely stared back with a total lack of interest.

"You were a very bad boy," she chided, even as she got out the can of gourmet salmon.

His only response was a big yawn to show her how unimpressed he was with her annoyance. Then, with his tail up like a big gray-striped victory flag, he strolled over to the counter and began noisily demanding his meal.

"Ingrate," she muttered, even as her heart went out

to him, remembering how, until Charity had saved him, he'd been forced to fight seagulls for food on the beach.

He'd been a stray. Just like her. And also like her, he came with baggage. Which, she thought, as she watched him attack the bowl of food, made them two of a kind.

47

They ended up having breakfast in Emma's bedroom, where she held court, eating her scrambled eggs and drinking her milk from, unsurprisingly, a Disney Princess plate and glass set.

Mac's father had added smoked salmon and chives to the adults' eggs, which had Annie thinking about that smoked salmon pizza she'd been planning to serve Mac for his seduction lunch.

Not that he'd needed any seduction. And he'd certainly not needed any oysters. She realized she was smiling to herself when Mac caught her eye and winked.

It was too, too easy for him to affect her. He could make her hot with a simple look. Then again, she thought, as she slowly licked a bit of the cream cheese off her English muffin and watched the flare of heat in his gaze, she could do the same thing to him.

And wasn't that amazing?

After complimenting Emma on the two scrapbook pages she'd completed with Mac and Boyd's help, including a carefully hand-printed accounting of the drama she'd been through since the wrist she'd broken wasn't on her good hand, Annie promised to see her on the Fourth and left.

"So, I guess you'll be working all during the Matchmaking Fair," he said as he opened her car door for her.

"It should be a busy day. The oyster-shucking contest is right down Harborview at the pier. Which is within walking distance of us."

"Nothing says romance like putting on rubber gloves and shucking a mess of oysters," he said.

"Still, with a hundred-dollar prize, they've gotten a lot of contestants."

"You know there's a dance," he said as she slid into the driver's seat.

"We have a poster in the window." She buckled her seat belt.

"So, want to go?"

"I hadn't even thought about it."

Which was true. The last dance she'd attended had been at the tony Belle Haven Country Club in Alexandria, where she'd been required to smile like a Stepford wife while Owen deftly worked the room like an old-time evangelical preacher at a tent revival.

"Don't you have to work?"

"I'm taking the weekend off. Cody, the morning drive-time guy, is getting married and they're saving up to buy a house, so he jumped at the chance to get the extra hours by taking my shift for the next three nights."

"We have three nights? *All* night? Together?"

"Well, unless you get tired of me or your cat kills me first, yeah. . . . So, you want to go to the red, white, and blue prom with me?"

"Since I've never been to a prom, how could I possibly turn that invitation down?"

"Okay, I didn't do the prom thing in high school, either. I was pretty much a nerd and it took until after

I graduated for the rest of me to grow up to my radio voice. But how could you have never been to a prom? What, were the guys at your school blind? Or just terminally stupid?"

"Schools. And let's just say I was choosy." She smiled. "And I choose you."

"Handy," he said, ducking into the car to give her another of those quick, lethal kisses that could set her head to spinning. "Since I choose you back."

"I've got to go shopping at lunch today," Annie told Kim as they opened up the shop. "I promise to be quick. Do you think you'll be able to handle things?"

"The oyster shucking isn't until noon, so that should be fine. . . . So, how was he?"

"How was who?"

"Midnight Mac."

"I assume he's fine," Annie said, busying herself with straightening a stack of paper printed with candy hearts, just in case someone did get lucky during the fair and wanted to memorialize the event.

"Just fine?"

Annie sighed and turned back toward her. "What are people saying?"

"Only that he was seen driving back to town from your house this morning. And that your car was parked outside his grandfather's house a little bit later. And there's no point in trying to lie your way out of it because one, you're a terrible liar, two, you're glowing like you really got some action last night, and three, to anyone who knows what they're looking for, you've got a pink beard scrape down the side of your neck." Kim grinned wickedly. "And, I suspect, in a few other more interesting places."

Annie thought she was saved from answering when her phone rang. Until she noticed the caller ID.

It was Sedona, calling to make a lunch date. "If you're willing to have a quick takeout from one of the festival food booths, because I have a dress to buy. Yes, for the prom . . . I mean the dance.

"Yes, with Mac, and now, as much as you know I'd love to share all the intimate details, I've got customers."

She turned off the phone.

"Can we just get to work?" she asked, turning the sign on the front door to OPEN with more force than necessary.

Kim saluted. "Aye, aye, Captain Bligh."

48

Sedona, organized as always, had thought to call ahead to the Dancing Deer Two, so when she and Annie arrived, Doris and Dottie, the elderly twin sisters who owned the boutique, already had a selection of dresses pulled for Annie to try on.

Two minutes after their arrival, Charity and Maddy showed up. Followed by Kara, who, from her uniform and the gun and handcuffs worn on her hip, was technically on duty.

"What, does Sedona have everyone in town on speed dial?" Annie asked.

"No way are we going to miss your first date," Kara said. "Although I was engaged to Jared in high school, since he was at boot camp, he asked Sax to take me to the prom. That was the day I'd discovered I was pregnant. I wanted to stay home, but after I cried all over Sax, he talked me into going and I actually had a good time." Her eyes turned reminiscent. "That was the first time he kissed me."

"To cheer her up," Maddy said. "They weren't the sex bunnies they are now."

Instead of denying it, Kara merely laughed, giving credence to Maddy's teasing accusation.

"With your coloring, I'd go for winter tones," Doris, who herself preferred muted earth tones, suggested, getting right down to business.

"Oh, sister," the pleasantly plump Dottie, who tended toward cheerful pastel shades, complained. "That doesn't exactly say summer."

"There's a reason they call it basic black, sister," Doris pointed out, a bit stiffly, Annie thought.

Which had her mind returning to the dozen black designer evening gowns she'd donated to Goodwill when she'd left the Fairfax mansion where Owen was now living with wife number four. Who, being a blond size double-naught, couldn't have worn them anyway.

"You know, dear," Dottie said, "I was thinking of that red sundress you bought a while back. That looked lovely with your dark hair and pale coloring."

"Yes, it did," Sedona agreed.

"It was one of Dottie's better choices." Even Doris agreed with that opinion.

Annie thought about the way Mac had not only noticed the stoplight-red dress, but commented on it. Saying he'd wanted to stop and bite her thigh.

"Do you have anything like that? But a bit more formal?"

"I pulled it from the rack the instant Sedona called," Dottie said. "Let me run and get it."

She was back in a moment with a scarlet silk chiffon gown. Simply cut, strapless, with a skirt that flowed in a straight, fluid column, it was, Annie thought, as she tried it on in the dressing room, perfect. Except for one thing.

"That side slit's awfully high," she pointed out when she showed it to the others.

"Like the guy hasn't seen a lot more," Sedona said dryly. "It's a showstopper."

"Agreed," Maddy said. "You've got to get it. It's got your name written all over it."

"And I've got the perfect jewelry for it." Charity reached into her bag and pulled out a black velvet case. "My mother, God love her, gave it to me before she took off on that around-the-world cruise with my latest, and seemingly forever-after, stepfather. Apparently she's simplifying her life, seeming to forget that I'd have nowhere to possibly wear such a necklace in this town."

Opening the case, Annie drew in a sharp breath as she looked down at the diamond necklace that must have cost nearly as much as her house.

"Oh, I couldn't."

"Oh, you must," both Doris and Dottie said at the same time.

"It's perfect," Dottie said on a sigh. "You'll look like a fairy princess."

"And it would also go well with basic black," Doris said with her typical practicality. "Although I do have to agree with my sister that red is a more patriotic color for this particular holiday."

"My mother got it from one of her husbands," Charity said. "Number five, a self-proclaimed Russian count. So, it's not as if there's any sentimental value attached to it. And besides, as Mom found out when she went to sell it to some estate jeweler, those aren't really diamonds, just very good CZs. So, essentially, they're as phony as the guy's title. But they are admittedly gorgeous.

"Turn around," she said. "And let me fasten it on you so you can see."

Lifting her hair, Annie let Charity fasten the necklace at the nape of her neck. The tiers of faux diamonds cascaded down like falling rain. Moving in the political circles she had, Annie had seen some serious bling. But nothing that began to equal this.

"I can't," she said weakly, feeling her resolve dissolve like a sand castle at high tide as she studied herself in the mirror. The sane, new, self-made Annie reminded herself that she'd left the life of sparkly jewelry and formal designer gowns far behind her. These days she tended toward sundresses and jeans, and if she did wear jewelry, it was usually Claire Templeton's simple but lovely sea glass work that the sisters sold here in the store.

"This isn't the same as it was back east," Sedona said. She might not be psychic like her hippie mother supposedly was, but she was very good at sensing what her friends were thinking.

"You're going to be among friends, people who'll be thrilled to see you looking so happy. And while I count myself fortunate never to have met your ex, from what you've shared, Mac Culhane is nothing like him."

"No," Annie agreed. "He's the polar opposite." In every way.

"Consider it your coming-out party," Maddy suggested.

"Coming out of your shell," Charity added. "Maddy and I have been there, done the breakup thing, though I was a runaway bride who escaped on my wedding day, so I didn't have to live through a messy divorce. But we know of what we speak. You *need* this, Annie."

"You deserve it," Maddy said.

"A special moment to remember." Kara pressed her case.

"And," Charity said, "believe me, there's a lot to be said for watching a grown man swallow his tongue."

Even Doris laughed at that idea.

"I give up." Caving, as she always seemed to do

where Mac Culhane was involved, Annie handed over her credit card, thinking she could always live on cereal and cottage cheese for the next month to pay for the dress. Along with the strappy satin sandals and the ridiculously scanty underwear Dottie convinced her she had to have to go with it.

49

Feeling like the high school radio club nerd he'd once been, picking up the head cheerleader for the prom, Mac climbed the porch of Annie's house and rang the bell.

Then felt as if he'd been hit in the solar plexus with a baseball bat when she opened the door.

"She was right," he said.

She tilted her head. She'd piled all those curls up in some complex, yet appealingly messy style that had them looking as if they would come tumbling free if he just pulled out a few of those sparkly pins.

"Who?"

"Kara."

"You've talked with Kara?"

"Yeah. At Bon Temps. She was in there when I stopped by to ask Sax what kind of flowers to get you."

"You got me flowers?" It could have been a trick of the porch light, but he thought he saw her eyes glisten a bit at that idea.

"Yeah. Damn. I left them in the car." He jerked his head toward his dad's Prius, which he'd borrowed so she wouldn't have to go to the dance all glammed up in a pickup truck. "I'll be right back."

"That's not—"

He was back down the steps, reaching into the backseat before she could finish what she'd intended to say. "You may fool everyone else into thinking you're Midnight Mac," he muttered to himself as he retrieved the clear plastic florist's box. "But once a nerd, always a nerd."

"Here," he said as he returned to the door.

"Oh." She breathed out a soft, pleased breath that sent a cool wave of relief rushing over him. "You bought me Gardenias."

"Sax said they're traditional, and I guess he'd know. Seeing how he took Kara to their prom."

"I heard about that. So what did Kara say?"

"That I'd swallow my tongue when I saw you." He drank in the sight of her, looking like a red flame with a mile-long stretch of bare leg revealed by that slit in the side. "Which is true. But while I'm being real honest here, I've got to admit that I'm no doctor, but I think every bit of blood in my head has just flowed south."

She glanced down. Tilted her head again. And laughed.

"If you think you're going to get me out of this dress—"

"Oh, I most definitely plan to," he assured her. "After I show off my girl to every guy in Shelter Bay. And then, when I get you home, I'm going to make slow love to you. All night long. While you're wearing nothing but that necklace. And those do-me red shoes."

"Well, you did bring me flowers," she said, opening the box and holding it out to him to fasten them onto her wrist.

"A lot of the boxes the florist was making up were carnations. With a few roses," he said. "But I told him I needed the gardenias. Not just because Sax says they're traditional. But because they remind me of your skin."

"Okay." She sighed, which had her breasts rising in an intriguing way above that scarlet-as-sin strapless neckline. Then, dammit all to pieces, he watched her take a shawl thing down from a hook by the front door and wrap it around her shoulders, across the front of the mouthwateringly hot dress. "That just earned you the necklace-and-stiletto sex thing."

"How long does this dance last?" he said as they drove into town.

"The way I'm feeling right now," she admitted, "I doubt we'll be staying around for the after-prom breakfast."

He reached across the console and put his hand on her thigh, bared by the slit, which was conveniently on the left side of the dress.

"Thank God."

50

Annie had never been part of the popular crowd in any of the many schools she'd attended. Nor had she felt as if she fit in with any particular group during her college days.

After that humiliating freshman year, she'd settled down and applied herself to her studies, waitressing at a local coffee shop and working part-time at a bookstore to help pay her bills and student loans.

But as soon as she and Mac walked into the gym of Shelter Bay High School, which had been decorated for the Matchmaking Fair dance with lots of sparkly hearts, red, pink, and white balloons, and pink crepe paper, she was greeted by the many people that she'd become friends with since moving to Shelter Bay.

Sax and Kara were there, Kara looking nothing at all like a cop in a white Grecian-style gown. They were seated at a table with Charity and her photographer husband, Gabe, Maddy and Lucas, and Cole and Kelli Douchett, who was showing a faint baby bump beneath her pink dress.

Annie remembered that the youngest Douchett brother, J.T., who taught history at Coastal Community

College, was spending the summer in Ireland with his Irish movie star/screenwriter bride.

"We saved you guys a spot," Kara said after waving them over. "And, wow, I could spot that dress the second you walked in," she told Annie.

"Along with every guy in the place," Mac said, as he held one of the two remaining chairs out for her. Once she was seated, he took the chair next to her and put his arm around her bare shoulder.

"Good idea," Lucas said. "Claim her now before anybody else gets ideas."

"*She* just happens to be sitting right here," Maddy told her husband. "Meaning *she* can hear you."

He shrugged. Grinned. "Just saying . . ."

They chatted for a while, easily, as friends do.

"I miss Phoebe and Ethan," Kara said.

"Phoebe said they couldn't get a sitter," Maddy said dryly.

"More like they didn't want to come in from the farm," Charity replied.

"Not that much of a surprise," Kara said. "Phoebe's been through a lot, what with escaping that horrible husband, even after she and Ethan found each other. I think they just want to enjoy the family they both fought so hard for."

"Agreed," Maddy said.

The thought of everything Phoebe and Ethan Concannon had been through to achieve their happy endings had Annie wondering if, just maybe, she and Mac could end up the same way. After all, the reason the mayor had come up with the idea of the Matchmaking Fair was that it was rumored there must be something in the water in Shelter Bay that had so many people falling in love.

As she was falling in love with Mac, despite the little voice of doubt reminding her that unlike those fairy tales Emma loved, all the other times in her life when she'd wished for her own happily-ever-after, it had remained elusive.

"There they go again," Cole said, drawing Annie out of her introspection.

The others followed his gaze to the dance floor, where his and Sax's parents were slow-dancing cheek to cheek, plastered together like a pair of teenagers.

"That used to embarrass the hell out of us kids," Cole said.

"Now I just want to *be* them," Sax said.

"Don't worry, darling." Kara took his hand and stood up. "I don't think that's going to be a problem."

"I hope we're still that hot for each other when we're parents," Kelli said on a sigh as they watched Sax and Kara sway together, in perfect rhythm, as they'd always seemed to be. Even, apparently, Annie thought, back when Kara couldn't, or wouldn't see it.

"Believe me," Cole assured her, "that's not going to be a problem. Not even when we're grandparents."

And speaking of grandparents, Adèle Douchett and her husband, Bernard, were dancing as well. She looked younger than her seventy-some years in a flowing royal blue gown that swirled around her ankles when he twirled her. It crossed Annie's mind that were it not for Adèle's persuading her to volunteer at Still Waters, she might never have met Mac. And what a loss that would have been!

"They look so happy," she murmured.

"Sax said they've had some rough times the past couple years," Mac said. "With her fall down the stairs causing that dementia. But I guess she's nearly over that."

"She was tested two weeks ago," Annie confirmed. "And the doctor said her scores were now higher than a woman ten years younger. It's amazing how her brain was able to create new pathways with time and therapy."

"If only that would work for Gramps."

"You never know." She took Mac's hand in both of hers. "If it weren't for his tendency to wander and leave the stove on, he could still be on home care. It's so early yet—there's still time for a cure. Or at least more drugs to slow the progress."

"True. But I don't want to think about problems tonight," Mac said decisively. Pushing his chair back from the table, he held out a hand. "Dance with me?"

She smiled and put her hand in his much larger one. "I thought you'd never ask."

One of the first things Owen had done, when they'd started dating, was to enroll Annie in a ballroom-dancing class. Dancing, like everything else he'd done, was formal, stiff, and boring.

Dancing with Midnight Mac, she quickly discovered, was like making love standing up.

The intimate, even possessive way he held her, which kept any other would-be partner from even thinking of cutting in, caused that familiar heat to flash through her.

"Put your arms around my neck," he said, his mouth against her ear. "This isn't some cotillion where we both wear white gloves and behave like extras in a period movie."

She laughed at that. "I did that," she admitted.

He drew his head back. "You were in a movie?"

"No." Wouldn't that have shocked everyone? "I wore white gloves."

"Seriously?"

"Seriously. Long ones to just above my elbows."

"Well, that's just dumb. How could a guy do this?"

Taking hold of her wrist, he lifted her bare hand to his mouth and kissed it, right in the center of her palm, which she'd never before realized was directly connected to that dampening place between her legs.

"Or this?" Seemingly unaware that they were in the center of the dance floor, he skimmed his lips up to the crook of her elbow, causing her pulse to leap.

"I think if anyone had done that, they wouldn't have been invited back."

"Lucky you to escape," he decided as he released her hand, allowing her to lift her arms around his neck as he nuzzled her neck.

"Lucky me," she agreed wholeheartedly, as red lights swirled around them and the not-bad Barry White wannabe declared a woman to be his first, his last, his everything.

"You are, you know," Mac said.

"Lucky?" She leaned tighter against him, swaying to what she'd always considered one of the most romantic songs ever. Which was why it had been added to her luncheon seduction playlist.

"*I'm* the lucky one." As he kissed her, lightly, tenderly, he slid his leg into the slit of the dress and pressed it between hers.

"I knew this dress was a mistake," she said as his intimate touch caused embers to flare to life within her.

"That's a matter of opinion." When he lifted his knee, ever so slightly, as other couples moved around them, Annie was afraid she was going to come right there on the dance floor.

"You're my everything, Sandy from Shelter Bay."

Even as her heart felt as if it were about to float up with those red, white, and pink balloons on the crepe-paper-draped ceiling, Annie feared it was all happening too fast. Too soon.

"You don't know me," she said, realizing she was going to have to share her personal failure with him.

"I know all I need to know." He lowered his head

and as his lips brushed hers, he said, "I also know that I want, no, make that *need*, to be inside you."

And wasn't that what she wanted?

She would have to tell him. But not tonight, she thought, as she belatedly realized people were returning to the tables during the band's break. Tonight was created for romance. Tonight she was Cinderella. With red-hot-come-and-take-me-big-boy stilettos instead of those silly glass slippers.

"The music's stopped," she said.

"Now, see, that's where you're wrong." He skimmed the back of his hand down her face. "It's just beginning."

51

Annie stopped into the ladies' room for a moment when Mac went to retrieve her shawl, and although he knew some women could take forever in there, especially when they were holding a summit, as she, Sedona, and Maddy had at the restaurant, she surprised him by being in and out in a flash.

"Quick," he said.

"You're not the only one in a hurry." The proof of that was in her low, husky-as-hell voice that reminded Mac of Kathleen Turner in *Body Heat*. Which, in turn, cranked up the thermostat on his own body temperature.

The fog had rolled in from the sea while they'd been indoors, making it seem as if they were engulfed in a cool white cloud as they walked back to where Mac had parked the Prius.

"Are you cold?" he asked as her heels clicked on the pavement, bringing up that fantasy he intended to live out as soon as he got her back to her house.

"Actually, I think I'm burning up," she said.

"I know the feeling."

"It's a good thing you remembered where we parked,"

she said. "Because I can't see more than a few inches in front of me."

"We've got good fog lights," he said, in case she was concerned about getting back to Castaway Cove in such low visibility.

"I'm not worried. I was just thinking of something."

"Want to share?"

"Absolutely." He could hear the smile in her voice as he clicked the remote to open the front doors. "As soon as we get in the car."

He was treated to a weakening flash of long bare leg as she slid into the passenger seat.

When he joined her in the car, she caught his hand before he could buckle his seat belt.

"Wait." She reached across the console and pressed her hand against the front of the single pair of dress slacks he still owned. "Don't move."

The sound of his zipper lowering in the still of the night was the sexiest thing Mac had ever heard. Then, sweet Jesus, she freed his erection, which was at Defcon One maximum readiness.

"I don't think I could move if I wanted to." Which he so didn't.

"That's the plan."

Proving to be full of one surprise after another, she climbed over the console and straddled him and, without a second's tease or hesitation, lowered herself fully, hot flesh against hot flesh, onto him.

"Don't tell me you've spent the night going commando," he managed, while his throbbing penis expanded to fill that warm, wet, happy place and she reached behind her back and unzipped the dress. Which fell to her waist, giving his mouth full access to soft, perfumed female flesh.

"Of course not." She brushed her mouth against his

and bit his bottom lip. "That's what I was doing in the restroom. My panties are now in my bag."

That she'd planned this only made him hotter.

"I've got to warn you," he said, as she began moving against him in a way that would probably blow the top of any guy's head off, "this isn't going to last long."

"Oh, I hope not," she said, as she began to ride him, hard and fast.

With each slap of her slick, damp flesh, his hunger soared. One. Two. Three . . . He lost count, but didn't think either of them had made it to ten when she came, violently, setting off his own explosive climax.

Since it was too late for protection, and the fog was surrounding the car as thickly as if it had been wrapped in cotton batting, he stayed inside her. Right where, he thought, still dazed as hell, he belonged. She'd slumped forward, her head resting on his shoulder.

Mac ran a hand down her bare back. "If I'd known you had that in mind, I would have blown it right there on the dance floor and forced Kara to arrest me for indecent exposure," he said.

"It was an impulse," she said. "Did you enjoy it?"

"What do you think?"

She shimmied a bit against him, causing another sharp twinge of hot need. He was turning into an addict, Mac realized. And luscious, tasty, very hot Annie Shepherd was his drug of choice.

"I think we've now had the entire prom experience," she said on a light laugh. "Because I'll bet we're not the first couple to have sex in his dad's car in this parking lot during a dance."

"Probably not," he agreed. Which, for a fleeting moment, had him wondering again about the possibility of locking Emma into a chastity belt as soon as she reached her teens.

Then, because he was trying to be a grown-up, he

said, "I hate to bring up practicalities at a time like this, but we didn't use anything."

"I know." She sighed, as if he'd brought her crashing back to reality.

Way to go, Culhane, he thought as she reached behind her and zipped the dress again. He felt a literal ache of loss when she returned to her own black leather bucket seat. "But you don't have to worry. I'm not going to get pregnant. And you said you hadn't had sex since you left the the service."

"I haven't."

"So you would've been tested in your separation physical." She fastened her seat belt. "And I had a test myself when I discovered Owen had been cheating on me. So there's nothing to worry about."

"Yeah. There is."

"Oh?" She glanced over at him.

He reached into the pocket of his jacket, which he hadn't had time to take off. "Whether this is going to be enough for the rest of the night."

The string of condom wrappers was as long as a kite tail.

Her merry laugh sounded like sunshine in the fogged-in car. "We'll just have to try to practice restraint."

"Yeah." He clicked his seat belt, and pressed the ignition. "Good luck with that."

52

They might have three nights together, but that didn't mean that Annie didn't still have to go to work and that Mac didn't want to be there when Emma woke up.

So as much as Annie would have loved to stay in bed all day the morning after the dance, they were back in the kitchen, drinking coffee. He was dressed in the jeans and T-shirt he'd brought over, she was wearing her red sundress again, wanting to keep every memory of last night's dance alive as long as she could.

"What did you mean?" he asked. "Last night in the car when you said I didn't have to worry about you getting pregnant."

"Exactly that." Having known this was coming, she'd also decided, while they'd been driving each other crazy in the shower that morning, that the time had come to tell him about the real reason for the failure of her marriage.

So, haltingly at first, because it was much more difficult to tell someone she'd been so intimate with than to tell a girlfriend, she related the story of her marriage. Of her too high expectations, of how she'd pushed her husband into the arms of another woman.

"He should have been honest with you from the beginning." Mac was not going to let her take the blame. "If he'd told you from the start that he had no intention of having children, then it wouldn't have even gotten to the point of IVF treatments or adoption."

"Maybe he tried. And I just didn't listen."

"Okay. Let's try something. . . . Stand up."

Curious, she did as instructed. He stood up, too, face-to-face, his hands on her shoulders. "Annie. I know it's soon to talk about this. But you've gotten under my skin. In my blood. And my heart. Everyone in my family cares for you as much as I do. I'm pretty sure I'm falling in love with you. So, here's the deal. . . .

"I don't care if you can have a child nor not. What happened to you was a tragedy. Especially given that you always wanted to be a mother. But there are other ways to get to the prize. If you want to try to do it with in vitro, that would be okay with me. If you want a surrogate, hey, that's okay, too. Or adoption would be cool. Your experience is proof that there are lots of kids out there in need of a good home."

"That's what I told Owen."

"Forget Owen. He's an idiot douche. He's in the past and we're not looking back. And there's another thing. You want a child. I *have* a child." He smiled down at her. "See how easy that is?"

Despite the seriousness of their situation, she almost smiled back. But even with easygoing Mac Culhane, it couldn't be *that* easy.

"That's what Sedona said."

"She's a helluva smart woman. You should listen to her."

"But what if you want another child and none of those other things work out for one reason or another?"

"Do you always plan for the worst?"

"I think I do," she admitted.

"That's one of the saddest things I've ever heard."

"No. It's only practical. Everyone's always big on going with the flow. Well, it seems to me it's easier if you know what might be lurking around the bend."

"Me." He took her hand in his and brushed a kiss against her knuckles. "I'm what's waiting around the bend. And, hey, not only am I an only child, but I was kind of adopted, since my dad adopted me after my birth father died. And look how good I turned out."

"Another thing Sedona said. Maybe you two ought to be together."

"I like her. She's pretty, friendly, smells like vanilla all the time, and is smart as a whip. But she's not you." He held her close, this time not to arouse but to comfort. "She's not the sweet, sexy, also very smart, not to mention hot woman I'm falling in love with."

"You said you *thought* you were." She couldn't say the words. Not out loud. It was as if her saying them might ruin everything.

"I lied. I *know* I am. Hell, I've already fallen for you. I just didn't want to scare you off before I could convince you what a dynamite catch I am."

"I already know that." She wanted to say the same thing back to him. But for some reason, she was tongue-tied.

She'd decided, after leaving Owen, that she was probably destined to spend her life alone. Which didn't mean she'd be lonely. Her life would be—and was—full. It would have meaning. She'd have friends. She just wouldn't have a husband. Or children.

That had been her plan. Carefully conceived during her long drive across the country. Logical, she'd assured herself, as she'd crossed the Rocky Mountains. To a fault.

But she hadn't prepared for Midnight Mac.

And she definitely hadn't prepared for love.

Although she trusted him, she couldn't quite ignore what a lifetime of experience had taught her.

"Think on it," he said easily. "Meanwhile, want to have dinner over at the house tonight? Dad grills a mean burger."

"Why don't you and Emma come over here?" she heard herself saying. "I'll toss together something after work."

"Seriously? You'd cook for us? Like homemade food not from the microwave?"

"Of course." How hard could it be? Other women did it all the time. "What's Emma's favorite meal?"

"That's easy. Mac and cheese."

Relieved, she gave him her best smile. "Piece of cake."

She hoped.

53

Annie was standing in the aisle of the market, holding the familiar blue box in her hand, amazed there were so many choices to the staple she'd grown up eating, when Maddy suddenly turned the corner and came to an abrupt stop.

"What the hell are you doing?"

"What does it look like? I'm shopping."

"For what? A chemistry experiment?"

"As it happens, I'm cooking dinner for Mac and Emma tonight."

"Not with that, you're not." Maddy snatched the box from Annie's hand and put it back on the shelf.

"I realize you're a famous gourmet Culinary Institute of America–trained chef," Annie said, taking the box down again and putting it into her cart. "But Emma is six years old. She doesn't like oysters with bacon, or smoked salmon pizza, or truffle oil—"

"Truffle oil's become dreadfully overdone," Maddy countered. A bit huffily, Annie thought. "I only use it on the very rare occasion."

"Fine. My point, and I do have one, is that six-year-old girls like macaroni and cheese."

"*Everyone* likes mac and cheese. Especially if it's done right. Which you're going to do." She took the box from the cart and put it back on the shelf again.

Then she took her cell phone out of her bag and dialed a number. "We've got a 911 situation," she said. "Annie's cooking for Mac and Emma. . . . Yeah. That's pretty much what I thought."

"I'm not that bad," Annie complained. "I'm merely a novice home chef. Not a professional."

"You're a home defroster and microwaver," Maddy corrected, then turned her attention back to her conversation. "You have to save her, and that poor child, by e-mailing me the ingredients for your chocolate lava cake. Then e-mail the instructions to Annie. . . . Great. Thanks." She ended the call.

"While she's getting your dessert ingredients to me, let's start shopping."

For the next ten minutes she bossed Annie around the store like a drill sergeant ordering an enlistee through boot camp. Though, having tasted Maddy's lobster mac and cheese, Annie wasn't exactly complaining.

"This is Gruyère," she said, picking up a block of cheese. "It's from Switzerland. It's sweet but slightly salty, and really nicely creamy and nutty when it's young. As this is. It becomes earthy and more complex when it ages, but for Emma's palate, this will be perfect.

"It's also one of the best melting cheeses. I use it in the restaurant's mac and cheese, and to top my French onion soup and in what was called *croque-monsieur* on the menu when I was cooking in New York City, but is basically a grilled ham and cheese sandwich.

"And you need some extra-sharp Cheddar to balance it out."

By the time Sedona had e-mailed the ingredients for

what Maddy assured her was a cake even a six-year-old could make—which wasn't the most complimentary thing she could have said, Annie thought—she'd filled her cart with ingredients, including a variety of spices that Maddy assured her Emma wouldn't resist.

"On your way home, stop at Farraday's. They just got some fresh lobster flown in from Maine. They also had some good slipper lobster. Just tell them what you're doing and they'll sell you what you need."

"I am *not* murdering lobster. Especially for a six-year-old girl who won't even appreciate it."

Maddy rolled her eyes. "The lobster's for the adult version. And they'll take care of that for you and sell you the meat out of the shell."

"I'm making two dishes?"

"Let me throw that question back at you. Is Midnight Mac worth a little extra work?"

Annie sighed. "You win."

"Believe me," Maddy said. "While man may think he lives by sex alone, he also has to eat. And if it isn't true about the way to a man's heart being through his stomach, then why did you cheat and ask me to cook the fried chicken and potato salad for your basket?"

"I hate it when you're right," Annie grumbled. She'd admittedly changed the menu from the crab sliders and slaw she'd intended to take out from the Crab Shack when she discovered that Mac was bidding on her basket.

"If you two are as serious as you looked last night, you really need to take one of my basic beginning cooking classes," Maddy said. "If for no other reason than it's kind of hard on a romance when you give the guy food poisoning."

"Thanks for the vote of confidence," Annie muttered.

"Don't worry. You'll be great," Maddy assured her

as she pushed the cart toward the bakery aisle, leaving Annie to follow.

The dinner, which turned out to be as manageable as both Sedona and Maddy had promised, was a hit. Emma, whose cast was almost entirely covered with princess stickers, had declared Maddy's elevated mac and cheese the "bestest" she'd ever had.

Even Pirate had behaved. Although he'd meowed noisily while doing figure eights between Annie's legs as she cut up the lobster for the adult version of the dinner, he'd spent most of the time curled up in Emma's lap, purring like a small motor.

"Maybe we should get a cat, too, Daddy," she suggested as Mac helped Annie clear the table—something Owen had always insisted Annie leave for the housekeeper or maid. "When we get a dog."

"Let's just start with the dog," he replied. "Besides, a cat might decide to eat your goldfish."

"Oh. I hadn't thought of that." She went back to petting Pirate.

"You've got me looking forward to that basket tomorrow even more," he said as he put the plates into the dishwasher while Annie cleaned off the counter.

How was it that the simple act of cleaning up after dinner affected her nearly as much as last night's prom date? Despite the back-and-forth between the houses, she was beginning to think of them as more of a couple than she and Owen had ever been.

"I have a confession to make." She may have pulled off the mac and cheese and the lava cake, but no way was she not going to give credit where credit was due. Especially for something she would never, no matter how many lessons, be able to duplicate. "Maddy's making the chicken."

He shrugged and placed the soap packet in the dishwasher. "You do realize that I'm not buying that basket for the food," he said. "From the beginning it's been all about you. You could have put sliders from the Crab Shack in there and I would've been just as happy."

She laughed at that. "That's exactly what I was going to do."

He cupped his hand at the back of her neck and leaned down and kissed her. "Great minds."

She was kissing him back when Emma, who'd gone upstairs to the guest bedroom to retrieve some of the cat toys, returned to the kitchen.

"Is this your scrapbook?" she asked Annie, who, unnerved at looking up to see that her deepest secret had been discovered, dropped a glass, which shattered on the floor.

54

She'd gone as pale as the gardenias he had fastened on her wrist last night as she insisted on sweeping up the broken glass by herself. Annie was, he'd discovered, a woman with secrets.

When she'd called in with a fake name at the very beginning, he'd realized right away that she was holding something back, but not wanting to push her, he'd waited, hoping she would eventually care enough to share it with him. Which she had done this morning, when she'd told him about her inability to have children. That made him sad for her, but it didn't change the way he felt about her.

Except to love her even more for what she'd been through. And to admire the strong, confident woman she'd become.

"Emma," he said, using the dad voice he didn't pull out very often and still felt more as if he were imitating his own father whenever he did, "where did you find that?"

"Pirate chased a ball into Annie's bedroom," she said. "It was on the table."

Glancing over at this woman he'd come to love, Mac saw his daughter's lie in Annie's gray eyes.

"Emma . . . ," he said softly but firmly. "You want to try that again?"

"Daddy," she said on something perilously close to a whine. Her eyes filled with tears. But realizing that this was another of those damn grown-up situations, he held firm.

He went over to her, took the album from her hands, and placed it on the cleared kitchen table. "The truth this time." He looked up at Annie, who gave the faintest shake of her head. "And I promise, Annie's not going to be mad at you."

"I was just looking for more cat toys," she said, her voice quivering on the edge of tears. Mac suspected that wasn't the whole truth and nothing but the truth, but he decided it was close enough. For now.

"And?"

"And I looked in the bottom drawer of her dresser."

The obvious place anyone would keep cat toys. Not.

"It's okay." Annie stepped in to help him out. "And yes, it's an album I received when I was a little older than you."

She sat down at the table, and patted her lap, inviting Emma to sit on it. Which, with a little sniffle that Mac found an overdramatic bid for sympathy, his daughter did.

"I was a foster child," Annie said. "Do you know what that is?"

"Angel and Johnny were foster children," she said with a nod. "They had to move around a lot. Even more than when you're a military family."

"That's true. And they were lucky. They found their forever-after homes with Dr. Tiernan and her husband."

Watching her carefully, Mac noticed that her hands

were less than steady as she opened the album. "This is my third-grade school picture."

Her wild curls had been somewhat tamed into two ponytails. Although he could see that tension he'd learned to recognize in her eyes, she was smiling, revealing a lost tooth.

"This was a very nice family." Her voice clogged a little. With tears? She turned a page. "This is a trip we took here one summer. To Shelter Bay."

She was wearing a brightly flowered swimsuit with a little ruffled skirt, her hair a wild mass of black curls around her head as she stood on the beach with another boy and girl. The boy looked a year or two older and the girl was probably Emma's age. Except for the fact that they were blond and she was not, there'd been no way, looking at the photo, to tell that she hadn't been a full birth member of the family.

"And this was Disneyland. I loved It's a Small World." She was sitting in a white boat at the front of the line, waiting to go through the ride, revealing a timeline gap from the coast trip, since her face was now beaming with a joy so bright it made Mac's heart ache, knowing how this particular story had ended up.

"I love it, too," Emma said, clapping her hands. "I love all those dancing and singing dolls." Apparently forgetting she'd been on the verge of being in trouble for snooping in Annie's dresser drawers, Emma began singing the song Mac feared would become an earworm for the rest of the night.

"I went through it three times," Annie said, running her finger over the grinning little girl she'd once been. "And I'm still not sure I saw them all."

"We can go back. Can't we, Daddy?" Emma asked, looking up at Mac. "When my wrist gets all healed up, you and Annie and I can go to Disneyland and Annie can see any of the dolls she missed."

"Good idea," he agreed, wanting to take Annie in his arms and hold her tight, easing the pain he realized this must be causing her. Instead, he stayed leaning against the counter, his legs crossed at the ankles, looking far more casual than he felt.

Annie blinked. Twice. As if fighting back tears. Then taking a deep breath, she turned yet another page in the story that was her interrupted life.

"And this was at Christmas."

"Oh, you look so pretty! I love your dress!" Emma sighed at the red velvet dress with the white satin collar and cuffs. Annie was, as she'd been in the other photos, included with the children. The only difference was that this time a man and a woman were in the picture as well, suggesting it had been a Christmas card photo.

What little girl, he thought, at eight years old, wouldn't have believed that she'd found a home?

"Did you make this scrapbook all by yourself?" Emma asked, running her hands over the gilt paper.

"No. I'd never had one before. But my foster mother was a scrapbooker, and she made this for me to take with me when I moved to my next home."

"She didn't keep you?" Emma's eyes widened with stunned disbelief. A disbelief Mac feared Annie had felt as well when the social worker had showed up, yet again, at the house she'd believed she had settled into.

"That wasn't her job," Annie said calmly. Watching her carefully, knowing her as he did, Mac saw a thin piece of glass about to shatter. "She told me that her job was to take care of children for a short time. That way she could have more than if she kept them forever."

"I think it's probably time to get you home so you can get ready for bed, pumpkin," he told Emma.

Who, big surprise, ignored him.

"My mommy didn't keep me, either," she said with an amazing amount of empathy for a six-year-old. Mac couldn't figure out whether to be proud of her or to start crying like a girl himself.

"But I have Daddy. And Grandpa. And Poppy."

Before anyone could stop her, she turned the page, and what Mac saw tore at something elemental inside him. After leaving what she'd obviously believed would become her real family, Annie had continued the album.

"Emma," he said. More firmly this time. "We need to go so you can get up early tomorrow for the parade."

"No." Annie shook her head again. "It's okay."

And so, Emma, engrossed in the process of the work, kept turning the pages, making comments on the papers Annie had used and the coloring she'd done. Even Mac, who knew nothing about crafts, could tell, from the increasing skill in the work, that the pages had been created over a period of years.

All the picture-perfect families depicted on the carefully laid-out pages were fictional ones, cut from magazines.

"So," Annie said as Emma finally, after what seemed like hours, reached the last page, "that's how I ended up owning a scrapbook store. So I could help other people keep their special memories. And the story of their lives."

And their hopes and, in Annie's case, unfulfilled dreams.

"I'm glad you did. Because now I'll never forget all the fun adventures I had the day I broke my wrist."

Emma looked up at Mac. "You need to take a picture," she said. "Of the night Annie made me macaroni and cheese and I played with Pirate and we looked at her scrapbook."

Even as he did as Emma asked, Mac knew he wouldn't need a scrapbook to remember tonight. Because the story of Annie's life would forever be burned into his mind.

And his heart.

55

Over the years, Annie had suffered from stress head-aches. Although she'd done her best to hide it, one had struck the moment Emma came downstairs with that photo album she hadn't looked at in years. Yet had never been able to throw away.

Because, she thought, as she sat in the dark, waiting for Mac to return from taking Emma home and putting her to bed, it had represented everything she'd ever wanted in the world.

She didn't want to spend years in college and become a veterinarian, like Charity. Nor did she want to be a celebrity chef, like Maddy. Or even the sexiest baker on the planet, like Sedona. She didn't want to arrest bad guys and send them up the river for life plus ten, like Kara could undoubtedly do without a blink of an eye, then go home and cook dinner for her family.

What Annie wanted, what she'd *always* wanted, was a family.

Seemingly everyone had them.

So why did it seem such an impossible dream for her?

As maniacs pounded away with jackhammers at her

forehead, she went upstairs to the bathroom, where she turned the shower dial to hot, waiting for the water to warm in the energy-saving water heater Lucas had installed during the remodel of the house.

Although it took a little while for the water to warm up, the advantage was that, unlike an old-fashioned tank water heater, in this one the hot water never ran out. From the intensity of the headache, she feared she would need a lot tonight.

Because Annie hated taking pain medication, Kara's mother, a neurologist who was currently traveling the world with her husband for a world health organization, had suggested hammering the spot where the headache had centered with hot water for twenty to thirty minutes.

Annie had no idea why or how it worked, but it usually did.

Until tonight.

She was about to give up when there was a knock on the bathroom door.

"You decent?" Mac's voice called out.

"I'm in the shower. And how did you get in here?"

"You didn't lock the door. You're going to have to be more careful," he said as he entered the steamy bathroom. "Because Emma must have ruined Pirate for guard duty. The minute I walked in, he rolled over onto his back and demanded that I rub his stomach."

He casually kicked off his shoes, unfastened the metal button on his jeans, and lowered the zipper. "I think he's got identification issues, because that seems like a dog thing to do. . . .

"And have I ever told you how gorgeous you are?"

"Yes. And I hate to fall back on clichés, but I have a headache."

"So why are you waiting for me in the shower?"

As he pulled off his shirt, revealing the mouthwatering six-pack that could have won him the cover on that Hunks of Shelter Bay calendar the mayor kept talking about creating for promotional purposes, Annie explained the short version of the headache shower cure.

"I'm not going to knock anything that gets you naked and wet," he said, pulling back the steamed-up shower door. "But in case I haven't mentioned it, I'm really good at relieving stress."

He entered the cubicle, cupped her breast, and gave her one of those slow, deep kisses as the water washed over both of them.

"Where does it hurt?" he asked when they finally came up for air.

"Here." She touched her forehead.

"Then that's where we'll start."

He kissed his way from temple to temple, lingering in the center, where she'd touched. Then he ran his fingers over her wet skin. "You really are tense. I once interviewed a medic in Iraq who was into alternative medicine," he told her casually, as his mouth moved down her cheek, returning to her lips, before continuing. "Since you can't always use heavy drugs in a battle situation, he was big on using pressure points to help alleviate pain. "

He touched her everywhere, his hands heating her to an internal temperature even hotter than the water streaming over them. When he'd worked his way down to the tile floor, where he even ministered to the arches of her feet, he began his journey back up again.

"Mac."

"Shh." He turned her around so her breasts were flattened against the tile as his hands moved up the backs of her legs and over her butt, which had her wishing she'd spent more time doing squats with Kara at the gym. "I'm concentrating."

Which was more than she was able to do. Her

thoughts were as fogged as the warm and steamy room.

When his hand moved between her legs, a sound somewhere between a moan and a cry escaped her lips.

His mouth continued up her back, his hands massaging her shoulders, even as his erection pressed against her.

"Now here's the key," he said. "The trick is to get your brain concentrating on some other place."

His hands cupped her hips. "Ready to try it?"

"If you don't, Kara's going to have to arrest me for justifiable homicide when I kill you," she managed, every nerve ending in her body concentrating on that one place that was aching for fulfillment.

"Can't have that."

He slid into her, tight and perfect, as if they'd been made to be together in just this way.

Instead of hurrying, as they had in the car, he took his time, and as her palms pressed against the tile she'd spent weeks picking out, he moved, languidly at first. In. Out. In. Out. Deeper with each fluid, rhythmic stroke, until her lungs clogged and white spots began to float in front of her eyes.

Just when she realized that it was, indeed, possible to pass out from sheer pleasure, he went for it, diving deep, until she screamed his name, the sound of it bouncing off the tile walls like an echo. That, and her orgasm, went on. And on. And on.

He caught her as her knees buckled and lowered her to the floor of the shower, where he took her onto his lap and held her tight.

"How's the head?"

Head? How could he ask about her head when somehow her orgasm was still rocking her from the inside out? She wondered if whatever he'd learned from that medic had done something permanent to her. Like those erections they were always talking about on the TV commercials that lasted more than four hours.

"Uh." She closed her eyes, trying to focus on something besides that hot, pulsing place between her thighs. "Uh, it's still there."

"The headache?"

Headache?

"No. My head." She lifted her fingers to make sure it was still on her shoulders where it belonged. "Are you sure that was really a medic? And not some kind of voodoo doctor?"

"U.S. Army," he said. "But he was from Louisiana, so I suppose he could've learned it from some voodoo practitioner. Why?"

"Never mind." Her headache was actually gone, she realized. And those intense contractions were beginning to calm down enough for her to notice her surroundings. How long had he been in here with her?

"We steamed the room up."

"That's not all we steamed up." He shifted her on his lap and she realized that once again he'd managed to hold back, letting her take what she needed. Wondering if that was another trick the possible voodoo medic had taught him, she said, "I'm not a doctor. Or even a medic. But just maybe, if you got into bed, I could help you with that problem."

"You're on."

As she climbed off him and they both got out of the shower, turning off the still-hot water that had Annie thinking she really ought to consider writing Lucas a thank-you note for having suggested the tankless heater in the first place, he asked, "I don't suppose you've got one of those little nurse outfits. With the short, skintight white uniform and thigh-high white nylons?"

"Sorry."

"That's okay." He caught her hand as she began to

dry the part of his body still needing attention. "You're perfect, Annie." Although his tone had been teasing, his eyes were as serious as she'd ever seen them. "Just the way you are."

And the wonderful thing was, as they spent another night exploring yet more ways they could be perfect together, Annie believed him.

56

Charlie was already dressed in his uniform when Mac and Annie arrived at Still Waters.

"Ha! You owe me fifty clams, boy," he greeted Mac.

"Clams?" Annie looked momentarily concerned that his grandfather was having another reality lapse.

"It's a bet," Mac said, trying to shrug the subject off. "Ready to go?"

"Not until you pay up."

Mac cursed under his breath, pulled out his wallet, and handed Charlie two twenties and a ten. "Happy?"

"Am now," he said. "How about you?"

"Yeah." Mac took hold of Annie's hand. "I am."

"I told you she was a keeper," he said. Then he turned to Annie. "His first wife was a nice girl. Pretty, too. Miss California, or Rose Bowl Princess, or something like that."

"Miss San Diego," Matt said between clenched teeth. Charlie may be living in reality today, but Alzheimer's had definitely taken away any conversational filters.

"That's it. Anyway, like I said, she was a nice girl. With a daddy who was in the Navy, like me, so that was a plus. But she was never right for Mackenzie. And he was never right for her. I could tell that right off from the day of their wedding."

"Pops," Mac warned. It wasn't that he hadn't already told Annie much the same thing. But she didn't need to have his former wife thrown in her face.

"Not every marriage is meant to be," she said mildly. "And even when they start out right, some just take a wrong turn along the way."

"Not me and my Annie," Charlie said, crossing his arms. He swept a look over them. "And not you two. I told you"—he turned back to Mac—"this one's a keeper."

"I'm sorry if Gramps embarrassed you," Mac said later, as they sat on the curb of Harborview Drive, watching the Shelter Bay High School marching band strut by while blasting out John Philip Sousa.

"Don't worry about it. You know I'm a little in love with Charlie."

"I didn't realize I had competition."

"I wouldn't stand a chance. Because I'm the wrong Annie." Her gaze drifted to Adèle and Maureen Douchett, seated across the street, waiting for their husbands to march past. "I envy people who can stay in love for so many years."

"I suspect it's not as easy as it looks," Mac said. "But if my mom hadn't died, I think she and Boyd would've been like Charlie and Annie. Charlie's parents were married eighty years."

"That's a wonderful family history."

"Yeah. Another reason I felt bad when I screwed up the record."

She looked as if she was going to respond to that, but just then Emma, who was seated beside him, began jumping up and down. "There's the float," she shouted.

She pulled the cards she'd made out of the pink backpack she'd brought with her, and along with the other children, went running up, handing them out to the marching military men and women. One Marine lifted Emma up so she could hand a card to her poppy, who, for a guy in his nineties, looked damn fine, Mac thought. The second card went to her grandfather.

"Why aren't you in the parade?" Annie asked. "And don't say because you were just the guy on the radio." She ran a hand down his leg. "Don't forget, I've seen the scars."

"Easy." He put his arm around her waist. Instead of her usual sundress, she was wearing a red-and-white-striped T-shirt, white capris, and red sandals. While she might have left the stilettos and diamonds at home, she was still the sexiest woman in Shelter Bay and he couldn't wait to get her alone for a few hours of highly inappropriate sex. "I'm exactly where I want to be."

"Did you see?" Emma asked as she ran back to them. "I gave away all my cards. But I saved my most special for Poppy and Grandpa. "

"We saw," Annie said. "And you did great."

"I know. Poppy said it was the best card ever." Her grin took up most of her face. "I *knew* Peggy was wrong about no one wanting pink ink."

"I brought you something," Annie said, reaching into her bag and pulling out the package tied with pink and purple ribbon.

Emma's eyes widened. "You got me a present?" she asked as she excitedly tore away the pink-flowered paper.

"For your scrapbooking," Annie said.

"Oh!" Emma drew in a sharp, pleased breath, then held the pink Disney Princess digital camera out to show Mac. "It's my very own camera!"

"Wow. That's pretty cool," he said.

"It's better than cool." Emma hugged it to her chest. "It's amazing!" She flung her arms around Annie's neck. "Thank you!"

As she hugged Mac's daughter back, Annie felt a mental camera click, preserving this moment, and the day, forever.

The bidding for the lunch baskets began and Annie realized, when everyone seemed to wind up with the basket made by the person they'd come with, that although the rules stated it would be a blind auction, no one was paying any attention.

The Douchetts had all ended up together, as had Maddy and Lucas and Charity and Gabe. Across the expanse of green lawn, lost in their own world, Kim and her fiancé were feeding each other bites of what appeared to be crab sliders.

After agreeing to go to the picnic with Mac, Annie had found a red, white, and blue hand-stitched quilt in the Dancing Deer's expanded home-decorating section, and she and Mac spread it out on the lawn for everyone to sit on.

"This is damn good," Charlie said as he dug into the potato salad.

"Chef Maddy, from Lavender Hill Farm restaurant, made it," Annie confessed.

"Not surprised the girl grew up to be a famous chef," he said. "Her grandmother could always cook circles around everyone in town. This tastes a lot like what Sofia De Luca always made for potlucks. My Annie used mayo in hers, which was really tasty, but I've got to admit that the spicy mustard gives this an extra zing."

Speaking of zing . . . As she looked up into Mac's eyes, which were looking down at her as if she were a decadent dessert that he couldn't wait to taste, Annie experienced an entirely different type of zing in parts of her body she'd only recently discovered *could* go zing.

Unsurprisingly, Maddy's potato salad and her crunchy, moist fried chicken were delicious; they could have been served in any four-star restaurant in New York City. And the brownies Sedona had contributed as a change from her usual cupcakes were rich and fudgy and equally perfect.

As Boyd and Charlie talked with one another about other vets who'd been in the parade, and Emma went dashing around, snapping photos of seemingly everyone and everything, Annie thought how lucky she was that Mac had already professed that her cooking was not what it was about her that had attracted him.

The city council had contracted with a company to set up a Ferris wheel on the bay by the pier. After taking Charlie back to Still Waters, Mac's father, apparently remembering what it was like to be newly in love, took Emma with him in one of the cars of the ride, leaving Mac and Annie alone.

"I have a question that's been bugging me," he asked as the Ferris wheel stopped for a couple to get on below them.

"What?"

"Why Sandy from Shelter Bay? Why didn't you just give your name?"

"Not everyone does," she pointed out. "Unless his mother actually named him that, Cowboy doesn't."

"I'll give you that one."

"I'd never called a radio station before. And when I realized I had to tell you my name, Sandy was the first one to pop into my head."

"Why that one?"

"It's silly." She sighed as the wheel started turning again. Below them Boyd was making the chair rock just enough to have Emma squealing with delight.

"When I was little, kids at school used to do a play on my name and situation, calling me Little Orphan Annie."

"Kids can be cruel."

"True. But after a while I developed a sort of shell, so it didn't hurt as much."

"No?" He pretended shock. "You? A shell?"

"I did. Until you." Because it had been too long since she'd kissed him, Annie lifted her lips to his. The wheel stopped again, leaving them at the top of the world. At least their pretty corner of it. From here Annie could see her store. And Take the Cake, which, from the line out in front, appeared to be doing a brisk business.

Cole's blue fishing boat, appropriately named the *Kelli*, was tied up at the dock. And as they did most every day, sailboats skimmed across the blue bay, some of them going beneath the bridge, out toward the sea.

"So, anyway, when you asked me my name, that came flashing back, and I thought of Sandy."

"Little Orphan Annie's dog."

"Yeah. Silly, isn't it?"

"Not at all. Though if you'd used your real name, I might have made the connection faster."

"And we probably wouldn't have talked nearly as freely," she replied.

"Good point," he said, then ended the conversation by kissing her again. Then one more time, as the Ferris wheel came around to let them off, earning applause from the people holding their yellow tickets and waiting to get on the ride.

57

"I had a thought," Annie said as she made waffles for Mac and Emma the morning after the Fourth. They might be from a packaged mix, which Maddy would probably consider a cardinal culinary sin, but at least she'd managed to make a stack without having batter run all over the counter. "About your school uniform."

Emma's mouth turned down as she smeared a piece of waffle into a puddle of marionberry syrup. "I can't wear any pink."

"On the outside," Annie said. "But the rules don't say anything about what you wear under the uniform, do they?"

Blue eyes dazzled like sunshine on a summer sea as Emma caught Annie's drift. "No. They don't!"

"Well, then. When I bought my dress for the dance, I noticed that there's a new Tots to Teens section down at the Dancing Deer Two. What would you say to you and I having a girls' lunch out, then going shopping for underwear?"

"I'd say yes!" She knocked the chair over as she jumped off it and flung her arms, and the heavy cast that was on one of them, around Annie's neck. "That's the bestest idea ever! Isn't it, Daddy?"

The warmth in Mac's eyes, as they met Annie's, had her feeling as if she'd swallowed the sun.

"The bestest," he agreed.

"Are you going to be my new mommy?" Emma asked across the table at the Lavender Hill Farm restaurant.

"I think it's a little early to talk about things like that," Annie replied, hedging.

"Why?"

Wasn't that what her friends had been asking? What Annie had even begun asking herself?

"It's complicated. How was your mac and cheese?"

"Really good. But I like yours better."

Annie decided not to point out that she'd used this same recipe and, unsurprisingly, Maddy's was definitely the superior dish.

"Thank you. Do you want dessert? Or would you rather wait and stop for a cupcake after shopping?"

Emma took a moment to weigh her options. "A cupcake," she decided. "Why is it complicated?" Her smooth forehead furrowed into a frown. "Is it because of me?"

"Oh, no." Having been rejected so many times growing up, Annie knew that even as bright and cheerful as Emma was, and as hard as Mac was working to fill both parental roles, her mother's abandonment had to have left the child feeling more insecure than she sometimes let on. "I can't imagine a more extra-special daughter than you."

"Then why won't you marry my daddy?"

"You'll understand when you're a grown-up," Annie tried, not having the answer to that one herself.

Emma's frustrated sigh ruffled her corn-silk bangs. "I *hate* it when grown-ups say that."

"I know." Annie reached across the table and stroked Emma's hair soothingly. "But relationships take time if you want to do them right. Your daddy and I are in the getting-to-know-each-other stage right now."

"Oh!" The last of the worry and frustration on her small face cleared. "Like Belle and the beast did. Although he seemed really mean and grumpy at first, he let her read his books and then they had to become friends before they could have a romantic dinner and dance and fall in forever-after love."

"Exactly."

That seemed to settle the problem.

At least for now.

Later that afternoon, as they returned home with cupcakes, shopping bags filled with cotton underwear covered with pink flowers, hearts, and various Disney Princess designs, Annie considered making a thank-you card to send to those Disney filmmakers.

The days that followed were, hands down, the most wonderful ones of Annie's life. Although it still took some juggling to make time for Mac and her to be alone, and there were some nights that they barely got any sleep at all, for the first time in her life, Annie was learning to play.

Since summer days were long on the coast, they spent every evening together. Barbecuing, walking on the beach, even going out on Cole's boat for a private whale-watching trip. As if they were becoming the family she'd always dreamed of, those evenings were always spent with Emma. Less and less with Boyd, who'd begun seeing Marian Long, a widowed nurse he'd met while dropping by the hospital to visit a patient.

The possibility of the handsome, eligible doctor being taken off the market had not only cut back on the amount of baked goods flowing into the Buchanan men's home, but it had the couple claiming Mac and Annie's spot in the Shelter Bay spotlight.

"I tell you, it's the water," the mayor said one day when she'd been standing at Take the Cake's counter, waiting her turn after Emma and Annie. "One of these days I'm going to come up with a marketing campaign and bottle it. After all, this town was started by selling water from the hot springs as a miracle cure. What's more miraculous than falling in love?"

Annie couldn't argue with that.

Another evening, Annie was outside setting the picnic table while Mac grilled prawns for dinner, when Emma, who was tossing wadded-up pieces of paper to Pirate—who Annie had belatedly discovered knew how to fetch—asked, "Why is he named Pirate?"

"Because he was found on this cove," Annie said as she set down the coleslaw, which she'd actually made herself from one of the recipes she'd learned in Maddy's beginning cooking class. "It's called Castaway Cove because there was this pirate, Sir Francis Drake, who had the fastest ship on the sea."

"The *Golden Hind*," Mac volunteered from the grill.

"That was it. And actually, Sir Francis was a privateer, but that's pretty much the same thing as a pirate. He was just working for the queen of England instead of for himself."

"Like Daddy works at KBAY."

"Sort of like that," Annie said. "But his job was to run down other ships and steal their treasures."

"That's a pirate, all right," Emma said, with a decisive nod. "I saw them at the Pirates of the Caribbean at Disneyland. I wonder if he chased women like those do."

Annie ignored Mac's smothered laugh.

"I'm not sure about that," she said mildly. "He was

actually quite a gentleman, for a pirate. He'd force the other ships close to the land, then allow all the crewmen to wade ashore. This was one of his favorite spots to catch the ships, so they'd end up here. Which is why it's called Castaway Cove."

"I like that story," Emma decided. "We should make it into a scrapbook page. With a picture of Pirate."

"I think that's an excellent idea."

As she exchanged a look with Mac, she could tell he was thinking the same thing. That this moment in time was about as perfect as life could get.

But as life had taught her, perfection, like so many things, was fleeting.

A month after the Fourth of July, Annie received a call at the shop. "I thought I'd better warn you," Mac said. "We're having a funeral tonight."

Her heart clenched. "Don't tell me Charlie—"

"Oh, sorry. Hell, no. He's fine. At least Analiese said he is. Emma and I are going over to see him today. But Nemo died."

Nemo being one of Emma's two goldfish.

"Oh. Well. That's too bad. Is she terribly upset?"

"Not as bad as I thought she'd be. There were some tears. But I promised her we'd bury him in the backyard, so she's busy coloring a box to put him in."

"I have some stickers of goldfish. I'll bring them over to the house after work."

"Thanks." He paused. "You know what?"

"What?"

"Even burying a goldfish together just feels right."

When she didn't answer right away, he said, "We're going to have to talk about where we're going."

He'd tried before, but she kept putting him off. Because, she knew, she couldn't quite trust what might be around the bend.

"Tonight we're going to a funeral for a fish," she said.

"Annie—"

"I just need a little more time, Mac."

He sighed and she knew he had to make an effort to bite back his frustration. She couldn't blame him. As Sedona and the others kept telling her, she had no good reason not to move their relationship on to the next step.

Mac was not just sexy Midnight Mac, the deejay that women all over Shelter Bay probably lay in bed fantasizing about. He was a good man. A decent man. He'd already told her he loved her and she had no reason to doubt his word.

They had, as Emma pointed out about Belle and the Beast, become not just lovers but friends.

So why, Annie wondered as she greeted a customer who had come in for supplies to make a whale memory page, did she feel as if she were standing on the edge of a cliff where one false step would send her tumbling headlong over the edge?

58

"My fish died, Poppy," Emma told Charlie later that afternoon when Mac took her to Still Waters. "Nemo. Daddy and Annie and I are going to bury him tonight. In a box I made him."

"I'm sorry you lost him, Emma. And that's nice you're going to bury his body. But you don't have to worry. Because he's already up in heaven with your great-grandmother."

"Fish go to heaven?"

"Sure they do. They're actually happier there because instead of a bowl, they have a whole ocean to swim in."

"What if the big fish eat them?"

"Not in heaven," he assured her. "Believe me, honey, he's one happy goldfish right now."

"Okay." She exhaled a long, relieved breath. Then her brow furrowed. "Maybe if I took Dory out of the water, she'd die, too. Then she could be happy in heaven, with Nemo."

"No, you wouldn't want to do that," Charlie told her. "Because like my Annie always tells me, we all have to go in our own time. And it's not Dory's time yet."

"Oh. But do you think she misses Nemo?"

"Probably. But if my Annie can come visit me, he'll probably be able to visit her, too. And tell her all about all the wonderful things he's seen in the sea up there."

"She'd like that," Emma said. "Because I named her after Dory, from the movie, who likes to talk. So this way she'll still have Nemo to talk to."

That problem solved, she went on to tell him all about tonight's sleepover with her friend Peggy. A sleepover where she'd be staying for breakfast, Mac thought with anticipation.

Which should give him and Annie plenty of time to talk about their future.

"Nemo is *too* in heaven," Emma told her friend after her daddy had dropped her off for the sleepover. It was the last one they'd be having before she began first grade.

"Is not," Peggy said. "Goldfish don't go to heaven."

Emma put her hands on her hips. "Poppy said they do."

"Ha." Peggy tossed her red head. "Everybody in town knows your grandfather's crazy. That's why he's locked up in that home."

"That's not true." Emma's hands curled into fists. "Take it back."

It was Peggy's turn to put *her* hands on *her* hips. "Make me."

Emma was about to hit her, right in the eye, the way she did Kenny. Then she remembered what her daddy had told her about hitting people.

But her poppy had told her that standing up for family was the right thing to do. And Peggy had just said bad things about Nemo and her poppy.

"If you hit me, I'll tell," Peggy said. "And you'll get grounded. And probably even spanked."

Emma was momentarily shocked into silence. Then she said, "My daddy would never hit me."

"He might. My mother says that he was a soldier in the Army."

"Shows how much you know. Daddy was in the Air Force."

"It's all the same thing." Peggy's skinny lips twisted in a sneer that had Emma's temper shooting so high she thought it might take the top of her head off. Or make it explode like those fireworks on the Fourth of July.

"My mother says that lots of times soldiers have PMS," her friend-turned-enemy said. "And when they have it they can go crazy and shoot people so I should be careful when I'm over at your house."

"My daddy would never shoot anyone!" Emma shouted.

Her palms were hurting from her fingernails cutting into them as she tried her hardest not to hit Peggy and get grounded for her last week of summer vacation. Especially since her daddy and Annie were taking her to Seaside for the weekend.

"He was in the war," Peggy said. "People in war shoot people all the time. I've seen it on TV. And he got blown up, so my mother told my father that there's no telling what that did to his brain."

"You are such a liar." Her daddy was the smartest man she knew. His brain was just fine.

"And your family is crazy with people who shoot people and who think fish go to heaven," Peggy shot back.

That did it. Grabbing her rolling overnight bag, Emma marched out of the room, down the stairs, and out the door.

Headed for home.

59

Mac was as gray as a ghost and obviously frantic when Annie arrived at his house. Kara was already there, looking grim and official in her starched khaki uniform.

"What happened?" Annie asked.

"Emma's gone missing. I've got to go look for her."

"I've got deputies out doing that. And I've called in an AMBER Alert," Kara said. "Let me just get a couple more details about what she was wearing and we'll get a search party started. Believe me, there's a way to handle this, and just running out without a plan isn't going to make the situation any better."

"How could she go missing?" Annie asked, confused. "Wasn't she at Peggy's for the sleepover?"

"She and Peggy got in a fight and she left."

"Left? Peggy's mother allowed her to leave alone?"

"She wasn't there," Mac said. "She left the girls with her teenage daughter while she stopped by the casino in Lincoln City to play the slots on her way home from work.

"When she got home, Peggy was in her room playing Barbies. She's not sure how long it's been since Emma left. And her older sister, who isn't exactly the sharpest crayon in the box, was listening to music on her iPod while texting with her boyfriend and didn't even notice."

He raked his hands through his hair. "I dropped her off right after I fed her an early dinner. She could have been gone for two fucking hours. Maybe more."

"We'll find her," Kara promised even as the radio she wore on her uniform shirt crackled. "Let me get this and I'll be right back." Looking very much like the big-city police officer she'd once been before returning to her hometown to take over her father's job as sheriff, she stepped outside.

"I need to go look for her," Mac repeated.

"Someone needs to be here for when she comes home," Annie said, refusing to think Emma wouldn't come home. That was one outcome she wasn't going to consider. "Where's your dad?"

"In Portland. He took Marian up there to the symphony. He's on his way home."

"Okay." Annie wanted to be with Mac more than anything, but she also knew that there'd be no keeping him here while his daughter was missing.

Kara came back into the room. Her expression gave nothing away, but her eyes weren't positive. "Does Emma have a Barbie suitcase?"

"A rolling one." Mac literally swayed and grabbed hold of the back of the couch. "She took it to Peggy's. Why?"

"Because a man watering his front lawn found one lying on the sidewalk. On Bayview."

"Oh, Christ. That's a good mile from the Murrays' house," Mac said. "In the wrong direction."

"We'll find her, Mac," said Kara, who, along with being a sheriff, had a son and daughter of her own. "I promise."

*   *   *

Charlie knew he should be grateful to get out of Still Waters. Everyone was always telling him that the field trips were good for him. That they kept him engaged and out in the world. Which may have been true. But they also put him on a van with a bunch of people that he had nothing in common with except that they were all in various stages of losing their minds.

As he sat trying to ignore the chatter of the women sitting at the table in the sports restaurant just outside town where they'd stopped to eat after a sightseeing trip to the lighthouse—during which he'd been forced to listen to stuff he'd known all his life—he hunched his shoulders, bit into his burger, and tried to concentrate on the baseball game up on the TV screen over the bar. Which wasn't easy, since he couldn't hear the announcer over the women's damn voices.

He was about to tell them to tone it down when the AMBER Alert crawled across the bottom of the screen.

"Emma?"

Okay. Maybe her name on the TV was another hallucination like people said he sometimes had. He stood up from the table.

"Where are you going?" the orderly—*Jack*, Charlie remembered—demanded to know.

"To the john," Charlie shot back. The kid didn't look old enough to shave. What right did he have to be monitoring where Charlie went or telling him what to do? "Want to come along and hold my dick?"

That shut the biddies up.

"Just hurry up," Jack said. "Because the van's leaving in ten minutes."

"I might be old," Charlie said. "But it doesn't take me *that* long to piss."

He knew this place well, from the days when he'd bring fish into the harbor. His memory might not be what it once was, but he damn well could find his way to the john. He stopped at the bar while Jack flirted with the girl who drove the van that had brought them all down here.

He was wearing his WWII Navy vet baseball cap, which usually got him some respect. The Greatest Generation, they were calling him. How about the oldest? But the anchor tattoo on the bartender's forearm was a positive sign.

"Was that an AMBER Alert?"

"Yeah. Some little girl. Six years old." The guy shook his head as he drew a draft beer into a frosted mug. "Hope they find her. I've got a daughter just her age. Sometimes these things hit home, you know?"

"Yeah," Charlie said. "I know."

Only too well.

He glanced back behind him, where Jack the Jerk-off was still making lame jokes to the girl, who obviously had good taste since she was trying to ignore him.

Taking advantage of the diversion, Charlie headed toward the restroom and then instead of taking a right turn, turned and went through the kitchen and out the back of the restaurant.

He might not remember what he had for breakfast, but he did remember Emma talking about that cave where she'd suggested they could go if he ever felt the need to run away from Still Waters.

Charlie could not let himself believe that someone had snatched his great-granddaughter. For such an angelic-looking little tyke, she had one helluva temper. She'd probably just gotten pissed over something at her friend's house and was headed there.

So, he thought, as he cut through the woods to keep out of sight, then headed back toward the beach, Emma would hide out in the cave, the same way he and Ollie had hidden overnight on that island that time the engine on their whaleboat broke down.

60

"Okay," Kara said, laying out a map of Shelter Bay. "We'll start here." She tapped a pencil point on the place where Emma's suitcase had been found, "and work in quadrants. Because I know there's no way I'm going to keep you home," she told Mac, "you're assigned this one. And don't go all Lone Ranger on me, okay? Because this only works if everyone does what he or she is supposed to."

Mac didn't like the idea. At all. But he had to admit that it made more sense than just randomly driving down streets. Hell, shortly after they moved here, he'd lost Emma for five damn minutes in the Newport Fred Meyer store, which, until now, had been the scariest moments of his life, even worse than being blown up by the jingle truck.

"It'll be all right," Annie assured him as he left the house.

"You can't know that."

"No. But I believe it."

"What happened to always preparing for the worst?"

"That was then," she said. "Before you and Emma and Charlie and your father taught me to look for silver linings. I know she's safe and out there waiting for you to find her."

He gave her a quick, hard kiss. Then, as the sun began to sink over the ocean, Mac began to walk the section Kara had assigned him, in search of his daughter.

Emma knew she was not supposed to talk to strangers. But it didn't take her long to figure out that she was lost. Like really, really lost.

She'd been so mad when she left Peggy's house that she hadn't really been paying attention. And it wasn't as if she'd actually ever walked there before—she lived far enough away that whenever they had playdates, either her father or her grandfather or Peggy's mother drove.

So, even though she liked to think that she was just like the bravest princess of all, she was beginning to get scared. And cold, as she got closer to the ocean and the wind started blowing and it began to rain.

She'd lost all track of the time, and she wondered if Peggy's mother had gotten home yet. Had Peggy even bothered to tell her that Emma had left? Because what if no one was looking for her? What if no one found her before it got dark?

The longer she walked, the more Emma began to realize that she just should've hit Peggy. Because when she finally got home, she was probably going to be grounded for life.

She finally stopped at a big house on the top of a hill. She thought maybe since she could see the whole town and the harbor from here, she'd see her grandpa's house. But she couldn't, so it was time to admit she was in trouble.

The house had a sign out in front which read HAVEN HOUSE. And it had pretty flowers in the yard and a stained-glass front door that was reflecting the setting sun like rainbows. Emma rang the bell.

A woman who looked at least as old as her poppy opened the door. She was skinny and wearing jeans and a red shirt with a ballet dancer on the front of it. Which had Emma looking down at her feet, which instead of ballet slippers were wearing sneakers covered in gold sequins.

"Why, my goodness. You must be Emma," the woman said, opening the door wider.

"How did you know my name?"

"Oh, you're famous." Her warm smile told Emma that she'd picked the very best house. "I'm Zelda. Why don't you come in and have some cookies and milk while we call your daddy to come pick you up?"

"You know my daddy?"

"Only from the radio," she said. "But I know how to get hold of him. He's going to be very happy to hear you're safe."

"I was always safe," Emma explained as she entered the house. "I was just lost."

"And doesn't that happen to all of us from time to time?" Zelda assured her.

61

Annie had never been as relieved in her life as she was when Mac called to let her know that Emma had been found. He'd arrived back at the Buchanan house with her just as Boyd and Marian pulled into the driveway.

"Annie," Emma said as she squirmed out of his arms and went running toward her. "Guess what? I was lost!"

"I know," Annie said, kneeling down to hold her tight. "We were very worried."

"I'm sorry. I was a little scared, but then I met this really nice lady and guess what else?"

"What?"

"She's a famous ballerina who's going to teach me how to dance. Just like Angel!"

Annie looked up at Mac, who while obviously looking better than he had when he left the house, still showed signs of stress around his eyes and his mouth.

"Isn't that special?" she answered Emma, even as her gaze assured Mac that she knew ways to relieve that stress. Later.

*   *   *

The good news was that Mac had his daughter back. Safe and sound, thanks, in large part, to Zelda Chmerkovskiy. The bad news was that while Emma was still recounting her adventure, wishing she'd thought to take pictures with her new camera, Kara showed up at the house.

"I hate to tell you this," she told Mac, her expression echoing her words, "but your grandfather's gone missing."

"What?"

According to what the bartender had told Kara when she'd responded to the call at the sports restaurant, Charlie had had the bad luck to see the AMBER Alert about Emma, and had, for some reason known only to himself, decided to go find her.

Which had resulted in the second AMBER Alert of the day.

Were they having fun yet?

Emma, who'd been remarkably calm, though still angry at her former friend when Mac had picked her up at Haven House, burst into tears when she heard the news about her grandfather.

"It's all my f-f-fault."

"No," Annie, who'd stayed calm throughout the ordeal, assured her as she wiped away the tears streaming down Emma's cheeks. "It's just one of those things. Your grandfather used to wander off before you even arrived in Shelter Bay."

"Which is why he's living in Still Waters," Mac's father reminded her. "To keep him safe."

"I know. That's why I never should have told him about the cave."

"Cave?" Kara asked.

"The cave with the diamonds on the beach. I told him if he ever wanted to run away that would be a good place to hide out. And I'd bring him food and stuff."

Kara and Mac exchanged a look.

"I know the one she's talking about," Kara said. "I'll go check it out. Meanwhile, now that it's dark, I want you to stay put. Besides, your daughter needs you."

"Peggy said you had P-P-PMS," Emma told Mac. "And that you might shoot someone because of it. So I left because you told me I'm not supposed to hit people anymore."

Mac could practically feel the gray hairs sprouting on his head. "It's PTSD," he said. "And no, I don't have it, and it's good that you didn't hit her. But the next time you decide to leave someplace like that, I want you to call me, okay?"

"Okay." She snuggled closer to Annie. "Or maybe I could call Annie."

"Absolutely," Annie said.

"Okay. So, I'm not going to be spanked?"

"Of course not." Mac wondered what he'd ever done to make her think she might.

"Or grounded?"

"No." He was too grateful to have her home safe and sound. But they were going to have to have a talk about her tendency to fly off the handle.

"Do you think Poppy will be okay?" She sniffled and her eyes welled up again.

"Absolutely," Annie repeated.

As Mac thought about Charlie, out there in what had become cold, pouring rain, perhaps walking along the cliff in the dark, lost and confused, he only wished he could feel as confident as Annie, who he knew was as worried as he was.

62

"And isn't this a fine mess you've gotten yourself into," Charlie muttered as he stood in the center of a grove of towering Douglas fir trees.

Although he hated to admit it, even to himself, Charlie was lost.

Somehow, although he'd been walking for what seemed like hours, he had the feeling he'd been going in circles.

Then again, maybe that could be all in his mind. Maybe, he thought, he was actually back in bed at Still Waters and all this was just a bad dream. Like the one he still sometimes had of the *Lexington* sinking. Or Annie dying.

"It's not a dream, darling," he heard a familiar voice say.

He spun around, almost tripping over a damn stump, only to see her standing on a trail he hadn't even noticed while stumbling around through the trees like the old man he was.

"Are you real?"

"I suppose that depends on your definition," she said. "But I'm as real as I am whenever I visit you, and no, you're not dreaming and no, I'm not a hallucination."

"Are you here to finally take me with you?" he asked hopefully.

"I'm sorry." Her expression was the same one she gave him every time he asked. "But I've told you, Charlie, my love—"

"We all have our own time," he finished the damn words for her.

"Exactly." She reached out and ran her fingers down his cheek. Or perhaps it was simply a gust of soft sea breeze blowing in from the coast. Wherever the hell *that* was. "Just as you told Emma about her fish."

"I was looking for Emma."

"She's home. Safe and sound and with her father."

Relief flooded over him. "That's good news . . .

"I miss you." He felt his damn eyes filling up. "I don't know what to do without you, Annie."

"You're doing just fine," she said.

"We both know that's not true. I'm out in the middle of the goddamn woods in the middle of the night even more lost than when I was bobbing around in the sea after my ship went down. I miss you every day. And every damn night. And it's just not fair."

"I can't argue that," she answered.

"Ha! I thought once you got to heaven you had all the answers."

"And wouldn't that be lovely," she agreed. "All I can say is that my time isn't the same as your time. I can't explain it, but you'll understand someday."

"Why not now? If I just found the damn cliff and threw myself off it, would that finally work?" Remembering what Emma had said about Dory and Nemo, he realized he was now thinking like a six-year-old.

"It might solve one problem. But it would create a host more. Your grandson's doing better than he was.

Mac's fallen in love and he's learning to be a father. But he still needs you, Charlie. As does Emma."

And *he* needed his Annie. But she'd always been wiser than him.

"They're probably going nuts," he said.

"They've very worried," she agreed. "Which is why you're going to take my hand now. And I'm going to lead you out of the woods and help you find your way home."

"*You're* my home. You've always been."

"Just be patient a little longer and know that wherever you are, darling, I'll always be with you."

She led him to what he recognized as the Coast Highway.

"Now take this." She pressed something into his hands. "And wait just a minute. And you'll be all set."

And then she did what he'd been dreaming of ever since she'd had that stroke that had taken her from him.

She kissed him. Full on the lips, a familiar, wonderful kiss that had stayed in his mind all during the war and helped him make it back home to her. And at this moment, it warmed him all the way through.

And then, like morning mist over the harbor, she was gone.

At the same moment, a log truck came barreling around the corner.

Charlie looked down at what she'd pressed into his hand. Turned it on. And waved the flashlight like a beacon signal, bringing the truck to a stop with the squeal of air brakes.

The driver's window rolled down.

"Hey, man," the bearded guy called out to him. "Everybody in the state's been looking for you. So why don't you get the hell out of this rain and I'll take you home."

63

They were waiting for him. All but Emma, who, having arrived safely home herself, had fallen asleep, exhausted after her adventure, so they'd put her to bed.

"You had us worried to death," Mac said, looking pretty much like death himself, Charlie thought. But he'd be okay. Because he had *his* Annie.

"Sorry about that," he muttered. "I guess I screwed up."

"Well, you're all right," Annie said, putting her arms around him for the first time since they'd met. At least the first time he remembered her doing that. "That's all that matters."

"Absolutely," said Boyd, who didn't look that good himself.

"I thought maybe I was going to die out there," he admitted. "But Annie, *my* Annie, told me that it wasn't my time yet. That I needed to come back because you"—he shot a look at Mac—"can't convince this lady to marry you."

"I'm working on it," Mac muttered.

"Well, work on it a little faster," Charlie advised.

"Because, believe me, boy, life goes by pretty damn quick while you're not paying close enough attention."

Then he turned to Annie. "You're already part of this family," he said. "You've seen us at our best. And well, maybe today not exactly our best. But you stuck with us. You stuck with my grandson here because you love him."

She was holding Mac's hand the same way Annie had held his. In both of her soft, pretty ones.

"So," Charlie demanded, "why don't you quit keeping us all in suspense and just say yes?"

"I believe that's my question to ask, Gramps," Mac said quietly. But Charlie wasn't fooled because anyone could see the humor in his eyes. His grandson had always enjoyed life. And now that he was finally with the right woman, Charlie knew firsthand that he was going to enjoy it a helluva lot more.

"Well, then? What's keeping you?"

"Maybe I'd like some privacy?"

"Oh." That made sense, and although he'd like to hear the girl say the words, he guessed he'd be dancing at their wedding.

"Okay, then. Just make sure you do it right. Women like you to get down on one knee. It may seem old-fashioned, but it gets them every time."

"I'll keep that in mind," Mac murmured, this time exchanging a laughing look with Annie, who smiled back.

"Oh, one more thing," he said to his grandson's Annie. "My Annie says that it's mostly good around that bend of yours. And what isn't, you'll handle together. Because that's what families do."

"So I hear," she said.

Damn. He didn't mean to make her cry. But, from the way she was still smiling, even wider, Charlie took that to be one of those female crying things that he would never, even if he lived to be a hundred—which it seemed he just might do after all—understand.

64

Mac and Annie dropped Charlie off at Still Waters, then went on to Castaway Cove.

"How did he know that?" she asked as they sat on the porch swing, watching the moon begin to rise over the top of the Douglas fir trees, casting a silvery sheen on the water. The rain had lessened to a soft mist. "About my bend thing?"

"Beats me," he said, rocking gently, his arm around her shoulders, her head on his. "Sax said he had ghosts return from the war with him. Real ones, who drove around in his Camaro and ragged him and stuff, just like they did when they were alive. Maybe he's not imagining his Annie visiting him."

"Maybe not," she agreed. "Did you notice something else?"

"What?"

"He was dry. It was pouring rain out there, but he was as dry as if he'd spent the entire night indoors by the fire."

"Damn. That is something to ponder. But I think it can wait until later."

Leaving her for a moment, he went back to the truck and returned with a package.

"You got me something from my own shop?" Annie asked as she recognized the wrapping paper.

"Kim helped me pick it out." Mac was suddenly nervous. "I hope you like it."

Unlike Emma, who tore into packages, Annie carefully slid off the ribbon, then cut the tape on the ends and bottom with her fingernail, folding back the paper to reveal the gift he'd come up with weeks ago.

"A scrapbook?"

"Open it."

She did, then looked up at him. "It's blank."

"I figured we could fill the pages with all the days of our life together."

She didn't immediately answer. As her eyes filled, he could only pray that her tears were happy ones.

"This is"—she ran her fingertips over the ivory and black woven cover—"the most wonderful present anyone has ever given me."

"It's just a scrapbook," he said, even as he was relieved that she liked it. The past few days he'd begun second-guessing himself, wondering if she'd rather have a ring. But then he'd figured she'd rather that they pick one out together. Wouldn't she? He'd never been so conflicted in his life.

"No," she said as she looked up at him. "Scrapbooks are about preserving the past. This is looking forward to our future."

"Speaking of that."

And then, because his grandfather had never steered him wrong, Mac left the swing, got down on one knee, and said, "I love you, Annie. For better or worse. Whatever lies around that bend. I love you now, and I'll love you forever. Until, like it goes, death we do part."

He waited a beat, thinking of Charlie and his war bride. "And beyond. You've always wanted a family, and I want to give you one."

"You have," she said softly, her eyes getting all moist again.

"But here's the thing. My family won't be complete without you. So, would you make my grandfather, my father, my daughter, and me very happy, and just say yes?"

Her answer was in those remarkable eyes. And on those lips he could taste even when she wasn't anywhere in the room.

"Yes," she said. Her laugh was light and breezy. "Absolutely, positively yes."

"Thank you," he said. "You've just made my family very, very happy.

"As for me . . ."

And because making love to Annie on this swing had been his fantasy since he'd first seen it, hanging there beneath the porch roof, Mac sat down on the swing again, put the scrapbook on the table, took her into his arms, and kissed her as he pressed her down upon the pretty flowered cushions.

It was all either of them would say for a very long time.

Eight months later

"Happy?" Mac asked Annie.

"How could I not be?" She glanced around at the party in full swing at Bon Temps. "Everyone we know is here."

"It's a special celebration," he pointed out. "We're now officially, according to the State of Oregon, a family of five."

"And Charlie, your father, and Marian make eight."

Annie thought it was cute how Boyd was obviously so in love with his bride of six weeks.

"We Culhane men lucked out," he said when she mentioned that. "Gramps with his Annie, my dad with my mom, and now Marian. And topping the hit list, me, with you."

"We're both lucky," she said as she looked over at Emma demonstrating a slightly wobbly arabesque to her eleven-year-old twin brothers, Jordan and Justin.

Annie had met and fallen in love with the two boys while volunteering at Camp Rainbow, a summer camp for separated foster siblings. When Mac, who'd come to the camp for an afternoon of letting the kids play deejay, had met them, he'd fallen just as fast and, although they'd been in and out of state care since they were toddlers, he'd told her they'd better scoop them up before someone else realized how great they were.

Although the boys had been living with Mac, Annie, and Emma on Castaway Cove since September, today's party was to celebrate the finalization of their adoption.

Emma, who'd proclaimed to have *always* wanted a big brother, was thrilled to now have two.

She was flourishing in first grade, and growing up so fast that both Annie and Mac often wished children came with a *Pause* button. Over the past months of ballet lessons, her princess stage had been swept away by her new goal of becoming a ballerina. One thing hadn't changed, though, and that was why she was wearing a petal pink shirt with TU-TU CUTE spelled out in darker pink rhinestones.

"You need to hold Zelda," she informed Jordan, as she picked up the pug, the one she'd chosen from Charity Tiernan's shelter the day after she'd gotten lost. Which, she'd told Annie, had been a lot better than being grounded for life. "So I can get another picture."

"How many does that make?" her older brother asked as she plopped the dog onto his lap.

"Only about a gazillion," his twin suggested. The indulgent smile he gave Emma revealed his inordinate patience with the little sister, who followed them both around like a puppy. But still managed to boss them around in a style befitting an empress. Or a prima ballerina.

"We need to record everything for the family scrapbook," she said, pointing out what everyone in the family had been hearing since Annie had given her the pink princess camera that she was never without.

After another series of clicks, she looked across the room toward Sedona, who was pushing a wheeled table toward them, accompanied by cheers from the guests.

"Oh, wow!" Emma began snapping away at the stunning blue and white sheet cake with JUSTIN AND JORDAN, HOME FOR GOOD written on the top in white frosting. "That's so pretty!"

Mac had surprised Annie yet again by coming up with the idea for the single large candle in the center, representing their joined family, surrounded by the five smaller ones for Annie, Emma, their boys, and himself.

"You need to blow out the candles," Emma instructed her brothers.

"Let's all do it together," Mac suggested.

Holding hands, that's exactly what they did.

"This," Emma said on a deep, blissful sigh as the six candles sputtered out and Annie began cutting the celebration cake, "is the bestest day ever!"